I, MY ANCESTOR

I, My Ancestor

* * *

NANCY WILSON ROSS

RANDOM HOUSE

NEW YORK

Contents

*
* *
*

I have been here before:
I, I, my ancestor.

RALPH HODGSON

. . . for it is as his ancestor that the middle-
aged man of forty is entitled to regard the young
man of twenty who formed his mind.

C. E. M. JOAD, *God and Evil*

PART ONE

* * *

The Island

CHAPTER *1*

* * *

ON the shore of the island of Peachpit, so small its presence on any map appeared only as a speck, almost indeed like a flaw in the paper, the tide turned.

Nothing at the waterline indicated the turning. The very same stones, no more, were washed by the next faint diastole of the sea, though probably the little rock crabs knew and the embedded clams preparing to spout. Certainly the old man, asleep in the cabin among the firs and madrona just above the beach, must have sensed a change, some shift and stir in the atmosphere, some barely perceptible quickening of that twin pulse of air and water which dominated this island world, for he came awake at once saying to himself, "The tide has turned."

He awoke instantly, as a man will whose life habits are so regular that sleep neither drugs nor evades him. Lying on his back, his eyes closed, in a room bare of everything but bed, bench and table, he savored the mingling scents from the woods and beach: salt and cedar, leaf mold and barnacle, yesterday's sun still held by the pine needles, the morning chill in the fern roots.

"What good luck," he thought, "what good luck that I, an old man, can still enjoy all this morning fragrance."

He pulled his arms from under the blankets and gave them a long hard stretch above his head, pleasantly conscious of the response in his still firm body. He lifted himself on one elbow to look out at the water where it lay motionless in the inlet, a sleeping green snake between the two islands. His thoughts returned to the tide. He recalled having read somewhere that the people of olden times, with perhaps the exception of the Chinese and Icelanders, had never wondered much about the recession and advance of tidewater. Even the Greeks, those normally searching and questioning people, had paid this phenomenon little attention. Perhaps the Aegean, on whose shores he had never stood, was an almost tideless sea. Could that account for it?

"I must ask Clare to recommend some good new book on physical geography." He spoke aloud again, in a clear, almost formal voice, a habit acquired from years of solitude. "If there is one," he amended wryly.

Since he had no reason to hurry, he relaxed once more, listening to the concert in the woods behind him. As the light grew, the birds, past their first chirps, murmurs, half-finished phrases, sleepy and plaintive, were swelling their morning outcry to harmonies and complex improvisations. While he lay smiling, his eyes still closed, it seemed to him the sounds tumbled over and through each other like water in a mountain brook, whirling and dashing, swaying gently in little pools, sending up rainbows of spray: the spray, the song sparrow; the whirlpool and the ripple, the brown thrashers; the gentle pools, the doves.

Only the gulls did not speak. He raised himself again on one elbow and looked out through the madronas to the pilings of the old vanished dock where morning and evening his gulls stood. Although it was early summer and most of the colony had flown farther north, two of the faithful remained. Tatoosh, the murderer, the old white one, with half a claw gone, stood on his usual pillar, meditative, aloof. Fred, the clown, picked at his left wing with a thoughtful beak.

It was only in autumn that the gulls communicated. When the winds came down the inlet, blowing straight from the fresh snow on the Twin Brothers, they rose, turned, floated in ecstasy, keening and exchanging their brief prophecies in some private minor key. Then the old man, alone in his own November, stood on the bare beach and thought of the past. Looking at the gulls, he said, "Autumn is the season of their souls," for he remembered Old John, the last of the Squalchucks, who had told him that the souls of earthbound men came back in autumn to inhabit the bodies of the gulls. Repeating Old John's observation to his summer neighbor, Clare Powers, he had added, amused, "Only Indian souls, I'll wager." Gulls, he had insisted, were too calm to be inhabited by nervous whites.

He swung his feet over the edge of the bed, stood up and walked to the open window, stretching his arms again as he drew in deep breaths of the sea-sweetened air. He could see the periscope ends of giant mollusks sticking up through the sand. A geo-duck tide. Too far out for a dip this morning. He would use the cold shower he had rigged up on the back porch with a length of rubber hose and a rain barrel.

The shower water came straight out of the spring. "Wow! Owie!" he yelled. As he let his voice go he thought of Clare across the inlet. She said she sometimes heard him when the wind was right and it gave her the greatest pleasure to be awakened by cries from a man under a cold shower. Then she would burrow back into her bed, happy to prolong her feeling of drowsy sloth. He smiled, thinking how Clare loved to pretend she was lazy, a little pose he had heard Lawrence tease her about, accusing her of learning to recline in odalisque positions merely to deceive people about how hard-working, ambitious and single-purposed she actually was.

After the old man had clapped himself dry with the flat of his palms he went into the kitchen to light the fire. As soon as he had it nicely crackling in the wood-burning stove and the coffee in its ironware pot placed squarely on the back lid, he combed his thin gray hair, put on his blue jeans and shirt, and started down the beach to the point. It was a trip he made every morning of his life.

When he came to the place where the beach thrust out a long sandy tongue he sat down under his favorite pine, watching the morning clouds pull away from the snow-capped peaks that filled the sky at the inlet's end. A heron standing on one leg in the shallows nearby held his pose no more quietly than the old man under the tree.

Across the inlet a figure emerged from the green blur of the woods, a bearded man, long and thin, in weathered dungarees. It was Lawrence. The two men saw one another clearly, but neither, by voice or gesture, indicated it; part of an unspoken law of privacy strictly maintained between them.

The old man watched the distant figure move along the shore edge, half-eager, half-furtive, like a wary bird on the hunt. And so Lawrence was—he knew—on the hunt for whatever the early morning could show him in the shore grass, under the bleached logs, among the green gloves of seaweed and the black-purple disks of the sand dollars whose beds the low tide of the night had left exposed. These discoveries would reappear later, changed into sign and symbol, poetry and prophecy, in Lawrence's intricate paintings of the life of beach and thicket, the insect jungle among the grass-blades, the tossed and torn embroidery of trees facing the sea.

By now the cold blue mountains had begun to pale and then to warm with the reflected fire of the rising sun and he knew the boiling coffee would be thrusting against the lid of the pot. He rose to go back.

2

As HE was shaving with his old-fashioned, long-bladed razor he remembered this was mail day. Going for the mail every ten days was the one concession he made to the calendar, though in reality he made it to Minnie Bye, the post-mistress at Madrona Beach, who had worried about him so much when he first came to his island that he had made her a solemn promise to appear at fixed intervals. If he failed to keep his word she would send her son Clarence around the point in the old dinghy with emergency equipment: bandages of torn-up sheets, a flask of cherry brandy, a thermos of coffee, and maybe even a red-tailed hawk pie.

He got into the boat and pushed off. "A foolish trip," he said.

He addressed Tatoosh who nodded coolly. "Foolish!"—although there was quite likely to be mail for him, since his daughter, Jane, wrote regularly from the mountains of Guatemala. Winter, however, was the heaviest time for mail. He often found magazines and assorted reading material from summer people who got to thinking in their oil-heated homes on a raw rainy day what it must be like on deserted Peachpit.

When he had beached his boat on Madrona he stepped off briskly through the woods along the hard-packed trail he had made himself years ago, all his senses alive to the pleasures of the familiar scene. He knew every detail of the journey: where the thongs of cedar, lying deceptively close to the earth caught the unwary toe; where a single stubble of Oregon Grape, grown a little too high since he last clipped it, could send a hurrying man headlong. When the path dipped down into the cool ravine past a small gurgling stream, he kept his eye out for the maidenhair fern, the song swallows darting around the red-brown rot of old logs, the giant sword ferns, the beds of moss, the Devil's Club on the opposite bank standing so handsome and menacing with its large flat leaves. Some Indians, he knew, made a brew of Devil's Club, and old backwoodsmen suffering kidney complaints drank the brew, and stayed well. He thought of how many foods there were indigenous to this land from which the Indians once drew their larder and medicines, and how this lore of edible root, berry, leaf, twig, bud and flower was passing quietly and surely from man's knowledge. He sighed, wondering if it was not, perhaps, his duty to put down some record.

He had with him, as always, his binoculars and hand lens. From time to time, he paused and, motionless, looked through the glasses into some thicket to catch the flicker of wings or the gleam of a beady eye. Once he stopped to watch a warbler at a little distance thread her quick crisscross way from branch to branch through a spindly young fir, as though weaving some invisible design. When she thrust her head up through the opening of the top branches and looked about like one anticipating applause, the old man nodded his silent approval.

Halfway through the woods he sat down on an enormous flat rock, designated locally as The Squat. Lawrence often sketched here, and had cleared carefully to expose the truncated cone of an ancient stump. In one section of this relic from the days of giant trees, ants had tunneled a complicated kingdom, but the outer shell of the dead wood had grown a moss and lichen landscape. On this, the old man now eagerly turned his hand lens. Insect-size, he wandered over the mounds of mossy green hills, studied the extravagant pink and chartreuse gardens designed for a fairyland pleasance, lay flat on his back in gentle valleys beneath the minute elaboration of conifer, palm and parasol trees.

It was nothing new for him, this fantasy journey on the stump. It was part of his regular mail-day ritual; he claimed he always rose from it not only restored but again "life size."

3

The Madrona Beach Post Office and Store lay just beyond the edge of the woods in a bright dry meadow. A gray building, weather-used and sagging, it sprawled along the shore of the inlet, still somehow hospitable and inviting, though badly in need of paint and repairs. Once it had served as a hotel—now it was general store, post office, ferry waiting-room and home for the Byes. Its upstairs rooms were only occasionally put to use, mostly by fishermen who had missed the last ferry and had no way of getting far enough down the road to find the widely advertised beer and mattresses of the new *Rustic Lodge* at Four Forks.

The old man, emerging from the woods, came suddenly upon Clarence Bye lying at the meadow's edge with his hat pulled down over his eyes. He was not asleep, for at once he called out, "Morning, Tom Stewart," addressing him formally as he always did. Clarence pulled his shapeless glandular body upright. "Lazy kind of a slow-poke day," he commented, reaching for a fresh blade of grass to aid his speech.

"So I see."

Clarence's mild eyes sharpened, he grinned. "Ma sent me to gather berries for a pie."

"Berries aren't up to much this year." It was the opening gambit in a prescribed exchange between them of weather prophecy and proof.

"That's right. Kinda soggy."

"Too much rain in late May."

Clarence accepted, with a solemn nod, this irrefutable truth and proceeded to elaborate the theme. "Sure could do with a little rain now, though. Woods is dry as tinder. Signs failin' every which way this year. Never saw the beat of it. Oak over on the mainland showed green before the ash this spring. Sure thought we could count on a wet season." He shook his head mournfully at this betrayal of Nature. "Even the caterpillars—head ends longer than their tail ends and still no rain in sight. . . . Ma's expecting you," and he abruptly waved his visitor down the path.

When Tom entered the store, Minnie Bye was trying vainly, as usual, to lay a neat pattern on the chaos of elements implied in the term General Merchandise. "Those dratted bags of chicken feed!" she greeted him. "I'm like to lose my mind." Minnie was a small round woman, her hair a flat twirl held up with old-fashioned bone hairpins, her good open face shiny with soap, free of powder, and also of the warts, liver spots, and fierce solitary hairs that mar the faces of so many country women. Tom Stewart always enjoyed looking at Minnie Bye.

"I got a letter here for you," she said with an air of suppressed excitement.

As he took it from her, he noticed it was postmarked New York, and was quite sure Minnie, a great student of the appearance of letters—postmarks, size, weight, quality of paper, position of stamps, type of handwriting and other details—was dying of curiosity. To oblige her he sat down on a pickle barrel and opened the letter to report at once on the contents and put her mind at rest.

He was startled to find the letter was from his daughter-in-law —a name only to him, hardly even a face, though somewhere there was a faded snapshot of her standing by a perambulator which he supposed held his grandchild. "My dear Mr. Stewart." He imagined the pen poised after "my dear"—wondering: "Shall I say father? *Can* I say father? Is it proper, rude not to, cold?" Then the decision on the formal side, and quite rightly, he thought. "This is a difficult letter to write, but I feel I must . . ."

He had read only a few lines when he began to feel grateful to the stout pickle barrel supporting him. A tremble, the source of which he could not at the moment trace, began to pass lightly through his body.

It was a long letter. He read it all through twice and then folded the paper, returned it to its envelope and sat for a moment in silence. He looked over at Minnie, who was pretending to dust the shelves of canned goods, and said suddenly, "Well, Minnie, I've got some news for you." She held her dust rag suspended. "I may be going to have a visitor."

"That *so?*" Her voice was edged with excitement, her face thrust forward like a dog on a scent.

"My son."

Minnie stopped dusting altogether and looked straight at him. When he met her glance he saw her eyes were glazing over with tears.

"Laws!" she said. "Tom Stewart, imagine that now!" She turned away, lifting her apron. He was astonished; he wondered if Minnie Bye had always secretly pitied him, thought him a bereft and abandoned old man.

"I guess I'd better lay in some extra grub—just in case," he said quickly, hoping by his matter-of-factness to create a less emotional atmosphere.

She began immediately to bustle. "That's right. You make out a list. I'll help you. And Clarence—he can row the things around the point for you sometime this week. No need you carrying 'em over the trail, breaking your back. No sir! He can row your boy over when he comes, too. Don't imagine a New Yorker'd know much about following a trail through the woods, would he?"

"Very little, I imagine," he agreed, humoring her in her notions about the habits of those remote foreign people from the opposite ocean. "But he was born out here, you know."

Minnie nodded. "I know. Has something to do with the movies now, don't he?"

Again Tom was astonished. Where had she acquired this information? It had been a long time since he had discussed Philip with anyone; certainly not since coming to the island.

"Yes," he answered slowly, "something to do with the stories they buy for the films, as I understand it."

"How many years since you seen him?"

Tom stared; it was so unlike Minnie Bye to ask prying questions that it took him a moment to answer.

"Too many years to count," he said gently. "Too many years."

She again lifted her apron; he had never seen her so affected. In fact, he couldn't recall a time he had caught a tear in her eye about anything.

He hurried out of the door and down the trail, still holding the letter in his hand. Minnie called after him once, but he did not answer.

4

IN HIS walk home from the post office he had come again to The Squat. But this time he did not study the insect pleasance. Instead he sat down, his hands slackly clasped between his knees, looking, without seeing them, at the scuffed toes of his heavy moccasins. For a long time he stared ahead, until the silence, broken by his passing, closed around him again, the slow, sweet, silent breathing of the sun-warmed wood.

He took the New York letter from his shirt pocket and read it for the third time. "My son may be coming to stay with me." The idea remained impossible to grasp. He tried to imagine clearly what had happened to Philip, but even the violent facts so clearly set forth in his daughter-in-law's letter could not entirely account for the proposed visit, this possible impending intrusion of his lost son into his hermit's existence. He rose and continued on his way down the trail.

Just at the wood's edge, in the middle of the path, lay a large white tree-fungus. Printed on its soft leathery surface in childish letters, as though scratched with a twig, were the words: *"Tom, want to see you. If not on beach, right back. Clare."*

Tom turned and walked to the place where she often sat. He found her typewriter on the sand on its cork pad, and her canvas back-rest against the big tree, but she was not there. He put down the basket Minnie had given him and prepared to wait.

"Too much has happened," he thought. "It's too late to be renewing an acquaintance with my son. My whole way of life . . ." he stopped, ashamed of his thoughts even as he admitted their truth. His island life had a form, a deliberate design into which he had woven his existence. Any outsider would be slow to comprehend the casual, contemplative pattern of his days. And yet Clare and Lawrence—once he had been equally reluctant to include them.

He remembered the April day four years back when their halloo across the inlet had interrupted his clam digging. Shading his eyes he had looked across the salty shimmer to where they stood, a tall bearded man and a slim girl. "Mr. Stewart?" the man was shouting through cupped hands. "Mr. Stewart?" He had dropped his digging fork, stepped into his boat, and rowed over.

He had seen at once they were city people. What they wanted was information about the old half-burned, abandoned homestead that stood to one side of the trail he himself had made on Madrona.

"The Byes, down at the store, sent us to you," Lawrence had explained.

Tom had known why. Although the Byes owned the deserted homestead, they had little use for money and would never dream of selling land near him, of threatening his close-guarded privacy, without his approval. He had not been very encouraging to the two young people until Lawrence had begun to speak. Tom never passed the charred and blackened house now without remembering how Lawrence had that day described its sinister beauty—here misty and shadowed like an autumn fog, here gleaming like a polished jewel. There had been a genuine urgency in his voice. Lawrence had finally stated that he "had to own the homestead, had to live in it," that the place had taken to "haunting his canvases." It was the first hint Tom had had that the man before him was a painter.

The girl had spoken up then and said she too wanted land over here, but no half-burned house for her, thank you! She needed something very modern, easy to take care of. She wanted to be free of "things." She wanted "time, more time." Her voice had been crisp, faintly truculent.

Tom had noted at once that she spoke about Time anxiously, almost fearfully, as though of a machine that had broken down beyond repair. When he had remarked on this, the two young people had begun to talk rapidly about modern life, about the "theme of Time" and how it seemed there was something wrong lately with Time itself. Didn't he find it so?

Interested, he had puffed on his pipe, looking into the blue distance. "No," he remembered saying, "the truth is I've come to feel there's plenty of Time for everything. Almost, you might say, nothing *but* Time."

The painter had appeared thoughtful. Or was it doubtful? The girl, who was gazing off toward the mountains, had said rather sadly, "I'm afraid I don't know what you mean."

Tom had felt sorry for them then—sorry, older, wiser, perhaps a little fatherly. He had said, to his own amazement, "You'll have to come to the islands some winter night when there's a full moon. You could bathe then in an immensity of Time. I've a notion you'd never be the same again."

He had tried then to describe what he meant; how there weren't many of these nights of intense sparkling cold on the island, but how they did come, occasionally, with the moon hanging frostbound in a vast enameled blue arc, and the stars sparkling with icy fire. A crystal spell was laid on the earth then. Nothing moved. Even the water in the inlet waited without a whisper or a stir of tide. There was no dog to challenge mournfully the bright frozen mystery in the sky. No forest animal crept stealthily among brittle twigs around his cabin. Alone in this pure and clean immensity he felt all things with special intenseness and clarity, his complete solitude not something that cut him off, but rather something that bound him to the universe, a thing actual and perceptible, a pillar pointing from the earth skyward, uniting him to the eternal silent aloneness of the winter moon that moved by secret laws through the vast arch of space.

When he had stopped speaking and they were both silent, he had added that, feeling as he did before such an experience, he was often left with a deep regret: that he had no way of communicating what he felt.

"I have just one envy left," he had said. "My envy of the

poet, the musician, the painter. Yes, young man," he had repeated, turning to Lawrence, "I envy you."

After that he had invited them over to share his clams. He had even gone so far as to get out his greatest delicacy, Minnie Bye's Christmas fruitcake, a Byzantine confection based on chopped-up salt pork drowned in a pint of black coffee, whirled about at the end of a wooden spoon with raisins, nuts, currants, citron and long-neglected spices.

Ishmael, his talking raven, had been alive then, and the old bird sat at table displaying his talents, reciting with a little help all the counties of Ireland. "It's a song," Clare had cried, and to an improvised air sang, "Kerry, Cork and Down, Fermanagh and Tyrone." A charmer, Tom had decided, watching her.

He smiled now, recalling that afternoon; how Clare had said, when he commented on the way she handled the utensils helping him prepare lunch, that maybe it came from handling shards of pots and ancient bones—for she was an anthropologist. He had never known an anthropologist and the idea of having one for a neighbor attracted him, yet he had not entirely let down his guard. He had tried on them, as his final test for city strangers, the hibernating bear story: how he and Clarence Bye—the soft-spoken yarner who had brought them across that morning from the mainland on the Bye ferry—had spent a night lost in the mountains curled up for warmth against an unconscious bear.

"You may not believe it," he had said, "but I never felt more safe or secure in my life. Clarence assured me nothing would wake the bear except the coming of spring, and I believed him." He had poured them all more coffee before continuing. "Yes, men might learn something useful from hibernating bears. Something about conserving energy."

The young woman, seated cross-legged in his kitchen rocking-chair thoughtfully crumbing her fruit cake, had given him a sudden intense look. Her intensity had made him laugh. "Wait a minute." He had spoken up quickly. "I'm not about to pass on the secret of life that I learned in a bear's cave."

She had laughed then, too, saying, "But it sounds like a Norse myth."

"I guess it does," he had admitted. "No, all I meant was—

getting rid of your body for a while, that's quite a trick! A lot harder for *human* critturs, I'm led to believe."

"Well, apparently there are men who have learned it." The young woman's voice was quiet but it had been his turn to look surprised. "You know you hear strange things among the Indians sometimes—even yet—degenerate as they've become," she had added, then asked abruptly, "Have you lived here a long time?"

"Quite a spell. More than twenty years."

She was plainly astounded. He had seen that to her, probably in her very early thirties, twenty years was like a lifetime.

"I'm an old man," he had said smiling. "Over seventy."

They had both exclaimed their disbelief.

"Do you practice yoga?" the painter had demanded.

"God forbid! I've read a few books on it, but how could I understand them, born as I was in County Antrim, Ireland?"

"But it's really remarkable you're over seventy. You certainly don't look it."

He had been pleased about that, he remembered—had admitted to them that from close observation of animals he had come actually to suffer at the way humans moved about, stooping, slopping, flat-footed, angular, lumbering. He had immediately noticed how Lawrence carried his head, in a sort of airy graceful way, like a listening bird.

"What luck to have an island all to yourself for twenty years," the painter had murmured when he finished. "You must have done something very fine to deserve it."

"No. Oh, no. Got it for my sins, I guess. So that I could repent of them and regret them at long leisure."

He had spoken lightly but something in his tone had given the words an almost melancholy weight. There had been a sudden silence. He had smiled, wondered if the smile was convincing, and the girl had asked a little quickly, "Do you go out often—leave the islands?"

He had shaken his head.

"And you're never lonely?"

"You mean do I get 'cabin fever?' No, I can't say I ever do. Not any more. Once maybe—but not any more." And then deliberately he had changed the subject. Looking out the window he had cried, "the canny bonny creature," and he meant the mother robin who was carrying off just then from below her nest in the corner of the porch the telltale bits of blue from broken eggs, before these fragments could inform an enemy that her babies were hatched.

The painter had jumped up saying that the construction of birds' nests was always a marvel to him. He and the girl had taken turns standing on an applebox to study the nest, while the mother robin chirped and whirred nervously at a distance and the great open mouths of the fledgelings gaped like orange wounds. Lawrence, to his surprise and pleasure, had commented on how the mother robin always plastered the nest with the mud from her beak, tramping it with her little feet; how she sat and turned around and around in the cupshape form getting the proper fit for her breast. They had talked, then, a great deal about birds, and he had led them to the wren's nest in the pocket of his old sou'wester. "One year it was one of my rubber boots. Fairly inconvenient, that! No bird like the wren for sheer whimsy." He had even showed off a little, imitating the simple love call of the chickadee—a high note, two lower ones—until he had persuaded one to fly down and perch on his outstretched arm, gazing with its head cocked as though questioning whether another bird could really be hidden inside.

When the chickadee had darted off to recite its name from a hazelnut bush he had suggested that they go over and examine the old house together, for he had made up his mind to let them purchase the Bye land, hoping only that the fact they were lovers—of which he felt sure—wouldn't lead the old-timers to ill-will and gossip, or to a refusal to sell them milk, eggs and vegetables.

5

THEY had been his friends and summer neighbors for four years. Lawrence came to Madrona every spring when the dogwood bloomed. Clare came later, as soon as her university classes were over. He wondered again if his son—undoubtedly a very conventional man—could ever fit into the simplicity and remoteness of their island life.

He reached behind him and broke a branch from the ocean spray that stood at the wood's edge. A bushtit darted out, revealing her hidden nest, but today he did not look for it. He sat absently studying the minute delicate perfection of the velvet flowers as though they were the faces of intimates. "Plan of five," he said, knowing it well from his magnifying glass; another of the not yet correlated affinities within the great cryptogram of Nature, another of those distinct numerical plans—the five, the three, the six, the seven—revealed in the world of flower, snowflake, berry . . . "Twenty stamens, five pistils."

He had spoken aloud and Clare Powers, appearing now suddenly from her house, asked, "What's that, Tom?"

"Hello, Huck." He grinned. "Just talking to myself again." He dropped the flowers in her lap as she sat down. "Ocean spray," he said, "cousin of the rose, cherry, strawberry, apple and plum."

"I'd have never guessed it." She lifted the lacy plume to her face.

He watched her, still smiling. Huck was his name for her when she wore, as she did today, her rolled-up jeans and striped sweater. Once, having seen a photograph of her in a newspaper, wearing white satin and pearls, he had said he could never call her Huck again. But he always forgot. He thought how young she looked now in the naked light, with no make-up, her long hair in pigtails. He saw staring out at him the willful and difficult child she had been. For on many occasions she had admitted to having been a problem child. "All because of pressure, pressure," she invariably cried, still with remnants of resentment and anger in her voice. "Do this, do that! The victim of projection—my mother's unlived life. I should have been a boy, then my preoccupation with snakes, toads, tree houses and adolescent vestiges of fertility rites would have been accepted as normal."

"Here's your mail," he said, reaching in the basket. "Yours and Lawrence's."

"Thanks." She hardly glanced at it. He thought how much she had changed since coming to the island and said so.

"Have I? But of course I have." Still she was pleased.

They were silent for a few moments. He leaned over and tried to oblige an overladen ant by laying a twig-trestle between two rocks, but the ant, after due consideration of the short cut, continued on his tortuous route around the big rocky hill. He laughed again, shaking his head as though at some private joke.

"Did you want to see me about something in particular?" he finally asked Clare.

"No, just hadn't seen you for a while—saw your boat, knew you'd gone to the store, and that I could trap you for a moment, at least, on the way home. You know how I like any excuse to be interrupted."

"That's not my impression of you."

Here was the perfect lead, he told himself, for speaking about Philip, about the letter. He wanted to tell her, and was astounded at his hesitancy and reluctance. Instead of speaking out he lay back on the sand, folded his hands on his chest and said, "I was thinking, as I walked through the woods just now, how people haven't the patience to study Nature any more. It's a peculiar thing. I don't know—maybe it's a bad sign."

It was so unlike Tom to linger, particularly if he saw her typewriter or signs of work, that Clare was surprised. She thought he looked saddened, almost depressed, and wondered if he had had bad news. But she knew better than to ask. When he was ready he would tell her.

"What do you mean—a bad sign?" she demanded. He always waited for the challenging eye she turned on him, and the crisp lifted voice.

"Well, you know what the Bible says about God watching Adam to see how he named the animals. Maybe that's a clue to an ancient wisdom. The animal world, like the plant world, I guess, is man's responsibility." He broke another branch from the ocean spray. "Sometimes it looks as though man's neglecting it, moving farther and farther from it, losing the power to read what it has to tell him."

After a moment when she said nothing, he added, "However, it's been remarked that ignorance isn't not knowing, it's knowing so many things that ain't so!"

She laughed again. It was a somber face, he thought, almost

brooding in repose, but with laughter the light flickered over it like hard sun on moving water.

"Still," he said, going back to his original thought, "the men in the laboratories are turning up some pretty lively stuff these days. You didn't come to my sermon on the onion, did you?"

Clare shook her head, smiling again. "No, but I heard about it."

"Poor Mrs. Hooper, she took it hard. She might accept God in a grain of sand, or heaven in a wild flower, but danged if she would accept either of them in an onion!"

"You can worship God in an onion," he had cried, holding one up to view in the pulpit of the old crumbling church at Venus. "In the very element that makes the eyes water they have found forces that can kill germs and heal wounds." He had said a lot more: about the seeds of life to be found in death; about mold and penicillin; about man the catalyst on whom Nature waits to have her secret properties revealed. But Mrs. J. Lowell Hooper remembered only the blasphemy of worshipping God in an onion. She had written him an angry letter from her white-trimmed brown-shingled summer place on the mainland. If there had been any Board to which she could have made complaint, Tom Stewart might never have spoken again in the Venus church.

But there was no Board; there were no trustees, no elders, no salary. The property on which the abandoned church from the ghost spruce town stood belonged to the Byes. As far as they were concerned, Tom Stewart could say in its improvised pulpit anything he pleased. And so he did. "Tom Stewart's crazy sermons," he knew people called them, but just the same a rather surprising congregation appeared to listen in the summer months. Particularly the Turbans, his name for those transient touring ladies from California who pressed up to him with their tie-and-dye scarfs, amber beads, long earrings, Siamese cats in baskets. With distended eyeballs, dry unused finger ends, they closed in, clutching . . . "The mysteries," they murmured, "the hidden, the secret, the occult, the esoteric" . . . With these ardent devotees he could not always stem his impatience. "Mysteries, ladies, mysteries!" he had once cried in irritation. "You need not visit Tibet to study the mysteries. Explain to me the mystery of the chlorophyll in the leaves of your own backyard." And snatching up a branch of mountain laurel that stood beside the collection plate, he had nipped off a few leaves and shoved them into the white-gloved hands. He had been ashamed of himself immediately afterwards; but now, much later, he rather enjoyed the memory of their faces.

In the silence that had dropped between him and Clare he could hear the singing of the warming day; the sands where the tide was creeping, the leaves of the trees stirring faintly behind them, and somewhere a cicada's monotone promising heat.

He forced himself to speak.

"My son Philip may be coming to stay with me."

As soon as he had spoken he sensed Clare's amazement. It had the same quality as Minnie's in the store an hour before. "Why, Tom," she cried. "Your son? How wonderful! Or is it?"

The abrupt change in her tone made him smile. It was one of the reasons he was fond of this girl—her forthrightness.

"I don't know," he admitted honestly. "I haven't seen him since he was thirteen. Don't think we understood one another very well at that time."

He stopped. "At that time"— Memory rushed up in him until for a moment he felt queasy, almost sick. "Needn't have him here," he thought. "It's not necessary. I can easily get out of it." But he was instantly ashamed of his thought and forced it from his mind.

"Is he coming on a sudden whim?" Clare asked, breaking his silence.

"Oh, no, that's the main point of it . . ." Tom hesitated. The facts in his daughter-in-law's letter still seemed so remote from the sunny peace of the beach, the birds, the leaping fish, the mountains on the sky, that he could not bring himself to speak of them. After a moment he said simply, "He's had an accident, Clare. Some sort of nervous reaction. The doctors think what he needs is complete peace and quiet."

"Well," Clare said, "that he will certainly get here—if he knows how to rest."

Tom met her glance for a moment and caught there a curiosity he had not seen since their first meeting. She was wondering, he suspected, about the break in his life that had deprived him all these years of his son's acquaintance. Could he speak of it; should he? The roots went back so long, so deep, so twisted and interwined, back, back, even to Ballymeaney . . .

He let his eye wander toward the gnarled, out-thrust limb of the old fir on which now a heron was making an awkward landing, braking its wings against the air, thrusting its legs down like sticks.

He rose abruptly, forgetting to say good-bye, and walked away over the small stones near the shore, and then over the large rough and barnacle-grown ones the low tide had revealed. He got into his boat, holding the basket with the blackberry pudding and cornbread Minnie Bye had given him. He put the basket down carefully on the bottom, waved at Clare, picked up his oars and pulled toward Peachpit.

All the way across, the rush and slack of the water under the boat, the regular creak of the oar-locks, carried into his mind sensations he had not experienced in many years. Doubts, questions, splinters of half-remembered scenes he had thought behind him forever, came glancing off the surface of his memory like the light off the moving water, caught and lost in the same moment. He was startled when his boat nudged the sand in the shallows below his cabin.

After he had beached the boat he sat a long time on the prow looking at the familiar pale stencil of the mountains. At last, as though he had made up his mind to something important, he rose and walked up the beach to his cabin.

He went to a closet and got out an old battered suitcase, brought it to the kitchen table, opened it, and began to rummage through its miscellaneous contents: faded photographs, bundles of letters, yellow foolscap. Finally he found what he was looking for—an old, thick, leather-bound book with the word *Accounts* written on it in a gold Spencerian script. He opened it. The pages of the old book were empty. At the top of each page, where the date was to be entered, the year read 190—. He shook his head slowly, eyeing the blank space, sorting his memories, then took pen and ink from the shelf and sat down on one of the plain kitchen chairs, the account book opened before him. He sat a long time. Finally he began to write, "I, Thomas Cameron Stewart." As soon as he had written this he laughed aloud, scratching out the four words—with extra force on the letter "I." He began again, "It was just after one of the periodic Irish famines . . ."

He continued to write rapidly.

PART TWO

*   *
* *
  *

East 72nd Street

CHAPTER 2

*
*   *
*

THE man running the apartment elevator in the late hot night
was a stranger. Probably a substitute, Philip Stewart thought as
he got in, someone must be taking his holiday early.

"Good evening," Philip said. He corrected himself lightly, "Or
make it good morning." There was no response. The surly type
—or deaf maybe, he decided, then aloud, "Fourteenth floor,
please."

Abruptly the old man thrust his neck forward like a startled
turtle to inquire, "Whassat?" Philip repeated the number more
loudly.

The metal box, acid green with a black-satin bench, began to
move slowly upward, the whirring fan in a corner muddling the
stagnant air. Why does it move so slowly? Philip asked himself,
then his drink-hazy mind began: "I am in the wrong elevator;
the wrong building; there is no building, only this vault in space
with the strange attendant moving me to an unknown destination."

Instantly, with a speed born of training and experience, plus
the chronic cynicism that was the inevitable result of his job—

his well-paid search for the disappearing "new" in idea or "angle" —a part of his mind informed him coldly that this sickly romantic thought was by no means original. He had read it somewhere; seen it, perhaps in a play. Yet he did not let go of it, finding it now definitely, morbidly, appealing.

He pinned his glance to what he could see of the profile of the unknown attendant. It was only the face of an ordinary old man with dead-white skin hanging in loose pleats, "a plastic suet quivering over the hard collar of a summer uniform" (he was forming fragments of that elaborate, imaginary and tragic story on which he still occasionally found himself at work in his head) "a face of final defeat, of utter loneliness, the human voice reaching dimly through deadened ears. Old age . . ."

Philip shivered suddenly, feeling the perspiration on his body grow clammy, and, as though at a signal, heard again the girl in the night club repeating her haunting refrain: *One and one and all alone and ever more shall be so.* Eyes as green as ferns and a dress of artful demureness, she fingered her guitar and sang, with calculated nostalgia, through the blue mesh of night-club cigarettes, above the tapping of ice cubes in glass cylinders, songs from a day when people embraced and parted beside the Bonny Doon, on the slopes of Old Smoky, in the foggy foggy dew. *One and one and all alone and ever more shall be so.* The refrain came at the end of a great number of verses. There had seemed to him, at the time, only one possible response to this unsolicited prophecy so obviously directed at him: "Waiter, one more please, all around!"

The elevator had come to a stop. The old man patiently waiting. As Philip stepped out he lurched a little and, embarrassed by this and by his delayed response, tried a hearty "Good night." There was still no answer. The lighted box dropped from sight down its greased silent well, leaving him alone, flatly deposited in another box, larger, dimmer, also painted green. He looked around —for an instant a man seeking escape.

As he inserted the key into the lock he could not help noticing that his hands were trembling again.

He felt for the light switch, turned it. The antique carriage lamps on either side of the door bloomed dimly, revealing the foyer and his own reflection, softened by the aqueous depths of Great-Aunt Hetebel's concave mirror. Peering in the old blurred glass he was relieved to be able to tell himself that he felt worse than he looked. He looked, indeed, in spite of his wilted clothes and the liquor he had been consuming since four-thirty in the afternoon, almost ruddily healthy. This he attributed in part to his faithful winter use of a sunlamp and to a recent week end of bright May weather which he had spent entirely out-of-doors. He was thirty-nine and he looked just that, no more, thanks to his haircut and his still lean jaw. He could not see in the mirror the incipient pouch below his belt, and the ones under his eyes were minimized by the lighting. "You'll pass," he said to himself, with extra emphasis and satisfaction, in order to dispel the memory of the moment in the evening just behind him when the girl from Ann Arbor, Michigan, in the black-satin suit bought expressly for dining out in New York, had pushed away his experimental hands with a firm, flat, "Please!"

As he stood loosening his tie he observed with distaste the three candles under the antique mirror. Wilted by the extreme heat they lolled in their elaborate sconces like the extended tongues of the strangulated. Why did his mind persist lately in serving up such gruesome thoughts? ("Nerves, hypertension, cut down on your cigarettes" . . . It was the voice of his doctor six months before.) Irritated at the memory he flung his necktie toward a small Victorian sofa which for more than five years had been receiving whatever he chose to drop on it as he entered the apartment. But the necktie, as though possessing a will of its own, sailed farther and higher than the sofa to loop itself over one of the six prints framed in black glass that took care of the wall space.

He frowned. This, too, was the kind of thing that happened to him of late with increasing frequency. Commonplace objects had a way of assuming special significance, stepping over from their world into the human one.

It was plain to him now that the necktie had chosen to convey a message. He was forced to look where it indicated. "The Summersault Hunt," he said aloud (his mocking name for the antique hunting prints from Somerset). But, because the necktie had commanded, he followed the hunt's progress around the wall. Blessed by the curate, the riders took ditches and fences, careened in full cry down lime slopes, held up the brush to view. The length of wilted foulard half-concealed the last scene, the one where the gentlemen (presumably) in at the kill, gathered, laughing somewhat theatrically, around the dilapidated remains of the fox.

Philip took a step nearer this last print. Was it here then, the sign, the metaphor: himself as hunted fox? He winced at the cliché. "A little over-stated, don't you think?" he inquired of the necktie. "Kindly avoid all excessive hyperbole, exaggeration. Also banality." There was no response. The necktie did not so much as quiver. Then it must be something else. He tried again—groping among shifting images, his hand pressed to his forehead. The prints seen as reminders?—the choicest of wedding gifts back in the Thirties when he and Ellen had been married . . . Was that it? Or the prints seen as relics, survivals of an England whose final disappearance had been symbolized for him when his wartime London landlady, a harassed contemporary pilgrim on a trip to Canterbury to visit an ailing daughter, had been buried alive in the bombed ruins of Chaucer's . . . The necktie fell to the floor. Ah-ha! So he was getting warmer. The necktie, the prints, were leading him slowly, surely, to some emotion that he wanted not to feel.

He stood, rocked back a little on his heels, unbuttoning his shirt, concentrating hard until he brought up the face of Jennie Bogson, his London landlady. Survivor of powdered eggs, bread queues, Liquid Apple, V-bombs, Jennie Bogson had survived also the Canterbury incident relatively unscathed, still scornful, "Them Huns!" Philip closed his eyes. He saw himself saying his final good-bye to her after V-E Day in the cold hallway in Upper Brook Street with the waxed paper over the still-broken windowpanes. He felt her creased and calloused middle-aged palm in his, heard her looping, loping, adenoidal Cockney voice: "A packet of good needles, sir, if it isn't too much trouble; and yes, indeed, sir, chocolate-pudding mix *would* be a proper treat." Her last words to him, wrung from her by his importuning, "But Mrs. Bogson, you know I want to send you something!" The false and easy voice of one who is going back to all the creature com-

forts. What manner of man was he who only once since returning—in all these months, stretching now into years—had sent a
package to that grimy London address where he had cowered
beneath a bed on bomb-shaken nights?

He turned out the hall lights and in darkness groped toward
the living room, seeing this act as a penance for nameless, countless failures.

As he entered the living room his heart did a quick leap. At
the end of the room a menacing red glow burned outside the
wide windows like the distant view of some mighty conflagration,
and although it was only the million lights of Manhattan reflected in the lowering canopy of humidity—a phenomenon in
which he had often found a bizarre beauty—tonight he wished
there were curtains to draw against the sight.

But the curtains were down, for it was almost summer, and the
apartment's annual stripping and shrouding had already taken
place. He looked around the shadowed room. A crypt, a mor-
tuary without bodies. Across the pictures, cheesecloth masks; the
floor bare; the big rug rolled up at the room's end, a long dark
cylinder from which the scent of camphor could be detected by
anyone who sat at the nearby piano. An unlikely occurrence, he
thought, crossing to raise the windows, since Pam and Ellen were
away and he came to the apartment only to sleep. He lived—
which is to say ate, talked, entertained, did business—in six or
seven well-known eating and drinking spots in mid-town Manhattan. For whom then the linen slipcovers with their writhing
tangle of assorted tropic vines? For whom the inherited mahogany
with its dark weight, its polished surface, restored leg, plugged
worm hole, and faithfully copied brass handle? This was, indeed,
a question. He looked accusingly at the antique barometer (never
consulted on the fourteenth floor of East Seventy-second Street,
New York City, kept not only because it was a "museum piece"
but also because it so nicely divided the wall space with an old
banjo clock). To his surprise he saw Great-Uncle Logan's rheu-
matic index finger—the middle joint a twisted rosette—irascibly
tapping the wooden frame as though demanding a more suitable
answer on a wintry New England morning.

"Ghosts," he said aloud, "ghosts." And not just dead ghosts, either, for the very flowers he had bought for Ellen's homecoming (or instructed Rosemyrtle to purchase) looked more funereal than festive. Would Ellen so regard them?

He had come home to go to bed so that he would be in good shape to greet his wife on her return in the morning. But now he was home the idea of lying down seemed impossible. He was too restless, too keyed-up, he told himself, even as he admitted that beneath this tight surface was an exhaustion so complete his very bones were soft with it. "You'll wonder why you're home the moment you get there," Dick Hill had said, affably, drunkenly, protesting his departure. "Maybe. But I've got some thinking to do." "You say things or thinking?" "Thinking," Philip had replied with, he hoped, simple convincing dignity, and had left them and come uptown, slurring alone through the hot rubbery streets in the open cab.

And now here he was, and what the hell? The sense of futility as familiar as a well-worn garment fell upon him. He completed the stereotyped pantomime of the half-shrug, the reach for the cigarette, as he dropped down beside the radio in the corner and automatically turned the dial. The warning humming sound was followed by a voice of vivid optimism crying, "Hear it foam!" The wild wave rushed in over a rocky promontory, carrying away the announcer, a city boy unused to the caprices of high tide. Philip flicked off the dial in disgust.

He put his head in his hands then and sat hearing nothing but the throbbing of his own blood until the sound became part of the gigantic, muffled pulse of the city spread out below him. *Nothing is outside us. But we forget this at every sound.* A face attached itself to the words; a face wearing rimless nose-glasses; a name: Professor Harmon, the instructor in Philosophy IV sixteen years ago. Zarathustra—*Also Sprach.* "Who was that character Zarathustra, anyway?" he asked aloud, mumbling the name over and over.

2

IMAGES of the evening just behind him began to flicker through his consciousness. They returned broken, blurred; with the spastic rhythm of silent movies: Dick Hill's terrace in the Village in late afternoon with the men stretched out in deck-chairs, their shirts dissolving on their backs in the unseasonable heat, the paunches of their not old but sedentary bodies straining at their pigskin belts; the faces of the women beginning faintly to show the ravages of luncheon martinis; those two girls fresh from Smith or Vassar with their bones locked in that prescribed young career-girl torpor, that panther use of muscles from hip to ankle—where learned?—like models without the deadpan or the patent-leather bandbox, but with the prescribed, laconic emphasis on certain words, always the least important: "But I *mean!*" "But *yes!*" And the one from Ann Arbor in the black-satin suit, the unmodulated vigor and assurance of the hinterland. . . . "Get a job and write in my spare time." "Oh God, oh God, oh God! That's not perspiration, that's tears." "Why don't you just have soda this time around?" she had suggested with co-ed sisterliness.

He saw them all—he among them—weaving their flickering course through the voice-shrill Village side-streets, past bars and grills, past pizza joints and spaghetti grottos, past cheap wineries and the pale occupants of the narrow houses who, in the heat wave, seemed to erupt from every doorway, every window, and spill down the steps. They were seeking someone's newest discovery, that quiet garden restaurant with the disheartened vines, the ritualistic red-checked tablecloth, the electric lights formed to resemble candles masquerading as stalagmites. Once seated, cold lobster had been recommended with chilled white wine, followed by lacquered pastries with bitter, black chicory—all to be eaten, drunk, dawdled over. And later there had been more cold drinks, and hot trumpet—for Ann Arbor had read about Eddie Condon's band in the *New Yorker*—and that was where he had finally left them, their voices in protest dissolving behind him into one long piercing trumpet tone. And now here he was . . .

Thinking! He was supposed to think. He had given his word to Ellen to "think" about their problem. Beer might help. Beer. He rose from the chair and ran an elaborate slow-motion football interference past the furniture. In the kitchen he found the thermos of black coffee Rosemyrtle was always instructed to leave. He unscrewed the top and almost without tasting it drank a scalding cup. He decided next on food. As he opened the icebox one of Rosemyrtle's illegible notes of information fluttered to the floor. With great effort he leaned over, picked it up and read aloud: *"Dere Mr. Stewar this chez best can do delicatess man say no Bell Prayse come in now see you mondy."* He released the paper and it fluttered again to the floor. How could a woman so ignorant cook so well? He got out the icebox staple—cream cheese mixed with sour cream and chives—and with precise and measured gestures spread a plate of crackers for himself.

Edgarbergen appeared suddenly, sliding with arched back and tail hooked high through the kitchen door. "Hello, Ed," Philip said, but Edgarbergen only walked to the corner and regarded with disdain the convenience that was nightly laid for him, strips and crumples of newspapers in a flat aluminum pan. "Don't you like the choice? Here! Try this!" He removed the front page of Rosemyrtle's tabloid, a blown-up profile of a general. He held it up for the cat to view. "Better?" He added it to the contents of the pan. "Don't sulk! Colored comics Sunday, if you're good," he promised and returned to the living room carrying the beer and crackers. As he stretched out on the sofa he wished Ed would come in and at least rub his fur against his leg. He called once half-heartedly but the cat did not appear.

A breeze had sprung up—rain in the Catskills probably. It brought into the room the thick urban scent, hot rubber, baked stone. He looked fretfully around the shrouded room, hating everything his eye fell upon. "I have never had a home." This mournful and unreasonable pronouncement filled him with mawkish self-pity.

His mother-in-law, Lily Slade Inc., had "done" their apartment and it exemplified the special blend of period accuracy and calculated whimsy which were her infallible stock in trade. It was considered a decorating "triumph" by the adherents and disciples of the widow Slade—a closed fraternity of perennially sunburned men with lilting voices, and uniformly shrill and ageless ladies in chic tailleurs. The rooms had even been reproduced in color in one of the glossy fifty-cent magazines, a copy of which had lain for some months on a table in the apartment where Lily had carefully placed it. "In the well-modulated idiom of the

East Seventies," the piece began. "The three-ply charm of the
Stewart apartment . . ." Philip, reading it aloud, had suddenly
flung it the length of the room. "Now don't be nasty, darling,"
Lily had said, rescuing it from the floor. "You don't know what
I went through to get that article published."

Lying on his back munching the crackers and brushing the
crumbs from his bare chest to the floor, Philip brooded momentarily on his mother-in-law, trying to shift onto her the whole
weight of his shapeless irritation—hearing her clack in in her high
heels crying, "Loot, loot!" followed by her Jamaican handy-man
carrying two Lowestoft cups minus handles filled with dwarf ivy,
or brandishing a Chippendale firescreen delicately unthreaded by
time and moths. Why in God's name had Ellen never taken a
stand on her mother's eternal interference, instead of shrugging
her off with, "Oh, Mother's like that!" or, "You can't do anything with Mother!"

Well, maybe now Ellen *would* take a stand on her mother—for
once that calm façade, which had so disconcertingly cracked
before his eyes this very spring . . . He sat up on the couch
suddenly, almost overturning his beer in his haste. He got to his
feet, wanting above all to blot out this memory, determined to,
yet knowing that he could not continue to avoid it. He began to
look for a cigarette; found one in a silver box on the table that also
held Great-Aunt Hetebel's miniature. He picked up the miniature as though it offered him, in this moment, a visual sanctuary.
He stared at it with a vacant fixity, thinking how little it conveyed of that monumental quality of the woman who had been
the central figure of his adolescent years. Nothing here revealed
that bust measurement of a Valkyrie, nor the slow sure hands,
nor the padded mothlike wings of her pale eyes; the mouth, here
but a tinted vise, suggested nothing of the soft voice that had
issued from it, with its inconsistent New England way of dropping and adding "r's."

"You're to blame for the Lily Slade Incs., of the world," he
accused the miniature, determined to keep his thoughts focused
on something other than his wife. "Those Alternate Thursdays,"
he reminded the placid face, referring to Aunt Hetebel's agreement (yielding to civic and patriotic pressure) to open the doors

of her Massachusetts house, a structure unarguably both Early and Colonial, twice a month from May to October, to interested visitors.

He could see himself, a reedy raw boy, lonely, puzzled and curious, that first summer in Lynnport, watching the visitors arriving. In the hallway was Aunt Hetebel, greeting the tourists on budgeted hegiras, the Garden Club ladies, the shrewd appraisers and envious detractors who followed her massive frame on the prescribed tour from parlor to library to dining room, while she indicated the inherited treasures, murmurously shared the scraps of assorted family legend: the chair on which Herman Melville sat to write his appreciation of *Mosses from an Old Manse* (an upstate New York relic—never, however, a fact mentioned in proud Massachusetts); the *very* table on which Charles Dickens rudely rested his British elbows among Yankees even as he praised in ill-bred astonishment the degree of interior bloodiness of the well-browned roast of Sunday beef . . . "You don't say! Think of that now!" Uncle Logan, behind his half-open door, wearing his hearing-aid, silently practicing Brooklyn and Nebraska accents to imitate later at the dinner table.

"You old devil!" Philip addressed his dead great-uncle. He did not need a likeness or memento to remember Uncle Logan. He could recall him quite clearly enough; in particular the day he had burst into Aunt Hetebel's upstairs sitting-room in the Lynnport house without permission or invitation, invading her secret private world with a peremptory Rap! Rap! like thunder on the closed door. In he had stomped. Philip and his great-aunt were standing before the very cabinet around which Lily Slade had, years later, created her artful effects on the north wall of the fourteenth floor of East Seventy-second Street. In this cabinet Aunt Hetebel kept her collection of minuscule objects, of motley period, source, and worth, which Philip always thought of as her Tiny World. Aunt Hetebel was dusting them with a small camel's-hair-brush which she held poised, fixed in a dancer's gesture, as Uncle Logan advanced upon the two of them with an air of evil purpose.

"Well, well, what's this? What's this? What's going on here?" He knew very well. He thrust his gnarled index finger into Philip's lean ribs and turned it with a corkscrew gesture twice, quite painfully. "What's your favorite, boy? Got one?" Philip had. With a timid hand he drew it forth, a little Nipponese box with a delicious scent and a tiny door that slid back with perfect ease to reveal a legless round-bellied little man with a black beard, who bobbed up eternally smiling, no matter how long you held him down. There had been something joyous to Philip about the bouncing roll with which the little weighted man always regained his smiling balance.

"Good choice!" boomed Uncle Logan. "Good boy!" His voice, in approval, sent a chill through Philip's young frame. At once his great-uncle launched into a mixture of homily, platitude, and something very like a veiled taunt, pointing the moral: "Never stay down, my boy—adversities—obstacles—perseverance," above all, "the right attitude." Under the jumble of phrases lay something humiliating, even faintly alarming, in what was seemingly implied: the necessity to fulfill expectations, to pay off obligations; again—not the first time—the wing-brush of dark hint, the unmentioned shadow out of his pre-Lynnport days, giving Philip the sinking heavy conviction that *whatever* it was (that lowering shape from the past) he must make an extra effort to overcome its ill effects.

As soon as Uncle Logan left the room Aunt Hetebel calmly continued her dusting. She made no comment on the intrusion or the sermon. Philip, watching her large soft hands move the small objects with such delicate care, promptly transferred his love to a small, painted, crystal bottle with a jade cap. Something told him that here was an object from which Uncle Logan could draw no moral theme.

The little snuff bottle stood on a shelf in the old cabinet. He had passed it on to Pamela, for he had already caught glimpses in his gangling daughter of Aunt Hetebel's impassioned feeling for the tiny and the curious; the wing of a beetle, a thumb-size watering pot. It never ceased to amaze him that such tenuous yet distinctive traits should re-emerge so strongly from the murky enigma of the genes.

The thought of his child filled him with sudden acute distress. Immediately the night-club singer with the guitar started again in his head: *One and one and all alone and* . . . But he did not hear her out, for the Venetian blinds began to speak, tapping the sides of the window: *Clock, clock-clock, clock-clock.* Here in the fading night there was something sinister in their movement. Their insistent ticking was like a metronome, like time passing, like the count of his own pulse. He looked once more at the radio dial, tempted. A voice in the room might help. He walked toward the radio, then stopped. Could he endure the standard whimper and whisper, the violence and banality, the teasing sensualism of rhumba bands, lover-crooners, mystery murders, or even news? No, above all, not news; not that flaccid, well-fed, well-oiled voice keeping the world posted on its dooms and disasters!

He dropped down again onto the sofa and tried to tell himself that there was no reason for his formless depression, for the sense of unease and anxiety that hovered, waiting to pounce. Ellen was coming home; she had written to say so. "Feeling better about things." Her own phrase. But she hoped he had "done some thinking too"; hoped he had "thought it over." He had not. His first days of relief to have her out of the apartment, to have the subtle unspoken pressure of her criticism lifted, had given way very quickly to pessimism, to this same shapeless persistent anxiety he was feeling now. He went to bed with it, got up with it, lost it only briefly at a spot midway in drinks. *This* side of the magic place, *that* side of it—no good! Just that one middle position—all too brief a space, and impossible to hold, for try as he would he could never keep himself from slipping to where a sensation that he unwillingly thought of as guilt claimed him.

But he must think. He had promised to think, think, think . . .

3

THE blow had fallen without warning. In the late spring he came home early one evening without stopping anywhere for a drink. He couldn't remember why afterwards, though the circumstance was fairly unusual. Ellen came in a few minutes after he arrived and her surprised tone, "Well, for Heaven's sake! Home already?" might have prepared him in another household, but not in his own. "Do you want dinner early?" she had inquired, as though this alone could explain his being here at this hour.

"No, not unless you do."

"I?" She shrugged, implying, What difference can it make to me?

They dined at seven-fifteen. She had put on a white-linen jacket cut rather like a coolie coat and she wore it with pale-blue trousers. She had kept her figure, Ellen, and it gave him pleasure to note that there were no gross bulges inside the pale-blue slacks. She had a new haircut too, shorter, with free wavy ends all over her head. He felt the mild response which in the last years passed with him for sexual stimulation and he thought, with sincere pleasure, of the fact that he was home early and able to join her in her six-thirty highball.

"That's nice," he said, indicating her costume. "New?"

"I've had it for years."

He felt slightly chilled by the flat tone of her reply, but he laughed. "Sorry. You must be wearing it with a new air."

She made no comment.

Dinner passed without incident. Pam ate with them. She asked some leading questions about fractions. He tried to encourage her by assuring her that he had been stupid at math himself. Rosemyrtle stood in the kitchen doorway and advanced her views on rising prices. Nothing seemed different or special. Yet right after their coffee Ellen began. She began with a long monologue. He was feeling drowsy as usual after his dinner and, in the beginning, he only half-listened, so that she was well into it before he understood what was happening. As a consequence it had come back to him since only in fragments, without coherence. Indeed he had asked himself subsequently if his immediate failure to grasp the meaning of the scene—the effect it had had on him of mediocre familiarity, altogether lacking reality—could have been due to his over-acquaintance with the same type of situation, a stock incident in the pages of those books and magazines he must forever read in search of fresh material. Could this really account for the fact that, to begin with, he had been so firmly cushioned against any human or emotional response? He found the notion hideous, yet could not shake it off.

Ellen had begun by accusing him of living essentially a bachelor's life. That much he remembered clearly. He came and went, so she said, on his own volition. Dinner was often postponed, or put off, or grew cold, awaiting his will. When he did spend an evening at home he spent it idly reading the back numbers of current magazines, yawning with loud baying noises and going to bed early. She insisted that she was not making an attack on him. She was merely describing his way of life—a way of life that she didn't much care for, and if this was how he had to live, then maybe they shouldn't go on trying it together.

It was at this point that the scene snapped out of formula and got intensely real. He could still feel the shock that had gone through him. In thirteen years of marriage he had grown accustomed to Ellen's temperate attitude toward everything. He sat up suddenly on the sofa where he had stretched out. When he looked at her he saw her face was pale and rigid.

Before he could speak she had added, looking down into her lap, locking her hands together, pressing their knuckles until they turned white, "I've even asked myself whether there could be someone else." He stared at her constricted fingers in amazement. He remembered thinking how fine her hands were, small-boned, delicate. "Someone else?" he repeated, without comprehension. And then exploding, "Good Lord, of course not! What makes you . . . ?"

"Or maybe more than one," she interrupted. "After all, I know you drink with different people every night."

He still couldn't believe it was happening. He tried to make her laugh, asking her what she'd been reading lately, but she refused to accept his joking. Suddenly he found himself bitterly angry. He had begun to talk, to defend his ways on the grounds of necessity, reminding her acidly and unnecessarily that part of his job as Eastern story editor for *Suprema Films* consisted in wooing people into letting *Suprema* have a look at literary properties before other studios.

"Look," he said, "do you want me to give you a blow-by-blow account of the way I spend my days?" As she answered, protesting, No, that wasn't it, he hardly listened, for suddenly in a near panic he thought, What if she had said Yes? He saw himself in his office enclosed by the four dark gray walls, the two framed splatters of high-keyed color (the race-track Dufys; Goldstone's choice, someone else was always decorating the rooms in which he lived). He saw the high expensive polish of his large blonde desk, the telephone. It rang, he answered . . . Yes, sure I'll speak to him. Hi, boy . . . No, I'm out . . . Ask if I can call him back. . . . Don't disturb me for an hour. . . . Or it didn't ring and he made the calls. People came in. The usual quota of Hollywood refugees. Office staff. Goldstone. "Mr. Stewart is in conference with Mr. Goldstone." The mornings passing quickly with a buzz and bustle, a not disagreeable tension. After lunch, the let-down, the slack season, with him sitting in a glazed trance after that extra drink, pretending to be present. Might as well have given up and napped until five o'clock when he set forth again to do business in the bars. . . . Could it be that all this dubious, exhausting, occasionally exciting, over-strained routine led, by paths too peculiar to trace, to the eventual luring, baiting, capturing of the material from which Hollywood created its mammoth myths? It was as though he had turned a switch, and a reel of film, long ready for showing, had begun to run itself off before him; the days, the years, telescoped in a dream sequence.

Hastily, to center himself (for the feeling of unreality, of split-off segments of himself in action, with him also as spectator, was abruptly threatening) he began to talk again, using a tone of half-sarcastic emphasis as he begged leave to "remind" his wife that the raise in his salary, which had certainly not been unwelcome, had come about solely because he had taken the trouble to cultivate Dick Hill, a self-admitted, semi-reformed "lush" who had managed in a lucid interval to write *The Turn in the Stair*. Maybe, he admitted, with what he hoped was disarming candor, he did see a lot of second-rate people who drank too much. He probably drank too much himself. This was the price his job exacted of him. If she would only try to adopt a "realistic attitude." . . .

Ellen interrupted at this point to remark, with what he considered female inconsistency in its highest reaches, that she herself would like a job and that the happiest period she could remember was the war years. (Formula again! The current fictional complaint of wives.) He replied in kind, aware that he was following the prescribed childish dialogue. "Sure! You were glad to have me out of the way!" At once (he was pleased to note that she did not deviate from the accepted verbal exchange) she denied that her pleasure had anything to do with his absence. Not that—for she had worried about him horribly—but because of her hospital job. She had felt really useful, important and needed, and now this feeling no longer existed. . . .

Something increasingly acid and indignant in her voice snapped him back into focus and for a moment he had a sensation of honest misery. But since he did not feel able to sustain it, or examine it, he spoke with forced lightness.

"Well, darling, I can hardly start another war to solve your problem—though it may be taken out of my hands. . . ." Her expression stopped him. "Look here," he said irritably, "there must be plenty of things that need doing by women with time to spare."

"Certainly," Ellen cried, "if I want to be a volunteer worker in some Cause, a Good Works Busybody"—she hesitated—"but I've heard you often enough on the subject of *that* kind of woman."

He shrugged. "Well, you went to college. What are you trained to do?"

As he shot this question it occurred to him that he had hardly been trained at college for his present occupation. But Ellen was not quick enough to pick him up on that—or else she deliberately ignored it. She admitted hopelessly, "Nothing." She might as well have had no education, she said. Certainly home-making in a city apartment with one ten-year-old child who went to day-school, and with the doubtful help of a part-time colored maid, could scarcely be called an engrossing occupation. . . . It all fell into formula again and his dulled ears refused to focus until suddenly he realized that she had made the startling suggestion that they might have another child.

"Good God!" he cried. "What for?"

He had never seen her eyes so cold. She turned them on him, two implacable surfaces. Her voice when she spoke again was toneless, all feeling wiped out. "Is it so strange to want another child?"

"No," he answered quickly. "Of course not. I just thought . . ." She waited.

He tried to speak. What was it he thought? What accounted for the sudden irrational feeling of being trapped that the notion of having another child gave him? He only knew that everything in him cried out against it. The revelation shocked him. He was no more prepared for this discovery than he had been for Ellen's original remarks.

After several moments in which he did not finish his sentence Ellen asked him quietly, "Thought what?"

"Thought Pamela was—was probably enough." He spoke lamely.

Her face was averted now. Nothing of her emotions was revealed in the cool profile with the faintly cleft chin, the fine straight nose he knew so well. "It would do Pam good," she said at last. "She's always asking me why we don't have a baby. She'd like one."

"Well, of course, since Pamela is going to support it and raise it," he said with another attempt at humor, "she has every right to ask us to produce one." Ellen did not smile, and immediately he felt ashamed of himself. After a moment he said awkwardly, "Look, Ellen darling, if you really want one, of course we'll have one."

At that she burst out sobbing, jumped up and ran from the room. She ran into the guest room and locked the door. He could hear her crying as he stood turning the knob, begging her in a low tone to let him in. But she made no answer.

Pamela appeared in the hall suddenly, tousled with sleep.

"What was *that*, Daddy?"

"What was what?" He tried to sound offhand.

"Thought I heard a door slam."

"You're dreaming, darling. Back to bed with you."

He put his arm around her bony shoulders and led her back to her room. She got into bed and he pulled the covers up around her. It had been a long time, he realized, since he had tucked her in. A feeling of failure as a parent thrust at him. "Look, do you want to say your prayers or anything?"

"Goodness, Daddy." Pam's pointed face stared up between the spindly stretch of her twin braids. "What for? I haven't said prayers since I was eight."

"Oh, sorry. Forget I mentioned it."

Her arms shot up and got a stranglehold around his neck. She was not normally a demonstrative child and this impulse startled, even frightened him. "I think you're beautiful, Daddy," she said intensely.

He felt profound embarrassment. "Yep, I'm the Clark Gable type, all right." He took her arms gently from around his neck. "Get to sleep, chipmunk."

"You haven't called me that in ages," she said ardently, snuggling under the covers.

"Do it from now on," he promised.

He went out and poured himself a double Bourbon. Christ! Pamela too! That was too much! Where did children get their frightening psychic antennae? Why should the door closing behind Ellen have waked Pam? She had slept through many a noisy evening party. He drank the whiskey in one long gulp.

CHAPTER 3

 *
*　*
 *

THE next day he and Ellen met formally for lunch. He broke
an engagement to do it because, as he was having breakfast she
came in and said—her voice still tense, her face clouded—that
she wanted to try to get "it" settled.

"Well, let's for God's sake have our scenes outside the house,"
he said stiffly. He told her about Pamela's nervousness the night
before. Ellen's expression did not change; in fact, she seemed
almost to restrain a shrug. He was baffled by her behavior, and
irritated. The fact that she appeared at the breakfast table (an
unusual occurrence in itself) simply to start his day wrong appeared to him an act of gratuitous ill-will.

"Where shall I meet you for lunch?" he asked, as calmly as
he could.

"You mean you're free today?"

"I can get free."

"It doesn't matter," she began indifferently, and then, "Why
not Vanni's?"

"Vanni's at one," he said.

43

Vanni's was an Italian restaurant he had gone to frequently in his days as a young magazine editor. Since starting work for *Suprema* he hadn't set foot in the place. Film maneuvers had to be carried on where two could linger over a fifteen-dollar lunch well out in the public gaze.

He arrived early at the restaurant and as he sat waiting for Ellen, smoking under the fading nostalgic grandeurs of Lakes Como and Maggiori, he thought with a superiority of which he was unaware, that Vanni's was still the haven of the Aspirants, the over-shrill and over-still Not Quites; the middle-aged woman fresh from an outlying province in definitely the wrong hat, lunching with her first literary agent; the studiedly disheveled young man from an undergraduate essay contest frightening a junior editor with his post-Guernica anarchy.

He had just noticed with a shock of recognition and something surprisingly like dismay, the single framed photograph at the far end of the room, when Ellen entered, her white hat gleaming like a startling exotic flower in the dim interior. He was relieved to see that her face had ironed out since morning. After he had repeated the ritual of the "Very dry, very cold martini, no lemon peel, no onion, olive in one," he said, making his voice determinedly cheerful and impersonal, "When did Vanni's become a shrine?" He pointed toward the face in the photograph that he had just noticed: a prematurely middle-aged and angry Kewpie in shell-rimmed glasses which had the look of being borrowed from a man with a wider brow.

"Soon after he died," Ellen said.

As he waited for their cocktails, Philip began to speak in studied phrases about the celebrity in the imposing frame. It was the establishment's one famous patron, a literary figure of the Twenties (never known to Philip, or his generation, except by reputation) who each noontime, for many years, had crept pallidly to a corner table to eat his poached eggs on toast—"quite simply," Philip said, reviewing the facts for Ellen's possible diversion, "because this place was the only restaurant within easy staggering distance of his apartment. I think he lived next door—or upstairs."

Ellen glanced politely at the photograph and murmured.

Philip clung to the subject. "Why do geniuses so seldom look the part?" he demanded. "Why do you so seldom see a face any more that has in it either power or beauty?" He recognized that a nervous distrust of Ellen's calm exterior held him to the theme with somewhat disproportionate fervor. "The most powerful modern men—Molotov, Bevin, with an 'i', Bevan, with an 'a', most of Hitler's crew—faces like unworked dough."

The drinks came then and they both reached quickly for the cold glasses.

After his first gulp, Philip proceeded compulsively with the theme of Vanni's as a "shrine." "I can review every step of it," he said. "Every calculated move"—and he went on in a light flat voice developing the theme: The Celebrity languishing for want of a public to read his neglected prose, finally put his head in a gas oven and kept it there for the prescribed length of time. There had followed imposing obituaries during which so many eminent critics and radio personalities rapped on their breasts and condemned themselves for neglect, that Vanni thought it worth his time to get the Bachrach photograph of the man's early youth and hang it above his former table. This bit of senti-ment, dictated by Vanni's business acumen, brought immediate tangible results. Columnists around town made fitting comment, and newspaper and magazine authorities on Where to Eat in-variably worked in a mention of the photograph while recom-mending the chicken canaloni.

He looked at Ellen then for corroboration and she said, indif-ferently, "Yes, that's the way it was."

With his second martini he continued his exaggerated half-humorous, half-serious, attack on Vanni's. He found as he talked that he was becoming almost immoderately depressed. How had simple, unpretentious T. Vanni picked up the "disease," the "sickness," the "deadly germ" which had led him to a small-scale imitation of those fishbowl West-Side restaurants where it was impossible to escape the publicized egos of Broadway and Hollywood? "If not in person, then hanging on the walls, grin-ning down at you like bats."

This change in the simple restaurant of his early New York days made him feel like a wanderer long absent who, on revisiting his home, perceives some shameful and unexpected degeneracy. For a moment, as the second martini blurred his senses, he saw himself in this same dim booth years before, when he had brought each day to any scene in which he found himself, a fresh curiosity. How furtively he had once studied couples seated as they were, wearing about them that intangible aura of the intimate, the personal: parting, recriminating, making vows over the basket of tired breadsticks tough as kindling wood. Once these glimpses into strange lives had set his pulses up a notch, put his head to weaving numberless situations and plots. Now he merely glanced to see if any of the current actors were known to him. Here they were not. His sphere had—what? widened? contracted? merely shifted?

He looked across at Ellen then and saw to his amazement that she was crying. For a moment he wondered if he had spoken these last thoughts aloud. He stared, shocked, as she pried the dewy pink clams from their little shells, swallowing them in childish gulps, her tears dropping soundlessly onto the parsley garnish.

"Ellen, please, for God's sake! Don't!"

"All right," she said in a stifled voice almost immediately. "I won't . . . I've stopped."

And she had, in that remarkable way women manage to turn tears off and on. In silence they progressed through lunch to the fruit compote and coffee. Then, laying aside the pit of one of her plums with an air of finality, Ellen said, "Phil, I have to go away. Our life doesn't make any sense. You've changed—or maybe it's me."

Oh, no, he wanted to say angrily, It's me, all me, remember? It's my fault, or at least it was last night. But he didn't speak and she went on in the same inexpressive cold voice, telling him her "plan," which was simply to take Pamela to a farmhouse near her summer camp, enter her in the camp as soon as it was open, and then go away by herself somewhere. She said she wanted to be alone, "To get quiet inside and think." As she talked he felt his resentment mounting, though he did not entirely know why. It did not once enter his mind to try to dissuade her. He too, he thought to himself, would be very glad to be alone.

"Whatever you want," he said indifferently. "It's up to you."

He was paying the bill as he spoke, she was pulling on her gloves. She gave him a dark glance, heavy with unspoken anger, but said no more. Outside the door, beyond Vanni's stained awning, the unseasonal heat slapped up from the concrete. "Well, you're lucky to be getting out of the city," he commented. At once he was aware that he had said this to make her feel guilty.

"Yes, I'm lucky all right." Her tone was sardonic, expressing anything but gratitude.

He hailed a cab. She said she would walk. They parted with no further words.

2

ELLEN had been gone not quite three weeks. Now her letter had arrived saying merely that she was leaving Pam with the farmer's family and was coming home to see him; she hoped he was ready to talk about "it"—that personally she felt "much better about things."

And so here he was, presumably getting ready to welcome her. It was two-thirty in the morning; he was hot; he was half-drunk, and alone in their apartment, the place to which he had forced himself to come in order to think about it all and, if possible, make some sense.

The unventilated city smell invaded the room once more, a sickening odor that led him to reach for the forgotten beer beside his couch. It had already gone flat but he drank it as purposefully as though he expected to find some pearl of wisdom in the bottom of the glass.

He returned the emptied glass to the floor, folded his hands under his head and lay back again on the sofa. He said to himself that actually his marriage was no different from those of their friends. The Battle of the Sexes: the male routine against the female routine; which was duller, which the more unrewarding? How many times he had heard these fruitless arguments. All women were angry—that was plain. Even the girl from Michigan this very night had appeared already prepared to resent her eventual life as a modern mother. He remembered that she had talked at some length, early in the evening, about how women could be seen neurotically overcompensating for their angry frustrations by their fervid intensity about progressive education, braces on the teeth, vitamins, posture. . . . Or was he the one who had made that charge? He mocked himself, yawning. P. B. Stewart, the social theorist. Anthropological Study of the Upper and—or—Middle Middle Class by a Disgruntled Member of it. Notes from the Age of Anxiety . . .

What was wrong anyway? Were there men who knew, who could say accurately where it came from—this vague, unexpressed, but persistent tick of worry that now possessed him, this dissatisfaction with himself and the world in general? Was it true that something intangible but real had gone from modern life, some hope, some sense of eventual fulfillment, some security and expectation? Or had he simply been brought up to expect too much?

He only knew that nothing had worked out quite as anticipated. As an undergraduate the future had seemed reasonably radiant. From his position as an editor of the college literary magazine it appeared only a few steps to—to what? Just before graduation he had fallen in love. He had taken the first two of the prescribed steps: a job, marriage—though, to be sure, handicapped and delayed, and, perhaps, even made permanently insecure by the fact that he had walked out with his diploma into the years of the Depression.

The first job had not come easily. So many polite secretaries, so many polite letters, yet no heartening summons: "Come at once. $5000 to begin with" in the box at the Williams Club where he lived while waiting. Growing feelings of panic. The iron claw closing on the solar plexus every morning. Illegible scrawls by post from Uncle Logan: "Never cry quit . . . Never stay down" (the moral of the legless weighted doll) . . . "The challenge, my boy . . . perseverance . . obstacles overcome by . . ." It all came nicely from Uncle Logan who had never earned a cent in his life; only dwindlingly inherited.

Philip recalled the day when, growing desperate, still with no job, he found among the few remaining notes of introduction one from Aunt Hetebel to Miss Jemma Bates, editor of *The American Women's Friend*. He had not taken it seriously before. All the factors involved in it had seemed quixotically remote.

> *Dear Jemma:*
> *I am sending my brother's grandson, Philip B. Stewart, in to see you. You will remember last December we were speaking about my mother's (Philip's great-grandmother's) letters from Mt. Holyoke to your Aunt Charity in Zululand. I think Philip has some of the same ability to express himself.*
>
> > *Affly.,*
> > *Hetebel*

Zululand! His great-grandmother! *The American Women's Friend!* He had to laugh. On an impulse he called the magazine. After the usual wearisome explanations he got an appointment with Miss Bates.

Aside from his long-dead great-grandmother the only thing about the bright young graduate of Williams College that appeared to interest the elderly editor of *The American Women's Friend* was the fact that he had been born in the Far West. Philip was about to say he hadn't been back since he was thirteen and had no desire to return (for he had long since learned that there appeared to be some nameless yet quite perceptible stigma attached to birth so far from the Atlantic seaboard) when Miss Bates—the Manhattan transplanted spinster, born in a rectory in Cambridge, Mass.—uttered a loud cry of pleasure and started down the Grand Canyon on muleback, assuming he knew every inch of the way. Allowing Philip no chance to protest his ignorance, she took him by bus up the Oregon coast, gathered avalanche lilies along the snow line in Paradise Valley, hired a buckboard to go watch the Hopi Indians bring rain on a sun-baked New Mexican mesa. As she described red bodies painted with black and white lightning, stamping on the earth brandishing bundles of living rattlesnakes, she had cried, "Life! Life!" thrusting at him an over-sized Western apple, kept on her desk in a myrtle-wood bowl . . . "get away from Eastern provincialism—regional astigma-tism . . ." She gave him a job.

There was general relief on every side when he could finally announce the big news that he had been hired by *The American Women's Friend*, though, to be sure, Lily Slade had laughed, twisting her Teclas, crying, "Oh, *no!*" and wasn't it a shame it couldn't have been a magazine like *Vanity Fair*. Philip, too, had been embarrassed about the job to begin with. Before long, however, he had met enough male graduates of other leading universities engaged in making truth palatable and fiction cockle-warming for the American housewife (a hypothetical unit of society about which personally they knew nothing at all) that he no longer felt embarrassed by his pro-fession.

And so the routine had begun, the steps, the moves that had led him to this summer-stripped room on East Seventy-second, this hot night, this mood of drunken despondency. He saw what he supposed college alumni magazines would refer to as his "career" as so many moves on a graph, short leaps like hop-scotch: his lucky transfer to *Fullers*—which presumably enjoyed male readers—to handle fiction instead of non-fiction; from there to Public Relations for the A.T.C.; and then the last, the latest move, through a door marked *Suprema Films*, "Story Editor." He spoke the words aloud. They seemed bereft of all possible meaning and he tried to push his imagination ahead in time, around a bend in the hidden road where he could almost see the word "Producer" blinking on and off invitingly like a neon road sign. Then, of course, there was that other goal, deferred monthly beyond the payment of the current bills, when he retired on his own at last to do some long-postponed "writing."

This last thought catapulted him at once, with a fresh de-spondency, into the consideration of a further possibility. P. B. Stewart—oh, yes, it was possible, quite possible—could lose too many properties and get the gate.

The word "properties" gave him a sour taste. It was the same every time he used it or even thought about it. He groaned, flopping down farther on the sofa, erasing his mind, deliberately making it a blank. But on the blank the words of the telegram he had sent Ellen, in reply to her letter, now appeared, and he read his own phrasing with detached interest: *Your message made me terribly happy. The accused quite ready to talk. All my love Philip.*

Happy! The word now seemed excessive to a degree. Yet at the moment he had written the telegram it had, apparently, exactly described his feelings: the relief, the upsurge of good-will. Happy! No, this was definitely a word to be discarded from the modern vocabulary. Why he could not even in honesty apply it to his own child, to so-called innocent youth! At ten Pam seemed to him more often troubled than joyful. She brooded. She yearned. Her gray eyes searched her parents over-anxiously. Her gaiety, when it came, was too high-pitched. She worried with an almost neurotic intensity over everything from her marks in arithmetic to whether her hair should be worn in braids or hanging straight. And she frequently talked about the atom bomb as if it was a firecracker in the next room that might go off.

"Were you like Pam at that age?" he remembered having asked Ellen some months ago.

Ellen had thought a moment. "Probably not. At ten I was being fed exclusively on *St. Nicholas* and *Chatterbox.*"

"Meaning?"

"Oh, you know—Arthur Rackham mice in cutaways—the girls of St. Bridget's camping at Loon Lake."

She dropped it at that, leaving him to supply the mental image of Pamela's favorite fare; adult picture magazines with bloated Untouchables dead in the gutter sharing a page with Lana Turner in her new chinchilla ear muffs.

3

SUDDENLY the sofa, the heavy heat, his thoughts, were unbear-able. He jumped up, walked across the room, his head swim-ming from the sudden movement, and dropped down again on the arm of the sofa beside the bookshelves. He sent his eye wandering feverishly along the rows of books, hoping to find one that at least he would wish to open. But all the titles on which his running glance fell seemed to him like discarded parts of his own life: A *Farewell to Arms, The Great Gatsby, Butterfield 8, Point Counterpoint* . . . Not that he could recall in detail incidents or characters from these novels, but their remembered atmosphere seemed as deadly familiar as his own daily routine. The very bindings exhaled a depressing colorless miasma. He tried a higher shelf where the leatherbound "classics" waited in sets, their pages stuck together with humidity and neglect. On the way up his eye was caught and held by a small shabby volume: A *Portrait of the Artist as a Young Man.* The book seemed, indeed, to project itself at him, acting of its own will, like the necktie in the hall an hour before.

He took the book from the shelf and opened it. It was heavily marked. *Why don't we talk this way?* written along the margin on one page in indelible pencil, his own handwriting. What way? Like whom? Ah yes, Stephen Daedalus and— what were the names of those other Dublin university students, those searching, philosophical young Irishmen who had once lived in his mind as vividly as real people, thanks to the young professor fresh from a Rhodes Scholarship who had guided him through a course called Contemporary Literature?

Philip began lightly to turn the pages. Lynch, that was one, Lynch always secretly rubbing his groin and cursing with the word "yellow." And Cranly. And Stephen again. While walking and drinking together these young men spoke to one another about the "tragic emotion." What is it? they asked. They tried to define pity, terror; they discussed "aesthetic feeling." On all their talk there had fallen for Philip then an unearthly classical poetic light, like the light that fell perhaps in ancient Greece. Now with increasing eagerness he followed the marked passages: the talk about mother love, the sacrament, Aristotle, kinetic feeling; the student who wrote his name in pencil on the backside of the Venus of Praxiteles. A singular peace seemed to drift toward him from this lost world of subtle mockery, expansive ideas, abstract argument. Someone spoke "jerks of old verse" and again, sixteen years later, Philip found himself approving the underlined phrase. And:

> "Weep no more, woeful shepherds, weep no more
> For Lycidas your sorrow is not dead,
> Sunk though he be beneath the watery floor . . ."

Lycidas? Who was he? A golden name, a drowsy golden name evoking bright echoes here by the parchment and alabaster lamp in a tired brain blurred with alcohol. "Beneath the watery floor" that's where he was; he, Philip-Lycidas, not dead but sunk. Sunk was the word! "Thought is the thought of thought." Ah yes, and so here, in this sultry, heat-spun city room, he must read of others reading about others reading, back and back through time—the thinkers and the students. Why must they always have been uttered in the past—all words capable of ringing the sweet secret bell in the head and heart? Back and back from the present, like perspective lines meeting on the far horizon, went the thoughts of the thought of thought. He pinned his filmed eyes on that invisible point where the lines met. They exerted a hypnotic spell.

He began to nod, was about to close the book, when a passage leaped out at him. *Was your father . . . I don't mean to pry . . . But was your father what is called . . .* Instantly he came wide awake; aware of a long-forgotten, inner tremulousness. His own father, a stranger, pushed out of sight and mind, never understood, not spoken of, seldom written to, the hidden Thing in Uncle Logan's homiletics and innuendoes . . . He held the book nearer the lamp, read on:

> *Was your father, Cranly interrupted himself for an instant, and then said: I don't want to pry into your family affairs. But was your father what is called well-to-do? I mean when you were growing up?*
> *. . . Yes, Stephen said.*
> *What was he? Cranly asked after a pause.*
> *Stephen began to enumerate glibly his father's attributes. . . .*
> *A medical student, an oarsman, a tenor, an amateur actor, a*

shouting politician, a small landlord, a small investor, a drinker, a good fellow, a story teller, somebody's secretary, something in a distillery, a tax-gatherer, a bankrupt and at present a praiser of his own past.

"I wish I could describe my father in such fancy terms," Fred Dillon had remarked in his high thin voice, reading the passage aloud to Philip over a beer across the state line in Hoosick Falls, where his crowd did their off-campus drinking. "I'd have to say: Stock Exchange, and let it go at that. Or maybe I could add: Golf at par, worrier, drinker of whiskey with plain water and makes a fetish of it—the plain water, I mean. Something he picked up shooting in Scotland."

Philip had been startled. He had known Fred all through college but had never become accustomed to his easy sophistication, his constant manner of light artificiality combined with utter frankness. Fred was tolerated by his class at Williams because he was reputedly the richest undergraduate among them, and because years at a boarding school in Switzerland had left him an expert at tennis and skiing. These seemingly male attributes made it possible to overlook the way he pitched his voice and his habit of waving his hands from the wrists as he talked. Philip did not trust Fred, did not really like him, yet he had to admit no one else he knew read as widely and remembered as much. It was always hard to find a subject to hold Fred's attention.

On this particular day, when Fred made his remarks about his father, Philip, to his amazement, heard himself saying—almost as though someone else were using his mouth: "I could do better by my father than that."

Before the words were out he was regretting them. Fred was instantly on the alert. He loved gossip, and admitted it.

"Your father? Didn't know you had one."

Philip tried to be off-hand. "Didn't you?" Then realizing he would have to offer something further, added coolly, "I never see him. Haven't for years."

In the brief silence he observed that Fred was doing what he always thought of as "twittering." It was a way he had of puckering and dampening his lips as though getting ready to chirp, or lick the last drops lovingly from a brandy snifter. Plainly Fred had caught Philip's regret at his impulsive statement, for in a voice guardedly avid he asked, "What would you say about *your* father?"

Philip, fearful of any revelations that could become a part of Dillon's Packaged Tid-bits and aware that only extravagance could save him, forced a laugh, then leaned forward with the sly, intimate air of someone about to launch into an enormously funny story.

"My father?" He began to recite elaborately. "Religious fanatic, student of useless subjects, reformed anarchist, heavy drinker of Irish whiskey when he can get it, interminable reciter of Shakespeare, Milton, Eugene Debs—and the Holy Bible."

Fred was delighted. He squirmed around with open pleasure on the hard bench. "He *sounds* all right. What does he *do*?"

"Do? Hah!" Philip felt so pleased with himself over the way he was handling the scene that he pushed to the limits. He felt his eyebrows moving up superciliously, falsely; felt his mouth assume an expression between a sneer and mirth, as though all his features were being manipulated by some outside agent. "Doesn't do anything, my old man. He's a rather special character."

"So I judge. You mean he's retired?"

"Permanently," Philip said. He laughed. "Permanently—he retired before he had even begun." And then, noting the suddenly strained expression on Fred's face, the sickening idea crossed his mind that Fred might be thinking his father had embezzled and gone to prison like Buzzy White's father a year before. And as soon as he thought "prison" he thought "jail" and remembered the dark buried truth: his father *had* once been in jail, and not for anything as spectacular as the grand scale, Big Deal thievery of Buzzy's father.

Thomas Stewart's brief time in prison had not been headline news, but it had remained the family disgrace, never to be examined, never to be mentioned; the terrible occurrence that marked, as far as Philip's childhood memory could recall, the

final step in the tragedy of his father and mother. Dim fragments came back out of that night when he had lain in his
bedroom listening to his mother's stricken voice, to his grandfather—No words coming clearly from grandfather, only *clang,
clang, clang*—insistent strokes like the school triangle affirming
the end of recess. His mother's words wrapped in cotton bat-
ting, "Yes, Papa, I will, Papa." The thick hammering of his
own heart under the blankets. Then, later, his father home
again and the bedroom door tightly closed. Behind it silence.
No one going in or out. After school Philip had seen his sister
Jane hit Bill Cary with her book-strap, crying, "Liar!" Philip
had run past, avoiding Jane, suddenly afraid of her constricted
shadow on the October sidewalk.

Although in that drab beer parlor near Williamstown a
queasy inner tremble had risen in him from this rush of buried
images, he had become so adept down the years at pushing
away unpleasant thoughts that he was able to lift his glass quite
casually and remark to Fred, "There's nothing alarmingly wrong
with my father. He's just a maverick—a special kind of political
and literary, maybe even religious, *bum*."

The fanciness of his description again struck uncomfortably
on his ear. He hoped it had thrown Fred off the scent, but he
was not sure when Fred, looking straight at him, said, "Funny!
I always thought you were an orphan."

Philip shrugged. "I know. Most people do. I am, to all in-
tents and purposes. Aunt Hetebel and Uncle Logan have been
my family."

Mention of the Lynnport menage had the desired effect.
Fred's features slid back into their usual composed yet sly expression. There was nothing novel to him about the Jessups.
He had been to their house; knew it was included in a volume
of Historic Colonial Homes; had been impressed with the
scenic dining-room wall-paper and the collection of flip glasses
in the morning room. (His divorced mother in Cincinnati also
collected flip glasses.)

"Oh, well," he said, lifting his shoulders, "family life is really
always a bloody mess. It's high time it was abolished!"

Since that time Philip had never talked to anyone about his

father—except once or twice, and then not in any detail, to Ellen in the early days of their engagement, after Lily Slade had done a little deft prying. The truth was that his father had been so long out of his life, had played so little part in it, that Philip seldom thought of his existence. He wondered why the memory of the Dillon episode had returned with such clarity tonight—of all nights.

He made one last attempt to trace the steps of the evening's pattern, but it was no use. The whole thing began to go around and around in his head like a fiery pinwheel. The necktie's riddle in the foyer leading to Jennie Bogson, to guilt, Ellen, liquor, Pam, prayers; then resentment: no home, Lily Slade, Inc., Uncle Logan's index finger in his ribs . . . What the hell! He would go to bed. Better a clear head tomorrow with which to meet Ellen than a ready-made confession now, or a program of vowed reform.

He rose shakily and put out the lights. Fumbling his way into the bedroom he struck his foot once on a chair, cursed, and fell heavily into bed.

CHAPTER · 4

＊
＊　　＊
＊

BUT he did not sleep. As his head reached the pillow he saw
his father's face rise in front of him, a startlingly clear image:
the pale hair, thin above the fine domed forehead; the bright
questioning eye; the straggle of light mustache; the silver-
rimmed glasses in one hand, and in the other an open book
above which a voice exhorted, reveled, turned phrases on the
tongue like rare wine, crying, "Man, man!" the "beauty" or the
"wit" or the "pity" of it!

Philip pushed up on the pillow, his body rigid, staring into
the darkness, hoping his father's image would vanish from
where it seemed fixed in the stifling air. He was reaching to
turn on the light when the open face and burning eyes abruptly
disappeared. Now in the room only the lyric Irish voice remained, rocked gently between the lingual and the labial, the
blurred prick of the consonants, the delicate bleat of the vowels,
half boxed, half airy—"Clooth-na-bare . . . Lough Neagh . . .
Ballymeaney." All at once Philip found himself ten years old
hiding behind a door in Milltown, watching his mother and
father performing like actors in a tense and ugly scene.

"By God, you will!" his father was shouting in an unfamiliar, brutal voice. His hand was raised. *Was* he going to strike Mother? Philip's eyes were clenched shut, tight as fists.

Then his mother: "Hit me, why don't you?" Her voice unafraid, taunting, cruel. "Why not strike me? Let your children see you. Your son's standing right now behind that door, watching you!"

His father had groaned, turned and flung the door back and dragged Philip out. With the flat of his hand he had struck him twice, hard on the head, then slammed from the house. Philip had stood quivering, stunned by this unexpected violence until his mother whirled on him. "Go on outside. Go along! Get out of the house and leave me alone!" Then she had begun to cry wildly.

For a moment Philip had been paralyzed; his parents had never acted toward him like this; he turned and ran from the room, from the house, across the yard, across Lane's yard, on, on—"Hi, Phil, wait!" Charlie Lane had called, seeing him. Philip had dodged out of sight behind the cedar hedge. A criminal running for his life, he had come finally, panting and exhausted, to the shelter of the Carys' abandoned barn. There he had climbed into the hayloft and lain sick and trembling. Even now he could remember in detail the atmosphere of that deserted barn: the cold feel of the hay in the early spring dampness, the cobwebs, the silence, the musty dusty sweetness of the smell, the prickle under his bare legs, under his neck, in his nostrils, and the scalding blur of tears—tears that seemed to start with a sickening wrench from his bowels and gush upward to his eyes, his nose, his mouth, as though wild water had broken through channels too narrow for its terrible anguished force.

Oh, yes, his mother and father had quarreled before, but never like this—never with this cold violence; his mother standing like a monument in the park, his father the same. The quarrel had actually begun in the presence of the scissors-grinder. Father had said, "Flora, how about an extra plate for lunch?" in an easy light voice, standing inside the kitchen doorway, with the scissors-grinder just outside in his old dirty green-black coat looking suddenly ill-at-ease and bashful, not animated and fiery as he usually was. And Mother had said, her sentences flat and turned down at the ends like Miss Banning in the Fourth Grade when she listed those who were to remain after hours, "I'm sorry, Tom, I really haven't got any extra today. It's chops." "Nonsense," Father said. "Of course there'll be enough." "Well, to be sure, I can go without my lunch," Mother said. Philip also outside, sitting on the grass, caught the scissors-grinder's uneasy eye. At once he nodded reassuringly at Philip, twisting his beard into a rough spiral of gray wool as he spoke loudly through the half-open door, "Never you mind, Mrs. Stewart. Don't you bother, Tom. I'll go along to town." "But not a bit of it," Father said, coming down the steps from the kitchen. He was angry. "I won't have it." He went on protesting while the scissors-grinder lifted his pack and went out between the lilac bushes, his hobnailed boots going squish in the spring mud and his beard looking like a goat's tuft because of the way he had twisted it. Father went on protesting, but the scissors-grinder shook his head alternately from side to side, meaning "no" to Father, and up and down toward Philip, meaning, "Don't think a thing about it, lad." Father followed a few paces down the road and stood gazing after him, his head bent like someone listening for a faint distant noise. Then he came back quickly, jumped up the steps into the kitchen, and it all began.

2

THE barn faded, the air turned raw, and now Philip Stewart, lying in the humid summer of New York City's Seventy-second Street, heard the tolling of a fog horn off Indian Henry's Reef, three thousand miles away in space and many years in time. They were standing in the cemetery beside his mother's open grave, his father, his sister. The autumn soil heavy with moisture was falling with a nauseous thud onto the lid of his mother's coffin. Through the wooden top, through the mud, the boy Philip saw his mother's face as he had last seen it, ready to crumble like wood ash on the pucker of cheap white satin in the open coffin. The minister made a gesture and Philip's father took the shovel and he too began placing muddy earth on the wooden box. Philip could not bear it. He turned violently away and, as he turned, a flight of small birds passed, tearing the thick foggy air like cloth. They were blackbirds; he never forgot they were blackbirds.

He slid down under the sheet, holding his mind hard against the return of any further images of that drab and ugly frame house in Milltown where he had spent the first thirteen years of his life. Since his mother's funeral he had never gone back to it even in his mind. He refused to admit even now that any memory had returned. He closed his eyes again, determined to blot out Milltown. By sheer will he was able to melt the distant sound of the bell off Indian Henry's Reef into the gentle insistence of the chimes a long-departed Bachelder had brought back from Ceylon, summoning Aunt Hetebel and Uncle Logan and their grand-nephew in to a pleasant dinner.

It hadn't been easy—the transition; a young barbarian from the easy-going ungenealogical West must be crammed with information about his Eastern relatives, those remarkable Bachelders and Jessups, Seymours and Logans who had juggled commodities and culture like two bright balls of equal weight in the period before and after the Civil War. Philip had cried in his bed many nights, smarting at Uncle Logan's quips, aching with homesickness and loneliness because Aunt Hetebel's eyes had been fogged with inattention at dinner, her "good night" at bedtime sounding faint and distant above her knitting needles like a stranger's voice heard across an empty field at twilight. He had lain curled up in the four-poster with the carved pineapples, confused and miserable, unable to question his choice, to think of Jane or his father, or even clearly to remember his mother. On only one point was he certain: he had done what his mother had told him he must.

"Go to your Aunt Hetebel," she had said, lying back weakly on the pillows in that swift last month of her life. "She wants you. She has written to say so. Don't let your father prevent . . ."

Philip had shivered with the feeling that some terrible doom hung over him in case his father prevented; that his mother was trying to save him from some insupportable fate. But in the end his father had offered no objections.

"Make up your own minds," he had said, not unkindly, not indifferently either, but as though he were merely an interested onlooker not vitally connected with the plans being made for, or by, his children. They were in the living room waiting for Aunt Hetebel who, after the funeral, had gone into the bedroom to bathe her eyes.

"I'll stay with you, Papa," Jane said at once, her dark glance bottomless in a white face that stared at her brother.

Philip looked down and away, fingering for protection, as strangers carried his mother out the front door, the taw he had found in the grass beside the steps.

"I don't believe your aunt thinks you should." The voice of his father contained no clue. It was like drinking milk when you weren't thirsty. You couldn't taste it; it had no sensation.

"I'm past sixteen," Jane's voice, defiant.

Still Philip did not speak. Closing his fist over the taw and ramming it hard into his best-suit pocket so surprisingly without grit, he knew he would go with his aunt, and that both his father and his sister knew it.

Aunt Hetebel came into the room; the moths of her fluttering eyelids were stained the palest rose. From her fresh handkerchief came the breath of crushed mimosa which was to scent the rest of his childhood and adolescence. Jane brushed past him, going outdoors. "Coward," she whispered. "I hate you."

The words were like the time Joe Cary threw the stone at the stray cat and hit Philip instead. They were as terrible as the slamming of his parents' bedroom door—the time he had wakened in the night hearing voices. Their ugly finality wiped out forever memories of the moments he and Janie had hidden together, two against the Enemy, lying with fast beating hearts in the willows in the loitering sweet dusk of June, playing Indians and Pilgrims with the Parrish boys.

His father said no more, not then, not later. He remained carefully polite to Aunt Hetebel—so much so that on the boat going to Seattle to take the train East, Aunt Hetebel had said, after settling herself in a corner of the salon to look out at the pier to which Philip could not bear to turn his eyes: "He is a handsome man." And after a little silence, with a sigh, "What charm he must have had!"

Aunt Hetebel had taken a long look at Philip then, and he had felt with unease that his best suit was too short in the sleeves, and that the polish applied with such force to the toes of his shoes had not quite taken away their scuffed look.

"I think you are a Bachelder," she remarked. She spoke with satisfaction. It was his mother's name.

His mother had had a way of saying the name too—"I am a Bachelder. . . . You are a Bachelder." There were moments in his childhood when Philip had imagined those nine letters to be invested with a special power of some kind; almost magical. He had been, personally, quite willing after his second year in Lynnport, to agree to drop the Stewart and call himself Philip Bachelder. To the amazement of his great-aunt and uncle his father had refused consent.

"Shouldn't have bothered to ask Tom Stewart in the first place," Uncle Logan had growled. "Just gone ahead and done it. A lot of chance he'd have had, fighting anything in a court!" . . . Bachelder. Cyrus Bachelder; grandfather: the sign above the mill visible to every ship entering the harbor; on thick white stationery, and on a rubber stamp . . . Bachelder, Philip Bachelder, Bachelder . . . the city's muffled roar faded slowly as he drifted into sleep.

3

WHEN—how much later he could not have said—he awoke suddenly, he did not know where he was. He could hear his heart against the wall of his chest and he put his hand up. Why was his heart pounding? Where was he? With infinite caution he turned his head, straining his ears and eyes, trying to get his bearings in the dim room where now the first hint of dawn was spreading like a pale stain. For a long moment he lay tense; then through the open door he saw it: a light, gone almost the moment he glimpsed it. A flashlight. And instantly he became aware that the door between the inner hallway and the living room was closing very, very gently.

"Ellen?" he said aloud, sitting up straight. There was no answer. As soon as he had spoken he knew it could not be Ellen. Who, then? He waited. He could feel himself beginning to tremble. Finally, very quietly, he eased himself out of bed and groped his way to the corner of the room where his golf clubs were. He reached into the bag, carefully extracted a mashie and tiptoed through the hall. At the closed door he stopped a moment to listen, then jerked it open with one swift gesture.

The living-room lights went on in a blaze and he found himself facing a pistol—behind it a young man in an open shirt and faded army trousers. The pistol was pointed coldly, firmly, at his chest. As Philip stood motionless, the young man moved away from the light switch, took the mashie from Philip's hand and flung it behind him without looking. It fell on the marble hearth of the fireplace with a harsh clatter.

"What's this?" Philip asked, feeling his voice quaver. He took a step forward.

"Don't move, Jack. And put your hands up! Got any money?"

"Not much."

Philip's heart, after its first wild leap, had grown quieter. Now that he knew what was happening, he felt suddenly detached, an actor playing a familiar role. It almost seemed that he had written the scene himself, planning the movement, polishing the dialogue. "Unfortunately I spent most of what I had buying flowers." He gestured with one elbow and his head toward the phlox and gladioli. "For my wife. She's coming home tomorrow. Didn't get to the bank Friday, due to circumstances beyond my . . ."

"Quiet!" The young man's voice was flat, final.

It's really perfect, Philip thought. If I didn't write it, I shall certainly do so. What's to prevent my playing it too? After all, what has Spencer Tracy got that I haven't—dry, lovable humor, a whimsical throw-it-away bravado . . . He now felt no fear of any kind.

"Where is it?"

"The money?

"Yes."

"In my wallet."

"Get it."

Philip started to lower his arms. The pistol gestured.

"Walk! I'll follow you."

With his arms above his head Philip preceded the pistol into the little hallway. The pose struck him as absurd. The young man found the light switch and they walked into the bedroom. "Where is it?" he repeated.

Philip nodded toward the mahogany chest of drawers. Among key rings, crushed cigarettes, match cases, a soiled handkerchief and a pocket box of aspirin tablets, lay his wallet. The young man picked it up. It opened to the picture of Ellen and Pammy when Pammy was two years old.

"My wife and child," Philip said. He continued to admire his tone. (It's Cary Grant, he thought, not Spencer Tracy.) "That a German gun you've got there? I was in ETO myself for three years."

"Quiet, Jack!" the young man said again.

"We'll have to get you some fresh lines," Philip suggested amiably. The young man did not appear to hear, he was pulling out the money. Philip could see what there was in the wallet: a twenty, two fives . . .

"Honestly, is it worth it—the risk—for that little?"

"This all?"

"Sorry, old boy. That's it."

The young man began to open the top bureau drawers. He found the stud box, removed the pearl ones, considered and threw to one side the black agate intaglio cufflinks that had been Uncle Logan's. "Where's your wife's stuff?"

"Unfortunately it's with her—what she has—which I don't think would interest you much."

The young man walked to Ellen's dressing table and began to rummage through the powder boxes, the compacts, handkerchiefs. There was something brutally precise and cold about his hands fingering, appraising, the intimate small paraphernalia. He had turned his back to Philip now in complete indifference. Philip, studying him, became aware for the first time that he wore no mask. This cool bravado—did it imply that the young man expected only to encounter weaklings, those who would be sure to play it safe? A pulse in Philip's head began to pound.

"God damn it!" he shouted. "What in hell do you think you're doing!" He dropped his raised arms.

The young man whirled around. Philip saw the gun tighten in his hand, saw the fingers close on the trigger, heard the click. Nothing happened. The young man looked surprised. He took two swift steps backwards and pressed the trigger again. Again there was only the faint puzzling click. Philip rushed him. From the sides of his eyes he noted the open door, the bag of golf clubs, the telephone. "God damn you!" he heard himself shouting again. As he lunged he saw the arm for which he was reaching come up swiftly, then down hard with brutal jabbing strength. He heard the loud crack as the gun butt struck his skull. The shocking noise went rocketing on and on; it hurtled down an endless well of dark space, carrying him with it—a crumbling heap somewhere at the center of its far-off, jangling reverberations.

PART THREE

*
* *
*

The Hospital

* * *
*

WHEN he opened his eyes, saw it was daylight, and that Ellen was leaning over him with someone who appeared to be his doctor, Bob Scott, it struck him as rather far-fetched. Then he half-remembered and tried to speak. He wanted to say, "No fight," because Ellen might believe he had been drunk and quarrelsome, but he could force no words from his mouth. He felt indescribably nauseated. Once he tried to sit up, pushing his elbows hard on the bed, but the faces of Ellen and the doctor retreated until he saw himself again dropping down the immense well where the rushing air of the heavy fall blotted out everything.

It was another day before he was coherent enough to discuss what had happened. He learned then that Ellen had found him unconscious on the bedroom floor when she came in from her train at eight Saturday morning, that he had a concussion, had barely escaped a fracture, would be hospitalized for an indefinite time.

When the police appeared at the hospital for a description of the assailant, Philip made an effort to recall the man behind the pistol. "Looks like a hundred other guys." He repeated this several times, aware it was an ineffectual description, yet the only comment that now seemed to him entirely accurate. When the detectives brought photographs of possible suspects, he could only shake his head. "Don't think I'd recognize him," he mumbled. "Looked just like any ordinary guy—like any guy in a gas station." Pressed for further details he added, "Clean-cut character—but sort of sullen." Finally they left him alone.

The truth was he felt complete indifference to any attempt to run to earth this young man who, it was reported, had successfully looted several apartments in the same building that hot Friday night. He felt no wish to be avenged, nor could he imagine how he had got worked up enough to oppose the robbery and get his head cracked. How had there risen in him an anger strong enough to prompt such a foolhardy act? Why had the young thief's casual assumption of his helplessness so violently enraged him? And beyond this insistent question there lurked, in a remote corner of his numbed mind, a question equally perplexing, even more significant and meaningful: Why had the gun not discharged?

Within a week They—for thus he now split himself off from the activity around him; he in his impregnable, horizontal uterine case, everyone else vertical, active, responsible—They, on their feet, brought him an explanation. A Negro in Brooklyn was caught in a similar attempt at robbery. He too carried a German pistol which had not discharged. It was discovered that American bullets did not quite fit the gun. The Negro also wore khaki pants, an open shirt, no mask. He confessed that he had got his gun in ETO, off a dead German. It was a literal and logical explanation of Philip's escape, but somehow he could not accept it, though he thought about it daily.

2

SLEEPING, drifting, dreaming, he lost track of time. At moments it seemed only a day, then again a month, that he had been lying in bed, his swollen head completely detached from his body, brooding, distant, signalling its presence only occasionally. He

ate, slept, defecated, urinated, spoke, was silent, all by command
of automatons in white who passed in and out with thermome-
ters, pills, bedpans, needles, trays.

Sometimes he found himself on the train with Aunt Hetebel.
He was trainsick. It was the first day. He had begun to be trainsick before he got on the train—long before—in fact at the very
moment Jane ran out of the house and did not reappear. She
wasn't even at the dock with his father to see the boat leave for
Seattle, and although her face was not among those idly staring
from the pier he could nevertheless see it clearly, the ink-blot
stare she had given him. The ugly words she had whispered, as
she brushed past, turned and turned in his head and would not
stop: "*Coward, I hate you!*" They were taken up by the train
wheels grinding up a steep grade: *hate you-hate you-hate you*
(very slowly, painfully) then quickly, in a steamy rush, *hate-hate-
hate.*

He sought relief out the moving train windows. Giants' teeth
of black rocks hurtled past the heated panes and suddenly *Conti-
nental Divide* and the altitude, written in dark plain letters on
a white board, shot up from the rocky wilderness. "Aunt Hetebel!
Look!" She looked, then shuddered, ringing for a fresh pot of
tea into which to drop one of her mysterious white pellets. "Quite,
quite incredible! How they ever made it I can't think!" And she
closed her eyes, longing, no doubt, for the neat, contained, minute landscapes of her paper-weights and miniatures far away in
Lynnport, Massachusetts. "Who?" Philip asked. "How who
made it?" "The pioneers," she answered briefly, as though exhausted by the mere contemplation of the ordeal. "The people
who went West on foot."

Philip knew about pioneers. People prided themselves; wore
ribbons: *Survivors of Jameson Pass 1865; Descendants of First
Settlers.* On the Fourth of July Mr. Pearse, the County Super-
intendent of Schools, rose in the flag-draped bandstand and spoke
pulpit words about "Our Pioneers," after which the Men's Quar-
tet of the Elks Club always sang "The Wide Missouri," "Clem-
entine" and "Juanita." Mother, however, wore no ribbon, and
Father had never so much as appeared. Even Grandpa had remained at home on the terrace across the bay where the pulsing

bleat of Bill Daly's cornet, *Ask thy soul if we should part?* could only reach him salt-strained, mercifully muted.

"Was Grandfather Bachelder a pioneer?" It had never been said.

"I don't believe so." Aunt Hetebel took out the cards for solitaire, roused herself to answer more fully the restless boy on the green plush opposite. "Not technically—as I understand it. He went West in the 1870's. Told your Uncle Logan once in a letter that that was late for what's called true pioneering." She spread out the cards, flick-flick-flick, the impassive cool profiles of the kings, the leering jacks, the queens more sly than stately.

"But even then it was still very exciting—and trying, I suppose." She paused, holding red diamonds suspended, placing them, "We have a letter he wrote Mother—that is your great-grandmother—describing buffalo. I believe they shot them from the train windows. There were already trains then—very crude."

"Why didn't you come with Grandfather?"

"Mercy me!" cried Aunt Hetebel pulling up the padded moth-wing lids in astonishment. "With my brother? I shouldn't have been allowed. And anyway, I was many, many years younger than your grandfather." She considered an ace of hearts, her mouth pursed like a string bag she was drawing in slowly, then with the air of sharing something faintly embarrassing, added, "Your grandfather left for the West the year I was born."

"Then why didn't you come later with Great-grandma when she came West to visit?" Philip pursued.

Aunt Hetebel's reaction to this question reminded Philip of the forked retreat of snails when he took up a twig and gently drove them back into their striped houses.

"I'd just been married to your Uncle Logan," she said primly. "Your great-grandmother had done her complete duty and was free to go live with her favorite child."

There was something puzzling here—something, Philip thought, as puzzling as the solitaire now being played out before him, a mystery as complete as the expressions of disappointment, self-criticism, or triumph with which Aunt Hetebel conversed with herself. Was Aunt Hetebel disapproving of her own mother: did she find something lacking?

"But didn't Uncle Logan ever want to see the West?"

"Oh, dear me, no, never!" said Aunt Hetebel very positively.

And again after a moment, as though she felt constrained to apologize for her over-hasty assertion of her husband's lack of interest in travel in his own land, she added:

"As a matter of fact a Jessup once *was* in the Northwest. His name was Singleton. His family were in the tea and fur trade. Your uncle read me fragments from a journal he kept on a trip to Canton in his youth."

"When was that?" Philip asked, wondering why he had never heard of Singleton's visit.

"Around 1790, I believe," his aunt said calmly. "He also visited Hawaii, ate *poi*, and saw the hula." And in the small black notebook among Uncle Logan's locked-away treasures a firm hand with the blackest India ink had deleted some of young Singleton Jessup's comments on the hula and Northwest squaws. But the young Philip, on the adherent green plush flying through the Montana landscape, did not know this. In fact he was finding 1790 so remote in time that already he had lost interest in the single Jessup who had set foot on the Northwest shore. Grandfather was more interesting. He had known Grandfather . . .

"When Grandpa ran away," he began, touching again on the whispered piece of family legend he and Jane had always found difficult to believe—but Aunt Hetebel interrupted with the tone of one who corrects an important mistake: "I wouldn't say your grandfather ran away, if I were you, dear. It was only that he was a young man full of life and the spirit of adventure."

Philip stared. Grandfather full of the spirit of adventure? Grandfather—that heavy-footed man who carried a stick and dragged one leg? He said nothing more. Aunt Hetebel finished the game, made some of the cards into a fan and dreamily stirred the air before her face. "It is strange to me to think that both my brother and my mother lie buried so far from home."

Again a puzzle. Grandpa's home had certainly been the house above the bay in Milltown. How could she say then that he had been buried so far from home?

In the new silence Aunt Hetebel did nothing. She sat as though waiting. It was oppressive in the compartment. It smelled

of stale plush, hot steam pipes, mimosa and sodden tea leaves—
the last, when you dared lift the lid and sniff the dregs, like the
end of rain in a strange country. Aunt Hetebel released a sigh.
It floated pensively between them.

"I believe your mother was really Cyrus's favorite, in spite of
everything. So much the youngest and the only girl."

The word "favorite" also struck without conviction on Philip's
young ear. Grandpa Bachelder was as cold as a lizard that did
not dart. "Don't forget to kiss your grandfather, children,"
Mother always said anxiously. They obediently pressed lips to
an old leather boot. "Ah, children." That was all. Never, "Here,
buy yourself some licorice whips, or whatever you want," like
papa's friends met occasionally in the town. "I wouldn't tell
your mother about Mr. Magee's fifty cents." No, Grandfather's
hand never moved toward his pocket; it rested heavy with a black
seal ring on a thick flank. "Well, Flora, how are you feeling?"
Could she have been his *favorite*? Philip thought not.

"Mr. Pug was Grandpa's favorite," Philip said.

"Mr. Pug?" Again the startled glance fluttered toward him.

Philip tried to describe Mr. Pug, how he was unlike any dog
in Milltown, how he had a sad pushed-in-face which made it
hard for him to breathe without snoring, yet how he was gifted.
He was able, Philip said, to hold chopsticks in his paws and blow
one faint note on a Chinese flute. Actually he belonged to Old
Sam, the cook, who had got him for payment of a gambling debt
from the mate of a boat briefly in harbor from Hong Kong. The
flute and the chopsticks had come along with him in a black
lacquer box with a red tassel. Mr. Pug always ate his meals on
the dot with Grandpa and used to carry the matchbox in his
teeth for Grandpa's cigar. When he died—no longer able to pull
the air into the constricted passages of his nose—Grandpa had
turned away blowing into a white silk handkerchief.

"He sounds an enchanting creature," said Aunt Hetebel of
Mr. Pug. "And you described him very well." She regarded her
grandnephew for a moment with interest. "You have quite a gift
for expressing yourself. Perhaps you will be literary."

"Papa can recite whole plays of Shakespeare," Philip said.

Aunt Hetebel's face tightened. "I know, dear. It is an impressive but not very useful gift." Again the moths left her lids and fluttered whitely between them. "Your poor mother," she murmured. "Such a pretty girl—such a tiny waist—only eighteen inches, I believe."

It was the first time Philip had ever thought of anyone's waistline. There was a black braid belt with the buckle of a foxhead and grapes. Philip remembered the day he had shown Ellen the belt. "Heavens!" she had cried, trying to span her own waist with it. "Not even Pammy could wear this." "Nor her shoes, either," he had said, seeing his mother's little high-buttoned, white-kid boots resting on the Sunday grass while Papa in the hammock read aloud from *The Lady of the Lake*.

3

FROM his hot pillow in the hospital Philip looked fixedly at this light and airy scene of Sunday happiness, striving to hold it before him as an omen, a promise of peace. But soon the scene flickered, faded, disappeared, leaving him alone and frightened.

He was in a dark tunnel that closed in around his bed, conveying him back in time again to that first trip with his aunt, the day the train had come, without warning, to a stop in a long underground mountain passage. He could hear the engine far ahead in the darkness whistling, "Help! Help!" shrilly, and he remembered the rocky barren landscape through which they had passed and knew no help could come from its empty waste. The engine whistled again and again. The only response was a tumble of dirty water past the window. Finally the cars began very slowly, creaking and jerking, to limp forward until at last they had emerged from the black tube and he saw again the unbelievable daylight.

In his feverish state he made a confused identification with the engine of this childhood incident. It seemed to him that he too had begun to cry Help! Help! in some bleak and deserted terrain. He was in a bed, he was also in a tunnel, lying without strength, weakly in the darkness. What was it that had finally got the engine moving again? Would he ever know? The command had been issued and, far to the front, the wheels had responded. Did that mean that he too was, perhaps, exempted from any effort? Surely he could not be blamed for not moving when he was bed-fast, ill, an invalid.

This argument with himself, this silly and childish rationalization, created for a time a sensation of relief and almost blissful irresponsibility. But when he began to struggle mentally with the relationship between his own confused cry for help and his will to move forward, the feeling of relief vanished, leaving him bathed in perspiration, and the victim of a new, and even more terrible, fear.

Something had entered the tunnel behind him, and, though he could not turn his head to look—dared not—he was acutely aware of its presence; a Thing, a force, implacable, irresistible, conveying with cold and logical malice the knowledge that he himself had to make the effort to move toward the tunnel's mouth. No excuses would be permitted; no mercy shown. If he failed he, and he alone, would have to take the consequences. And the chief consequence was that, if he did not move, he would be *pushed*, with destructive violence and without proper warning, into the dazzling glare at the tube's end. (This seemed to him in his fevered state, a far more frightful experience than remaining forever in the darkness.) There was nothing to do, then, but start moving slowly toward the light—the light that far away, flickering and dim, shone only on a landscape of cold and ancient stone convulsions, not on the grass, the hammock, Papa and Mama and Sunday poetry.

4

SINCE clocks in the hospital had lost all meaning, it seemed to Philip that the experience in the tunnel went on a long time. He was most aware of it in the early morning, before coffee and the tart clarity of fruit juice had interrupted him on his crawling journey. He was very grateful to these aids in the silent secret contest between him and the Thing. He slept and woke, crawled and rested, and finally there came a morning when it was surprisingly eleven o'clock—the first time an hour had registered on him since coming to the hospital—and he knew he was out of the tunnel for good.

But again he had hardly taken a free breath, congratulating himself on victory, before a new demand—equally compelling, and requiring an energy beyond physical exertion—appeared to threaten him. He lay in a vast open space with an empty movie screen before him. There was no place anywhere in which to hide from the demand of that blank white space. It had invaded his hospital room and there it intended to remain—insistent, vacant—ordering him to animate its dead surface. No matter how he turned his head or shut his eyes he continued to see it— in front and behind him, all around, stretching to infinity, an endless expectant emptiness.

How could he summon the energy or the imagination which this new task required?—for now he saw his brain like layers of bleached convoluted tissue, bloodless, lifeless. The more he tried to force it the more impossible it seemed that he could ever again use this dead-white, scarred, and pitted moonscape that had been his mind. And yet he was certain he would not be let off. Whatever mysterious powers had ordered him to fill the vacant movie screen would never excuse him simply because his brain was no longer alive, had become merely an unreal image, a chart in an anatomy book.

Then, from the very center of his body, from some place in his abdomen that seemed to prove itself, surprisingly, a source of shrewd intelligence, he found a solution. He could not hide from the demand so long as he lay exposed on the earth's surface. Not even a tunnel could hide him. There were only two movements, two possible directions of escape: up or down. *Up* was a special kind of activity, requiring talents he did not possess. *Down* was easier. This he could manage. Instructed by the mind he had discovered in the region of his navel he began to sink deeper, deeper, ever deeper into the mattress of his bed until it became the ground, then the soil, the sub-soil—down and down, past the seeds of plants and the roots of trees, past the beetles, the moles and the earthworms, until at last he lay on the unyielding stone finality of the earth's underpinning. "I can't be found," he assured himself with feverish persistence. "I am hidden. I won't stir. They can't make me!"—and he was amused to hear his voice, out of the blind still tomb, talking quite normally to those who entered his room never suspecting how far he had removed himself.

5

HE SENSED, however, that he must in some way appear unnatural to Ellen and his doctor. He could see the anxiety in Ellen's eyes when she approached the bed. Her reading aloud to him was, he felt sure, an effort to divert him from his clever practice of teleportation.

He deliberately and even cruelly mystified her by asking her to reread the letters of sympathy he had received since entering the hospital. To him these letters were immensely comic. He never tired of hearing how he had served his friends and acquaintances briefly as a happy topic of amazement and horror: someone whom they knew well, a perfectly ordinary comfortable citizen, practically murdered in his own apartment by an assailant still nameless, faceless, terrifyingly at large. There was a wry humor in the thought of himself, a man with an uneventful, undramatic, padded and protected existence, as the central figure in an attempted murder, a successful robbery. Dick Hill, Goldstone, his mother-in-law had all chanced to use in their letters the same phrase: they spoke heartily and happily of his "close call." He would lie in his stony hide-away, in his self-discovered darkness, below the creeping roots and the stealthy worms, and repeat to himself in mockery: "Close call! close call!" Then the words became instead, "Last call!" and this mawkish phrase seemed to him even funnier and he would smile. Twice Ellen, at these times, asked suddenly, "Are you in pain?" He wondered if his face was twisted in some inner agony of which he was unaware. Or had there merely rested on his features the cliché of the "mirthless grin?"

CHAPTER 6

*
* *
*

THE doctors' and Ellen's first choice for a cheering outside influence was Goldstone.

The day Goldstone came was a rainy Saturday afternoon. As a concession to other men's country habits, Goldstone, who never moved from his penthouse overlooking Central Park West, had donned white flannels and a vivid light-weight tweed jacket, cut extra long and with an extra deep vent. Philip observed the jacket attentively. He had for years been accustomed to ragging Goldstone about his taste in clothes. It was, in fact, a part of their relationship, as definitely established as a daily greeting. He spurred himself now to make the usual bantering effort.

"What's that you're wearing?"

"What do you mean?" Goldstone looked down happily at his tie, bright green, a pure silk with handpainted clouds and sailing ships.

"No, not your Countess Mara job—I mean, your fur-bearing tweed."

"Oh—my jacket? Oh! I knew you'd like it."

"Jacket! I thought it was the newest thing in light summer topcoats."

Goldstone grinned. "My boy says this is *the* length now."

Goldstone's only son went to Lawrenceville. He was very proud of the fact, but worried when he learned the boy was no athlete, that he preferred chess to football.

"I know," Philip said. "It's an exact copy of a $45 Brooks Brothers item which your tailor was glad to stitch together for only $150! I'm sorry about your tie, too. It's so conservative! The nurses here are great ones for wardrobe details."

Goldstone wagged his head happily again and dropped down beside the bed. He felt reassured; everything was as usual. "How are you anyway, old boy?" His shrewd dark eyes liquefied with sympathy as he crossed his stubby legs, one pulpy hand nursing a shrill green sock.

"Goldy, you wouldn't believe the nightmares I have," Philip told him softly. "I think I could write the kind of violent story treatment now that even you wouldn't like."

"Zat so? What kind?" Goldstone was now faintly uneasy. They had warned him to keep the talk light and gay. "Never mind," he said quickly. "Don't tell me."

"I won't. And you needn't ask me what the hell I've done to rate nightmares, either. The answer is, nothing, and I know it!"

Philip had never spoken to Goldstone with this kind of bitter detachment and he could see he was puzzled. Though they were not always—or even frequently—in agreement, their relations had always remained on a certain prescribed, intimate, yet impersonal, social level. Whenever Philip wished to talk Goldstone into sharing some enthusiasm, he followed an established routine; a series of gags accompanied by hard facts. Goldstone had opposed his hunch on *The Turn of the Stair*, but when Philip had bulled it through and, in Goldy's vocabulary, it had begun to "roll," it was Goldy who had seen that Philip's salary was raised.

Philip said again deliberately, suggestively, "These nightmares I'm having . . ."

Goldstone cut in, keeping his voice light, affecting a rather touching, unconvincing twinkle, "Nightmares, eh? Maybe you're the suggestible type?"

"Suggestible?"

"Influenced by all these first novels by bombers and pilots we've been getting. Don't they all have postwar nightmares?"

"Culver Military Academy plus the Apocalypse in seven hundred and fifty pages," Philip said. He used a mechanical unnatural voice. It was a line he had thought of that morning. Abruptly he let go of his private check-rein; allowed the words to come rolling out: "Is it me, Joe Jo-Jo from Greenfield, Indiana, lying camouflaged in the jungle, or am I really the steamy thicket I've been fixed up to resemble?" (Another of his nightmares—one of the worst—when he saw himself as an indistinguishable part of the light and shade of tropical forests, become the very shadow and substance of the jungle in which he lay waiting—motionless, soundless—to kill or be killed) . . . "Twenty-two ways to do it," he said loudly. He shot a glance at Goldstone who was now looking both worried and ill-at-ease. "Twenty-two ways to kill a man without making any noise, Goldy. You might think Jo-Jo could relax, mightn't you? But how can he? The Japs lying hidden in the same thicket may know twenty-*seven* ways—including Jo-Jo's own favorite, which involves piano wire and the jugular vein."

When he stopped speaking, Goldstone looked around anxiously, obviously embarrassed. "Yeah, you've been reading too much."

"Could be."

They were both silent. He could feel Goldstone struggling not to say, "The war's over, my boy." Philip knew he would regret having acted this way. He could not imagine why he had. Suddenly Goldstone was staring at him with genuine concern, for a moment the doors in his eyes opened and seemed to show a passageway leading to another Goldstone; to a man who perhaps wanted more than the pat, marketable answer. He was asking gently, "How do you *honestly* feel, Phil?" It seemed to Philip then that he really wanted to know.

"Okay. I'll tell you exactly," Philip said. "Like lying here for the next year—I'm just too tired to die yet—like lying here and then asking somebody to give me some lethal pills of sure-fire potency."

He had carefully phrased his answer, avoiding any direct un-compromising word like death or poison. But he saw he had really frightened Goldstone now. The doors in his eyes closed hurriedly, and again the face assumed the masked look of the man in the silent swivel chair behind the expensive desk.

"That's perfectly natural," Goldstone assured him. "You've had quite an experience, old boy. Don't make light of it."

Then, without waiting for an answer, Goldstone dived com-pulsively into office talk: what they were dickering for, who was in town, a few racy bits of special prurience from the Hollywood scene, what they were paying for *Street That Leads Nowhere*, how such and such an agent was applying peculiarly female bitchery to a contract situation, how her bluff was being called. "We'll get it for $25,000. Wait and see!" "Maybe the guy who wrote the book needs the $40,000?" Philip suggested. Goldstone looked up, pleased, hoping for a gag. But when Philip's face remained serious, he said quickly, "Sure. Who doesn't?"

He went right on: *Bus Ticket to Miami*. Great new talent! Really fresh . . . *Two Plus*—mystery with a stunning new twist. Change the title, of course . . . The talk had for Philip now the precise accuracy of a phonograph record played so frequently that each word and pause, each defect in recording, each scar and flaw, was known and intimately anticipated.

But after his first forced attempt to show interest, he could not keep it up. He felt a great scream had begun to gather itself above his head, and that when it swelled to enough force it would scream itself out and destroy forever his easy comradeship with his business superior, his senior officer: little, shrewd, kind, tough, ambitious, materialistic Goldstone who talked Left and lived Right, who supported PAC with one hand and purchased imported caviar, old brandy, and two-hundred-dollar suits with the other.

2

No, the Goldstone visit was not a success. That night, toward morning, Philip again awoke, rigid with fear and horror. This time he did not call the night nurse. She no longer had anything, he felt, which could aid him. Desperately he began to search through time past, time ahead, through memory, through anticipation, for something that would soothe his ragged nerves.

Finally, in memory, he came to rest in the Lynnport kitchen where Nelly had just made fresh bread. The indescribably sweet delicious scent filled the room. The loaves stood cooling on a side table, covered with a white cloth which he went over and lifted, looking down at the brown crusts. He picked up a loaf, closed his eyes, smelled and smelled in ecstasy. Nelly caught him at it, and, for a wonder, wasn't cross. Instead she grinned and came over and cut him a generous slice, standing with her perpetually distended neat round belly in its spotless gingham pressed against the table edge. Next she took down the butter from the lower shelf of the cupboard, where it stayed in a blue bowl all day long to be more easily spread, and got out the strawberry jam, made generous sweeping motions with her knife: smear of buttercup yellow, smear of strawberry pink; handed him her creation with a "Here now! Git!" spoken in the ghostly fibreless voice of the deaf. He went out slamming the screen door—the one door in the house he dared close with force—whistling to Bruce, his collie. He was, for a moment, so happy with his dog, the day, the smell of fresh-cut grass and bread, that he yelled, whooped, ran wildly up the slope of the garden to jump the clipped privet hedge at the top.

The Lynnport house might not have failed him had he kept to his memory of the kitchen and his own room. But there rose, unbidden, the picture of the afternoon he had gone to sit, at the request of Uncle Logan, in the library beside the shelves containing the books on Napoleon.

That day Uncle Logan was haggling with a dealer. The dealer had come all the way from New York to make an offer for Uncle Logan's entire collection of Napoleonana. Uncle Logan had no idea of even considering the offer, but he was quite willing to spend a dull afternoon bargaining; particularly since the man who wanted the Napoleon collection was someone in Detroit, rich enough to pay any price, self-made enough to want to keep it low.

Uncle Logan spoke of Napoleon with many a hah and snort, with much nose-trumpeting into a large, very white, very fine

linen handkerchief, and a constant twitching of his half-para-
lyzed left hand with the seal ring on the little finger. Sometimes,
for emphasis, as he hunched near the fire to read aloud, he would
strike the legs of the yellow damask wing-chair against the
polished fender.

"You listen to this, Philip, my boy. This is instructive. This is
the credo of Napoleon. You won't get this in school, my lad,
only the public facts, not the man's private theories," he said,
clearing his throat elaborately before launching into "Napoleon's
own words."

*"A man such as I does not concern himself about the lives of
millions of men. . . . I have spilt blood? I had to: I shall perhaps shed more, but without anger, and, quite simply, because
bloodletting is a component of political medicine. It is necessary
one should always talk of liberty equality, justice and disinter-
estedness, and never grant any liberties whatever . . ."*

"Ah, the old fox," said Uncle Logan breaking off. "And here
it is in a nutshell," he cried. "His point of view: *'I am not a man
like other men and the laws of morality or custom cannot be
applied to me.'*

"Ah-ha, *ha!*" said Uncle Logan, delicately fingering the tuft
of dark hair that grew from the mole on his right ear. "Ah-ha, *ah!*
Yes, indeed! Napoleon was a great cheat at cards, you know.
Cruel in many small ways, too. Used to keep his attendants three
hours in a hot steam bath. Loved to pinch the noses and ears of
children and women. Good hard yanks he used to give them,
too. No heart, the man, only ambition. Josephine the only
woman he could ever abide. Ever read his remarks about the
marriage bed? . . . Welter of sweat and . . . Well, never mind,
never mind! Josephine appealed to him, no doubt about it, but
he was perfectly willing to let her go to get an archduchess in
beside him . . ."

Philip at sixteen, home on a holiday from school, restless, undetermined, inadequate, sat politely in the stiff chair, unable to
protest, wondering: But if all this is so, why has Uncle Logan
spent a small fortune collecting all he can find on the life of a

card-cheat, woman-hater, puller-of-the-noses-of-children? What was so instructive about Napoleon's private credo? Did something in Uncle Logan respond to his heady assertion that he was "not a man like other men" and should not be so judged? Did he and the anonymous millionaire in Detroit—whose agent, a precise gray little man with glasses attached on an imposing black cord, alternately tittered and looked pained at Uncle Logan's comments—did they both secretly long for the power to indulge in sadistic impulses large and small, ranging from nose-tweakings to a forced winter's march of exhausted troops through the Alps?

Something terrifying and portentous was here, Philip thought, something too baffling to lend itself to any ready answer—a certain inconsistency he had already dimly perceived in the rules of conduct applicable to young men growing up in Lynnport, Mass., and those applicable to the world's great. "History's verdict," said Uncle Logan—a favorite phrase. But was not Uncle Logan himself a part of history's verdict on Napoleon, sitting now in his cosy book-lined room crying "Hah" with a sort of reluctant yet pleasurable admiration at the foibles, crochets and downright wickedness of a dead celebrity? Philip had left the room at the first opportunity.

As this scene rose now before him, he turned uneasily in the hospital bed, unable to find his way with any comfort back into the old Lynnport house. No matter what door he entered, he had to get to his own room at the top of the house along the hallway that led past the library; and there, beside the dying fire, sat Uncle Logan, the book dealer, and Napoleon—waiting for him with their chuckling, old men's cynicism.

3

THERE was only one road of escape—one safe, happy, uncorrupted lane of memory—the one he had known intimately as a boy. He lay back, concentrating hard . . . He was in bed, in his room in Milltown; ill, feverish. It was summer and very hot, and his sister Jane sat beside him saying, "Close your eyes and think of November." She closed her own eyes. "Remember," she was saying dreamily, "in the woods, the fungus . . ." He had held his eyes tight shut while Jane summoned up the cool rain-swollen November of the north Pacific slope. Far off he had heard a cowbell knocking faintly on damp gray air, the light heavy with the weight of rain-soaked firs pressed darkly upon it. The shrill monotone of the chipmunk, plundering against January, pierced the chill woods; and from the earth, padded with moisture and cinnamon pine needles, there rose no other sound. The fading blue of Oregon grape, the glistening lacquer of its leaves, alone still carried any remembrance of summer sun. All else belonged to rain and autumn; even fluted whirls of fungus, springing white and naked from the moist soil, grotesque and strange as those sea creatures belonging wholly to the realm of water, revealed unwittingly at lowest tide . . . I, *Philip Lycidas, sunk though I be beneath the watery floor.*

He rocked in the tide of rising sleep.

Then, abruptly, the woods also failed him. The shrill familiar chitter of the chipmunk was drowned by a high piercing tone; thin, menacing, otherworldly. At once Philip knew its origin: the supersonic whistle-pistol, no larger than a lead pencil yet capable of killing, with inaudible sound, a dog at sixty feet (Bruce and Mr. Pug lay together dead under a mock-orange bush); capable of inflicting severe burns without developing heat; capable of raising the temperature of a chemical two hundred degrees in one second without transmitting warmth. (He had read about it in the science section of a Sunday newspaper.) And now these rays of highest frequency, of soundless sound, flooded his consciousness and drowned out all other noise, taking from him his pleasant world of fantasy and desire. He pushed himself up on his pillows, straining to hear the yellow apples falling in the moonlight on the orchard grass, the chestnuts, striking dried leaves in the late afternoon, the first peepers strumming in the marshes, or an April bird calling—trailing its name through the rain. He could not hear them. They were gone forever. The supersonic whistle grew more intense, more shrill, high, pervasive, piercing his head like a great hot needle until the whole universe was drowned in its manic shriek.

His damp hand at last found the cold bell.

"Stop that noise!" he shouted.

The nurse cut into the room with a brisk stride. "Stop what noise?" She put her heavy hands on his shoulders, as she did so pulling the pillows down a little—a trick to get him to lie back on the bed.

"The whistle!" he shouted.

"What whistle?" Her calm enraged him.

"You mean you can't hear that whistle?"

"There isn't any whistle, Mr. Stewart. You've been dreaming again."

"Dreaming?" He found this supremely funny. He laughed and laughed. "Listen," he said, suddenly fierce. "I'm not dreaming. You are. And everybody else. But I'm not. I'm cold sober. Sane. But the rest of you—you're all strictly bats. You're going around acting as though you didn't see anything, hear anything, smell anything! You mean to say you don't *smell* anything either?"

"I smell the very beautiful roses your wife brought you today," she said with her standard syrupy inflection.

He was abruptly calm and resigned. "That's right. Just bring me the nursing bottle. That's all I need." He lay back on the pillows, but in a moment he had shot up again. "You have the nerve to stand there," he shouted, "and tell me you don't smell the stink of those ovens? Not bread, oh, no, not Nelly's bread, baby, this is another kind of bakery, another kind of kitchen . . ."

He was in the Nazi crematories, the film he had seen of the Nuremberg trials: the crates of human hair and teeth, the piles of human skin. "Waste nothing!" a man on a podium was shouting. Was it *his* voice? Uncle Logan's seal flashed on a brass knuckle and in his own hand a golf club changed into a gun. "It's only a movie," he tried to say and the gelatin sea would soon part magically and let him escape along with the Children of Israel in the fifteen-cent Saturday matinee in Lynnport, Massachusetts. "Only a movie!" but there was no comfort for him in this false assurance.

He felt himself being carried away by some dark wild torrent of anger and fear. He began to shout more loudly. Once he saw the nurse pressing the bell and tried to strike her hand, but he was too late. She grabbed his wrists in a professional clasp, pressing down with her body weight. Almost immediately there was an orderly in the room. Philip tried to fight them both. He screamed, protesting the needle that was descending near, nearer, toward his rigid arm.

CHAPTER 7

*
*   *
*

NEXT day the memory of his struggle with the nurse and orderly came back to him with a kind of thrashing white horror. From Ellen's face, even from Bob Scott's, he could see they had both heard what had happened. He wanted to speak out, talk to someone about his state of mind. But Ellen of course would only be alarmed; and Bob—he did not want to discuss his mental condition with any doctor posing as a friend; he was sure in advance that he would resent whatever professional attitude Bob would choose to adopt, the soothing or the challenging, the Don't Worry or the Be-a-Man counsel.

In the afternoon Ellen came in again, as usual with some knitting, and sat near the window. He could see the film of moisture on her forehead and the look of strain she was trying to force from her face.

He endeavored to keep his voice casual as he said, waving his hand around the room, "All this is being terribly expensive, isn't it?"

"Don't worry about it, darling," she answered—too quickly, he thought. "Just get well."

Her last words dropped on him like a physical weight. He wanted to cry out against them and the burden they suggested, to protest, roll wildly on his bed, groan, make a scene that would command her sympathy. With a great effort he held himself steady.

"I don't think I'm improving."

"Bob says you're doing wonderfully."

"Does he?" Now he would have to tell her. "Look! I'm not doing wonderfully. I'm washed up, Ellen. I simply can't face going back to the office. I never want to see it again—or any one of the people—or hear them talk. I—what can I do about it?" In spite of the effort he was making, he could hear the panic and tension under his voice.

"Don't go back."

He looked at her in amazement. Her tone was strong and quiet: the voice, it seemed, of a sympathetic stranger. Even her appearance, that natural streak of blonde hair that winged across her brow, alerting and quickening her serious face—Who was she? He closed his eyes, knowing it was fantasy and indulging it. Yes, she was a stranger who had come to help him, a wise, tolerant and beautiful woman drawn to him by his need, a super-*She*—the woman behind every myth who asked nothing and gave all. Or was it gave nothing and took all? . . . A strange line from nowhere came into his fevered head, "Since the Lady Ishtar descended to the land of No-return" . . .

He heard the voice repeating, outside his private world, "You don't need to go back."

He held onto the vision of the strange woman—Garbo, Nofretete—his eyes closed. "I don't?" he inquired dreamily. When he opened his eyes again and realized that it was Ellen, Ellen his wife, who had said this remarkable thing, he cried out, "You mean that?" His voice held the relief of a man who has just received a last-minute reprieve.

"Of course I mean it."

For a moment he felt a gratitude so intense that his eyes filled with tears. He saw Ellen turn away. Almost at once he became cautious again, skeptical: Could it be another trap? Aloud he asked, "But what will you—what will *we*—do?" To prevent her replying too quickly and easily again, his voice took on a sharp edge. "We can't 'suck with the bee and bed in the cowslip!' "

It was an expression from the days when, on Sunday mornings, they talked of the time they would give it all up, go off to Vermont or New Hampshire, buy a farmhouse where he could write and she take up her music again; maybe even give lessons to neighbors' children. There would be blueberries in the fields all around, and a detached barn that could be made over into a study. In winter they would be snowbound, able to reread all the classics, even Walter Scott, and maybe they would go out on snowshoes to look for rabbit tracks and leave suet for the birds . . . When he used the old intimate phrase, he saw her eyes blur faintly.

"We can manage," she said. "We'll find a way. Get well first."

He shook his head. Instantly the dull pain signalled him to be more careful. "But I can't get well while I lie here worrying." When she did not reply, he added, "I've wasted my whole life."

As he spoke these last words they seemed so tragic and true that he felt he might begin to sob uncontrollably. He put his arm across his eyes and lay rigid.

Ellen came over and sat down by the side of the bed. When she took his other hand and pressed it gently between her own, he twined his fingers through hers and held on hard.

"Do you have to talk about it now?"

He moved his head on the pillow. "Yes."

After a little silence he took his arm away from his eyes. Still hanging onto her fingers, he looked out the window. "I'm really washed up, Ellen. I never want to go back. I feel as though something in me absolutely quit with that blow on the head. It's not just *Suprema*—I haven't the stomach for anything that looks like work, or routine—or even thinking. I just want to lie down and . . ."

He broke off. "And die," he finished inside his own head.

She said nothing for a moment, then murmured, "I think I understand."

He searched her face. Did she understand? He was sure she did not. How could she? Protected all her life, the very protection she rebelled against, or said she did, had been her cotton-wool, her insulation. "Don't dramatize, Philip! You've not had it so hard!" Yes, it was true. He had been lucky—lucky even during the Depression. Or was it lucky? What about this sense of being caught and held all these years to a fixed round of meaningless activity? Was that luck? Was it a conspiracy of silence on the part of all men—this non-mention of the onerousness of their routines? Or was he alone in his feelings—unmanly, irresponsible? Perhaps he had not chosen right in the first place; had jumped at the first thing—The *first* thing? No, there had been no choice. He had wanted to marry. He had accepted the *one* thing that offered him an income after his graduation. It had been as simple as that. And now it was as complicated as . . .

Aloud he suddenly repeated to Ellen, "But what *would* I do— *we* do—if I did quit?"

He thought of the question when he asked it the second time, as some enormous and difficult test to which, without her knowledge, he was submitting her.

She hesitated.

"I mean definitely, *practically*," he added. He tried not to let his voice reveal how important he felt her answer would be.

When she spoke it was haltingly, as though she knew she might say the wrong thing. "I thought—that is, I've been thinking—you know, darling, you understand so much about what makes a successful movie—I've heard you talk about the 'formulae' and that sort of thing—and I wondered, why couldn't you go away and take a good rest for a few months (we've got enough savings; those war bonds, remember?)—and after a rest maybe you could write a story yourself that you could sell for a big sum and then quit for good and—well, just write the way we used to plan?"

He laughed; and the cracked sound of his laughter came back to him full of self-contempt. "You've been going to too many movies yourself," he said, withdrawing his hand.

"What do you mean?" She looked up with an expression between irritation and apprehension.

"Just that it's one of the strangest damned things in the world that none of us bright story-editors who know what's wanted—

or claim we do—ever seems to hit the jackpot with any ideas of our own."

"Maybe you just don't try?"

"Maybe that's it," he said dully. "Or maybe it's just that it's hard enough to handle what someone else shovels out, so your own pride can't take shoveling it out yourself. It's the only thing you've got left. Or maybe it's just another form of . . ."

He stopped. He had been going to use the word "death" again. Immediately the sick familiar sensation, the rush of uncontrolled and apparently unrelated images that now came surging regularly through his mind, possessed him: the useless heirloom mirror in the apartment, that never-consulted antique barometer, Rosemyrtle's turned-over heels ("What in hell does she do with that $45 a week?"), a half-empty bottle of Scotch, the muscular, crop-haired, hockey-playing headmistress of Pammy's school . . .

"We're lost," he said aloud. "All of us." He spoke with a flat and heavy finality. When Ellen this time did not ask him what he meant, he added more quietly, "Or anyway, I am. I'm having frightful nightmares, Ellen, all the time. I think I should do something about it—but I don't know what."

"A psychiatrist—if Bob agrees?"

He noticed how quickly the suggestion came. Obviously she and Bob had already discussed the matter. The thought made him faintly irritable. "Oh no, that's not necessary. Anyway, they're too expensive." He spoke with an indifference he did not feel. The idea of consulting a psychiatrist had already crossed his own mind; but he had dismissed it as something foolish, a little embarrassing.

"We aren't that poor, darling."

"We will be—if I don't get out of this bed damned soon!"

"But that's why I thought of it—to help you out."

"Help me out?" he cried. He bit back the words of anger and resentment he felt rising. "Why should I be the one? Why should I get up, get out, earn the living for both of us? What's it to me? And where's it leading? If I liked what I'm doing it might be different." He began to pleat the white cotton counterpane with tight fingers.

Ellen stood up. "I'll talk to Bob about it, darling. You're tired now. Try to rest. We'll work it out some way." She kissed him, walked to the door, then turned back. "About the psychiatrist, don't you really think maybe one might help?" He frowned and did not reply. "Let's think about it anyway," she said and left the room.

The moment she was gone Philip regretted that he had not said firmly, "No, no psychiatrist!" The idea, though scarcely novel, now seemed to him both exhausting and repulsive—for even Hollywood, that abstraction he had once pictured to Goldstone in a moment of disgust as a frenzied zoo-keeper trying to keep alive its valued over-fed beast, the public, had sent forth word that the psychological film could now be a part of the animal's diet. Actually, he admitted with a certain irony, he knew no more than the general public about psychiatry and psychoanalysis. His knowledge was hardly more than a tangle of flashbacks and Daliesque dreams, sadistic matinee idols with canes and the big beautiful Swede disguised as a lady M.D. He could not imagine submitting his own psyche to elaborate and expensive proddings and pokings. Nor could he imagine lying flat on his back in some analyst's office, revealing his life, revealing it every day at a definite hour, talking, talking, talking.

CHAPTER 8

*
*   *
*

"BUT wait!" Dr. Ermenthal said, and he held up the index
finger of his thin soft right hand. The gesture annoyed Philip
immoderately, although by now he had come to have less resistance to the little man: the accent, the pulsing tic in the tallowy
left cheek, the slanting shoulders, the stoop—all the outward
signs of a shattered physique that had caused him to say to himself on first viewing Bob Scott's choice, "What has this guy got
for me! He belongs in the next bed!"

"But wait!" One of Dr. Ermenthal's two favorite phrases
meaning, "This looks like a blaze to me—weather-worn but certainly hacked here once," or "This is spoor," or "I think I hear
water." The other signal was "Ah-ha" quite different in tone,
faintly, unpleasantly triumphant—or so it seemed. Only yesterday, on hearing it, Philip had knocked the contents of his bed-
table to the floor, pretending it was an accident, yet fooling no
one, certainly not Dr. Ermenthal.

The doctor sat in full view, an unrelated assortment of flesh
and bones in a nondescript suit—the position he had taken since

95

the first day when Philip had not allowed him to remain hidden from sight behind the bed. "I don't care what the rules are!" Philip had cried. His body had shot up on the pillows as though released by a hidden spring. He had rasped out, "Please sit where I can see you."

Dr. Ermenthal had made no protest. He had calmly moved the chair in front of the bureau and sat down, then spoken with unconcern. "Don't let the rules disturb you. This is not a chess game we are going to play."

The cheerful calm of that opening gambit (for, in spite of the doctor's disavowal, the whole procedure still seemed to Philip like a game which he—an amateur—had been forced to play with an opponent who knew all the rules) had given their initial session a quality not yet repeated. There had been something immediately reassuring to Philip about the way the little man just quietly moved his chair and sat down, spoke casually, leaned back, expressionless, his eyes so obscured by the thick-lensed glasses that only occasionally did you see a darting shadow like a trout in a deep pool.

Philip's first spontaneous resistance—revived many times since—had melted away. To his own amazement he had heard himself apologizing for his rude voice, and then had spoken blunderingly of the tunnel nightmare, of the threatening Thing behind him. After that he had gone on, compelled, to speak of other night-mares, the empty movie screen, the recurrent dream of himself as murderer and victim. As, one by one, he revealed these secret apprehensions he had felt within him a sensation like the melt-ing of ice, the falling of a wall, or rather—and this he had even admitted to the doctor—like the little Dutch boy in the old story who, holding his finger to the hole in the dyke, finally takes the finger away, knowing the very dyke itself will go.

So complete, indeed, had been Philip's release in this first hour that the deepest musculature of his body was affected. Try, as he had, to tighten and control the sphincter, it had been no use; he had been forced to ring for the bed-pan. His sudden need had embarrassed him, though Dr. Ermenthal casually remarked that it was not a bad sign—this physical response—and with many patients did not come so soon.

2

FOR five days they had been sitting in the afternoon light of the hospital room reviewing the possible reasons for Philip's state of mind, following any clue that presented itself as significant. Sometimes to Philip it was like walking up a hill through a thick grove, hacking away with a dull knife at the undergrowth, slipping, even falling all the way back down into the gully again, unable to find the path just hacked out. At other times there was an unexpected wide view—like a landscape from a plane on a clear day. More often it was like being in a solitary cell, underground, a man tapping the walls, slowly, painfully, hoping to hear the hollow tone that will tell him, "Here is a hidden door."

Philip had just said, in the tense and resistant voice he could not keep from using, "I might as well say it straight out—I'm on a hair-trigger about being pushed around by anybody."

It was then Dr. Ermenthal had said, "But wait!" and holding up the index finger had asked gravely, "Who is pushing you?"

Philip's voice flared up. "Everybody!" He was almost shouting. "Everybody and everything! Push, push, push! *Pressure!* Nothing but pressure! By God, I can't stand it!"

"That is evident." Dr. Ermenthal, with a swiftness for which Philip was in no way prepared, snatched the hand-mirror from the bureau and thrust it before his patient's face. "See for yourself —if you care to."

Too startled to resist this unexpected action from the calm figure before him, Philip found himself gazing back at his own image. He saw the eyes, broken in focus, blurred, filmed, the pupils clouded, glaring from a face darkened and swollen with anger. The shock of the reflection sobered him and at once he turned away. Without a word Dr. Ermenthal replaced the mirror on the bureau, sat back again in the wooden chair in his fixed imperturbable pose.

There was a long silence in which Philip could still see the angry contorted reflection of himself in the glass.

"I'm soul-sick," he said finally, as if hoping to explain once and for all the source of this embarrassing image of rage. But such dramatic words coming from his own mouth confused him. To prevent a too personal application he added hastily, "Every-body's soul-sick." . . . and then again quickly, "But of course we don't allow that word any more, do we—the soul? There ain't no such animal." With this last phrase he deliberately made his voice nasal, crude, ridiculous, as though hoping to prevent the doctor from replying with the heavy seriousness he had himself started to assume.

But Dr. Ermenthal held to the first lead. "I do not find any-thing wrong with the word soul-sick," he began calmly. "It seems an accurate enough description of modern distress. But then"—and his glasses looked straight into Philip—"not everyone is flat on his back in bed with his soul-sickness."

Again Philip felt the wash of hot blood that he could not con-trol. This was one of the doctor's meanest tricks—bringing every-thing right back to him. He was going to answer acidly when a sudden vision stopped him. He saw Dr. Ermenthal holding a forked willow wand, walking along with it, looking down, as though waiting for it to bend. Philip closed his eyes; opened them. How absurd! Of course the vision was not Ermenthal. All the doctor had in his hand was the yellow pencil with which he sometimes made furtive scrawls on the pad in the palm of his hand. No, it was a man he had seen once in childhood, with his father—a man trying to find water for a desperate farmer; a water diviner. Philip closed his eyes again. At once the willow wand leaped inside his own body, and, in leaping, changed into a needle on a magnetic compass—and this magnetic needle was pointing, faintly quivering, at something in a corner of his own mind.

He blotted out the picture of the water diviner, the needle; he spoke flatly, "Don't kid yourself, I'm not in bed with soul-sick-ness. I'm in bed because a man hit me on the head with a gun!"

"I know." The little man by the bureau seemed always in-furiatingly prepared for any remark. Again the glasses gleamed toward Philip. "But why did you try to attack an armed man? Wasn't that a rather foolhardy thing to do?"

Now I have him, Philip thought. He felt suddenly aware of

his size and bulk—even stretched out helpless in a bed—as compared to the gnomelike figure across the room. "Instinct," he answered superciliously. "What else?" He paused. "What would you have done?" He gave the "you" a little stress, as though to imply the doctor needn't think he alone could make the cracks.

Dr. Ermenthal separated his index finger from his folded hand. "Ah-hah! Careful!"

"What? Careful about what?"

He could hear the petulance under his question and was grateful when the doctor took no notice of it. Indeed the doctor seemed to be faintly amused as he said, "That word instinct—I worry more about the use of that word than about the use of the word 'soul.' Instinct." Dr. Ermenthal appeared to examine it somewhere out in space with a quizzical and regretful air. "It carries a terribly unfair burden—that abused word." He looked back at Philip. "Perhaps it is time we stressed the fact that human beings are not just animals with instinctual equipment. They are also—and uniquely—creatures capable of modifiable behavior." He paused, pressing his thumbs into a calm steeple.

"You mean to say that self-preservation isn't an instinct?" Philip demanded.

"Are you implying that you wanted to preserve your life when you tried to fight an armed man with a golf club? I would say it looks rather more as though you were trying to lose your life."

At this remark Philip felt his magnetic needle jump as though it had been dealt a shattering blow. He sat up straight on his pillows with an abruptness that made his head spin. His voice was pitched high. "That doesn't make sense! In fact, I don't think there's much here to argue about. So why discuss it?" He looked away toward the blank window, then back to the concealing glasses, "Any man would have done the same thing I did."

Ermenthal took off his glasses and, holding them by their frames, looked through them at the floor, "I believe," he remarked with special gravity, "at least I think, the usual phrasing is, 'any red-blooded male!' "

Philip laughed in spite of himself, and, having laughed, felt his irritation dissolving.

3

Soon the days began to revolve around Dr. Ermenthal's afternoon visit. Out of the monotony of the hospital, they emerged—these monologues, these occasional lopsided dialogues—like brief islands in an empty gray sea. Promptly every day at three there was a faint tap on the door, and the little man would enter, looking to Philip so like a studious gnome that he invariably asked himself how he could ever have got himself into a situation where a funny little Viennese doctor, still collecting American speech idioms with the air of a connoisseur, could be looked upon by him as a personal savior—for, occasionally now, this was the role he assigned to Dr. Ermenthal; though more often that of Tormenter, Chief Executioner, Grand Inquisitor seemed more accurate.

Whatever his shifting judgment of the calm figure in the plain wooden chair, Philip had to admit that Bob had been right in his conjecture that he would find Ermenthal more endurable than one of his own countrymen in the same role. He could very easily summon a picture of an American contemporary, an imaginary Dr. McSmith, seated by the bureau as Ermenthal now was, wearing a dark-blue pin stripe, a properly subdued expensive tie, carrying around him (an unshakable aura) the ten rooms in Bronxville, the two children, the cocker spaniel pup, the Buick sedan . . . "Don't pretend to me, Doc, that you've got the good life, because I don't believe it for a moment." No, Ermenthal was infinitely preferable; the stranger from an unknown background, making possible—easier certainly—the close intimacy they were daily establishing.

"You say you feel guilty—and you ask me why?" Dr. Ermenthal was saying, creating instantly in Philip—with his repetition of the word—a sharp regret at having let the admission slip from him, since it offered the doctor an unfair advantage, permitted him to dwell on guilt as an established symptom. He would have given anything to recall the word, but it was too late. "Guilt!" the doctor was repeating. He carefully did not look toward the bed. "I should say your sickness was by no means unique—in fact, a fairly universal one. We might call it the sickness of modern man—a collective guilt. The legend of Cain and Abel! Yes, as modern men, we have all been guilty of killing our brothers."

Something unusual in the voice made Philip glance sharply at the face across the room. Now, in place of the impassive neutral mask, he thought he caught a fleeting expression of such bitter sadness and weariness that he forgot himself for a moment and began to wonder about the doctor's personal history; the reasons for the pallor, the stoop, the tic.

Ermenthal was continuing, "No one agrees about when—or why—or how—man began to feel guilty. Original Sin?" He offered it as a half-question—left it hanging in the air. "You and I cannot settle that—the question of the origin of the feeling of guilt. Perhaps we cannot even settle it for you personally. For one thing, our time is too limited."

Philip stiffened, waiting for, expecting now, the "plug" for the extended period of analysis; the three-year prescribed routine he had been told once was standard. He had been expecting it for some time, although Bob Scott had insisted Dr. Ermenthal had been chosen because he was, supposedly, willing just to "keep his eye on the steam valve for a few weeks"—Bob's phrase for it; delivered with the superior air of one who says, "All you need is a little talk with the camp counselor—the headmaster— Daddy . . ." Philip's response, at the time, had been so bitter he had almost refused to go ahead. Now he waited, expecting the suggestion for a full analysis to follow on the phrase about their "limited time." He half-hoped it would come, allowing him an outlet for that constant surcharge of formless hostility of which he was beginning to be uncomfortably aware. But Dr. Ermenthal merely continued to speak in the same vein as before, gravely, reflectively, almost as if to himself.

"We are all sick because we cannot escape the knowledge of our crimes as men. We are daily reminded of our guilt—re-minded by every radio and television set, by every newspaper and magazine. Within a matter of minutes we know—we are forced to know—the worst that is happening between men anywhere— no matter how remote the place."

He shook his head solemnly, looking at Philip as though he wanted to express his personal sympathy. "This is a great strain for a modern man—whether or not he knows it, or admits it."

Familiar as the ideas were, dinned from pulpits, from radios, the glib prophecies of Armageddon, somehow coming from the little pale man beside the bureau in the unadorned hospital chair, the words had an unexpected apocalyptic weight and force. Philip did not want to look at Dr. Ermenthal now. He looked instead at the flaming red maws of the gladioli in the vase behind the doctor's graying head, and it seemed to him, in this instant, that the very flowers were about to utter loud cries and spring from their curved green stalks. He closed his eyes. When, a moment later, he dared open them, he saw with relief that the gladioli appeared normal again.

The doctor was continuing, still looking away out the window, his hands clasped loosely in his lap, the light on the glasses obscuring his eyes and giving his whole face the expressionless masked quality Philip sometimes resented.

"Yes, we can no longer escape sharing all things with all men, almost in the moment of their happening." Ermenthal removed his glasses, wiped them methodically. "Because of its virulence, this ancient sickness of collective guilt appears today like something very new and disturbing. Disturbing it is—but new it is not." He returned the glasses to his nose. "Your dreams—I mean your dreams about the prison camps, with yourself both prisoner and keeper, murdered and murderer—actually such disorders are a part of the most ordinary psychological phenomena. Because people do not speak of them—or can dismiss them with vague words like nervous tension, apprehension—does not mean that they do not feel them. And you, as a sensitive man, the creative type—you would be bound to have it strike more deeply and forcibly . . ."

"Creative?" Philip leaned forward. "Me? Nobody leads a more uncreative life than I do." He spoke with scorn.

"That is probably quite true." Dr. Ermenthal's face did not change. "It does not alter the fact that you are essentially, basically, a creative type."

"I don't know where you get that!" Yet even as Philip spoke he realized he wanted it to be true.

"I have talked with your wife," Dr. Ermenthal said quietly.

"I presumed you knew that I had. She has told me about your early ambition to be a writer . . ."

"Oh, God!" Philip laughed. "Jesus!" He turned his head away in weary disgust. "Look," he said, "there's not a man in any advertising or publishing or radio or movie office in New York who didn't think once he wanted to write. *There's* a mass psychosis if you want to see one." He felt absurdly pleased with himself for the term he had used so glibly.

"So?" Dr. Ermenthal said calmly. "That may well be true. But it need not concern us here. We are thinking of you." Because of the way he spoke, without flippancy, with grave dignity, Philip turned back, quiet, very attentive now. "Perhaps it is not exaggerating to suggest," the doctor continued, "that you have never been what you want to be—whatever that is. Perhaps you were brought up to believe, educated to believe, in solid material success; that the one good life is to be a successful man with a steady job and a handsome salary."

His voice was now faintly ironic, and Philip again thought that he caught something almost taunting lurking in its depths.

"I guess I can't deny that." He was interested to see that this admission gave him a good feeling, like the semi-ridiculous wave of self-esteem that comes with any outlay of co-operativeness. He was silent.

After a few moments Dr. Ermenthal, with the air of a man who is now bringing an argument back to its original starting point, said, "I have spoken of collective guilt . . . Thousands of people read crime magazines and tabloids. They fill their minds with stories of so-called normal fathers killing their babies, honor students beating their old landladies to death for no apparent reason, and well-known athletes caught in sodomy. But then they go to bed and sleep soundly—or soundly enough. They will probably tell you they don't even dream. The subways every night, all the commuters' trains, are full of men and women vicariously torturing Jews, stabbing their mistresses, poisoning their husbands, knifing, slugging, forging—but they do not suffer so severely from their preoccupation with violence that they cannot eat a hearty supper and get to their jobs the next day on time. You, however—you are suffering, have suffered, from what you have read, seen, thought. It has temporarily paralyzed you, and so I say we must look at the personal, the *individual* genesis of *your* guilt."

"It's Bach," Philip said to himself—"the way he builds it—the theme, the contrast, the repetition, so measured" . . . What he said out loud was, "But I thought we weren't going back to mud-pies and bed-wetting."

"I do not think we have to," said Dr. Ermenthal gravely. "No, I think not."

Philip again spoke half-flippantly, "But I suppose we're going to uncover something just beyond the anal or the oral periods—something, say, like a good flourishing Oedipus complex or . . ."

Abruptly Dr. Ermenthal raised his right index finger, he seemed even to check an impulse to shake it in reproof. "But wait!" His voice was stern now. "We will at all costs avoid the cliché." He looked directly at Philip and Philip felt no impulse to smile. "Let us try never to speak of the darkest passions and terrors as though they were titles for articles in some undergraduate review." He leaned a little farther forward as though trying now to reach Philip through an impalpable barrier. "Remember, all these psychological names, all these terms you can hear on every quiz program, were given to living realities, to what were, still are, mysterious, often tragic, processes of the ego." He paused. He remained silent for a long minute and then said, "So, then, we are talking about you—not about Greek myths."

Inside himself Philip accepted the reproof, though he was not sure he cared for the doctor's teacher-pupil expression of it. But he said nothing and, when the silence had lasted to the point of awkwardness, Dr. Ermenthal asked, his voice gentler now, "Tell me, what did you do during the last war? Where were you?"

Philip thought, Here we go! Now for the "truth serum"; Man Under Influence of Sodium Amytal Relives Experience of Seeing Buddy Blown to Bits by Hidden Mine. "Sorry. Can't oblige," he said.

"Can't oblige?"

"No foxhole, no Pacific atoll. A flat in London and nothing worse than the V-bombs . . ." (And once more he saw the torchlights playing on the rotting sandbags, the boarded windows of London in 1944; the corpses tossed up out of an old East End graveyard in a direct hit.)

"Very fortunate," said Dr. Ermenthal.

He made a small hasty note in the little book that lay hidden, as always, in his curved palm.

4

It was difficult, Philip found as the days went on, indeed impossible, to maintain a single fixed attitude toward the doctor. He despised himself for his changing moods, for this turning like a weathervane with every passing wind. Within one hour he would be cravenly anxious to please Ermenthal, wishing to astound him, uttering cheap witticisms, attempting to deceive him, struggling with a hostility that verged on hatred—all in the face of an unvarying, kind neutrality that made him long to create a scene like a hysterical woman, anything to break the smooth surface of the little man's imperturbability.

Whether or not it had been arranged—and he had his suspicions because Dr. Ermenthal had said he had spoken with Ellen, and Philip sometimes imagined them talking behind his back, treating him like a helpless child—Ellen usually came in on the heels of the doctor's departure. Often Philip found himself venting on her the irritations and frustrations he had held in check in the doctor's presence. Ellen was usually extremely patient, so that afterwards he upbraided himself for his attitude. But one day she surprised him, answering his remark that he was sorry he had ever agreed to see Ermenthal, with the cool comment, "You can stop any time." Her tone seemed to imply that the problem was entirely his.

It checked him a little. He tried to measure the quality of the remark. Did it reveal real or feigned indifference?

"There's nothing wrong with me, anyway," he said, "except that I don't want to go back to work—and I think that's pretty frighteningly *normal*."

He waited for her to say it wasn't normal not to work, but she said nothing for a moment. When she did speak it was only to remark, still coolly, "But Bob feels sure Dr. Ermenthal can help you."

"How? By endowing me with a million dollars?"

"I don't think you don't want to work, darling," she said more reassuringly. "It isn't in the least like you."

Perhaps she was indifferent, but at least she was determined, he saw, to be pleasantly reasonable. Sitting near the window—her face still turned slightly away—she began to talk in a soothing monotone about the ways there were in the modern world to get straightened out—particularly if it was your profession that was wrong, or if you had chronic depressions: "Rorschach tests . . . examinations to determine aptitudes . . . hypnosis . . . sodium pentathol . . . electric shocks . . . insulin shocks . . ."

How in God's name, Philip asked himself, had Ellen acquired all the information she let drop so casually. It was amazing! Tap the average American woman on any subject—nuclear fission, hormones, Totem and Tabu, Picasso, neurosis—and out streamed a gush of hard bright facts. But what good did it do her? He looked at Ellen in the flat white light from the window—she had turned back toward him, revealing to his scrutiny a face in which soft beauty was hidden under a film of tension. The modern woman's face. His wife's face. A woman who had once loved him, given him sympathy, tenderness, looked up to him; and who now seemed to live altogether on another plane of existence.

```
    *
*      *
    *
```

CHAPTER 9

WHEN Philip began his session with Dr. Ermenthal the next day, the old perverse wish to disturb the little man, to throw him off whatever scent he was following, led him to ask, "Would you like to know why I made up my mind to see you at all?"

"Certainly," said Dr. Ermenthal. He laid his black Homburg carefully on the bureau. "It might have some bearing."

Philip told him then about the girl from Ann Arbor in the black satin suit, the one he'd been out with the night before he was hit, the one who'd said all men were "babies," "young souls," and that he, in particular, was "pre-Atomic." "She called me a 'coward,'" Philip said, "and then turned on me and said, 'I hate you.'"

"Why did she call you a coward?"

"Because . . ." he stopped. "I'm getting confused. She didn't call me a coward. That was Jane, my sister Jane, years ago when I was a kid."

Dr. Ermenthal made a note in his small book.

"Anyway, I didn't give a damn about that Michigan girl," Philip went on, "although I made an automatic pass at her. But I have thought several times about what she said—so I guess it got under my skin." He heard the eastbound train grinding up the steep side of the Rocky mountains: *hate you-hate-you-hate-you-hate-hate-hate.* He could feel Dr. Ermenthal waiting for him to say more. He had the feeling of having now opened a private Pandora's box. Once you had used a word like "pass" you were bound to be needled for more information on your sex experiences. It was what they were all secretly looking for—these twisted analysts, licking their lips, just like aging Oxford Groupers in a "sharing" fest. Only analysts didn't share; they just sat and lapped it up.

He had always been shy about speaking of any emotional problem. He wondered if this secretiveness resulted from his mother's early example in repression, or whether it was something he had picked up from Aunt Hetebel's conventional—almost virginal—reticences. Whatever he had learned as an adolescent about physical things he had learned either furtively or crudely. When he took a class in psychology while still in his late teens, he had been hoping to get at some direct truths. He remembered a certain Glossary—a list of terms it was suggested the students memorize (though other terms, the ones about which he was most curious, were carefully ignored). He could see some of the words in that—for the most part dull—book even now: *manic-depressive, masochism* ("from Sacher-Masoch"), *masturbation.* Then there were the ones he had been required to define: *abreaction,* "the process of discharging repressed emotion connected with painful past experience by describing the experience vividly to an analyst"; *aphasia,* "inability to speak." (Simple as that!) *Electra complex* (never heard of any more—lost in the semantic shuffle); *voyeur, ticquer* . . . Ah ha! "persons suffering from a tic or muscular spasm." Suddenly he felt easily superior to the little man before him with the pulsing nerve in the pale cheek.

"The truth is," Philip said, facing Ermenthal, "I'm breaking up—as a man, I mean." Hurriedly, at random, he projected a jumble of facts about himself: how he couldn't drink as much as he used to; felt no immediate results from liquor and then suddenly, whamo! he was out. No pleasure in it—merely a city habit. He also confessed that for months he hadn't really felt acutely or painfully anxious to possess any woman; that, although he had made a pass at that self-assured refugee from co-education the night of the accident, he hadn't had his heart in it. "As a matter of fact, Doctor," he said, "it's something of a relief to see my appetite slackening off. I might as well admit it."

"Perhaps to be relieved about the loss of sexual appetite is not quite healthy," Dr. Ermenthal replied slowly, but without emphasis.

"You mean I'm *repressing* something?" Philip mocked.

"Not necessarily."

"Then maybe I'm sublimating it—you know—rising above it because of the vital energy I pour into my creative work."

Dr. Ermenthal ignored the mockery.

"Sublimation, repression—these are hard words to untangle in every instance, though, to be sure, they both exist." He was silent again. Philip was quite unprepared for the question with which, after a moment, Dr. Ermenthal faced him. "And your wife—what about her in all this?"

Philip's protective inner door shut with a clang. "Better ask her about that," and then he added defensively, "No, you'd better not. I don't want you two hashing me over." When Dr. Ermenthal said nothing, he went on with increased edginess, "I know you'll think that makes my guilt about *something* very apparent—not wanting to be talked about behind my back." Still Dr. Ermenthal said nothing. Philip saw his own inner compass turn and quiver, pointing, pointing. He knew the direction. It was the scene with Ellen about the child she had asked him to let her have. Feeling as though a hot flame was licking up his brain as he formed the words, he blurted out a garbled account of the spring evening on which Ellen had broken down so completely. When it was all out he felt relieved. He lay back on the pillow.

He was even ready for the question that Dr. Ermenthal, after a long silence, finally asked him: "Do you have any idea why you did not want the child?" the voice was casual, so casual, Philip, for a moment, half-believed that Ermenthal understood what could prompt a modern man to resist the idea of responsibility for the birth of another human creature.

For the second time Philip surprised himself—almost before he was aware that he had remembered—by giving an answer he did not know was in him. "It has something to do with my feeling about a home—that I have no home—have never had a home—and therefore, I did not want another child."

He had choked up on the word "home." Something caught in his throat. A feeling of self-pity that he found mawkish but could not control flowed through him. At the same time he had the terrifying conviction he had now put himself entirely at the mercy of the adversary by the bureau and must act quickly to protect himself.

"Not that that's so unusual." His voice was falsely glib. "It makes me a pretty typical American. All Americans are rootless, aren't they? Come to think about it they act—always have —just like the postwar wandering Europeans—maybe more so. I suppose that's because a part of every generation in America always moves away from its birthplace. Take my great-uncle's house in Massachusetts where I grew up . . ."

He went on to tell how, on Uncle Logan's death, following Aunt Hetebel by just six months, the inheriting Jessup (pleading sinuses and the necessity of Bermuda) had cold-bloodedly sold the old place to a Duncan Hines restaurant famous for fish chowder. As he talked, making a light and amusing anecdote of it—pleased to see a flicker of appreciation on Ermenthal's mask—he suddenly remembered how deftly, years ago, he had led Fred Dillon back to the historic Colonial Home in Lynnport.

He had the uneasy sensation that Dr. Ermenthal was reading his mind at this moment and he boldly introduced early pictures of Milltown. ("Who says I'm avoiding Milltown? I can mention it perfectly easily.") But he did not speak of the little cramped house where his mother had died. He told only of his grandfather's home on the terrace above the bay; and this detoured him easily, perfectly naturally, into a discussion

of the peculiar veneration that had been accorded the objects
his great-grandmother had sent or brought from the East. Such
objects, he told Dr. Ermenthal—suggesting that he, a European,
might find something significant in the fact—were treated in
homes in the Far West with a sort of religious awe, like sacred
relics; survivors of the dark perils of passage by way of the
Horn or overland by rough wagon trails and single-gauge railroads.

Then, since Dr. Ermenthal still appeared interested, he introduced the question of the contrast between this so-apparent
American trait—the worship of age for age's sake, the self-
conscious pursuit of antiques (he sketched in his aunt's Alternate Thursdays)—and that other obvious aspect of the national culture pattern, the unnatural fostering and protracting
of youth into old age—"The American addiction to adolescent
rituals," Philip said. He liked the phrase. He saw Ermenthal
make one of his quick scribbling notes, and felt that, perhaps,
Ermenthal too had admired the wording. He expanded the
theme into specific instances. The very same human being, he
said, who would proudly present a hero-grandfather's powder
horn to the Elk's Club, or lend a talented—and probably frustrated—grandmother's seaweed and grass-seed landscapes to a
D.A.R. bazaar, felt no shame at drunkenly parading the streets
dressed like a musical-comedy Turk, or engaging solemnly in
pseudo-mystical practices, assuming mythological titles, wearing Greek robes and crowns, quite like any little girl engaged
in Make-Believe . . .

When, exhausted, Philip stopped talking, he was relieved to
have Dr. Ermenthal, with an expansiveness unusual in him,
take up the subject and carry it on.

"Your national culture has few layers. It does not go down
deep. Too little planting and digging, too much emphasis on
quickly picking the fruit. Not enough questions: Where did
the plant come from? Is it healthy, useful, beautiful? Only,
quick! More fertilizer! Force-feed the growth, get a result you
can weigh, slice, sell. And so too many Americans have become
spectators, observers, journalists—not creative workers. So music,

art, entertainment, education get *packaged*— isn't that the word?"

Philip nodded. "It's one of the terms. 'Canned culture.' 'Dish it out!' e.e. cummings said it once and for all in a poem I haven't thought of in years: 'Land above all of Just Add Hot Water and Serve' . . ."

"A *poem?*"

Philip had to laugh at the doctor's expression, seeing him surprised as only a man can be to whom the word "poem" suggested geniuses like Goethe or Heine. He watched him make a careful note. "Ermenthal the Anthropologist." For a moment he felt something almost like affection for this earnest, compassionate, sickly little European.

Dr. Ermenthal continued to hold the pencil in his hand horizontally. Balanced between his middle and index fingers, he addressed his further remarks to it.

"Too few aesthetic solaces in America for the ordinary man. Here he does not even have them in his church. The suffering Christ, machine-made—stamped out in a mold and sold by the gross . . . No, religion is not as dangerous here in America as Lenin once found it in Europe. Here it is the movies that serve as opium for the masses." He shot Philip an apologetic half-glance as he spoke the word "movies." "Here in America, underneath a canopy of stars, in a Moorish palace warm in winter, air-cooled in summer, you may sit in the dark for fifty cents and lead a new life."

He slid the pencil back in his upper coat pocket.

"Did you know," Philip asked, "there's been some talk of showing Hollywood's religious movies in Sunday schools—to build up attendance? Might set a good example, you know— seeing the stars in holy garb every Sunday morning. It can't be true that Bing Crosby hangs out at the Santa Anita race track. He's really Father O'Dwiddle and may be found at any time of need in the vestry of the local church."

Ermenthal's face lit up like the face of a specialist who has just heard of some rare specimen to add to his collection, "Ah-ha!" He appeared so relaxed, so momentarily off the scent of any of his patient's buried secrets that Philip, without being aware of what was happening, found himself circling back tentatively toward the magnetized zone of personal revelations.

"I'm certainly one of the rootless ones!" The abrupt admission made his heart whir and falter. It seemed a momentous confession. "I'm going somewhere—presumably—but I don't know where, and lately I don't seem much to care."

For a moment he dared not look toward Dr. Ermenthal, not wanting to reveal the terror his own words had created in him. But when the doctor made no comment Philip finally turned to him and found only the familiar expressionless waiting face. Against this solid and sustaining impassivity, he now hurled the Great Question. "What am I after?" As he asked it he heard the blood racing in his head, swelling toward him like the sound of the sea in an ear-cupped shell. He rushed forward, carried on a wave of desperate courage. "Is it happiness? I suppose so—yet the night that fellow hit me with his gun I was thinking about that very thing—about happiness; how you never see it any more, or feel it. Even children look worried and haunted. Or do I imagine that?"

Still Ermenthal did not speak.

"What about this happiness idea anyway?" Philip persisted tensely. "Is it something I—we—all of us—should give up as an illusion?"

"No," Ermenthal spoke firmly. "That I do not believe."

After a moment he added, "It is, of course, quite possible for a man to entirely lose his capacity for happiness of any kind. This is very serious. Such a sickness strikes into the very sources of life. Should it happen to enough men it might mean the end of the experiment on this planet."

"Experiment?" The word startled Philip.

"Experiment," Ermenthal repeated simply. He left it there.

But Philip would not allow him to drop it. "That sounds pretty mystical for one who claims not to be a mystic."

Ermenthal looked at him in surprise. "Oh, no, not at all mystical."

He did not explain further and, as Philip lay gloomily attempting his own analysis of the remark, Ermenthal said in quite a different tone—the tone with the hidden pressure that

Philip had come to recognize, always with an inner tremble of alarm:

"You have told me very little of your father and your sister."

Philip's pulse quickened but he replied with outer calm. "Not much to tell. You know I haven't seen them in years. I believe we mentioned that, didn't we? My sister lives in Guatemala. My father is a hermit. Lives on an island off the West Coast . . ." His words tapered off into silence.

"Your wife," Ermenthal said softly, "told me that when you were delirious you spoke of your father more frequently than of any other human being."

The resentment of Ellen, of this behind-the-back carrying of tales, flashed up through Philip again. The word ABREACTION, in large letters, appeared in front of him, followed immediately by APHASIA, glittering and glinting, coming on and off like a red arrow of warning. He amazed himself by the calmness of his reply.

"I was thinking about my father the night of the accident. He'd been in my mind." He was going to leave it at that when Dr. Ermenthal inquired with what seemed to be matter-of-factness, "For any special reasons?"

"I—no, I don't think so. I was glancing through A Portrait of the Artist as a Young Man—you know, Joyce's—and so got to thinking of Dublin. . . . My father came from Ireland—northern Ireland." He let the words slide away again. He lay with his eye on the clock, waiting. Thank God there was not much time left! Ermenthal always got out promptly when the hour was up.

But now the doctor made no move to go, nor did he even offer a word to break the silence. Philip glanced over at him and saw again the man with the willow-branch searching for the secret spring.

Suddenly Dr. Ermenthal reached into his pocket and produced a slip of typewritten paper which he unfolded with a determined air. "I have here," he said, "something I would like to read aloud. It is a communication from your father."

Philip felt his whole body constrict.

"Communication to whom?" he asked. He knew his voice sounded tense and uncertain.

"To you. It was included in a letter to your wife after she wrote him the details of your accident."

"Well, why didn't she give . . . ?" he stopped. "Go ahead. Read it," he said stiffly. He was annoyed again by the thought that Ellen and the doctor were secretly deciding his affairs, censoring his reading-matter even to the point of personal letters. And Ellen—why had she written his father? She had never written him before.

Dr. Ermenthal lifted the piece of paper and began to read slowly and with apparent enjoyment:

> "For Philip:
>
> One evening while an enlightened man was at his prayers a thief with a sharp sword entered his home demanding money or his life.
>
> 'Please don't disturb me,' said the good man. 'You will find some money in the drawer,' and he went on with his meditation.
>
> A moment later, however, he added over his shoulder, 'Leave a little, will you? I have to pay some taxes tomorrow.'
>
> The thief made no reply. As he was leaving by the window through which he had entered the man said, 'Why don't you thank a person when you receive a gift? It's only good manners.'
>
> The thief mumbled something unintelligible and disappeared.
>
> Some days later he was caught and the robbed man was summoned as a witness against him.
>
> 'This man is no thief,' he said positively. 'At least not as far as I'm concerned. I freely gave him the money and he even thanked me for it.'
>
> However, the thief was proven guilty and went to prison. As soon as his term was up he sought out the enlightened man in order to become his disciple."

Dr. Ermenthal folded the paper, put it on the bureau and leaned back, clasping his hands across his stomach. Philip could see that he expected some comment, but he did not know what to say. It was not clear to him why his father had bothered to write this parable, or why Ermenthal had chosen to read it aloud. The story had interested him mildly, and yet he had found its moralizing irritating. More than that, it teased faintly at some memory out of his early life in Milltown, a memory he could not capture. He seemed to remember this kind of indirect approach as one his father had always enjoyed, a method for throwing people off the track of his meaning only to trap them later, when they least expected it, with the point of his homily.

When Philip made no reply, Dr. Ermenthal began to talk again. To Philip's surprise the doctor did not mention the parable. Instead he took up once more his familiar philosophical observations, speaking like a man dictating an essay, or like one who has learned English late, and from books.

"As an uprooted European," Dr. Ermenthal was saying, "I have had the opportunity to live—a stranger, with a stranger's sharpened vision—in several cultures alien to my own native one. This has made it possible for me to realize something I had long suspected—that conflicts and neurosis can grow out of the very climate of a culture. In fact, a certain type of culture may determine a certain type of conflict. So I, at least, believe, and so do some others in my special field."

When he paused a moment to make the church steeple with his thumbs before continuing, Philip asked himself, "What's this? What's he driving at now?"

"And so, in your case, I allowed you today to talk at such general length about America," the doctor went on. "I did this because I feel that the very culture you were describing so vividly—the materialism, the disgrace of non-conformity, the mixture of traditionalism and hooliganism, the emphasis on youth, the stigma of the 'provincial'—all this is the climate in which you as a human plant have grown. This soil and this atmosphere have created you, and they now contain the seeds of your illness and of your possible destruction as a man—a human being."

He was as solemn, as grave and terrifying, as he had been the day he spoke of the mushroom explosion on the home television set.

Philip waited rigidly, wishing only for silence; wishing Ermenthal would leave, fearful that he was now on the track of something ominous and final, altogether inescapable.

The doctor reached out and touched the folded piece of notepaper on the bureau. "Now about this man," he said, "your father . . ."

Philip could feel his body tighten, preparing its shell of protection. "What about him?" He held his voice firm.

"I would like to hear you talk about him. In him I am very much interested."

"Why?"

"I think I would find him a very congenial soul."

Philip wanted to keep his voice light, but it sounded constricted as he replied, "I don't know why you say that. You know nothing about him." Ermenthal did not answer. He had picked up the piece of paper and seemed, from his expression, to be reading the parable again with pleasure. "Anyway," Philip went on, feeling his throat stuffed with cotton as he forced the words up and out, "You've probably met plenty like him in your lifetime—social rebels, out and out non-conformists."

"I've not met so many, alas!" Ermenthal said quietly. "Tell me, why is it you never see your father? What really happened there?"

It was unlike Ermenthal to ask blunt questions. Philip looked at him, aware of his own hesitancy to answer, aware too of his confused sensations, fear, shame—even—curiously enough—gratitude at the doctor's warm mention of his father. But he said, "I thought the other day you said something about factors in a neurosis not necessarily lying back in the 'unfinished business of childhood.' Wasn't that your phrase?"

"It was."

"Then why should I try to exhume my father?"

"Because he is not a part of the unfinished business of childhood. He is still alive—alive in you." Ermenthal paused and Philip turned away. He could feel his pulse quickening again. He wanted to make some further protective protest but the words would not come. "This isn't just the theme of the prodigal son," Ermenthal continued gently. "Nor the psychological stereotype of the son searching for his long-lost father."

"What is it then?" Philip demanded thickly.

When Dr. Ermenthal did not answer immediately, Philip had the impression that the question was being thrown back on him. He was shocked when, with terrible force, he heard the answer burst from his own lips. "I've always been ashamed of my father."

As the words came rocketing back to his own ears he had the sensation that an old neglected wound was opening deep inside him, opening like some night-blooming witch's flower that has no seed, a dark and bloody aperture no surgeon's needle could ever stitch together again. And at once he saw his heart—in grotesque and melodramatic exaggeration—trickling blood like the eternally gory Sacred Heart of Catholic iconography. Once more the chill of that agonized hour in his childhood when he had hidden from his parents' violence in the musty abandoned barn threatened to close in on him. He fought down a swelling need to weep. He took a deep breath: "That's not all of it. My father was in prison once." It was exactly—he thought—like the sensation of tossing a hand grenade and wondering if you've thrown it where it will only do *you* injury. Now you can only wait for it to go off. He counted to a slow sixty and then looked at Dr. Ermenthal. His face was impassive except for the pulsing tic in the cheek that seemed sometimes, when the light blotted out his eyes, to be the only sign that he still breathed.

"For what reason?"

The question, put so calmly, came as an immense relief. Suddenly this part of the story was easy ground.

"For being a political agitator. Doesn't sound very American to a European, I suppose. Resisting arrest was, I believe, the formal charge. They only kept him in jail a short time. It was in the days of the I.W.W.'s—if you've ever heard of them." Ermenthal nodded. "He wasn't a member, just a sympathizer."

When he stopped he was aware that a heavy weight had gone from him, had floated off as suddenly, as impalpably, as a lifting fog. "My father was in prison once!" At last he had spoken it.

"But it sounds very American," Dr. Ermenthal said solemnly. "The America which was once the haven of all free and rebellious spirits."

Philip looked over at Ermenthal again with gratitude. In a flood of relief, he saw how his father's experience—so outside the accepted American norm as to be considered an overwhelming disgrace—actually connected his father in spirit with thousands of people over the face of the earth who had differed with those in power and paid the heavy price for it. Philip wondered, in this moment, how he could ever have felt and harbored such absurd shame. He put his hand over his eyes. "I can't believe it," he said shakily. "It's all suddenly so inconsequential."

It was not the word he wanted to use. Ermenthal did not allow it. "Not at all inconsequential." He made the denial with gravity. "He is obviously a man with a special set of values—one you did not, could not, understand as a child. One, perhaps, which you do not understand even now." He eyed Philip thoughtfully.

"That's probably true," Philip agreed. "Personally I don't have any set of values. And I wouldn't say my father's set worked any too damned well either." He stopped and looked over at the clock. "It's after four."

"I know," Ermenthal answered pleasantly. "Today I have an extra hour." Philip thought the little doctor suddenly appeared inordinately pleased with himself. He tried, in response, to drop his resistance.

"All I know about my father is this," and he began, slowly at first, then with increasing ease and candor, to resurrect the fragments of fact and memory about the man he had not seen for twenty-six years.

He told Ermenthal about the attempt Uncle Logan had made to have his name changed to Bachelder; how his father had bluntly refused permission; how his refusal had been a signal for the flagging of the periodic correspondence between the Lynnport household and the one in Milltown, how Jane's per-

functory notes had ceased altogether. As for his father, he had
always answered all communications, but had never written on
his own. At Christmas Aunt Hetebel, with Philip's assistance,
had regularly sent off boxes from S.S. Pierce and Filene's in
Boston and his father had replied with holly, cedar and kinni-
kinik from the Western woods. "Guess he thinks we don't have
any evergreen," Uncle Logan regularly growled. Aunt Hetebel
dutifully made wreaths of the greens for Philip's room. Finally with the deaths of his aunt and uncle the boxes stopped.
"Now," Philip said, "the exchange between Father and me has
come to only an annual greeting card, with a few lines of handwriting. And from Jane, nothing—not a line since she was
graduated from medical school."

Dr. Ermenthal was listening with close attention. When
Philip seemed to have completed the miscellany of fact, suggestion, and uncertain memory, he asked, "How is it you're so
convinced about your father's non-conformist attitudes?"

Philip looked up, startled—puzzled himself to know when
and where he had picked up the conviction that his father was
a dangerous radical. He did not remember any direct statements about him: indeed every reaction he remembered from
Uncle Logan, Aunt Hetebel, his grandfather, was shrouded in
evasions, in dark hints rather than in open accusations. Yet he
seemed to have known always that his father was a malcontent,
an eccentric, perhaps an "atheist." Yes, he had known that as
far back as the Milltown years when father was still Daddy, the
miracle man who could handle bees without being stung, recite Macbeth, tell stories of Irish heroes, and play anything you
asked for on his violin.

CHAPTER 10

*
*   *
*

IT WAS their last hour together. Philip was to be dismissed from the hospital in three days. Dr. Ermenthal was departing tomorrow for his summer holiday.

There was some subtle difference, Philip felt, in the doctor's attitude today—something freer, less formal. He had just risen, walked as far as the window, looked out, walked back toward the bureau and stood for a moment touching the green in one of the vases with the ends of his delicate fingers. This movement, so unlike his usual fixed pose and calm attentiveness, aroused again in Philip the question of Ermenthal's identity. What about Ermenthal? Was he married, single; what were his tastes and habits; what was he really like behind this studied self-effacement—this man who for weeks had been hardly more than omniscient voice and ear?

"There's no use my trying to say how you've helped me," Philip said with intense earnestness.

"Not at all, not at all," Ermenthal replied, stooping, bowing, the tic in his cheek pulsing lightly. "Do not speak of it. I am sure your head will soon be quite well, and I hope you will begin to have quite different dreams."

Philip repeated the words he had used that morning to Ellen. "A little loafing in the sun is all I need now to put me right." It was his answer to her repeated suggestion that he take a trip west to visit his father.

Ermenthal was now standing so near that Philip could see behind the glasses into his eyes. Something flashed there—amusement? warning? The doctor shifted his head to one side.

"What is your hurry?" He spoke very deliberately. "Something may want to happen inside you with which you will not be able, successfully, to interfere. And this may take time."

He dropped his head, clasped his hands together, added quietly to the linoleum at his feet, "The ego is a continent—a dark continent, unexplored, terrifying, large, beautiful . . . You have only just begun the journey."

Philip spoke lightly, checking any threat of agitation. "Well, I'm sure I couldn't have a better guide."

Ermenthal looked at him penetratingly and then away. "No guide can go with you all the way," he said, "not with you, or anyone." To Philip it sounded like a dark prophecy—a warning. "Somewhere you have to go alone. Life itself is, finally, your only guide."

'But I don't want to go alone!' Philip cried to himself in panic, out of his unreasoning fear that he was going to be lost without this daily meeting with Ermenthal, who had become more than a paid counselor, closer than a friend. There was no one else before whom he could lay the endless and insistent questions that rose in his mind now when, for the first time in years, he had the opportunity, even the desire, for reflection. Yes, he needed Ermenthal, could not get along without him. In fact he resented the idea that the doctor had chosen this particular time to go on a holiday. He thought with apprehension of the change of atmosphere he must endure upon leaving the hospital, this place of protection to which he had become so accustomed. He wanted to cry out, "Please don't go. I'm afraid. Can't you postpone the trip? Must you go just now?"

Aloud he said, nervously, "I can always reach you if I need you, can't I?"

Ermenthal spoke calmly, reassuringly. "Of course. I'll leave my address— though I don't feel you will require it. Perhaps you will be going west, anyway?"

He made the last sentence a question. At once the feeling of nameless threat, of unwelcome pressure claimed Philip. He knew by now how much both Ermenthal and Ellen wanted him to go see his father and he felt an obstinate wish to thwart them. He could not entirely account for his deep resistance to the idea but it was there, firmly fixed. He argued with himself about going a dozen times a day: "I don't want to. I haven't time for it. I can't afford it. What will it mean to me anyway? Besides, I'm too old to be getting acquainted with my father."

He answered Ermenthal with forced lightness, "No, I doubt if I'll be going west. The only place for me to go is back to my job." He attempted a weak grin. "Unless I can persuade someone to crack me on the head again."

Ermenthal looked through his glasses, nodding slowly—a series of small movements, tapering off gently like one of the Billikin dolls that were a craze some twenty years before.

"Very lucky you were! A desperate young man entered your apartment, struck you on the head, tried to kill you, gave you another chance at living your neglected life." He spoke half-humorously, half-seriously.

Philip sat up a little farther on his pillows. "Maybe he did kill me," he ventured. "Maybe I actually died when the trigger clicked and the gun didn't seem to go off."

The light shifted on the glasses that so effectively concealed Ermenthal's eyes. "Maybe."

"Or maybe I had been just wanting an excuse to go to bed and stay there. That idea has certainly crossed my mind."

Ermenthal nodded again, non-committally. "It need not have been a gun-butt, of course."

"You mean I might just have fallen downstairs, or stepped in front of a car?"

"Yes." Ermenthal looked faintly amused. "I have told you— your psyche always wants to take care of you. It tries to warn

you. It will even break your leg or put you to bed with a severe
cold or skid your car as a warning. Or, if pushed too far, it
may take over altogether and start running the whole show.
Sometimes with disastrous results."

He was still speaking half-humorously, but Philip saw in his
remarks the opportunity he had been waiting for; the chance to
ask another of the Big Questions that—out of fear or perversity
—he had so frequently postponed. Because it was their last
hour together for an indefinite period, and because he now felt
he could trust the doctor, he gathered his strength and said,
"There's something I've been meaning to ask you." He heard
his voice carrying that faint glaze of unease that dropped over
it whenever he spoke of things not touched on in daily life by
anyone he knew. "Do you believe in fate? I mean, could there
be a plan somewhere that includes me personally?" He felt he
was blushing like an adolescent caught in profound feelings of
which he is ashamed. "This sounds like awful YMCA crap, I
know . . ." Something in Ermenthal's face stopped him; returned him to the sincere voice with which he had begun.
"*Could* there be something which did give me a second chance
—if that's what I've been given? You seemed to imply just
now . . ." He broke off.

He observed how carefully he had avoided the use of the
word "someone" who had given him his second chance—choosing instead the word "something." He realized how without
meaning to him was that concept of a personal God on whose
doctrine he had been conventionally—but unconvincingly—
raised.

Although Ermenthal had been about to depart he returned
to his chair and sat down. He did not speak for several moments. Philip had long since come to believe that these pauses
indicated a struggle continuously going on in the doctor between a rigidly imposed psychoanalytic training and discipline,
and a natural wish to speculate upon all questions, to expand
with imaginative, non-professional freedom.

"I am not a religious man, as I have said before," Ermenthal
began at last. "Great mischief has been done by self-declared
religious personalities, so I wish to deny any possible charge

that I am one." He paused. "A little intrusion of my ego that
I hope you will pardon."

In the few times Ermenthal made any statements about himself, he always bowed a little, with an air that was not quite
mockery, though bordering on it. These mannerisms to Philip
were hints and vestiges of a vanished society in which actions as
prescribed and formal as dance measures were part of ordinary
human intercourse. Coupled with the doctor's scientific knowledge, his mixture of uncompromising realism and intuitive perception, of European sophistication and an enduring unshakable air of shy naivete, they gave his personality its distinctive
archaic stamp.

When he continued, it was still not toward a direct answer.
It was going to be—Philip saw—one of his rare philosophical
musings.

"Today's *Zeitgeist* is still materialistic. Matter is still king, although we are beginning to learn all over again—in new ways,
of course—the old truth that, in reality, matter is as mysterious,
as inscrutable, as any invisible power. Still, the Spirit of our
Age—it has not yet stopped dictating to us that we must deny
the existence of all which lies out of reach of our contemporary
materialistic explanations."

He repeated the words "contemporary materialistic explanations" slowly—not looking at Philip, acting more as though he
repeated them for his own benefit, either to impress them on his
own mind or to examine them for any possible weakness.

"Not in the world of physics," he continued. "No, there we
allow mystery. We cannot deny it. But in the realm of the
psyche—there we are still afraid of the mysteries. We have been
afraid for a long time now to allow the psyche too much influence, too much power. Perhaps because in other centuries
she possessed more than her proper share, creating thus what
we now call superstitions."

He paused again, added speculatively, nodding his head as
before, "For this neglect, this contempt, the psyche may now
be taking revenge." He smiled gently at Philip, folding his
hands across the middle button of his dark sack suit.

A pose more commonplace, more homely would be hard to

imagine. Yet Philip, watching him with a sudden feeling of tenderness and affection, recalled the emotion that had filled him once or twice in old churches in Europe during the war years when, in search of some vague, some vanished, college memory about "the Gothic," he had wandered through cold gray naves, lit only with the murky red and purples of stained glass, and paused to look up into the stone face of saint or angel, feeling, as he did so, a power and beauty flow from the carved visage into his own heart, briefly warming and stirring it with perceptions of the lost spiritual life of man.

Ermenthal was going on quietly: "As to an ultimate meaning beyond our lives—here we can admit only one truth: that after six thousand years of speculation we still *know* nothing. It is necessary that we admit this painful truth from time to time to keep ourselves in equilibrium. At the same time, we should perhaps admit something more. We should admit that mysterious patterns do appear in our lives, and their recurrent themes can seem to us frequently to possess a design. Perhaps this is a design of our own psyches, or souls, and perhaps its origin lies outside them somewhere."

He made a brief impatient gesture with his left hand. "*Inside, outside*—impossible your language. Mine too, for that matter—perhaps all language—impossible for expressing what I am now trying to express; a thing that both contains and is contained . . ."

He again broke off and was silent for some moments. Then in a different tone, quiet, halting, yet positive, he continued:

"As to what happened to you, it was in you already. You were groping for it, *needing* it, we might even say. Had you been less unconscious, less buried, it might have happened, as I have said, with less violence. In your case it took a concussion —near death—to crack the bars of your particular prison."

Philip's heart began to beat—the dull throbbing he had come to recognize as a sign that some word of Ermenthal's, or of his own, had struck deep. Prison! Was he then going *back* to prison? Back to the fixed unvarying routine his ordinary life, in retrospect, had seemed to hold? He leaned forward, not wanting to miss anything Ermenthal was saying in the quiet voice with the slur of accent, hoping the doctor would find some word, some satisfactory last-minute admonition to which he could hold during his absence, on which he would rebuild his wavering faith in himself.

"That the psyche is something more than merely the product of certain biochemical processes—that I believe," Ermenthal went on, as though sensing Philip's unexpressed need. "As to whether it is contained in a Larger Spirit, a God, a Plan, a Higher Consciousness, that I am not prepared to assert."

He paused, waiting, perhaps expecting mockery or denial, but Philip was silent. "Yet I will say that there is, or appears to be, some source from which guidance can come—a new direction, for those prepared to receive it. I will not call it God, for I do not know. But also I am prepared to suggest that a belief in God is not merely, as someone has said, a fossil of the medieval mind. This very need—which you have just indicated in yourself—this need to believe in something beyond yourself—may be a requirement as basic to the truly healthy man as salt to his body."

He stressed the phrase "truly healthy man."

Philip became aware of the picture the two of them made in the bare white room, with its scrubbed floor and all the specified antiseptic equipment of the ordinary hospital room. He saw his own body stretching out, long and thin under the white covers, and the compressed small body of Ermenthal seated by the bureau in the hard wooden chair.

"I see," Ermenthal went on, in the voice now of a man in the presence of an intimate, "I see the ever rising and falling tide of spiritual interest rising again in the postwar world. This —it has little to do with organized religion. Perhaps even, one might say, the churches get in its way—for there the old truths lie too deeply buried under schism and dogma. This present tide of spiritual unrest rises—is, in my opinion, increasing rapidly— because thousands and thousands of human beings in the last few years have found the set schemes of their lives destroyed forever. This had to lead to new searchings, fresh doubts, and perhaps—we can at least hope—fresh affirmations."

Philip reached for one of his still limited quota of cigarettes. "Then you mean to say," and the old questions and anxieties stirred faintly in him again, "that only through violence on a large scale, through war, for instance, will there come, *can* there come, increased spiritual growth for man?"

"Far from it," Ermenthal said quickly. He leaned forward. "Far from it," he repeated positively. "*You* could have avoided your concussion. You wouldn't have had it if you had used your head instead of your fists. And just so—you could have used your intelligence and your will, years ago, to stay off the path that led finally, inevitably, to this loss of relationship with your wife and child, to this loss of inner identity, to this wish to escape into automatic, hypnotic daily routines, into drinking, aimless drifting, half-death. What you could have done in your personal life, all men could do, *can* do, both personally and collectively."

He had never spoken with more directness and firmness. For a moment he was silent. Then, rising, like someone who has completed a mission and must go on (at the thought a faint chill, that later seemed premonitory, passed across the surface of Philip's body) Ermenthal concluded. "This is—all of this talk —perhaps quite outside the proper realm of the psychiatrist." He spoke almost apologetically, and then added, smiling, "If, however, there are any seeds of help in it for you, you are welcome to them."

Once more he approached Philip's bed. They shook hands and, for a moment, Philip felt a fleeting sensation of embarrassment, both in himself and in Ermenthal, as though the termination of their strange intimacy was not to be easily achieved, or lightly passed over.

"I'll see you in the autumn," Philip said. It was not a perfunctory remark of farewell. It was more like a promise he was making to himself.

"If you feel you need me," the doctor said.

And then Ermenthal did a strange thing. He put out his hand and lightly, very lightly and gently, touched Philip on the top of his head. It was almost a fatherly touch, or the gesture of

a schoolmaster to an eager pupil, and by it Philip suddenly
sensed the span of years between them—or was it merely the
span of experience? When Ermenthal said good-bye, Philip
could feel the hoarseness rising in his own voice, an emotion he
could barely control. Ermenthal went out then, softly closing
the door.

CHAPTER *11*

*
* *
*

ON THE day Philip was to go home, an hour or two before
Ellen was due, Bob Scott came into the hospital room, his face
grave.

"I think you're well enough to hear this, Philip, and anyway, since you're reading the papers you'd probably come on
it . . . Ermenthal is dead." He paused a moment, and then
went on in the same subdued and shocked voice. "He went out
rowing somewhere off the coast of Maine. A squall came up and
he was drowned."

Philip sat on the edge of the bed without moving, unable
to speak. When Ellen entered, walked straight to him and took
his cold hands in hers, he saw she knew and had come to the
hospital early because of the news. "I can't believe it," Philip
said then. "It isn't so!"

"I know. It's unbelievable." She added, "I was counting on
him, too."

These last words seemed to slip from her unconsciously. At
the time Philip did not particularly notice them. It was only

later that they came back, carrying with them the weight of all her unspoken worry.

Bob at once began to talk about Ermenthal—in a way he never had. It was strangely as though he now felt safe in discussing the doctor as a human being. He explained to Philip why—after first suggesting Ermenthal to him—he had asked not to have anything said about the choice. It seemed Ermenthal was not quite a Grade A guaranteed member of the selective psychoanalytic fraternity. Once he had been, but in mid-career had turned heretic, breaking with his former colleagues, men to whom he referred later—not with bitterness but with a certain wry irony—as "mechanics" or "dentists of the psyche." Ermenthal, Bob said, had unsparingly attacked in print the set vocabularies, the unyielding procedures, the fixed time spans for "cures," the premature formulation into unquestioned dogma of the Master's findings. "It took a lot of guts. He must have known they'd fling him out of their organizations for the things he said and wrote. They really tried to crucify him. It was tough going for a while, but he gradually got followers—other dissidents and questioners. In the last year or so the tide had definitely begun to turn his way . . ."

Philip only half-listened, finding it all meaningless. It seemed to him the tide had not turned for Ermenthal; it had, instead, run out. He was relieved when Bob left. He got up, dressed, sat numbly in Ermenthal's chair—as he had always thought of it—while Ellen put the last things in his bag. When she had finished he walked, without a backward glance, from the room.

The ride home was torture; the heat, the smells of pavement and carbon monoxide; the crowds of people, limp with fatigue, greasy with sweat, hurrying for transportation at the day's end. The sight of the faces, the bodies, thick-packed; expressionless, anonymous units of human freight staring zombie-eyed from the buses, streaming down the subway steps—all the broken and frenzied interplay of sound and movement of a great city in summertime—seemed like snatches from his nightmares. He saw a group of half-naked children leaping around a gushing water hydrant a few blocks from his own quiet street. Their screams of delight seemed grotesque, like deprived and greedy yells of protest uttered against time and the shutting off of the forbidden water. As he watched—held up by traffic—their contorted faces leapt into the white air like fragments from a modern Goya's notebook. He pressed his body back in the cab.

He entered the cool foyer on Seventy-second Street with relief. But at once the solicitude of Louis, the old doorman, the welcome of Michael in the elevator, filled him with impatience and mild disgust. He was a marked man now; he had been in all the papers; no doubt Michael had even started a scrapbook for his grandchildren. Certainly he would insist on speculating on the moves of that still anonymous thief for all the rest of the months and years Philip would be entering the elevator. The prospect seemed beyond endurance.

Upstairs he had to face the clucking and clacking of Rosemyrtle, every morbid aspect of the accident reviewed. He tried not to appear impatient, aware of Ellen's anxious glance, her apprehension lest he be irritable. As soon as he could he got into bed, after which Rosemyrtle brought him iced tea and his favorite cocoanut cookies. He pretended to doze until suppertime, then, accepting a meal on a tray, he complained of weariness so that he could continue to be alone.

2

He lay in the quiet room with the shades drawn thinking of Ermenthal. Ellen had found an item about him in the evening paper and Philip had torn it out and put it under the ash tray by his bed. He read it over and over until he knew every word of it, yet each reading seemed to him to reveal less what he wanted to know.

"Physician and psychiatrist, Dr. Karl Ermenthal—of a distinguished Viennese family of doctors and scientists . . . The boatman said that Dr. Ermenthal appeared to handle the boat like an expert when he took it from the dock . . . Had with him only a book, sun glasses, a cap with a green visor . . . The doctor seemed quite

cheerful; told the boatman he intended to row to some
secluded spot and read and sunbathe . . . No motives
. . . No letters . . ."

Only silence. The capsized boat, found floating off shore; and
as yet, no body.

Why? Philip asked himself. Why this man—of all men? How
could one accept this sudden grotesque accident? "There is a
sense in which one can state quite positively, *there are really no
accidents.*" Ermenthal himself had said this. "All action may
be said to be symbolic."

Last seen in a little boat on the open water . . . He, Philip,
had dreamed of just such a circumstance the night after his
second talk with Ermenthal. He had seen himself in the dream
setting out in the teeth of a storm in an open boat, and Ermenthal had told him that this was an image frequently employed
by the unconscious to express impending change, a symbolic
formulation of a new phase of an individual's journey through
life. He could remember Ermenthal saying this, and, at the time,
it had appeared to convey a very direct meaning. Now it only
deepened the mystery. Indeed, everything Ermenthal had said,
the platform of faith he had placed under him, had gone as
suddenly, as completely, as Ermenthal himself.

Philip now felt himself hopelessly abandoned. Even the death
of his mother years ago seemed less of a personal deprivation
than the disappearance from sight and sound forever of this
man whom he had known for only a few weeks of time. Ermenthal had given him the belief that he might learn some of the
answers; that it was possible to escape his growing sense of personal bankruptcy. Now there seemed no possible answers anywhere, nothing to guide him through the gigantic irrational
drama in which a man like Ermenthal could sink beneath the
waters of the sea, leaving no trace, no explanation; serving only
to deepen, with his disappearance, that hateful and inescapable
dualism, the eternal presence of death in the midst of life.

At nine o'clock Ellen tiptoed into the guest room. "I'm
awake," he said at once.

She turned on the light. "I've brought you your pill." She

looked at him warily, trying not to reveal her anxiety. "How do you feel? Anything you'd like, darling?"

"No, not a thing."

"Can you sleep?"

"I think so."

"Well—good night then." She leaned over to kiss him. Her lips were sweet and cool and he had a fleeting impulse to cling to her, to ask her to stay in the room with him—but instantly he dismissed the feeling. Ellen could not help him. No one could help him. Of this he was once again—and finally now—convinced.

He grew a little sleepy from the pill. Later, somewhere between consciousness and sleep, he began to struggle with a movie script called *One Month in the Life of Philip Stewart*. He could hear Goldstone arguing—swiveling in half-circles in his soundless chair, his little legs dangling a fraction of an inch off the floor, his socks echoing the shrill cry of his cascading necktie. "But you can't have him never see the guy again—the one that robbed and slugged him. Audiences won't go for that. He's got to get what's coming to him. He's a thief—just remember that. And also you can't have this psychiatrist flash on, do a little fancy talking and flash off again, falling out of a boat and disappearing without a trace. Okay, maybe it *is* life—but it certainly ain't the movies, chum, and it's not what people expect." Philip forced himself to wake up. This much, then, had been accomplished. He could move himself out of these half-waking, half-sleeping nightmares now if he tried.

3

But, as he lay wakeful and restless, he realized that a strange new thought was forming in the depths of his mind; that Ermenthal's death was linked up somehow with the solution of his own personal dilemma. His top mind assured him that such a thing could not be; that he was investing this tragedy with a special personal import; and that anyone to whom he confessed it would surely see in such a notion only a dangerous and unwarranted inflation of his ego. For surely, unarguably, the continuation of Ermenthal's career was more valuable than any possible contribution to the common life of humanity which he, Philip Stewart, might make in the late thirties of an aimless and misdirected existence. How then could there be any possible connection? A *sacrificial* connection? The idea was preposterous, quite beyond the bounds of reason or rationality—yet Philip, as he tried to shake off the idea, recognized it taking root in him as a conviction.

For the first time in his whole life he began to think about the mystery of the death of Christ—Christ who died, so it was affirmed, for all men; and he wondered what the story meant; what the truth was. Was it merely myth, legend? Yet myth and legend—they were also, in a sense, truth; at least so Ermenthal had said. For did they not spring out of man's own image-making? Was it—the Christ story—some gigantic needed symbol, of which the death of Ermenthal was also shadow? Did the death of the little Viennese who had served briefly as his teacher cause these psychic reverberations in his, Philip's being, because of the great archetypal symbol of a Christ, the son of God and Man, dying for all men—any man?

He could feel the sedative struggling to take repossession of his nerves and he tried to help it by lying back flat on the bed, counting slowly, counting waves swinging on a shore—but at once the waves were revealing, as they broke, the cruel jaws of man-eating fish, a hat with a green visor, illegible pages from a water-soaked book. Then the long dark nose of a carp thrust itself at him out of the churning breakers—beside it, above it, a man's profile with the beard of Christ of the colored Sunday-School charts. "Fish brain and human brain" said a voice, and he saw himself looking at an illustration in a book on the structure and function of man, the human animal—a book that Ermenthal had brought to the hospital one day after the session in which Philip had revealed his sick imagery of a "dead" brain . . . "A fish has only the brain stem, the seat of the reflexes and instincts" read the caption. "Man too has this structure, which is the *core of his personality*, but in addition he also has the cerebrum, the seat of the higher intellectual faculties." The words seemed to be coming now from the mouth of the bearded profile in the illustration, wearing the diagram of its own brain structure like a fanciful embroidered cap of curling leaves, sweet-breads, harpstrings, nut kernels, sea shells, small gas balloons, turbines and embryos. And the mysterious haunting words of the accompanying text: "Between the Pukinje cells lie the large Golgi cells whose *function is unknown* . . ." Function un-known, meaning unknown—everything unknown. Nothing fixed, final; no harbor, no anchor . . . Philip saw his own body, wear-ing his brain like an embroidered cap, tossed up by a giant comber and thrown, to be broken on the coral reef along with the bearded Christ of the physiology book, the giant carp, Er-menthal's dark-rimmed glasses.

4

AFTER he admitted to himself that it was not going to be pos-sible to sleep he got up and crept into the living room to the book shelves. But Ellen heard him. She came from their bed-room tying her blue robe about her as she walked through the door. He noticed again how worn and anxious her expression was, and he went toward her, put his arms around her and dropped his chin on the top of her head. "Oh, Ellen!" She clasped her arms about his waist and they stood there in the humid room seeking reassurance. Philip felt that something which wished to come from him was paralyzed; as though ice had formed on a once free-flowing stream.

Awkwardly, after a moment, he freed himself. She did not cling. "I was looking for a Bible," he said hesitantly.

"A Bible?" She seemed puzzled, faintly alarmed.

"Don't look so frightened." He gave a tight laugh without humor. "I couldn't sleep, so— My God, it's really fantastic! If you want to convince anyone you're hopelessly sick, or batty, just ask for a Bible or start reading religious works!" He heard his voice rise, the scorn and anger in it—though at whom or what it was directed he could not have said.

Ellen made no direct reply. She only murmured that there must be a Bible around somewhere and began to search the long shelves. "Will this help?" She handed him a little Episcopal book of Common Prayer she had once carried to school chapel.

He took the book and looked at it, shook his head. "I'm afraid not. I don't want to pray—I was after information—information about the life of Christ. Do you know anything about him, really?"

"Well, just what you do, I guess." Her apprehension had given way now to something very like embarrassment. "You might try the Encyclopaedia," she suggested, tentatively, "or here—maybe this would have something." She held up to view a *History of Western Philosophy*. "Betsy James lent me this. She's been taking a course at the New School for Social Research. There's something in it about the History of Christianity—as a philosophy, not as a religion."

"You girls!" he said. "On your toes every minute!"

She did not pick up the old challenge. Together they walked back into his room. He put the two books on the table, certain he would not touch them. As Ellen tucked in the rumpled sheet at the foot of his bed, he noticed again the sadness in her face. He put out his hand and touched her arm. "I'm sorry I'm so low. It's Ermenthal's death. I can't accept it."

"I know." For a moment her eyes, which had been avoiding his these last weeks, or so he thought, looked directly, softly at him. "But there must be other men like Dr. Ermenthal. You'll find someone else, darling."

"Oh, God!" he cried violently. "Is no one indispensable in the modern world? Are we all, for God's sake, just so many interchangeable parts? Sure there are other men—but . . ." He broke off abruptly. "Never mind," he said in a different tone. "I'm making too much of it. Sorry."

She turned off the light and sat down on the edge of the bed. He reached out a hand and she took it and held it lightly without speaking. They were both silent for a long time. Philip thought of the night she had rushed into this room, had locked the door behind her and fallen on this very bed sobbing bitterly. Only a short time ago but already something that had happened in another existence. If he had not had the accident could they have entered one another's arms now without restraint? There was no way to be sure. He wanted to question her, to confide in her, to try to discover where along the way of their joint lives they had lost connection with one another. But he could not. He lacked the interest, the strength to do so. Without meaning to, he groaned aloud.

At once she asked, tightening her clasp, "Does your head hurt?"

Her voice seemed to him as automatically, unfeelingly solicitous as that of his former day nurse.

"It's my head all right—but not the skull. The worm in it!" He felt her fingers slacken. He pressed them in quick apology. "I'll try to stop it. I'm talking like a fool."

"You're not over the concussion yet." It was all she said but somehow under it he could feel her disapproval. With his free hand he clutched at the sheet. Suddenly he wanted her pity, her approval and love.

"Ellen, I'm in no shape now to talk about what I feel but— don't give me up! I'm going to be all right. Don't despair!"

The melodramatic word "despair" surprised even his own ears. He could not imagine a year ago ever using such a word about their lives.

After a moment, "I don't understand you at all," she said.

He too waited a moment. "Do you understand yourself?"

"No," she said, "not any more."

Had she meant to she could have said nothing more calculated to move him to pity. Her words, the voice in which she spoke, were full of an infinite, terribly young sadness, and he imagined her now as she had looked the night he first met her, when she came with Jerry Edwards to a fraternity dance his junior year. She seemed to him, suddenly, no older than she had been then. She had had a special kind of shy eagerness that had delighted him, coming upon her, kind, gentle (but not dumb) after the aggressive maneuverings and outspoken critical comments of Toni Jessup who had been insisting that he try to dance the beguine. He could never bear to make a public spectacle of himself and he had been sure that he was one as he lugged—refusing to yield to the rhythm himself—the prescribed stiff spine, sandwiched feet, and undulant hips of Toni around and around the hall.

"I think the beguine is sort of silly anyway," Ellen had said when they had their dance. He had looked gratefully into her yellow-brown eyes, at the bird's wing of bleached sun-streak flying away from her brow. He had loved her, it seemed to him, instantly. Between that delicate, gay, yet wistful girl and this delicate, withdrawn and tearful woman, there stretched only some fifteen years of quick-paced time. What had effected the change? Where had she gone, that girl who had seemed the only possible one for him? Had he ever known her at any time, even for one moment?

He was aware that they had been silent for a long time, ever since her "not any more."

He pulled her head down beside his. He could not keep from groaning once more out of bitterness and misery. Then neither of them moved or spoke. They lay with their heads on one pillow, her body's length stretched close to him. But, in spite of this physical intimacy he knew, felt, they were actually so far apart an icy wind was blowing from the bottomless chasm that separated them. And as he lay wanting—he could not say what— sympathy, reassurance, devotion, pity, he could feel her withdrawing even farther. He could feel her, as though by an act of will, pulling herself away, determinedly extending the space between them. He realized with astonishment that she would be glad to be rid of him for a while, free of his half-expressed worries and fears, his tedious self-examination, his new inability to face his daily life. And chillingly he had a faint fleeting prevision of what it meant to be alone—all alone. This seemed to him the real specter, the real ghostlike gray and grinning terror whose shadow he had felt falling coldly near him since he was a boy.

"Ellen!" he cried in sudden panic. "Ellen, don't!" He put his arms around her and pulled her closer. "Hold on, Ellen," he begged. "Please do. Give me time! Let me see if I—if I can find out where I got so mixed up!" He could hear the terror in his voice.

PART FOUR

* *
* *
*

Journey to the Island

CHAPTER *12*

*
*   *
*

ALL day the vast country had unrolled its marvels beneath the wings of the great metal bird. Philip, looking out and down in sun and shadow, in green and purple, in blue and gold, seeing the sprawling deserts and checkerboard farms stretch into peaks, lakes, cities, had been surprised at only one thing: that he had not felt with deeper force the dramatic incredibility of such a flight. For, like the other passengers, he had thumbed through magazines, yawned, dozed, eaten and drunk whatever the crisp stewardesses thrust before him at fixed intervals, all with hardly more than an occasional glance out the window and with never a comment on the miracle of a day spent hurtling through space.

At sunset, in a twilight of undersea green, they came sailing down the mighty gorge of the Columbia River, bouncing a little in the warring currents of air, sea-cooled from the west, desert-parched from the east. The landscape now seemed not to belong to the earth but to some fearsome and weirdly beautiful planet viewed only in swift passage by rocket-men. Against the bland afterglow, the black and purple peaks, cones, spears, mounds, rocks, glaciers, each asserted a personality born of its own form,

143

its own special manner of reflecting light, of riding or splitting the air.

The greatest of these solitary snowcapped giants Philip's seat companion readily identified: Rainier, Hood, Adams. Philip followed his urgent finger toward the mountains. Painted implausibly by the dying sun—plum, pink, cerise, indigo—they possessed for Philip the stylized unreality of those exotic views of Fuji with which Japanese painters of the nineteenth century shocked the Occidental eye. The trip would be worth it just for this, he thought, his whole being shaken from its passively receptive groove by both the unfamiliarity and majesty of the airy landscape.

And then, suddenly, they were in the Seattle terminal: the thrust and counter-thrust of rivet-machine voices, greetings, complaints, and the too-solid bodies shuttling the hot space, pushing and claiming, "Porter, here, porter!" Philip's head began to swell and float. He had a momentary vision of himself in a plane flying on and on, never landing.

By the time he reached his hotel, he found the wait in line at the desk almost unendurable. When at last his room door closed on the bellhop, he fell face down on the bed and into a drugged sleep.

2

HE SLEPT half the next morning, though he had intended to get up early and start for his father's island. When he wakened for the third time and looked at his watch, instead of rolling over and burying his head once more in the pillow, he thought in irritation, "God, I'm late for the office again!" Then he saw his suitcase on the valise rack. It took him a few moments to remember where he was.

He emerged into the bright morning, blinking at the sunlight bouncing off the sloping stone streets. He caught a whiff of the sea and was half-inclined to follow his nose down to the port. But, reminding himself of the hour, he went as directed to the Travel Service. There he found an astonishingly pretty girl with natural brown hair (after New York he never expected anything but bleached blondes in public places) who was eager to help him. She shuffled through a pile of maps like a card-trick expert, chirping booster phrases at him about "beauty," "off the beaten track," "unique," until finally tapping a pencil against her white teeth she said, "Here's the island of Madrona, but I don't see anyway to get there."

She noticed Philip's frown. "Don't worry," she said. "There must be *some* way." She smiled and jerked up the telephone; her desire to be helpful radiated across the desk. "Hello, Liz," she called into the phone, "this is Betts. Say do you remember how Fritzie Bates got to that island last year where the old Indian does his smoked-salmon job?" The conversation lasted a long time and went considerably beyond the subject of his itinerary, yet Philip had to admit it was cheerful to hear about smoked salmon and old Indians. At his elegant breakfast that morning of *croissants* and chicken livers à *la Victoire*, he had felt convinced that every semblance of the Last Frontier had vanished.

The girl put down the telephone at last. "Two ferries a day to the part of the Sound you want to go to. But I'm afraid you've missed the morning one."

"Oh, God," he groaned in such a strained and worried way the girl looked at him sympathetically.

"Maybe you could rent a boat," she said, "if it's terribly urgent."

He saw she meant "life or death." "Oh, no," he said, "it's not that urgent." He remembered the last interview with Ermenthal, the darting glance behind the thick-lensed glasses and his pointed remark about "hurry." He tried then to relax his tight muscles, to smile. He leaned with deliberate nonchalance on the counter. The girl was still watching him, waiting.

"I don't know what the hurry is," he said. "Actually I'm staying with—with someone on a little island called Peachpit—right near Madrona. If I get to Madrona, I guess I can make it the rest of the way by rowboat."

"Peachpit!" she smiled with genuine pleasure. "That's cute. I never even heard of it. Just shows you. Learn something every day." She whisked out a fresh map—a more detailed one—ran the scarlet spear of her index finger up and down a moment and then cried out in triumph, "Here it is! Yes. Right across from Madrona. Looks nice and remote. Kinda off the beaten track. See?"

The girl's enthusiasm was so infectious that Philip found himself looking eagerly at the dot on the map, as though he might summon from it some picture of the island.

"Says here Unoccupied," the girl went on.

"Well, it's not. My . . ." he stopped. Why couldn't he tell her straight out his father lived there?

"Lawrence Warren lives over on Madrona," she said.

"Who?"

"Don't you know who Lawrence Warren is?"

Philip said he didn't. The girl seemed briefly shaken. "Why, he's a famous painter. Lots of Eastern people ask about him out here. There was a picture of his house in the Sunday paper once—I kept a copy." She ducked down behind the counter.

Philip became impatient. "When does that afternoon ferry leave?"

"Oh you've got *hours* yet. Five-thirty," the girl said and brought up a large black scrapbook and spread it on the counter. "I keep things like this to show people. You know, kinda human-interest things." She opened the book. "Here's his house. And this is Mr. Warren. And that—that's the Indian devil mask he hangs on his gate to keep people away. He says the Indians charged it for him and it's as powerful as an electric current."

"He sounds insane," Philip remarked. He wondered how close Madrona was to Peachpit.

The photograph showed several blurred abstract paintings— and a tall young man in a startlingly pale blonde beard, standing, essentially faceless, between two doubles for the All American Mom, complete with noseglasses, pearls, cameo brooches, veils, wristwatches, feathers, upswept coiffures, pagoda hats and formidable bosoms. The caption read:

LAWRENCE WARREN BEING HONORED BY THE PRESIDENT
AND VICE-PRESIDENT OF THE LOCAL CHAPTER OF THE

WOMEN FLORAL PAINTERS OF THE PACIFIC NORTHWEST
UPON THE OCCASION OF HIS WINNING THE NATIONAL PRIZE
FOR METROLA VEGETABLE SHAMPOO.

"Metrola Vegetable Shampoo," Philip muttered. The way he said it was designed to make her laugh, but the earnest girl entirely missed it.

"They give big prizes every year," she said with as much enthusiasm as though she expected to capture one herself. "Lawrence Warren's had lots of honors. He's in the Museum of Modern Art in New York. And his picture's been in *Life* and everything like that."

"You don't say." His irony, he saw, was equally lost on her.

As she chattered on, Philip, glancing again at the scrapbook, saw the photographed corner of a modern-looking cabin, caught the words: "*Lawrence's nearest neighbor. . . .*" What am I getting into? he asked himself, his heart sinking. How close were the islands anyway? Did his father have any contact with these people? The undercurrent of anticipation he had felt from the moment he smelled the sea was gone now and the thought of the day stretching ahead of him with nothing to occupy his mind seemed unendurable. He cursed himself for lying in bed and missing the morning ferry.

"What can I do between now and five-thirty in this town?" he asked impatiently.

The girl looked at him a moment without speaking, as though trying to assay what sort of character he really was. What did she see? he asked himself. "Enter an old man of forty"? He looked furtively toward the mirror on the wall behind her, straightening his shoulders under the gray flannel suit, "And don't say the movies," he said bluntly, "for I'm a refugee from the movies."

3

"THOUGHT you wuzn't comin' back," remarked the "Special Chauffeur" of the hired car; a designation which indicated that he had at his tongue's end certain pertinent information on the age of the Totem Pole in Pioneer Square, where hand-carved walrus tusks could be purchased, or west coast oysters sent home by express.

"I liked it," Philip admitted climbing into the taxi from the Public Market which the Tourist Bureau girl had insisted he visit first on the itinerary he had allowed her to make for the empty hours until ferry time. "Be sure to get out and take a *real* look," she had urged, sounding very much like Aunt Hetebel preparing him for his first trip to Europe, worrying for fear only the façades of the Louvre and the Uffizi would claim his heedless eye. He had found the girl's enthusiasm infectious enough to force him from his bored impatience, his unwillingness to spend a day viewing the local sights. As he got back into the taxi, waiting near the market, he offered the driver a lump of black-walnut fudge in a pink-striped sack bought from a garrulous old lady he had come upon, surrounded by stalls displaying dressed rabbits, salt-rising bread, fireweed honey and watercress as large and unreal as velvet shamrocks. "Yes," Philip said, "it's quite a sight," and it was true that the polished glint and gleam of thousands of scrubbed vegetables, stretching from him in seemingly endless lines, attended by cheerful guardians of every racial strain from Japanese to Finnish had caused his spirits to rise remarkably. He had strolled along exchanging grin for grin. Downstairs among a wealth of unfamiliar objects—the antlers of elk, goats' milk cheeses hanging in rows like miniature punching bags, a man painting Mount Rainier in a snow storm on black velvet— he had found for Pammy a paper Chinese dragon and a toy totem pole. He had also found a postcard for Goldstone showing an alarmingly developed young woman in a bathing suit whose torso conveyed the message: *Greetings from the Puyallup Valley.* He laughed out loud imagining Goldstone's pronunciation.

"Where to now?" the driver was demanding.

"Well, let's see." Philip consulted the girl's list. Again he was aware of that absurd but warming feeling of co-operation with invisible elements that he remembered having become aware of at times with Ermenthal. He had no opportunity to trace the tenuous filaments of this emotion to their source; the driver's eye was on him. "How about the Indian Museum?"

The driver looked sceptical. "Wanna see it? Okay. Nothing much in there." But he drove off and they threaded their way through traffic, across bridges, up and down hills and came to a stop on the university campus before a soiled gray structure growing unclassifiable architectural bulges like enormous stone wens. "Left over from the Alaska-Yukon-Pacific Exposition of 1908," the driver apologized. Funds, presumably had not yet extended to Gothicizing the repository of Indian relics.

Philip's first impression on entering was that the driver's negative view had been justified. He found himself confronting cases that displayed only miscellaneous varieties of dead life from the sea and the land. What had they to do with Indians: a ballet of Thurber starfish, rows of spiraled, spiked, coiled, striped and spotted shells; lumps of unfamiliar minerals sliced and polished, showing fanciful patterns like sunsets in late August, the ceilings of Santa Sophia, moonlight on the cliffs of Dover? He paused before a case of mastodon fragments: tooth and jaw, tibia and fibula: *Ten million years ago and six feet tall . . . crossing by a land bridge,* and turning a corner, found himself looking straight into a huge staring black eye; the central theme of an Indian blanket spread out in a glass case. *The eye of the Thunderbird,* announced a card. The black pupil gazed fixedly at Philip. It was as unmoving, as implacable, baleful, terrifying as an eye seen suddenly through a chink in a shutter. "The cosmological eye." He turned his back to it, reaching in his pocket for a piece of paper. Resting his elbow on the case behind him he began to write.

"Don't lean on the case, please."

He jumped like a guilty child. "Sorry." He looked into a pursed mouth, glass-caged eyes. His creative impulse fled. The woman who had spoken turned her back in the detached and non-human manner of all people who deal with the public seeking information, cultivation, or the passing of a leisure hour, and walked briskly out of sight on her sensible heels. He could not even remember what had prompted him to search his pockets for the envelope on which to scribble.

He walked outside and got back into the taxi. He read the note he had scribbled; found it meaningless. Lowering the window he let it sail out, saw it flutter and bounce and come to rest in the gutter.

"Volunteer Park?" asked the driver.

"What's that?"

"Oriental museum."

"Oh, God—not more culture!" He was impatient again, convinced he was wasting time; his destination seemed to be receding.

"Oughtn't to miss the view anyway," the driver said forcefully. "You've got plenty of time yet."

Philip shrugged. No use resisting these aggressive types, he decided. He sank back and let the taxi carry him to the Park, where the driver hopped out, opened the door and stated firmly, "You can see better if you get out."

"See what?"

"The mountains."

"What? Again?"

But as he got out it was not the mountains that immediately commanded his eye. He was confronting the most curious sight he had yet seen—archaic stone animals, giant-size rams and camels, standing in somber and massive incongruity before a "modernistic" white façade.

"What on earth are they?"

"These here are animals from the Ming tombs. Come from the sacred city of Peking, they say. . . . Peking, China," he added.

"Very impressive," Philip muttered. He stood in the hot sunlight staring at the primitive simplicity and beauty of the stone figures for several minutes—his back to the mountains over which the driver had exercised such proprietary airs. "I think I'll take a run inside."

He had the galleries to himself. There was no one to disturb with voice or footstep the atmosphere of ancient unshakable serenity which, despite uprooting and transplanting, lingered among the objects from the Far East. He wandered slowly until he was stopped by a Chinese scroll, an artfully rough and simple brush painting in fading ink strokes, beautifully mounted on antique silk brocade.

Philip found himself caught, forced to look at the picture: a seated man leaning easily against the bole of a pine tree— half-turned away from any possible observer—gazed into space, empty except for a hint of far mountains. At what was he actually gazing, this quiet man? And what power had the long-dead painter possessed to pull the onlooker's eye so compellingly into that empty space, while at the same time identifying him with the lone figure against the pine? There was so little to the subject, so amazingly little; yet to Philip in this moment it seemed more satisfying than any painting he had ever seen. He thought of those crowded canvases of the Renaissance filled with roiling and active life, that he dimly remembered. In none was there the sense of hidden mysterious force that came toward him now out of this ancient scroll—this figure of a solitary man resting serenely against space.

He stood before the painting a long time. As the minutes passed he became aware that somewhere inside him a nerve, an interior coil, was slowly loosening its tension. But immediately, as though in response to his awareness, he felt the coil tighten again, and with this renewed tension he felt again the familiar thrumming of tired nerves in his upper spine and head. What had given this perverse signal to his nerve ends—this message of resistance to the very thing he most wanted and needed: to let go, to drop, to float, to be at rest like the man gazing serenely into empty space? At rest! How could any modern man dare be at rest, to rely even briefly on tranquility in his shifting, exacting world? Yes, he was afraid—afraid of letting go, of letting his guard down—afraid of the empty space, the empty apartment, the lonely road, the inaccessible beckoning mountain. Far safer to stay coiled like a spring, ready for action or reaction.

He felt lonely now. The museum seemed frightening and unfamiliar, far away from his ordinary life; strange, as his whole day had been. He hurried outside. As he climbed into the waiting taxi the radio was offering a clack and clang of bell and triangle, brass and strings—some exaggerated comic parody of a familiar air from light opera. The driver started to switch off the dial. "No, leave it," Philip said quickly. "Leave it. I like it."

CHAPTER *13*

*
* *
*

THE *Oyster Queen* was ready to depart. Her ample lower
deck nudged the scaling pier to receive the line of cars that
waited, bulging with pup tents, sleeping bags, picnic hampers
and deck chairs, to cross an arm of the inland sea. Somewhere
in the green smudge of the far shore there waited, it was plain,
a land for campers.

He stood in silence a long time watching the splendor of the
dying day. A few gulls were dipping and gliding in the ferry's
wake. Around him he heard the remembered nasal burr of
Western speech, and he wished he could feel with more intensity the emotions that should certainly accompany a return
to the country of one's childhood. He was sure they were there,
the feelings—only buried, glazed over. Perhaps it was his exhaustion, for the day had tired him immoderately. Perhaps he
had seen and done too much for a man not yet recovered from
a severe blow on the head.

Now the *Oyster Queen* was approaching the shore and he
became aware of a slow scent of salt and cedar, of burning

brush and tide flats, moving toward him on the still clear air. Without knowing why, he felt a clutch at his throat and the prickling sensation of tears forcing their way to the surface. He turned from the deck, feeling weak and a little ridiculous, and hurried back into the cabin to the circular counter.

"Coffee, please."

Without a word the attendant tipped up one of the pyrex pots and poured the thick tasteless liquid. "We're landing," she said, as she put the coffee in front of him and nudged the sugar bowl.

"I know, thanks."

He hardly touched the coffee, but it was something to do, to sit and stir it. As the ferry slowed for landing, he felt it in his whole body, the grinding and bumping at the dock. He had to summon his will to rise from the stool, leave the lights, go down the steps to the dark lower deck where passengers and cars disembarked.

As he carried his two bags along the narrow gangway leading from the pier to the village, he realized with a twinge of apprehension that he had missed the opportunity to ask about the next stage of his journey. Surely someone in the cars now rolling past him would have known. In the easy, hospitable way of the West he would have been passed along until he had the information he wanted. Now it was too late. The people and the cars melted away into the twilight like puffs of dandelion before the wind. He watched the red eye of the last vacationer's car flash its warning and disappear. Suddenly he felt farther from his father's island than he had in Seattle, or even in the hospital room in New York City when he had talked about the trip with Ermenthal.

When he put his bags down to take a look around the dusty village, he realized he was alone. Somewhere in the distance an old dog barked without protest or conviction. He could see a few houses set well back in weed-cluttered yards, their lights all at the rear—supper lights—and he could imagine the start that a sudden hand on the back door could give. He felt hesitant and undetermined, like a child who finds himself in an unfamiliar place with night coming down. The sensation of the ballooning head, which he had had so often since the accident, threatened him again.

He was standing before a weathered porch, with broken steps rising from the hardpacked path. Squinting in the fading light at the sign over the entrance he could just make out *General Store and Post Office*, and beneath it, lettered in an even more distant day, *Hides and Gold Dust*.

He stepped onto the sagging boards, his feet loud and citified, his hand tentative on the insecure wooden knob. As the door opened there was a clanking rattle of announcement overhead, and immediately the rear wall split open to reveal lamplight and a little bald man. A dog rushed out silently from behind a burlap curtain, a fat black-and-white terrier who circled Philip, sniffing.

The little bald man had been gnawing on a bone. He held it in his hand and his jaws worked on the interrupted bite. "Howdy. What'll it be?"

Philip again put down his bags. "I want to get to Madrona Island. Can you tell me how?"

This simple question had the effect of putting a match to a string of firecrackers. Still holding the sparerib in his left hand, speaking with a chattering echo from ill-fitting teeth, the little man delivered a series of crackling sentences.

"Early morning stage your only chance. Last stage to Venus left ten minutes ago. Ferry was late and Prentiss wouldn't wait. Doggoned independent cuss, Prentiss. Just got married awhile back. Married a French girl he met on the other side. Says she gits scared if he ain't home by nightfall. Doggoned if I see what he'll do about it come winter. Gits dark mighty early up here come December. I suppose mebbe he'll give up the job. Not much in it for a young fellow."

He returned the bone to his mouth and allowed his upper and lower plates to beat a delicate tattoo of sound on it as he nibbled the last well-browned bits.

"Well, then, I'll need a place to spend the night," Philip said wearily. "Have you any suggestion?"

"You mean for a bed? Sure," said the old man spryly. "I can put you up here. Extra room out back. My daughter Fay's.

She's a cashier at the Hans Brinker Bakery chain in Seattle. Don't get over as often as she might."

"That's—that's good of you." Philip looked cautiously about him. The place seemed clean enough. "And—about food? I hate to bother you but—I haven't had any dinner—I mean, supper."

"Well, now, doggoned!" said the little man shaking his head. "Doggoned if I didn't have the notion not to give Lottie that last sparerib. Something said to me, Don't you do it, but she sat up there begging so cute that I . . . Tell you what I'll do, though, I'll fry you a couple of eggs. And I got some country ham. How's that? Ought to take the cramp out, anyways."

"That sounds wonderful. Thanks," Philip said gratefully. "I hate to bother you, but you see I've never been . . ."

"I know. You're a stranger. I can tell. Sticks out all over you." He picked up one of Philip's bags with surprising agility. "Come on back."

The old man lifted the burlap curtain and Philip preceded him into a small room crowded with a kitchen stove, two rockers, a wooden table covered with flowered oilcloth, a couch that appeared to double as a bed. But what lent the room its appearance of confusion and disarray was the cluttered wall space. Every available inch was plastered with calendars. Philip felt, at first, that he had stumbled into another museum, that the pattern of his day was now complete.

While the old man sliced the ham into the spider skillet, Philip, rubbing his tired eyes, studied the assortment of gaudy symbols and reassuring iconography which leading merchants and institutions annually pass out as reminders that they stand ready to serve the faithful during the coming twelve-month. All were here: sport, play, sex, nostalgia for the past, rural virtue, Nature's marvels, and the blessings of organized thrift. Noble setters pursued invisible birds through waving rushes; coy kittens pursued balls of twine under rocking chairs, hyperthyroid maidens in sweaters too small for them invited unseen males; abandoned stagecoaches rested picturesquely under ancient elms; brawny men and women with perfect teeth harvested oversize fruit that had never been touched by scab, scale or worm; an impossibly cobalt lake reflected an equally improbable sky from the crater of an extinct volcano; Greek-temple bank façades promised courteous service and one-and-a-half percent on everything but loans. Dead, indeed, the man who would not respond to at least one of these stimuli.

"Quite a collection, ain't it?" the old man cried, observing Philip's interest with delight. "My daughter gets 'em for me every year."

"You must have a pretty busy day at the end of each month," Philip said.

The little man cackled with pleasure. "Yep, that's right. Yep, that's good. I'll have to remember that one for Fay."

He walked over toward the kitchen stove still cackling, then suddenly he turned back and clapped his right palm forcibly to his bare forehead with a resounding thwack that startled Philip. Gazing at his visitor with stricken eyes he cried through the ghostly clatter of his teeth: "Holy mackerel! Wait a minnit. I'm thinking—your name's not Stewart, is it?"

"It is."

"Can you imagine that now!" cried the little man, in dismay. "How could I be so slow with me wits? Clarence Bye's been here every day for the last three looking for you on the morning ferry. Somehow we didn't figure you'd ever take the night one. No one does that doesn't live over here—except maybe crazy week-end campers. . . . Well, sir, I'm not going to have the pleasure of giving you my daughter's bed, after all. I'll have to call Minnie Bye right up. Tell her you're here."

"Wait a minute," Philip cried, as the little man jumped toward the wall phone. "Who's Clarence Bye? Who's Minnie? And why can't they wait till morning—if I can?" Although he had no wish to remain here longer than was necessary, he knew he was exhausted, and in his weakness he could not bear to face any more strangers. He reached for a rocker, dropped into it. "I'm pretty tired," he said.

"Bet you are," the little man agreed heartily, "but you don't know Minnie. She wouldn't like it by a darn sight, not by a darn sight. No, siree, I'll have to let her know right away," and he shot over to the wall, gave the telephone handle a loud cranking honk and after a pause shouted into the mouthpiece:

"That you, Sadie? This is Jim Everett. Sadie, see if you can get the Byes at Madrona, will you? Company they're expecting just hove in here. Yep, took the late ferry. Didn't know about it, a course. Yep, darned shame, all right. Well, see what you can do. I'll be waiting right here."

He hung up with the air of a man who has settled an important piece of business. "Might as well relax," he said cheerfully. "It'll take Clarence Bye a good two hours to git here—even lickin' up the road—maybe nearer three."

Philip repressed a groan. In his exhaustion all his impatience to arrive at his destination had left him. What if he refused to budge from this place tonight? They couldn't make him move, after all. He could tell them he had been sick. But he said nothing for he knew he lacked the energy to resist the plans that had been so mysteriously woven around his coming. He remembered the bottle of whiskey in his Valpack. He went over and took the bottle from its case, asked his host if he would join him in a drink.

"Nope, thanks," said the little man, his spry voice rising above the sputter of the ham now filling the room with its spicy odor. "Took the pledge. Took it a year ago. Joined the Jehovah Witnesses and made a vow to give up spirits for a year. Year's up September 24 at nine in the evening."

"Well, here's to September 24 at nine in the evening." Philip raised the bottle and took a long swallow. The liquor burned its way to his empty stomach. When the telephone rang again he was willing not to interfere with any arrangements that had been made for him.

"Minnie?" the old man yelped. "Yep, he got here. Took that afternoon ferry. Yep, it's a doggoned shame. I told him he could stay here. All right, all right; figured you'd want it that way. Well, I'm giving him some ham and eggs. That oughta hold him till he gits to you. O.K. We'll be right here waiting for him."

He hung up, shaking his head.

"Strong character, Minnie Bye." He began to dish up the eggs. "Might as well give in first as last. Doggoned if I ever see how she had a son like Clarence—soft as suds water. People will tell you he ain't right in the head—summer folks, that is—but don't you believe it. Clarence could run circles around any of 'em. Does act kinda queer sometimes, but no harm in him, not a mite." He put the eggs and ham before his guest with a gesture courtly in its grace and attentiveness. "Hope they'll suit you."

"They look wonderful." Philip tried to respond heartily, but the thought of a two-hour trip on unfamiliar roads through wild country with a man who was touched in the head—the idea crossed his mind again that his excursion West was a stupid impulse from which he would probably return home broken beyond repair. Something in his expression must have betrayed his apprehension, for the old man said at once, "Don't you worry none about Clarence Bye driving you. Drives that car straight as a nailer. Runs the Madrona Ferry, too. Done it since he was fourteen, after the old man died. Got struck by a trolley, his pa—over in Tacoma where he went to collect a bad debt. Doggoned shame. Fine fellow, old Bill Bye." Having passed out his assurance, he became silent.

He did not speak again until Philip had eaten his ham and eggs. Then, as Philip lit a cigarette, Jim Everett pushed forward the applebox that served to hold cedar chips and small alder logs for the stove. "Git your feet up," he suggested kindly.

"Thanks," Philip said, complying. He noticed the box read *Skookum Gems from the Yakima Valley*.

"Skookum," he repeated aloud. "I remember that word. Chinook, isn't it? I remember my father saying, it'll be a skookum day."

"Guess your pa probably knows a lot of Chinook," Jim Everett said. Philip imagined that the look he gave him was a questioning one.

"Why would he?" he asked, tilting back with an air of unconcern.

"Well, he knew a lot of the old-time Indians when he first come up here," Jim Everett said. "Some of them still spoke it. He used to talk to 'em by the hour—so I've heard. Gave him a funny reputation with some people. Now my daughter tells me they study the Siwashes up at the university. Can you beat it?"

Philip could think of nothing to say, and after a moment, chuckling, Jim Everett remarked, "Man of mystery—that's what someone called your father in here just last week. Man of mystery! I had to laugh."

"Why a man of mystery?" Philip asked. He was really curious to know.

"Oh, pshaw, how would I know?" said Jim Everett. "Guess any man that lives alone and shaves every day is mysterious to some folks."

This was his last remark about Philip's father, though he now took over the general conversation with the air of an expert. He displayed little interest in learning anything about his visitor's views or way of life. The homely and garish intimacies out of his own existence were more satisfying to him, and—he calmly assumed—more entertaining to his visitor.

He was full of talk of the "old days." For two hours he reviewed the incidents out of an active life that remained high-lighted in his memory. Philip, who at first had resisted this garrulousness, soon found himself listening with pleasure. Jim Everett could remember well such things as Chinese New Years in the rough and ugly port town where he grew up: the kites and dragons, incense and firecrackers, the exotic shimmer of the lanterns, the unfamiliar wavering beauty of the lighted paper—green and pomegranate—a breath of romance in the drab, ugly setting of a pioneer town. (Philip could see it clearly, this brief spurious blooming on foreign soil, a thin fading echo, like Mr. Pug's note on the flute, from a legendary world where gentlemen with fingernails eight inches long hid lumps of jade up their sleeves merely for sensuous pleasure, invited friends for blossom-viewing on nights of full moon . . .)

"Saw them get the last Chink with a queue in the Northwest," the old man exclaimed. A cruel story, prankish and adolescent, of loggers full of "blue ruin" whiskey operating with scissors stolen from Bob the Barber.

"And Chinese slave girls," he chittered on, licking the enticing words from his liquorless lips. "Mamie Wong kept 'em. She had the best house." (There they were, eyes like velvet flowers, luring incautious Occidentals to their anonymous pleasures.) "Rough, tough days," he gloated, only pretending to deplore the methods of shanghaiing, or the fake "dentist" near the port, with the sign, DON'T GO TO SEA WITH BAD TEETH. "Did a land-office business. But no one who ever come in, ever come out— woke up later with an almighty splitting head in the hold of a ship!" He beat his thigh in glee with the palm of his little gnarled hand. The stories drew nearer home, became more common-place. "Father of Edie Everson across the road told me—Edie herself, no better than she should be . . ."

2

PHILIP had long since forgotten the clock when he heard the noise of a truck drawing up outside. There was the heavy clat-ter of boots on the porch, the door opened and a red-faced man of some thirty years with a thatch of stiff, sun-faded hair, a body strong yet soft-looking, with sloping shoulders and abnormally wide hips, stood grinning in at them through the sacking curtain.

"Sure burned up the road that time!" he exclaimed with genuine satisfaction. He spoke in a high, sweet voice.

"Shake hands with Clarence Bye," said Jim Everett rising promptly. His voice indicated regret, as though at an untimely arrival. Philip put his hand into a large hard palm, looked for a moment into a shy and gentle blue eye. "Welcome home," said the piping voice. Home? "Thanks," Philip answered, a little late.

Clarence seized his bags in an excess of fervor as Philip turned to Jim Everett to say good-bye and pay for his supper. "No, no. Them ham and eggs is on the house—if you can call it that." The old man cackled again as he followed Philip out onto the porch where he extended his little withered claw. "Wellsir" (he ran the two words together, avoiding thereby any suggestion of a distinction in status), "it's been a real pleasure. Real interestin' to talk with a stranger. Suppose likely I'll see you when you leave to go back."

Philip nodded, smiled, and stepped down to the old battered truck that stood in the gray light steaming and clattering.

"Take it easy now, Clarence," the old man advised.

"Sure thing."

Philip climbed in one side, Clarence hopped in from the other, and with final good-nights they lurched off into the darkness, taking the same road the campers with their tents and fishing-poles had followed several hours before.

They drove for some distance in silence. After the heartiness of his first greeting Clarence appeared to have grown shy. Philip was glad, for he had become aware again of his fatigue, his help-lessness in the hands of these determined strangers, and he had nothing to say. It was Clarence who finally spoke.

"Been killing snakes all day," he volunteered.

"Snakes?" Philip's voice was guarded. He recalled the old man's supper remarks that city folks did not always find Clarence right in the head. He wondered if Jim Everett's further judgment that Clarence could run circles around these same critics would prove only an opinion rooted in local loyalty.

"Snakes," Clarence repeated. He drove headfirst into his sub-ject. "Mrs. Burridge, she's got the old Adams place—summer folks, you know—she's scared plumb to death of snakes. I told her she ought to see a doctor. Understand doctors can cure people of being scared of things. Eb Wiley got cured of being scared of the insides of a tank. Yessir, got cured in Georgia dur-ing the war. Said the doc found out he was scared because Gert and Charlie put the old rowboat on top of him when he was a kid and sat on top of it all morning while he was under howling. Eb got so's he could finally drive a tank all over northern Africa and right into Germany. That's a fact."

"Interesting," Philip murmured. For the first time he thought of Ermenthal with amusement, imagining his enjoyment of this tale of a psychological cure. "How'd you get rid of the snakes?" he asked, after a moment, when he saw that Clarence considered the snake-killing incident covered.

"Oh, easy thing! I just picked 'em up by their tails and tossed 'em off over the tops of the hazel bushes—about a hundred feet. That way you don't have to out and out actually kill 'em—something I'd as lief not do to any living crittur. You just kinda snap the fluid in their spines up into their heads and it kinda addles 'em. They get confused and can't think straight, don't know how to feed themselves and just plain starve to death before long."

Philip shot a side glance at Clarence, but his face was serious and earnest. If this was a leg-pull for tourists he gave no outward indication of it.

"I suppose there's lots of wild life here."

"Quite a likely amount of it. Yessir. We'll probably see deer along this road tonight. Even a bear maybe—though it's early yet. Appletime in about a month—that'll bring the bears around."

"Are the bears dangerous—I mean fierce?" Philip was aware that he was making the sounds of a dude, but he wanted now to keep Clarence talking.

"No, not many of 'em. Not if you treat 'em halfway decent. Old Purly Barrett met one of 'em when he was comin' home drunk one night above five years ago and he spoke sharp, called her a dirty name. She up and slapped his face, pushed his lower jaw around toward the back of his head. Doc Sawyer down at Venus fixed his jaw for him, but it's always stood off kinda funny ever since. Wouldn't a been so bad if Purly hadn't been such a big talker. But he always has a lot to say, Old Purly has. His jaw'll fall outa joint and hang there a minnit, but he's got so's he can snap it back so quick he hardly loses a word."

This time Philip laughed out loud. Clarence gave no visible sign of appreciation, except that his girlish voice rose higher above the rattle of the truck as he continued:

"Had a Spaniard come in here once prospecting. Leastways, said he was a Spaniard—a Basque, he called himself. Brothers was sheepherders over in Eastern Oregon. He had the biggest ears I ever saw—kinda like dinner plates—saucers anyway; stood straight out beside his head like tree fungus. He tangled with a bear once over on the peninsula. Bear got his left ear. Joe got the ear back, all right, but it wasn't much good to him after that. He was in trouble, his wife didn't like his looks with only one ear. She finally got around to hiring an old Indian to whittle him a good one outa madrona wood. He was a real artist, that

Indian. Made it so's you could hardly tell the difference. Got some cedar pitch and stuck a lot of black bear fur in that wooden ear so's it looked just like the real one. Yessir, Joe carried that ear around in his pocket for years. Whenever he met anybody he'd haul it out and hold it against his head with one hand, and danged if you could tell the difference, if you didn't know."

Philip laughed again. He had forgotten the headache that had started up when he began this journey. He looked ahead on the dirt road; the pitching truck, the ruts and pockmarks, no longer annoyed him. The sight of unfenced land gave him a feeling of pleasurable remoteness. He drew in a breath from the dark woods: the smell of decaying logs and wayside ferns, of ripening berries, alder leaves and cedar bark, and, far off, dimly, the tang of the sea.

For a while Clarence was silent. Philip got the distinct impression that now his strange companion had sensed his fatigue; that he did not want to let his guest either grow weary with boredom on the long ride (hence the yarns) or weary with trying to listen to his thin voice above the truck's roar. A mile or two passed before he began to talk again.

"You was asking about wild life, Mr. Stewart. Some of it's died out. Had an old beaver on the island until about ten years ago. Nice friendly old fellow. Last of his family. Some son-of-a-gun from Hollywood up and shot him. Said it was by mistake. Think they've all got too much money in a hurry—those fellows— and it's made 'em all careless about other folks' feelings." (To Philip a vision of Mr. Mellar Kane, occupant of the top throne of *Suprema*, rose out of the darkness; his well-oiled, hairless, sun-tanned torso, squared off above his flowered Lido beach clout. He grinned.) "I wanted to keep Hollywood characters off these islands," Clarence said, "but your pa says it's a sin to generalize."

This last phrase rolled out with complete aplomb. Although unlike the rest of Clarence's remarks, Philip had the very strong notion Clarence understood exactly what he had said.

"Then there used to be the big gray squirrels," he went on, the asperity dropping from his voice. "Some disease took 'em off. A mystery. Nobody knows what. They were great for play. Saw a sight once I'll never forget. Just a year or so before the squirrels died out, I'd been cutting down a big cedar tree for my mother. Stopped to eat my lunch and take a little nap and when I woke up I saw the darnedest thing I about ever did see—a whole gang of squirrels—musta been near to a hundred—staging races on the cedar chips. Yessir, they had their tails up in the air to steer by and get some wind—like sails, you might say— and they were sure staging some real fast races."

This time when Philip laughed Clarence laughed too. Philip had the feeling he had stepped inside some invisible barrier, that he and Clarence could be friends.

"I suppose my father is quite a naturalist—I mean, knows a lot about animals and so on," he remarked rather lamely.

"Mr. Stewart's great for birds." There was an unmistakable note of respect in Clarence's voice. "I suppose you know about his raven, Ishmael. There sure was a doggoned smart bird. He could talk more sense than most men. I think your pa's often real lonely without him."

"What happened to Ishmael?" Philip asked. He wondered if Clarence knew how little communication he had had with his father, what strangers they really were.

"That's another mystery. Your pa left him home one day to guard the house while he went for the mail. When he came back Ishmael was dead right outside the house on the beach. Couldn't find no marks on him, but I always suspected the old gull—the one your father calls Tatoosh. Tatoosh was always real jealous of Ishmael, I thought. He couldn't speak a word himself. Always acted as though he didn't give a tarnation about Ishmael's talents anyway, but I'm not so sure."

Clarence's voice seemed unnaturally solemn. "He believes this story about the revengeful seagull," Philip said to himself in amazement.

Clarence was silent again, and Philip, in spite of the pitching truck, began to feel sleepy. He dozed, his head jerking about painfully when they hit the ruts. He would open his eyes then and see the paper-white undersides of leaves as the lights fell on the alders, the occasional ghost of an old stump wearing a crown of green. Then his head would fall forward again.

At last he sat up straight with the feeling that Clarence was slowing down a little.

"Sure bet you're tired, Mr. Stewart," Clarence remarked. "It's only a little bit of a ways now."

His voice was as tender and solicitous as a woman's. Philip's heart warmed with the feeling of human sympathy that came from the lumpish man beside him. He felt glad suddenly to be spending the night with the Byes; and then the thought occurred to him: this kindness is being extended to me because of my father. The thought confused him in some way that he could not explain.

They were descending a hill now. The outline of a shed roof appeared darkly against the sky. There was an open graveled place, and beyond, a pale band of water.

"Well, here's the ferry," Clarence said. "Just a minnit."

He left the truck running, jumped out, sprang on to the small ferry, made a clanking noise with the chains, reappeared, and drove the truck down the narrow passageway with a sure eye. When they took off, Philip stepped out on deck. There was not a light in view, not a sound but the slurring of the water under them. Overhead the stars hung very bright and near and Philip looked up, as he had not since childhood, for the Big Dipper, the Big Bear, and the Red Planet, Mars.

3

THE ferry was grinding again to a stop. They got once more into the truck and ascended another short hill, turned in a half-circle and drew up at the rear of an old building facing the inlet. "Here she is," Clarence said. Whether by "she" Clarence meant their destination or his mother, Philip was not sure, for as soon as the truck stopped, the door of the house opened and the round short body of an elderly woman appeared, holding a lamp high in her hand.

" 'Bout time," she called out cheerfully.

"Here he is, Ma," Clarence said.

Philip went slowly up the wooden steps. He had an absurd feeling that it was a homecoming; also that it was Mrs. Bogson standing there as she had stood in the hall in London's Brooke Street the wartime day he had come asking if he could sublet a flat; the same stance: competent, casual, analytical and friendly all at once.

"Glad to see you, Mr. Stewart," Minnie Bye said. She took his outstretched hand and gave it an awkward pumping motion. "We been looking for you for several days."

"I'm afraid I've put you to a lot of trouble." He followed her into the big kitchen. The room lay half in shadow, the light falling only on the cheerful stove and the blue checked oilcloth of the table. There was a cat asleep in a rocking chair, the glisten of green plants in the windows, the covered cages of birds just beyond the glow of the lamps.

"You're hungry, I'll bet."

"Well, I've eaten once but I could eat again."

His answer obviously pleased her. "I've got some fresh clam chowder here," she said. "And I could toast you some left-over biscuits, and there's fresh blueberry pie. Would you like buttermilk, or plain milk, or coffee . . . ?"

No, it was not Mrs. Bogson—not with this prodigality of food— it was Nelly in the Lynnport kitchen on one of her "good days." Philip felt the brittle tension leaving his spine. He sank into the rocker. "I don't think I'll ever move again," he heard, with surprise, his own voice saying.

"You don't need to." Mrs. Bye was pulling the iron pot of clam chowder forward on the stove as she spoke. "We could bring your pa right over here and put him up. I'm always trying to persuade him he ought to in the winters, anyway. But he says he's never lonesome."

"So I'm staying all winter, am I?" Philip said.

The Byes found this very funny. They laughed together, crinkling up their weathered blue eyes.

"You'll see," Clarence said. "This place'll git you. It gits lots of folks who don't expect it to."

CHAPTER 14

*
* *
*

HE WOKE and looked at his wrist-watch. Six o'clock, but already he could hear people stirring about below him. There were footsteps on old wooden planks, the smell of coffee, the clear sound of voices over water. He got up and went to the window. At the dock's end a small motor launch, badly in need of paint, rose and fell with the easy tide, and a man in the bow in faded pants and a red-plaid mackinaw was talking up to Clarence on the dock. Their voices, carving the salty morning air, speaking words he could not understand, seemed to come from another world, a childlike world, simple and uncomplicated. Philip had the disturbing feeling that he was a stranger here and could not possibly ever be anything else. Once more the apprehension at the thought of meeting his father swept over him. The ominous drumming in his temples began again faintly. He returned to his bed and curled down into the warm pocket of the blankets.

The room in which he had slept seemed stripped and barren in the cold morning light. The old wooden bed with the cheaply carved footboard had peeled its varnish, the white paint on the iron-legged washstand was flaking. Even the bowl and pitcher were without charm—a nondescript over-all pattern of entwined and writhing plant life of indeterminate botanical origin. He tried to feel pleased with the one picture on the wall since there was something about it that made him think of Christmas cards long ago; the kind that came frosted with a magic glittering substance like sun on snow. The scene someone had chosen to frame with impressive bands like so much gilded Swiss cheese showed a small house half-buried in drifts, with ruddy light from one window and an implausible opal moon. Before the door stood a sleigh with horses whose breaths rose alarmingly into the cold air, twice the size of the penmanship plume that indicated the chimney. It was certainly going to be a cold Christmas if the horses' breaths indicated the temperature, Philip said to himself; but it did not seem an amusing observation. Instead he again had the feeling of having lost something nameless and precious. Was it that Arthur Rackham mouse in his striped trousers and cutaway; was it his childhood?

He reached for his cigarettes on the floor beside the bed, and, as he drew the first smoke into his lungs, tried to recapture the sensations of the night before in the warm kitchen with the light on the checked cloth, his idle fork making patterns in the rich blue juice at the bottom of his second slice of blueberry pie. He had been drowning in sleep, like a child at the end of a day in the sun, yet he had hated to leave that homely room, full of warmth, the soft sounds of fire and kettle, the mingled scents of cookery, plants, cats, birds and humans. It seemed a complete world in itself and he had dreaded the creaking stairs, the glare of the single overhead light bulb on the naked walls of his bedroom, the cold rough sheets. Now he told himself that the sight of the kitchen again was all he needed, and he swung his long legs out of bed.

As he appeared in the doorway at the foot of the enclosed stairway, Minnie Bye looked up in surprise.

"Law's sake, up so early?" she greeted him. "I don't think you could have got your sleep out."

"I can't seem to sleep," he confessed. "Maybe I'll go back to bed after breakfast. There's no hurry—now that I'm here at last."

She gave him an odd glance, as though such an idea was out-landishly bizarre, but she made no direct comment. "Sit down," she suggested, "and I'll bring you your coffee. Buckwheat cakes do you?"

For a moment he did not understand what she meant. "Oh yes, they'll do fine," he managed to stammer.

As he waited for the cakes bubbling gently on the old iron griddle, he looked around him at the room with its windows bulging with miscellaneous plants in painted tin cans, the two silent canaries in their cages hopping compulsively with little scratching sounds from perch to swing to floor to perch again; the drowsy cat moving sleepily from chair leg to chair leg, rubbing its back and shoulder sensuously against the wood.

"Here kitty, kitty!" Philip said. The cat coldly ignored him; he felt embarrassed. "My little girl has a cat," he confided quickly.

"That so. What's its name?"

"Edgarbergen."

"Funny name for a cat," Minnie Bye said.

Philip was startled. Had she never heard of the original? What a marvelous thing that would be! He did not want to question her; he preferred to cling to the thought of such happy isolation. He beckoned again to the cat.

"*Her* name's Samantha Ann," Minnie Bye said. "How old's your little girl?"

"Ten."

"Nice age for a little girl." She set the buckwheat cakes in front of him.

He had almost forgotten their sour-sweet taste. He splintered crisp slices of bacon into the maple syrup, drank two cups of black coffee.

When he had finished he walked outside. There was no one around. The intense silence seemed now to have the quality of a solid, and his own steps as he walked the dock clattered offen-sively on the loose planking. At the dock's end he sat down on the steps and peered into the clear water. Near the surface a jellyfish was expanding and contracting, and below, on the sandy floor, he saw the pink and purple starfish of childhood memory. How magical they had always seemed when they appeared punctually every summer in the cove near his grandfather's house on the bay.

He leaned his head against the peeled log of the railing and closed his eyes, feeling the sun invade his neck and shoulders. As soon as his eyes were shut he realized the silence was not really silent; it was murmurous with a thousand minute mingled whispers, flutters, trembles, melodies: the birds in the distance weaving an embroidered web of sound, the humming of insects, a singing in the sands, a faint lapping and creak of water under the float. He began to sink lightly, softly, with a feathered fall, into the cadence of the warming day, into this benign and unfamiliar circumambience. He felt he could sit here forever listening, waiting.

And then abruptly he jerked himself up straight, as if some perverse instinct forced him to inquire, "What on earth will I do all day in a place like this?" He had asked Ellen this very thing before he left. "Read, swim, fish, walk, pick berries, dig clams," she had answered promptly. "Boys' camp," he had said. "Well, anyway, I envy you," Ellen had replied. She had spoken lightly, almost too lightly, before adding, "Seriously, if you don't feel like doing any of those things, why, then do nothing. That's what your doctor says, Do nothing." "I've never done anything else in all my life!" He had been self-conscious and bitter. Ellen's answer had been in kind. "Well, you've certainly made noises and movements as though you were busy, haven't you?" He had shrugged and not replied.

He was grateful when Clarence's appearance on the dock turned his thoughts away from Ellen. As they exchanged good mornings Clarence gave him a sharp glance. "You don't look so good, Mr. Stewart. Why'n't you try sleepin' a little more?"

"I think maybe I could," Philip agreed.

"Why'n't you lie in the hammick under the big madrona? Nobody'll disturb you. I'll show you where."

Feeling like a child in the care of a protective and affectionate Nanny, Philip followed Clarence back toward the old weathered building. They walked around the side across a neglected orchard, high with uncut grass, to the shore, and there, threading their way through clutching salal and Oregon grape, came to a big faded canvas hammock stretched between two madrona trees.

"Give it a try," Clarence said. "We don't need to go over to your pa's place till this afternoon. He won't be worried. He takes everything real calm. Said he'd expect you when he saw you."

Philip lay down in the hammock. The green cradle began to rock him, the green waters closed over him.

2

WHEN he awoke the sun told him it was noontime. He lay for a few moments taking the warmth again into his bones, listening. He could hear a persistent sleepy rustle. Raising himself on an elbow he looked about trying to place it. At last he saw that the sound came from the madrona, from the steady dropping of leaves on leaves. He examined the trees attentively; noticed where the cracking red-brown bark exposed the smooth green surface beneath. As he stared at the linear arabesques of the peeling bole, he wondered of what they reminded him; then he knew: it was the Indian designs he had seen the day before in the museum. He felt pleased at this discovery. Perhaps, after all, he was more conscious, more observant and alive, than he imagined.

He swung his legs out of the hammock and made his way back to the *Madrona Beach Post Office and General Store*. The Byes were as glad to see him as though he had been away on a long trip. He sat down at the kitchen table feeling rested and invigorated and, with relish, ate a lunch of pork chops, fried apple rings, cole slaw, home-made bread-and-butter pickles, blackberry shortcake with heavy country cream, unwhipped, spooned thickly out of a bowl.

CHAPTER 15

*

*   *

AT THREE-FIFTEEN, after his ferry trip, Clarence piled Philip's bags in an old flat-bottomed rowboat and started the trip to Peachpit. The sun was high and hot, the tide against them. In the hard glare Philip began to feel unwell. He was grateful to Clarence for refusing his help with the rowing. The now-familiar dread was rising again from the pit of his stomach.

The quality of the day, the hard sunshine, the dipping oars—It was a Sunday, long ago, in Milltown. He and his father were off to rent a boat for rowing on the bay. Down at the big dock there was a black-funneled ship in from Japan and they stopped to look at the little bandy-legged men moving about the decks in the early light. . . . But there was something else, something more, before that, before they rented the boat. The shapes began to swim up through the cloudy waters of memory. . . .

2

THE morning sun was shining flat and full on the silver roof of the Athena Oyster Company. Young Philip looked at the

roof, blinking, and as he turned away to rest his eyes there
appeared, reeling around the corner out of a street of decrepit
houses, dark and evil, where it was said the Chinese smuggled
opium for their gambling dives, the figure of Pearl Fiske. The
ugliness of Pearl Fiske's face! It had been so terrible—he had
seen her before—that he dreaded catching sight of her again.
He wanted his father to hurry by, not stop and speak to her.
Thinking about that face now—as the startled heron rose with
dignity from a half-submerged tree root and sailed off, a slow
feathered spear, along the bank—Philip realized that its ugliness must have been due to a scar, the kind of scar that acid
thrown in the face would make.

Usually Pearl Fiske was tidy, but this morning everything
about her hung awry. Her slip dangled, her stockings were
twisted, her high heels turned over crazily. Her bright red hair
—her one beauty—was pulled back as tight as the grim coiffure
of Miss Amelia Beatty, the third-grade teacher's, and on her
ruined face there rested, what he now knew to have been, the
contorted mask of a night's heavy drinking.

Here, in Philip's memory, there came a hazy place. Some
part of the scene dropped out, some revulsion at the sight of
the familiar town character blurred his recollection of the first
words spoken between Pearl and his father. But somehow he
had the notion Pearl had been bound for that boat in from
Japan and that his father had tried to persuade her to go back
where she came from. His father must have offered her some
alternative, or bribe, or reward, for she was saying in her
cracked and drunken voice, "That's white of you, Mr. Stewart.
Mighty white!" And then she had caught sight of Philip.

To his terror, to his horror, she had thrust out a hand toward
him, falling back uncertainly, as she did so, on her high broken
heels.

"That your little boy? Nice little feller. Scared, ain't he?
Scared of Pearl's face. Tell him she wouldn't harm a cat. No,
sir, not a cat. Not a cat."

The words apparently started some rhythmic association in
her befuddled head. "Not a cat," she repeated, staggering about
faintly on her wobbly shoes in the ghastly caricature of a dance.

"Not a cat," she cried, turning to face an imaginary partner. "Not a cat, swing a cat, swing your cat, down the middle . . ." Her movements became more awkward and uncertain; a broken puppet.

"Wait here, son," Father had said. He took Pearl firmly by the arm, slipping and sliding along with her until they disappeared around the corner into the Nisqually Hotel—the hotel Philip knew because he and Jane had been warned by their mother, as they went past to Grandpa's on the other side of the bay, never to so much as glance at it.

Philip felt ashamed and sick, afraid someone would come along and ask him what he was doing and where his father was, and he would have to tell. Everything was suddenly ugly: the barnacles gnawing eternally, silently, at the half-eaten, decayed pilings of an old abandoned dock; colorless blobs of jellyfish—revealed where a shaft of light struck the pale water—contracting, throbbing invisibly, as they secretly fed themselves.

His father was gone a long time, it seemed to Philip, but at last he reappeared, whistling serenely. As he held the boat for his son, Philip got a smell of his breath: it had whiskey on it! His father had stopped to take a drink with Pearl Fiske! Philip turned weak with his shame; with the thought of what his mother would do if ever she found out.

As they moved onto the choppy surface of the bay he could feel his father's glance resting on him speculatively. At last in a voice Philip found brisk and unrepentant his father had remarked, "Son, you mustn't judge people by the way they look, or always even by the way they act. Pearl Fiske is a sad human derelict. She should rouse your pity, not your contempt."

Philip had made no reply. He could think of nothing to say. He dangled his hand in the water, heavy with embarrassment, praying his father would say no more. To his relief, when his father spoke again it was only to say cheerfully, "I'll recite you a poem. It's about a woman called Bessie Bobtail."

He began in an unconcerned way, but Philip was not entirely taken in. He might be using this particular approach, this particular voice, to throw him off guard. He might still be out to prove something; the poem merely a device with which to make his point—whatever that point might be. Still Philip could not avoid listening with attention, for no one could help listening to his father if he wanted you to.

> " 'As down the road she wambled slow,
> She had not got a place to go;
> She had not got a place to fall
> And rest herself—no place at all!
> She stumped along, and wagged her pate;
> And said a thing was des-per-ate.' "

He gave the word "desperate" an extra special twist; breaking up the word into separate syllables and giving the "a" a long flat sound.

Philip could still remember every line of that poem; not from his father's recitation but because he had learned it to recite at school some years later. He had come on it in an anthology and had been amazed to discover the poem was not by his father but by an Irish poet named James Stephens. All the boys at school had found it a very funny poem, comic from first to last.

That Sunday on the gently rocking bay his father had recited all three verses in a voice growing faintly mocking, faintly sad, with one eyebrow raised at his son as though asking him couldn't he make the effort not to be so stiff, so much a Bachelder?

> " 'Her face was screwed and wrinkled tight
> Just like a nut—and left and right
> On either side she wagged her head
> And said a thing: and what she said
> Was des-per-ate as any word
> That ever yet a person heard.' "

Before the last verse his father paused. He dropped his voice. He let a sort of liquid feeling well up through the lines slowly. It was like looking at the spring water under the log back of Grandpa's orchard.

> " 'I *walked beside her for a while*
> *And watched the people nudge and smile:*
> *But ever, as she went, she said,*
> *As left and right she swung her head,*
> *—O God he knows: and, God he knows!*
> And, surely God Almighty knows!' "

There was no conviction in the last two lines as his father spoke them. They hung like a question in the warm air. Suddenly something happened to Philip's picture of God, that bearded Santa Claus without the stocking cap, hanging out of the heavens above red velvet portieres. The face of God seemed to grimace, to twist, fade, dissolve into mist; into the empty sky as on the evening of a gray day when the sun has abruptly disappeared, departing without color, bringing a night without stars, nor any promise of them.

Then his father began again to row. The oars lifted and fell, lifted and fell, through the salty water of the June bay. And there came over the boy, Philip, a curious and frightening feeling of this going on forever, like a spell, like an enchantment in a fairy tale: The dip of oars—eternal; the rise and fall of water around them, swinging toward the shore, retreating from the shore; swing of tide and swing of cat and Pearl Fiske's broken heels—eternal. This moment—with Bessie Bobtail Fiske and his father arm-in-arm disappearing together; and God (gone, like the Cheshire cat with an idiot's grin) and he, Philip, left behind, in fear and panic—lasting forever . . .

The same panic touched him now, looking up from his half-doze, seeing the water flowing, the green trees moving past slowly above the broken sandy banks, the strange young-old man with his womanish hips resting lightly on the seat of the rowboat as he pulled with his incongruously muscular arms against the resistant tide.

3

THE dinghy grazed the shore and, before it stopped, Philip jumped out. He had the feeling that if he did not get out immediately he would cower back and beg Clarence to return him to Madrona Beach.

A lean man in a blue shirt and faded corduroys was coming briskly toward them over the rough beach. Philip thought in surprise, "But he's not old." The body, the springing step— could he really be seventy-four?

Now that he saw the solitary figure approaching him a pe- culiar sensation took hold of Philip. The shore, the water, the woods and the sky seemed to swell and tremble with momen- tous suspension like a landscape in a delirium. The whole scene appeared reflected in a gigantic overblown bubble; their two converging figures enclosed in a bright translucent sphere. Philip tried, as the space between them narrowed with his father's firm steps on the crackling gravel, to check the sensation of unreality, saying to himself: "This is only my father coming toward me. After these long years, these last long two days, we are finally meeting on a lonely island, surrounded by the sea, guarded by mountains. . . ." Abruptly, the enclosing airy sphere collapsed; everything was once more flatly, familiarly normal. The old man was clasping his hand. And here was the remembered intense blue eye; not misted, thank God, just warm, friendly, quietly impersonal. "It's good to see you, son." The voice had not lost its lilting cadence.

"You too, Father." Philip felt his knees trembling. Sweat broke out along his spine and forehead. Was this then to be all of it—the few simple words, uttered without self-consciousness, or any seeming emotion? And was this, perhaps, the most re- markable part of it—this easy, quiet greeting? He hoped his father would not notice his own agitation.

"Was it an easy trip?"

"Very. Less than twenty-four hours by air, you know."

"The magic carpet. Here, Clarence, don't bother with the bags. We can manage. You'd better be getting right back. Your ma'll worry if you're late."

"It was a real pull today," Clarence said in his high sweet voice. "Had the tide against me all the way. Well, so long, see you soon."

Philip and his father stood watching Clarence go. As the

stretch of water between them and the boat widened, Philip felt as though abandoned by his last friend. He and this stranger who was called his father were alone together on an island in the midst of wild and unfamiliar land. He turned and saw a plain small house half-hidden in the trees that came down to the shore. Behind it, stretching away, only a dark thick forest.

The panic that had been rising within him suddenly flooded his whole body. "What am I doing here?" He had to check an impulse to cry out to Clarence across the moving water, to beg him to return, remain until he and his father had conquered their first embarrassment and could learn to speak to one another.

"I imagine you found Clarence pretty entertaining, didn't you?" His father's voice betrayed no emotion of any kind. He stood looking after the dipping blades of the oars with an expression of quiet amusement, perfectly at ease.

"His tales were a little tall," Philip managed to say.

"The Byes are good neighbors."

"Your nearest ones?"

"Oh, no, we've got some right across the inlet." He nodded in the direction of the opposite shore, and peering into the green gloom Philip could see the outlines of a low log house with modern windows. It appeared to be the house he had seen in the newspaper.

"Two of them," his father was continuing, "man who's a painter and a woman who works among the Indians. An anthropologist. They come every summer. They're great friends of mine."

Now that he had arrived, and had sensed the isolation, this information about the nearness of neighbors gave Philip a distinct feeling of relief. He leaned down to pick up his bags. His father insisted on taking the heavier one and they made their way across the sliding stones of the shore to the little house.

The house was without any special character: a structure built to keep out rain and cold, provide a roof, a place to cook, eat and sleep; the kind often seen in rural districts where the main, if not the only, concern is survival. The kitchen, however, was reassuringly cosy. Already Philip had a feeling of the importance of a stove's living presence in the houses he had entered the last two days. Here, on the newly scrubbed bare floor, it stood crackling with recent wood, the iron kettle on it humming in a contented monotone. Nearby was an old rocker with a cushion of checked gingham. (Woman's work, Philip decided.) Over the plain wooden table shelves with dishes extended, and, at the far end, a painted wooden cupboard with more dishes and a few books. At the back, through a gingham curtain that matched the cushion, there appeared to be a little ell, and here he saw firewood stacked, and shelves of canned goods. Near the stove was a green iron sink with one faucet, and just outside the door, an old-fashioned priming pump.

"This is the room where I live." His father paused deliberately in the center of the floor to give Philip a chance to take in his surroundings. "When you do your own work you finally reduce everything to a pretty small radius. In winters I sometimes even bring my cot right in here and sleep, particularly if it gets very cold—which it seldom does—if you remember Pacific Northwest winters."

Philip murmured something noncommittal about the winters. "It looks very comfortable," he managed to say.

"Your room's back here," his father went on, leading the way through the adjoining room where there was a wall of books, a little camp organ, a round table with a Paisley shawl thrown over it. The room smelled faintly musty and unused.

In passing through, Philip caught a glimpse of his own photograph in his ATC uniform, an enlarged dim snapshot of some woman riding a Western saddle (Jane probably), and several other faded unfamiliar photos. There was a painting of a horse feeding in a green meadow below a bulbous green hill, strangely shaped, planed off on top. He remembered that horse and that hill intimately. The painting had hung at home in Milltown above the piano. He could even remember what it said beneath: "She was born in Old Glen Wherry at the foot of Slemish Mount." Mount Slemish, where St. Patrick—a young man in exile—had served as a swineherd. He could hear his father saying, laughing, long ago: "That small romantic-looking building in the background is a brewery," and then some story—exaggerated, poetical, unfactual—about St. Patrick and the "Snakes," the Druids, whom he drove out of Ireland.

His father had walked on ahead of him. "Here you are," he said, opening the door into one of the two box-shaped rooms that led off from the small parlor. "It's small and plain but the bed's comfortable."

Philip murmured something again, putting down his bag.

"You've got the mountains," his father continued, pointing out the window. "I hope they'll not disturb you."

He gave Philip no time to question this curious remark, for he added immediately in a warm voice and with his blue eyes focused full on his son, "Why don't you rest for a few minutes before supper? You're looking a little fagged out."

"Thanks," Philip said. "I believe I will."

He needed very much to be alone. As soon as his father had gone, he went to the windows and looked out. The mountains! They seemed, in the declining light, to be advancing toward him through the sky. As he watched them, the splendor and immensity of their snow-capped peaks against the blue sky, his father's words came back to him. "I hope they'll not disturb you." What had he meant? That it was open to doubt whether he could endure this much beauty; so spectacular, so compelling and inescapable? That perhaps one had to grow accustomed to this kind of undiluted experience after years of intricate and scattered city life?

He turned away and lay down on the bed. At once he became aware of the sound of the tide outside the window, gentle, dreamy, yet insistent in its steady measured beat.

The next thing he knew there was a knocking at the door and a voice was saying, "Supper's ready." It was his father's voice and he realized then he had been in a deep sleep.

CHAPTER *16*

    *
*   *
   *

THE first morning on the island Philip rose at seven. Before he went to bed he had asked his father what time he usually got up and was assured he kept no regular hours. But Philip had decided to set his alarm for seven anyway, out of a childish wish not to appear lazy. At supper he had hardly been able to keep his eyes open as they ate the simple good meal of a meat stew and vegetables, with the berry pie that Mrs. Bye had insisted he take with him. In bed he had dropped off to sleep so quickly that it seemed he was still turning the key in the clock when consciousness deserted him. A moment later he jumped up, half-sitting in his bed, looking around to locate a terrible whirring and ringing—and it was morning.

He turned off the alarm and lay back weakly on the pillow. A new day. The alarm of a new day. The sour insistence of the mechanical summons brought to his mind a floating image of city lives stirred each morning with the jangle and whir of clocks: beds folding back into walls, stockings hung over radiators, milk bottles on sills in the gray drizzle, dolls won at carnivals and faded silk cushions with *Souvenir of Niagara Falls* stamped on in purple ink. He addressed the ghost of Ermenthal: "This morning the ringing of the alarm made me think of how people renew every day the trauma of birth; over and over the throbbing clock repeats the cry of protest with which the foetus, now inescapably a human being, accepts its destiny" . . .

Too fancy! he told himself. He sat up, swung his legs over the side of the bed and stood at the window. The air rushed into his throat like a purifying drink, and there were the mountains again, clear and sharp in the morning light. He knew, looking at them, that they would spend the day retreating, growing misty, tender, milky, wraithlike, until the late afternoon would start them moving toward him in the changing air. He wondered if they might not become to him, in the next weeks, as intimate as human creatures. At the thought he looked across to the opposite island at the half-hidden house of peeled logs on the shore; and again he wondered about the anthropologist and the artist and how soon his father would suggest he meet them.

The tide of the night before was going out slowly, leaving a wet expanse of sand, and on this sand two gulls strolled, slowly, arrogantly, with the indifferent air of crows, toeing in slightly, their rears swinging gently from side to side as they walked. The movement made him laugh. He dug into his bag for his bathrobe, put it on and went to the kitchen.

When he appeared in the doorway his father looked up from the frying pan, his alert blue eyes flickering with humor.

"Throw away that mechanical gadget, boy." He was turning bacon strips with quick thrusts of a long-handled fork. "I don't want my chipmunks developing anti-human attitudes, and there's nothing like an alarm clock to get their backs up."

Philip laughed. "Okay, to hell with all clocks!" As he said it he had a fleeting sensation of escape and release. But, a moment later, when his father put before him without question a bowl of steaming oatmeal and a cup of coffee, he found himself looking around for a newspaper.

"Don't you miss the papers?" he asked, as he accepted his

father's suggestion of honey and diluted canned milk for the porridge.

"I hardly remember now what it was like to read them every day."

"I suppose very little is missed if you don't."

"You'd be surprised how little. . . . How do you like your eggs—blind or staring?"

"Here!" Philip said, pushing back his chair, starting to rise, suddenly embarrassed to be waited on. "Let me do that."

"Take a day or two," his father said easily, "until you learn where things are. It's easier this way. I enjoy it." And he seemed to; the way he turned the bacon, dropped in the egg, handled the coffee pot. He did it jauntily, with control and style. For the second time Philip thought: It is impossible that he is seventy-four. His movements were edged and sharp, and he had none of that rheumy film of lingering sleep, or any of that reluctance to face the morning Philip remembered in the breakfast visage of his Uncle Logan during his last years. Maybe the old man practices yoga, he thought, taking a gulp of the strong coffee. His belly is as flat as that fancy young man's, a friend of Ellen's mother, who expensively demonstrated muscular controls one winter in an apartment in the Pierre. But I'll stay off all that, Philip said to himself. I won't run the risk of any homilies until I feel stronger.

"I make it a point to listen to some good radio summary around New Year's time," his father was saying, pouring himself a fresh mug of coffee and settling down with it in the chair by the stove. "It saves a lot of wear and tear—not harassing yourself every twenty-four hours with the spectacle of a sanitarium full of sick and crazy patients all preventing themselves from getting well."

"Is that the way the world looks to you?"

"Pretty much so." There was a certain reserve in the old man's answer. It gave Philip the reassuring feeling that his father was not waiting avidly for the opportunity to air his views, like so many people who lived alone.

"I remember you wrote that to Ellen. She and a doctor friend of mine both agreed."

"A doctor should be in a position to judge."

"This one was. He worked with sick minds."

His father put the ironware coffee pot on the table between them, "How could he pick and choose?"

Philip grinned. "He just took the ones that had caught on to their condition. That kept him busy."

He had an impulse for a moment to talk about Ermenthal, to tell how the doctor had urged him to come to the island, how he had died. He wondered about his father's views on fate.

"If you think you're going to miss the news we could try to repair the radio," his father offered. "I think I know what's wrong with it. I don't use it much in the summers. There's so much else to do."

Philip said No, he could get along without the radio. As he stirred the sugar into his second mug of coffee he wondered what his father meant by "so much else to do." He couldn't imagine what he found to occupy his time, but he did not ask.

Immediately after breakfast his father had a few puffs of his pipe, Philip had a cigarette, and then they washed up the dishes together.

As his father stacked them methodically into the enamel pan he said, without any trace of self-consciousness, "I have the habit of reciting when I wash up. Keeps my memory in condition," and without further remark he began. He skipped from one quotation to another without any discernible order. Some of the things he recited, Philip noted, were familiar: "Tomorrow and tomorrow and tomorrow, creeps in this petty pace from day to day"; "O wild West Wind thou breath of Autumn's being"; "Wee sleekit cowrin tim'rous beastie" . . . But there were an equal number of unfamiliar quotations. Some of them, to Philip's ear, had a vaguely scriptural sound, though they did not quite ring with true Bible sonority.

Philip found it soothing to stand and rub the towel slowly over the surface of dishes as he looked out into the moving green wall of trees, at the play of the light on the blue water, while, behind him, this fountain of words and phrases, easy rhymes, and slow, stately prose measures filled the little room, drowning the voices of the kettle and the fire. He remembered a story from childhood—one of which his mother had not approved—about his father being paid to recite poems in a San Francisco bar; and he grinned at the memory.

When the last dish was put away his father said he would feed the chickens. Philip, still in his bathrobe and pajamas, went with him to see the henyard, the small garden, the bee-hive, the orchard. He saw the woodpile with the cross-cut saw and the shed where the fuel was stacked for the winter.

"That saw keeps me fit," his father said. "No exercise on earth like a cross-cut saw for a man's belly."

"I could wish mine were as flat as yours."

His father forebore remarking that the cross-cut was always there. Philip had already observed that the old man was not likely to make the obvious comment. After the chickens were fed, his father walked off whistling through the orchard, saying he was going to look for mushrooms. His manner of leaving neither invited nor rejected company; he simply went. Philip watched him disappear into the woods on the opposite side of the clearing and then came slowly back to the house.

Still feeling too lazy to dress, he walked out on the beach to a sunny spot with a clear expanse of warm sand. He lay down, rolling his bathrobe for a pillow. Through lowered lids he watched the sidewise scuttle of crabs, the minuscule geysers of squirting clams, the occasional airy somersault of a fish in the inlet. Two gulls were drifting dreamily on the sky; behind him in the woods the noisy birds were beginning to quiet with the warming day. Far off, where the inlet widened to an open branch of the sea, he caught an occasional sight of a small boat heading up into these remote waters. How long it was before, overcome with drowsiness, he fell asleep he could not have said. It was past noon when he wakened.

2

AFTER he had made himself a sandwich in the empty kitchen —his father had not come back—he wandered into the little sitting room with its faint but not unpleasant smell of dampness. He looked first at the books. There were a number of well-thumbed specialized volumes on Birds, Butterflies, Insects, Flowers, and several on Natural History in general: *Mosses with Hand Lens and Microscope, Wayside Berries*, three old volumes of an *American Medical Botany*. There was a dictionary of Sanscrit next to one of German, and some volumes of the Pali texts of Wentz Davis, Suzuki on Zen Buddhism, Max Müller's *Sacred Books of the East*, a Bible, an Apocrypha, a Milton, a Dante, old volumes of Shakespeare, Spinoza, Goethe, Nietzsche, the Oxford Book of English Verse, the Irish poets. Nothing seemed particularly extraordinary to Philip except the Sanscrit dictionary, the Pali texts, and a book or two on ancient symbolism that carried sinister connotations from his early perusal of an old Faust of his uncle's with graphic illustrations of the terrifying activities of the learned doctor of Leipzig.

I don't suppose, he said to himself, the old man does any experimenting in his own kitchen with *Transcendental Magic, Its Doctrine and Ritual*. Still you could never tell. Solitude had a way of breeding strange traits. His eye fell on a *History of Ulster*. Stamped on the cover in bright scarlet was an open left hand; strong, tapering, dynamic; the head, heart, and life lines clearly marked. "*The heraldic badge of the northern counties of Ireland*." Philip held up his own hand and saw it was similar; the width across the palm, the thumb thick at the base, turning back at the tip, the long middle finger; width and length well-balanced—all in all, he supposed you might say—if you did not know its owner—the hand of a practical visionary.

He started to put the volume back on the shelf, but as he did so he noticed behind it the body of a dead moth. He was about to brush it onto the floor when something prompted him to take it up and examine it. A silver dust came from its wings onto his fingertips. Turning it on its back he studied it minutely. It had, he saw, a face—and this surprised him. The face was faintly whiskered like a grizzled old man who has not shaved, and there were round bulbs for eyes. One long antenna was missing; the other extended itself, a spidery gesture in space. The legs were bent, touching halfway down in a ballet form, and the silvered wings were closed protectively around the slender tube of the body. Suddenly this moth possessed for

Philip such mystery and sad beauty that he could not throw it away. Walking across to the table he laid it carefully on the Paisley shawl. As he laid it down he realized—and the thought provoked his wonder—that he never took time for such observations; that he could not remember when last he had looked with interest at leaf, stone, or insect.

After he had put down the moth he began to examine the photographs above the little organ. There was one of a group of men around an enormous Douglas fir. He recognized his father in the front row, wearing a white cook's cap. It read: *Fallers and self at Old Camp Thompson: record Douglas fir.* Alongside was another picture of the same enormous tree—or one of equal size—with two young men in work clothes and battered hats lying down feet to feet in the cut section of the tree. *Undercut of 12-foot Douglas fir: H. Sorenson, B. Hodges.* The faces of the two men wore a sheepish but amused expression. It had probably been somebody's idea of a joke; mixed with pride in the Bunyanesque achievement—little men against these primeval forest giants. How appealing they were, these faded pictures, done in the days before Chambers of Commerce or State Tourist Bureaus had started to send out their bright young men with the most expensive camera equipment to procure material for "Big, Best, Most Beautiful" propaganda.

Next to the two grinning loggers was a photograph of a group of young boys and older men in large sombreros, all carrying clubs and guns. *Colorado Coal Fields, 1914; Striking Miners.* In this picture no one smiled. Even the young boys had a look of mingled desperation and fear. How had his father come by these ghosts from a drama about which his son knew nothing?

There were other photographs, but now Philip's eye was caught and firmly held by a black-framed poem written in a strong crude handwriting and with an appended message in green ink: *Joe Hill's Last Will, written in his sell in the Utah Pen, November 18, 1915, on the eve of his execution by firing squad. Dear Tom: Jake wanted you to have this.*

Philip grinned at the Joycian "sell." He knew little about Joe Hill, except that he had been a wandering radical songwriter. Vaguely he made association with those other martyrs of the labor movement, Sacco and Vanzetti. To read the poem on the wall of his father's house gave Joe Hill and his dim history a sudden sharp reality. Although banal words, they were, after all, the last written message of a man about to die, and in the intimacy of the little musty room, with the old organ and the moldy books, they had the power to constrict Philip's throat:

> *My will is easy to decide*
> *For there is nothing to divide*
> *My kin don't need to fuss and moan*
> *Moss does not cling to rolling stone.*
> *My body? Ah, if I could choose*
> *I would to ashes it reduce,*
> *And let the merry breezes blow*
> *My dust to where some flowers grow.*
> *Perhaps some fading flower then*
> *Would come to life and bloom again.*
> *This is my last and final will.*
> *Good luck to all of you, Joe Hill."*

As he heard his father enter the kitchen he swung away almost guiltily from the wall. But, thinking he had been seen, he asked in an indifferent voice, "Did you know Joe Hill?"

"Very slightly."

"Is this the original?"

"Oh, no, it's a facsimile."

"Was Joe Hill really a martyr?"

His father stood leaning against the door jamb considering the question. "Yes, he was a martyr, all right. A martyr to a system that can make a gifted man a homeless wanderer."

Although he made the remark with no special fervor Philip braced himself for a sermon. To his surprise his father added calmly, "In my opinion, he committed the crime they killed him for, but that doesn't mean it wasn't injustice. To mete out justice you have to understand the roots of the crimes you judge."

He did not elaborate. He stood rereading the poem. "Yes," he said, "it's not much of a poem, but it served its purpose. It focused a lot of feeling, brought to bear some attention on flagrant ills. The best lines Joe Hill ever uttered were, 'Don't waste time mourning—organize!' "

"Why do you keep the poem on the wall?"

His father appeared to acknowledge the reasonableness of this question in view of his disparagement of the poem's literary value. "Because an old friend of mine gave it to me. And also I keep it there to remind myself about catalytic agents. Joe Hill was a catalytic agent in his own way. The sowing of little packets of his ashes all over the earth after his execution was a kind of symbolic deed of brotherhood."

"Too bad they weren't better ashes then," Philip could not refrain from saying.

"Oh, as to that," his father commented, "I would guess all human *ashes* are pretty much alike, wouldn't you?" He did not press it. "That's your sister, Jane." He indicated the woman on the spotted pony with the Western saddle.

Philip took the picture in his hands and studied it candidly. It was a stranger's face, a secret face, something was locked away behind it. It had experienced pain, but long before, so that a guard had been mercifully erected in the firm mouth and eyes that probed not for any possible answers, nor even in hope of them, but simply as a researcher, adding and subtracting, not seeking clues.

"Tell me about Jane," he said. The conventionality of the phrase struck his ears falsely. It could hardly pass as anything but counterfeit with his father, in view of all the circumstances of his long separation from his sister and the manner of their parting.

But his father did not appear to notice any triviality in the idle inquiry. "You'd be proud of your sister," he said simply. "She's a very fine woman." He acted as though this statement about Jane should, and would, cover everything that was necessary to know about her.

"Will she ever marry?"

"I doubt it. She's got her hands pretty full. As nearly as I can tell from her letters she's raising about twenty little Guatemalans single-handed."

"Do you think you'll ever go and visit her?"

"I'm too old to go gallivanting around to strange countries."

It was plain that his father felt, in spite of the warmth of his voice when he mentioned his daughter's name, a detachment from her; no wish to share her life. It struck Philip as unusual. He had seen a great many possessive parents who linked their existences forcibly with their children's and hung on hard, long after the need for the bond—in the child, at least —was there. Even Ellen's mother, whose life was not as empty as the lives of many of her contemporaries, was apt to give unsolicited advice and in general attempt to do what he called "interfere."

Philip put the photograph of his sister back on the table. It was not the time to talk about Jane. It would only mean stirring up memories perhaps as well left buried now that there was no Ermenthal to turn to.

"What's a bull cook?" he asked to lead the subject away. He indicated a picture on the wall of a thin-faced, staring-eyed blond boy. *Frankie Gray—bull cook at Camp T.* "The chief cook, I suppose."

His father grinned. "No, I was the chief cook. A bull cook is the unfortunate lad who does all the dirty odd jobs around a lumber camp kitchen. Frankie Gray was a nice boy. Had tuberculosis and didn't know it. Went fast when he went. I was with him when he died. Hadn't a soul in the world, poor lad, and never had had. Found naked in an alley when he was three hours old."

It was a perfectly commonplace story of the life and death of an unprivileged human being, and, though his father told it without any emotional or literary trimmings, it struck Philip with a peculiar and poignant force. It occurred to him that his father's life had been involved with many destinies beside his own. He could see them stretching back as far as Ireland's County Antrim; a motley lot, little men and big, derelicts, clowns, philosophers, poets and villains, speaking with a dozen accents and as many errors in grammar, with wild invective, cold passion, lyric beauty or plodding inarticulation, cursing or praising God and man, the Vatican, John Calvin and many a nameless woman. Smashing glasses in renewing temperance pledges, they gathered in open places in the forest to declare, "We, the People"; they stood on chairs to see a passing Queen. They died in poor farms, rotted in jail, threw stones, planted primroses, composed love sonnets by an attic candle-end, or hymns in a rat-run cellar. Questioning the wheeling stars, giving thanks for the crops, turning in an empty bed, they carved lines from Milton on a cedar shingle, or tossed confessions and maps from nameless Treasure Islands into the ocean in empty rum bottles. These were the men his father had met . . . How did he know this about his father, if real knowledge it was? He could not answer, but the truth of his own feeling struck into him like a pointed barb, and he saw his own life, by comparison, stretching down a series of stage-set interiors, of carefully arranged rooms where men with abdomens like bursting melons pivoted coldly in swivel chairs—a slow dance of power and commerce; or, another group, a lower echelon, the Servers—he among them—lolling on the spine's end, dropping careless ashes, idle phrases, each rattling his own ice cubes in his own liquor glass like some fateful necromancy of the forever paralyzed and the triply damned.

Yet even as he thought this he admitted, I really know nothing about my father—only scraps from memory, hints, fragments—and he heard himself saying aloud, "You know, it's a strange thing for a son to know so little about his father as I know about you." "Now he will begin to talk," he thought apprehensively, "and it will be too much for me. I won't be able to endure it." But the old man merely looked over and regarded him with a faint smile, half-quizzical.

"Is it so strange? I think it likely few men know their fathers. I didn't know mine until long after he was dead and buried back in Ballymeaney."

"Well," Philip said, relieved, "sometime I'd like to know about your life. If you can tell me . . ."

"Anytime," said the old man. "You say the word."

CHAPTER 17

* * * *

PHILIP could not wait to explore the little island. He felt an immediate necessity to discover for himself the boundaries of his father's world. When he announced his intention at breakfast his father approved. "It's not much of a trip—though take it easy. Some uneven ground in places. But no danger of getting lost—not with the mountains to steer by." He sketched a rude map of a suggested route: along the beach, past the salt marshes where the ducks came to provide him with his autumn fare, through a deep woods, a meadow, another, better cleared, wood, the orchard. He made Philip a sandwich with some corned beef and put in his pocket a small package of raisins.

"You won't come?" Philip asked, though he wanted very much to be alone.

"No, thanks," his father said. "I've some reading to do." He spoke as if he were preparing something special, or meeting a not too-pressing deadline—anyway, certainly like a man whose time is carefully planned. So far, his avoidance in conversation of anything personal with his son had been marked. Philip was grateful and thought again how unlike the average solitary old man he really was.

2

PHILIP started out back of the house, planning to make a circle and return by the beach at noontime to take a swim.

As he walked he made a mental catalogue of what he saw, to write it all to Pammy and Ellen in his next letter. There was the small chicken yard, the woodshed, the little well-tended orchard and garden. Near the orchard was a deep spring from which a brook—languid now in summer but lively, he supposed, when the rains came—flowed into the sea. Enclosing the orchard, held at bay by his father's axe and knife, were the remains of the forest: fir, pine, alder and madrona. Fringing it —and Philip remembered well the look of these Western wood-edges—there would be, in the months of spring, the airy spray of wild plum and wild currant, white against the dark wall of Douglas firs.

The trees in the orchard had not borne well that year, his father told him, but every tree carried fruit: peaches, plums, pears and apples. In the clearing back of the house he found a head-high tangle of blackberries—the bushes heavily loaded; and nearer the forest, huckleberries, already showing their misted blue fruit.

3

WHEN he had made the circle he sat down and ate his sandwich and raisins. He smoked a cigarette, then lay back on the sand and slept.

As the tide was high when he awoke, he stripped and went into the water. It was cold and clear—going out very shallowly over rough stones that hurt his feet. He looked down with some contempt at his city whiteness and tenderness, for he had seen his father that morning walk out barefooted over the barnacles to pull in his boat.

He let the sun dry him, thankful for the absence of biting

insects. Not even the salt marshes here seemed to breed mosquitoes. Stretched out naked on his shirt he began to add up what his father had. A house, and a rowboat, a collection of enduring books. His money, whatever its source (and the vague feeling of uneasiness again crossed Philip's mind) was obviously enough to keep him in the staples his little kingdom could not supply. His shore brought him clams and wild oysters. The sea gave him fish when he needed them. Across on the mainland, when the tide was right, were hard-shelled crabs for any man with a rake. He had fruit and vegetables, chickens and eggs, wild duck. Obviously he lived, by every possible standard, very well indeed.

His clothes had been reduced to a minimum. After putting away his own in the closet they shared together, Philip could pretty accurately estimate what they were: rubber boots, a sou'wester, heavy walking shoes, Indian moccasins, one wool shirt of eye-dazzling plaid, one pair of corduroy trousers, blue overalls, a large battered straw hat, some khaki pants and shorts, an old weathered felt with fishing flies in the band. There was a dark-blue suit of serge and a city raincoat hanging in a transparent garment bag that he was sure some woman had given him to keep the mold off his "outside" clothes.

Philip thought of trying to inventory his own apartment on Seventy-second Street. All the complications and over-extension of his life rose before him, reaching back even to Lynnport— those Thursday visitors of Aunt Hetebel's, pointing, appraising, dating, coveting. The same despair he had felt in the hospital returned as he considered the hopelessness of any escape. The conviction that he could not find a way out; had been doomed since Lynnport, that he was going to have to take up the threads of his life in a few weeks just where, so briefly, he had laid them down, created in him such panic that he got up from the sand, dressed and started toward home.

As he walked he found himself nursing a curious resentment. What right had his father to all this—beauty, privacy—the wealth that men in Philip's world had to be millionaires to achieve? Imagine having your own private island without doing a lick of honest or dishonest work to get it! It was unfair. Where had he got the island anyway?

When he came around the curve of the shore he saw in the distance his father seated on the farthest point of land, his back against a pine, gazing across the inlet at the mountains. There was something so fixed about his body, that, although it was the attitude of a man resting, Philip had the very strong feeling his father was doing something. At least he was occupied: that much was conveyed in the very quality of his pose.

Philip's memory returned hazily to the scroll painting he had seen in the Oriental museum in Seattle. Was there a similar bond here between the reclining man and empty space; an invisible polarity, as though one somehow completed the other, was an extension of the other? It was—Philip thought—almost like a *necessity*, the presence of his father; as though without him the mountains would not be there, or the sea deepening with the fading day; as though also (the other half of some puzzling universal equation) the figure under the pine would not be there without the sea and the mountains.

Indeed, as he stood looking thoughtfully at his father, he became once again merely a bewildering stranger—remote, inaccessible, one he could never hope to know. Yet, as Philip turned back quietly into the woods, he realized his momentary resentment had vanished.

4

THAT night at dinner, over his second bowl of fish chowder, Philip said simply, "You are a very lucky man."

His father did not seem surprised, nor did he deny the truth of the statement. "I agree," was all he said.

"How did you ever find this place?"

His father grinned. "It's quite a story."

After crumbling three soda crackers into his bowl he said, "In the old days when I was active in the labor movement I knew some pretty derelict characters. One of them was an Italian named Christ. He was a very heavy drinker, with a lot of guilt in his soul, and when he was recovering from a bad drunk he used to go and walk about with the Salvation Army doing penance and confessing his sins. I always thought he was a little unbalanced and finally I was proved right. At the end of one of his drunks it came to him overwhelmingly that he wasn't just named Christ, he *was* Christ. Immediately afterwards he got a message to burn down the Catholic church."

His father paused to laugh, moving his head from side to side as he nursed the memory.

"Early one morning as I was coming home from work—I'd taken a job night-watching because it gave me a chance to read; I remember I was carrying one of Müller's big books on Buddhism that morning—near the Catholic church I began to smell smoke and, a moment afterwards, who should I see but Christ coming out of the side entrance of the church grounds. He was walking pretty unsteadily and I went up and asked him what he was doing. He didn't recognize me—he was so drunk—and he tried to fight me. You know, violent and shaky at the same time. I was able to handle him—though I had to knock him out to do it. I used the book.

"By then the smell of smoke was getting stronger. I ran into the church and sure enough, right near the altar was a pile of oil-soaked rags. I ran to the rectory and a young priest answered the door. He was a good fellow, name of Conant. I came to know him later and we had some fine talks together. Well, he called the fire department and then he helped me drag Christ into the rectory basement where we brought him around with ammonia and cold water. I made Father Conant promise not to report Christ and he agreed, but he did give him a good jawing and a good scare (after all, he'd been brought up in the Church) and he warned him that next time it would be jail—and I don't know what all else in the way of eternal damnation."

At that his father broke down and laughed again so hard he had to take his glasses off and wipe them before he went on. Philip, watching him, became infected with his mirth and began to laugh too.

"He scared Christ so badly, so badly," his father concluded, returning his glasses to the firm blade of his nose, "that he decided to go away where drink wouldn't be any temptation. How

he found this island I don't know, but he did, and he home-
steaded it for a few years. Then he couldn't stand it. He went to
Seattle and killed himself with one final spree. And by George,
if he hadn't left me the island in a will he made that Father
Conant had witnessed."

"What a story!" Philip said, shaking his head. "Everything
out here's larger than life—the people *and* the yarns."

"Oh, your stories would sound just as tall to us," his father
said, reaching for his pipe, pushing his chair back from the table.
"In fact, taller. There's nothing strange about local yarns. They're
as commonplace as can be."

"And I suppose I'm to consider Clarence Bye's stories perfectly ordinary too?"

His father's blue eye glinted as he tapped the stubborn tobacco
down with a calloused finger. "Clarence does exaggerate a mite
once in a while. He's a born story-teller, and something of a poet.
You have to allow him extra license."

"Just how crazy is Clarence anyway?" As Philip put the question he realized he was extremely interested in the answer, as
though it might contain some clue to his father's hermit way of
life and his whole attitude toward it.

"Clarence crazy?" He appeared to give this idea serious consideration. "I don't believe I'd concur in that opinion."

He sat tilted back, sucking on his pipe. His face, Philip thought,
looking at it from the other side of the table, was still remarkably
firm, all the bones clear and defined, the flesh neither withered
nor sagged. "He must have been a handsome man," Aunt Hetebel
had sighed, looking back after she had said good-bye at the dock
more than twenty years before. He was still a handsome man,
Philip corrected her.

"Clarence just gets more messages of a contradictory nature
from the world than the rest of us do," his father was saying.
"He hasn't quite learned how to divide the 'what seems' from
the 'what is'—and maybe the truth is there isn't any division."

He waited a moment, as though to allow his son to question
or contradict if he wished, then went on, "But that's the kind of
an idea that's pretty frightening, except to a simple child-mind
like Clarence's. The rest of us learn young in life not to credit

our senses too far. Now if a porcupine speaks to me on the road, I'm not apt to answer him back, and I don't allow myself to wave when a poplar nymph beckons me on a moonlight night. But Clarence—he practices no such foolish restraint. He'll sit right down and have a talk with the porcupine and like as not dance with the poplar nymph, and be none the worse for it."

His father, having finished his pipe, rose and began to clear the table. Philip came over to help him.

Tom was a slow and methodical dish washer and he seemed to enjoy the routine. He did all his chores, Philip now realized, with an air of easy pleasure, without hurrying, without dawdling. It was a one-thing-at-a-time precision.

"No, don't fool yourself! Clarence is no idiot," he continued, scraping a dish with his thumbnail. "Far from it. There's not a person who knows him that wouldn't tell you how smart he is. Sometime I'll show you some paintings of the so-called idiots that the Zen masters of Japan used to draw. I always think of Clarence when I look at them." Abruptly he began to dry his hands on the towel. "Might as well show you now."

He had always been like that, Philip remembered. When he was home and Janie had asked at dinner the meaning of a word, up from the table at once he and Janie must get to consult the big Webster's that always stood on an iron stand right beside the dining table. "No time like the present for finding out," his father would say.

Now he brought from the little sitting room one of the mildew-stained books and opened it. Laughing men in rough kimonos with thatches of wild hair, rather like the thatches of the brooms on which they were resting, stood laughing and pointing—at a bird, at a book, at a leaf, at nothing.

"What are all the long faces about?" his father said, turning the pages with slow pleasure as though communicating with old friends. " 'Stop!' they say. 'Wait a minute! Quiet down! Watch some birds making a nest, or two cocks fighting, or leaves falling just when you've finished so carefully raking the path.' "

Awareness of his own ignorance suddenly rushed up in Philip. How many layers of experience there were to uncover—

in nature, in art, in history, in philosophy—for which no man
has the time (or at least for which he had no time). Impatient
with himself, he spoke irritably, "With all you know about
labor strife and the atom bomb and world wars and the rest of
it, you can't say this is quite the moment for a man to feel
justified in taking time out to watch birds nesting, or leaves
falling, can you?"

His father looked at him directly through the spectacles he had
put on when he opened the book. It was a long level look, and
it had in it something fiery that sent a childlike fear darting
through Philip.

"Let me ask you this: If you were on a very swift toboggan
going down hill—a toboggan with the whole human race on it,
and sure destruction at the end of the slope—and someone offered you a chance halfway down to get off and watch a sun-
rise, or sit on a rock by a brook, or smell mountain air, would
you feel you couldn't do it? That you had to stay on that
damned toboggan just because everybody was doing it?" He
paused, then added, "What's the sense in that? What purpose
are you serving? No, I say, get off the damned toboggan and
take a breath. Look at the mountains. Maybe you'll see a way
not to go on down with that toboggan, how even to get some
of the rest of 'em off it."

He closed the book decisively, laid it on the table, returned
to the dishpan, pouring in more hot water from the kettle.
Philip watched the bubbles form and blink out on the soapy
surface.

"Well, there I agree," Philip said, "though I can't see that
I'm going to get any clearer about my own place on the toboggan, loafing here on this island."

"What do you expect, man?" asked his father. His voice still
had an edge. "If you live like an automaton for over thirty
years, do you expect to become a thinking man in a month's
time?" He began to move a scrubbing brush back and forth
around the chowder kettle.

"Do you consider yourself a thinking man?" Philip made his
voice very small and quiet. He still felt apprehensive, as though
his father might let real scorn flash out of his words and that he,

Philip, would find this unendurable. To his question, however, he saw at once he was not going to get a direct answer.

"I don't believe we know much about thinking—any of us," his father answered. "The mind is certainly not just a physical function of the brain. It's an instrument of subjective power."

Again his words, the unfamiliar phrasing, carried him away from Philip. He became as much a stranger—wringing out the dish-cloth in his thin rough hands—as he had seemed under the pine tree gazing at the distant mountains.

"It's a mighty strange thing what's going on now with the brain," he said. "What do you see in every magazine you have the misfortune to pick up? Accounts of medical men removing sections of the brain, giving deadly injections, electric shocks— all sorts of special techniques to *reduce* the functioning, when what is obviously needed is redirecting."

As he hung the dish-cloth on its hook under the sink, "Quite a responsibility," he remarked, "removing sections of the brain it took men thousands of years, and a lot of downright painful effort, to acquire—developments that helped to separate him from the animal."

He walked over to the shelf above the table, took his hand lens from it, lifted his binoculars from the hook, "Man is certainly the creator of his own doom." Over his shoulder, he remarked, "Think I'll walk out a little." He opened the neatly patched screen door and strolled off under the sea-stretching madronas to the beach and so disappeared.

CHAPTER 18

*
*   *
  *

THE day after his exploration of the island the weather abruptly changed. Philip woke to a world muffled in fog.

After his first shock in discovering the unfamiliar clammy presence in his room, he found the cool gray morning a delight. This smell—he drew into his nostrils the sweet elusive scent of fog, salt water, damp evergreens—it was what he most remembered from childhood. A rush of half-formed memories took hold of him. Wet pungent woods, the mysterious, subdued woods of autumn with their beckoning pallor of fungus and toadstool, the plundering chipmunk of his hospital visions, silenced by the deadly sound-rays . . .

He pushed down the thought of that dreadful inaudible whistle of his nightmares; realized with relief that the image had seemingly lost its power to fasten upon him. No, here the world had not changed. The birds still sang even in the fog, and the water tapped the old pilings of the dock, where the barnacles feasted, with unchanging, unagitated rhythm.

Leaping like a boy from the warm cocoon of his bedclothes,

he thrust his body into his cold garments and dashed for the kitchen. He rushed to the stove, extending his hands to capture its warmth, and with his fingers stretching, his shoulders hunched in the luxury of that last shiver, he expelled from compressed lungs an exuberant "Good morning" to his father. In that moment he wished all mornings could be like this, with nothing to be seen outside the windows, the whole world confined to the limits of one warm and cosy room crackling with fire, humming with a kettle.

Breakfast had never tasted better. The bacon broke into crisp fragments, the butter melted deep into the browned toast, the golden honey sank sensuously into the pale porridge. He felt physically well, and aware of it.

When he had helped his father with the breakfast dishes and the kitchen chores, he went out to walk along the beach. The world dreamed in the fog; all sounds and colors hushed and muted; the very water, subdued and gentle, barely moved along the fringe of sand. A darkly glistening round head, bald and babyish, thrust up and disappeared, came up again, ducked again —a coasting seal.

Through the drifting mist he caught an occasional glimpse of the shore across the inlet, and he wondered about the still-unseen neighbors, imagining the young woman jumping out of her warm bed to start her fire with pitchpine knots. Strange, but now he had a growing curiosity about them, though only yesterday he would have asserted that city life had forever dulled his interest in any possible neighbors.

2

AT THE end of the beach he turned into the grove that led away from the shore near his father's pine, doubling back in a half-circle to the rear of the cabin. Between the beach and the woods, in the narrow open space where the salal, Oregon grape, and coarse grass grew, the spiders had left their water-glistening canopies—"fairy tablecloths" Pamela had called them the one summer they were all together at a rented farm in Vermont.

He began to think of Pammy tenderly, wondering how camp

suited her. Was she having as much fun as the Girls of St. Bridgets camping at Loon Lake whom Ellen had exhumed from that sheltered lost world of *St. Nicholas Magazine*? This island where he now was would be a perfect environment for a child; and his father, in his mellow old age, the perfect companion. But, even as he suggested this to himself, he doubted if his father would care to interrupt his solitude with the insistent demands of a child of ten.

He looked at the clouded world around him, suddenly frowning. Whenever thoughts of Ellen or Pammy stayed with him too long he was troubled. Now he began to walk more rapidly to escape the faint unease, the subtle irritation, that rose in him. As he emerged from the woods into the meadow behind the orchard, he stopped to watch how the trees seemed to push their way through the clinging gray filaments of the fog. Some vague and shapeless comfort came to him from the sight.

3

DURING the week the fogs thickened, and on the mornings of the densest mists the spiders outdid themselves in daring designs. Philip had never before seen webs of such variety and profusion. No longer content with laying simple carpets and scarves on the grass, the spiders branched boldly into the visible forms of higher mathematics, into geometric flights of exact fancy: polyhedrons, logarithmic spirals, skeleton prisms. There appeared on every shrub and weed exhaustingly intricate constructions; scaffoldings and cables, beams and flying buttresses, crossbars and suspension cords.

Philip remembered from childhood only the circling rose window of the web that legend had woven at the cave's entrance to save the life of Robert Bruce. Now, pressing his way cautiously through the damp meadows and the dripping woods, he cried out in amazement at the sight of transparent fairy balloons woven lightly—webbed frame and silk extensions—around the end of countless pine tips. He found minute ghost-trees, their interlocking branches threaded about the single stalk of a summer-dried weed, with a many-plied snowy carpet woven beneath. And there were any number of trapeze bars and safety nets for imaginary minuscule acrobats.

That all this beautiful and complicated architecture existed only for the capturing of insects of inferior cunning seemed an unending mystery, and when the sun, piercing the fog, turned these airy fabrications into iridescent baubles, he hurried home like a child to tap his father's store of information.

Tom, to Philip's surprise, disclaimed any great knowledge of insects. The insect world, he asserted, required a special kind of appreciation: all those hideous feastings and matings, those monstrous orgies, ghoulish rites and biological perversions, the frightful rapacity and individualism on one hand, the mysterious will to collectivism on the other. He quoted someone who had said that "Insects did not seem to belong to our globe, had come to us rather from some comet that had lost its course and died demented in space."

But though disclaiming knowledge of insects, his father's casual talk revealed so much to Philip that, for the next few days, right after his morning ramble, he sat reading by the stove everything the small library offered on the subject. He wrote a long letter to Pammy asking if there was anyone at camp to tell her of the marvel of a certain spider's telegraph wire from its hindleg to its distant web, of the meteorological equipment of caterpillars, of that incredibly complicated musical instrument, the bow of the cricket. It seemed to him important now to interest his daughter in the ingenious, though sometimes grossly fallible, calendar of the instincts by which the lives of unobserved creatures are so marvelously regulated.

4

ONCE during the days of fog, because of the morning cold, his father brought near the kitchen fire the eggs of a nesting hen. Philip, for the first time, was able to look on at the drama of the baby chick escaping its egg prison. He could hear the tiny prisoners tapping away at their shells, occasionally murmuring or humming or whining at their work—it was not possible to determine which. When he expressed surprise that they could speak from inside the egg, his father entertained him by silencing the hidden chicks, or getting them to chirp in reply to his whistles.

"Chicken talk," he called it, and seeing that Philip was amused and interested he took him out to the henyard where older chicks were already running around. There he proved, what Philip had doubted, the existence of a whole series of sounds ranging from the frail piping of contentment to the double note of sensuous enjoyment in response to a caress, cheeps of hunger and loneliness, squeaks and cries of protest, distress, and fear.

"Not that that means they're really bright," his father said, holding a ball of shrilling yellow fluff in a cupped hand, again failing to conform to the conventionally sentimental attitude Philip always half-expected of him. "A baby chick'll try to eat anything he sees that appears the right size—its own feet, or its brother's eye. And they always act surprised as all get-out when they discover about water—that it's to drink. The mother has to set the example. Sometimes it's downright comical to see her pretending to eat grain so the babes'll try it too."

("Yum, yum, delicious!" Philip saw Ellen with Pammy, lifting the spoon and crying "Lovely" as Pammy turned her dark suspicious eyes from bowl to spoon and shook her head, resting her baby hands, firmly closed into fists, on the counter of her high chair.)

"Have you always been interested in birds?" he asked his father. "I don't remember that you ever . . ." He quickly let it drop.

"Quite a long time," his father answered easily. "When you live alone and you're like me you're apt to get too immersed in print and that's not healthy. Birds are all around, easy to observe. They fascinated me as far back as a boy in Ireland. I remember the day I discovered that female swifts don't always want to return to their nests. I saw a husband chasing his wife around and around the steeple of the barn trying to get her to go back to her nesting. After that first time I often saw it. The female would dart out at twilight to stretch herself and snatch an insect or two for her supper. Sometimes the freedom was just too much for her and she had to be literally forced back to her job."

He was laughing, squatting without awkwardness or any apparent discomfort on the ground, holding the feeding-pan in his left hand, extending grain to the chicks with his right.

"You could easily distinguish the husbands. They were hot on their wives' tails, moving their wings in a special way and sounding a very firm chirp as they drove them to their duties."

"Do you derive any moral from that?"

His father grinned, lifting himself upright. "It's always dangerous to draw morals for humans from the behavior of animals. It's difficult, too. I've learned, however—and you can make of it what you will—the more brightly colored the female bird the less domestic. Among dogs, I've been told, the more highly bred the bitch the less maternal."

How he meant this to be taken he gave no hint. Before Philip could question him he added—again with the air of enjoying some private joke quite as much on himself as on anyone else —"Yes, it's not safe to draw human parallels from Nature, though it's sometimes entertaining to try. Take the sad case of the male nightingale. He's a regular golden-voiced Caruso until his chicks are hatched. Sings all the time. Gives benefit performances for his wife on the nest. The moment the babies arrive nothing comes out but a guttural croak. *Grrk-grrk*. Just alarm and anxiety, that's all."

They walked back together to the kitchen, and, as they came in, his father said: "There's one other thing about a baby chick maybe you don't know." He picked one up from the box behind the stove and showed Philip a tiny chalky nodule on the upper half of the soft bill. "See this? It's called the egg tooth. It'll soon disappear. But it's with this the chick makes his escape from the shell."

Philip was immediately certain his father had a motive in pointing out this phenomenal part of the chick's equipment. He decided to rise to the bait—if bait it was. "What I need is an egg tooth, I guess," he remarked half-humorously, half-seriously.

When the old man did not reply Philip was baffled. Almost as though he had forgotten his son's presence he stood regarding with an air of tender amusement the latest bird to emerge from the cracked shell. A very caricature of the woebegone; damp, bedraggled, with drunken eyes and lolling head, it seemed impossible that it could ever recover. But as they stood watching, it began to move jerkily, to lift its head, open its eyes. Finally it staggered uncertainly to its feet.

"Guess it's never easy to get yourself born," Philip remarked, and was amazed to hear the bitterness in his voice.

"Can't imagine how he ever stood it inside there," was all his father said. "Look at the size of him in comparison to the space he occupied." Apparently he found more interest in the familiar drama of the emerging chick than in the problem of a despondent man.

Tom began to clear the table. "Yes, an egg tooth's a mighty handy thing to have."

Philip looked up quickly. So he had heard, after all.

"Maybe I've got one and don't know it," Philip ventured, carrying his dishes to the sink. "But since I haven't got the uncomplicated instincts of a chicken I don't know how to use it —or even where it's located."

When his father made no reply, only proceeding as usual with the fixed routine of the breakfast dishes, Philip added experimentally, "I do know now that I'd like to break the shell."

"What is the shell?" his father asked. "That's the main question, ain't it?"

Philip had already noticed the occasional slip in his father's grammar. It came whenever he was asking in a carefully offhand voice any question of pertinence or directness. He was sure that by this easy method his father had at one time tried to conceal his education, the qualities that made him different from the men among whom he had worked.

"You mean what is *my* shell?"

"Well, I don't mean *my* shell, certainly," said the old man with a certain asperity.

Philip did not answer for some time. He was extra careful with the drying of the forks, massaging each tine with loving care. When he finally replied he was thinking out loud.

"Things have changed a lot in the last few years. I wonder if you'd find it so. I may be wrong—but among men my own age . . ." He stopped, realizing how he was temporizing; how much uncertainty he was reflecting.

"What I mean is," he continued more firmly, "I don't think young men expect to amass fortunes any more. There aren't the same number of magic hens around laying golden eggs . . ." This jaded metaphor, following on the remarks about the egg tooth, momentarily confused him. After a brief silence he went on, "I think people like me just—well, now they just hope to get 'through.' That's about all."

"Get through?" his father repeated. His voice was gentle and faintly puzzled. "How can they help it? They'll get through. It can't be avoided."

"You know what I mean," Philip said.

"No, I don't," said his father simply.

"Well, I mean, *get through*," Philip repeated tensely. "Get through life without too much . . ." He carefully skirted the word "suffering." After a hesitation he brought out the word "difficulty. And maybe even with some of the extras. Yes, definitely some of the extras."

"Extras?" His father appeared genuinely interested, as though he was hearing something extremely fresh and new.

"Yes, extras, like being able to educate your kids properly, spend summers in the country, own a decent car, afford a good-sized life insurance . . ." And Scotch, shirts made to order, a new fur coat from time to time for your wife, he went on adding silently to himself.

"Oh, I see," said his father. That was all.

After a moment's silence, "No answer, eh?" Philip demanded.

"I still say they'll get through," his father remarked, stepping outside to pour the soapy water on some plants in a box on the side porch. Coming back through the door: "They'll all die in their time," he added. "Time," he remarked with special emphasis, putting the pan away on the floor under the sink, wringing out the cloth. "Time! That's the place to look for answers. It's Time that's got us licked. We don't understand it."

"Do you understand it?" Philip demanded, his voice sharp with his wish to get a clear answer, to have his father's fixed attention for just one minute.

"A little," said the old man solemnly. "A little," he repeated, looking out the window and nodding his head up and down very slowly. "But I'm not bright enough to communicate much of it yet," and he walked out of the kitchen door and went briskly down the little pine-needle path to the neat white privy. Philip, looking after him with mingled amusement and frustration, saw that he took from his pocket a small book just before he opened the door to go in.

5

WHEN he returned some time later Philip was still seated in the kitchen by the stove, smoking, with his feet on the woodbox. His father had some eggs in an old felt hat and he reached up into the cupboard for a bowl to put them in. "I never see eggs now that I don't think of something a medical chap—friend of Clare Powers'—told me, about breeding deadly viruses inside eggs; part of the research for bacteriological warfare. He described laboratories with rows and rows of eggs, and a man coming along with a microscopic needle injecting viruses right into the sac in which the yolk is suspended. Ideal environment for controlled growth, of course. Somehow when you think about the egg, one of the primal life elements, deliberately put to the service of death, it's a pretty strange thought."

As his father spoke, Philip had a clear memory of himself years before looking at the colored plates of birds' eggs in the *Encyclopaedia*. There were only two blue ones—the catbird and the robin; and one plain deep yellow—the pheasant's, and all the rest were speckled and spotted and dotted, like the moss agates he and Janie searched for in Eel's Cove. He could see the delicate pointed ellipses of the illustrations on the gray background, and the caption at the bottom: EGGS OF NORTH AMERI-CAN BIRDS (LIFE SIZE).

"I remember when I was a kid wondering why the bluebird's egg wasn't blue," he said, musing aloud. "Or the robin red-breast's red. Maybe that's why I liked coloring eggs at Easter so much. I could get the color I wanted."

"I remember those egg-dyeings," his father said, half-smiling.

He looked off as though he really saw again the scene from the past. "And your mother knew how to suck out the egg without breaking the shell and she used them for angel's food cake. Old Sam, your grandfather's cook, taught her. Do you remember Old Sam?"

"Very well," Philip said. He was aware of the quickening of his heart beat. It was their first direct reference to the past they had shared so many years before. It seemed to have come quite easily, but Philip did not trust himself to speak further and his father, too, appeared quite willing to let the subject drop.

CHAPTER 19

*
* *
*

ONE morning, without warning, Philip awoke depressed. In spite of the green light, the sweet whispering airs from the inlet, he was reluctant to leave his bed.

A dream about Goldstone lingered unpleasantly in his mind. He was trying to tell Goldstone what he was doing, and, as he described his life on the island, Goldstone suddenly wore the face of his mother years before in Milltown, and Philip was trying to explain to her what he had been doing lying on his stomach all afternoon watching the dragon flies ("the devil's darning needles," so she called them, as her New England grand-mother had before her) stitching time in Miller's Creek. Philip could see now the flash, dart, and pause of their green metal bodies, the tips of wiry rushes along the bank stroking the water as it slid past them, the golden flecks and shadows on the sandy bottom. But none of this way of spending time was of interest either to his mother or to Goldstone.

Philip began then to think of Ellen, to count the days that had passed since the accident. Next, he began to divide their monthly budget into what remained of his bank account. He flung in the war bonds, went on adding and subtracting, and a cold sweat broke out on his forehead. What in God's name am I doing here? he asked himself frantically. I can't stay like this —marking time, floating, dreaming, fooling myself about "taking a rest" in a world where a rest only unfits a man to return to work. This life will grow on me—debilitate me. I'll never be able to go back.

Automatically, in his distress, he reached out for the cigarettes on the floor beside the bed. He would lie and smoke just one and then he would get up, take a dip, shake himself out of this dark mood—for, of course, he did have an excuse, he was ill. Hadn't they all urged this vacation on him—even Goldstone, certainly Ellen?

The cigarette lit badly—a long black flake of paper flaring up at the end. Philip shook it off with nervous impatience and it fled from him and was instantly caught in a cobweb that had formed under the window. He watched the ashy flake struggle like a living thing to free itself until finally its own struggle became its destruction and, breaking into shreds, it drifted into nothingness. He ground out the remainder of his cigarette in the empty clam shell by the bed and turned over on his side. Pulling his knees toward his chest, the sheet up behind his head, a piece of it between his teeth, he lay trying to think of nothing, to listen only to the pause and pull of the tide. Finally he slept again.

2

WHEN he awakened a second time the light told him several hours had passed. He entered the kitchen feeling guilty. His father stood by the sink pulling feathers out of a chicken he had just lifted from a pan of boiling water. He was quickly and deftly plucking the fowl, reciting cheerfully to himself as usual.

" 'There where earth, water, fire and wind no footing find. No moon shines there. There is no darkness seen . . .' " He broke off to say, "Good morning."

"I went back to sleep." Philip spoke apologetically, going to

the stove to ladle out a bowl of cornmeal and pour his coffee.
As he sat down at the table he felt it necessary to add: "I don't
know why I'm so dead tired all the time. I must be a pretty
stupid companion."

His father went on quietly plucking the chicken. "You've
probably been drawing pretty heavily on your energy reserves
in the life you've been living," he said. "And when you get
here to this quiet place you just sink and sink and the fall
seems bottomless. Shows how tired you really were."

A feeling of gratitude out of all proportion rose in Philip.
"It's very good of you to say that."

Something strained in his voice made his father look at him
quizzically. Philip felt the keen questioning eyes on him. "Drop
off your fears, son. What are you afraid of? Let go of all this
compulsive stuff about proving something to me, to yourself,
or *anybody*. It's bound to do you harm in time." After a moment he added—a little cryptically, Philip thought, though he
did not question him, "Every man's entitled to his forty days
in the wilderness."

He began then softly to whistle, an old tune Philip remembered from childhood: "The Irish Washerwoman." When the
melody sailed up into a high octave the old man's clear voice
never faltered. The incongruity of this music, following his last
remarks and the lines he had just been reciting, did not seem
to trouble him in the least.

Philip sat down at the kitchen table and, at once, his glance
fell on a filing-card leaning against the sugar bowl. There were
two separate notations on it: one in blue ink, one in black.
The first read:

> "Verily, I declare to you, my friend, that within this
> very body, mortal as it is and only a fathom high, but
> conscious and endowed with mind, is the world, and
> the waxing thereof and the waning thereof, and the
> way that leads to the passing away thereof."

Beside it was written the single word: *Buddha.*

Beneath, in black ink, under the heading, *Jesus Christ as
reported by St. Luke:*

*The kingdom of God cometh not with observation;
neither shall they say, Lo, here! or there! For, lo, the
kingdom of God is within you."*

Philip read them with one eye as he ate his cereal, "Now it begins," he thought to himself, "the sermon." But his father was still whistling the old cheery air.

"Lawrence Warren was just over," he broke off to remark. "He wants you to come to supper tonight with him and Clare Powers. I said I thought you might like to. I won't go myself. You'll get to know them better if you're alone."

Philip murmured. "That's very kind of them." He was not at all in the mood to row across the inlet and spend the evening with strangers, but he had no idea how he could get out of it. He watched the honey disappearing into the dish of porridge as he dropped it slowly in circles off the tip of his spoon. Nobody made porridge like his father, who considered it—("mush" he called it) one of the great culinary satisfactions.

"That girl in the Tourist Bureau—the one I told you about with her book of clippings—she had a picture showing the Indian devil mask Lawrence hangs on his gate to keep people away. Sounds thoroughly inhospitable. I'm surprised he'd invite me."

His father laughed, cutting open the chicken's gizzard, expelling the grit and pulling the tough gray lining away with his fingers.

"The truth is Lawrence is real gentle—too gentle. That's why he has to protect himself. Or else Clare does it for him. He seems to bring out the mother in women. Some men do."

At this statement Philip was immediately aware of a flash of resentment—almost personal resentment, irrational and apparently without basis. Yet he realized that this commonplace remark had created in him a wish to undermine his father's estimation of his neighbors. In a voice purposely suggestive, he inquired, "What's the relationship between the two of them?"

If his father was aware of anything special in his tone he gave no indication. "Oh, just good friends," he replied simply. He was wrapping the intestines in a piece of newspaper. "Chicken for tomorrow," he remarked. "Nearly always have chicken for my Sunday dinner. Shows how old habits cling."

There was clearly no way to pursue further the subject of the neighbors without undue emphasis. Philip let it drop. "Weren't you a vegetarian once?" he inquired.

His father looked at him across the room and laughed. "Two or three times. Always gave it up because I got too darned hungry. But I've done it all in my day: bran, fruit juice, raw carrots, raisins, kelp, buttermilk. Now I just eat what I like when I want and it seems to work the best. Guess that's the final test of the matter."

Then he did something Philip was beginning to accept as characteristic: he referred to remarks made some time before, as though his thoughts were long chains, linking up endlessly, no part ever lost.

"I think I should correct myself on those remarks I made to you a while back about energy. I don't think energy is limited. And that's not a mystical statement." (How like Ermenthal, flashed through Philip's mind; this quick denial of the stigma of mysticism.) "It's medical. A doctor from New York—the same one that told me about viruses bred in egg-yolk sacs—said that to me. Energy isn't like a bank account; something you draw on too far and it disappears. There's no limit to it; the fault lies in the receiving instrument."

3

BEFORE Philip could make any comment, and again in a different voice, he announced, looking out the window, "Here's Clarence Bye. He's come to take me fishing. The sole are running past the point. I thought we mightn't get back till late, and it would be a long day, so I didn't count on taking you. But anytime you want to fish just let me know." He spoke a little apologetically.

The idea occurred to Philip that perhaps his father had been finding him something of a burden; that it was a relief to have a day in the boat with simple-minded, cheerful Clarence and an evening alone in his own house. He wanted to say something then, to express some gratitude to his father, but he could not get the words out.

They went together onto the sunny beach to greet Clarence.

"Good morning, son," Tom said. He calls everyone "son," Philip thought. It's not a designation just for me.

Clarence got out of the boat talking.

"Ma sent a blueberry pie and some good store cheese. Best we've had since the war. Real Tillamook. Know that cheese, Mr. Philip?" He thrust under Philip's nose a slab of cheese wrapped in waxed paper. "Special kind of tang," he affirmed.

Philip murmured his appreciation.

"Folks all over the world order it," Clarence pursued, with all the enthusiasm of a paid salesman. "I even heard Madam Chiang Kai-shek took some back to China with her when she was here that time getting that loan and all them mink coats and so on. But Mrs. Bradley, over on The Point, says the Chinese don't eat cheese. She says they like decayed eggs for a relish. Or the brain of a duck on a toothpick. Well, there's no accounting for tastes, as Ma always says. I remember how Ebie Beale—he was the Beale that was nursed by their pet cougar after his, Ebie's, mother, died bearing him—well, Ebie never could tolerate cow's milk. Claimed it turned his stomach. His pa always said it was because they tried to wean him from that cougar with a milch cow they borrowed in the emergency from someone over on the mainland. You shoulda seen that Ebie. He hollered and took on so when they tried that weaning—and so did the cougar, Bertha, who was nursing him—that they give it up. Bertha was before your time here, Mr. Stewart, but I remember her. She was shore a good cat. Gentle as they come. She'd been a pet from babyhood. You know the Beales adopted her when she wasn't moren'n a week old, after they'd killed off her ma by accident."

Tom nodded absent-mindedly during this recital which Clarence had continued as they walked up the beach to the house. Clarence and Philip went inside while his father collected his battered straw hat and fishing equipment. As he was reaching in the cracker tin for a handful to take with him, Clarence said, "Don't bother about no lunch, Mr. Stewart. Ma fixed for us both."

"That's the best thing you've said yet." Tom grinned. "Water canteen?"

"Got it too."

"Then we're ready." He turned to Philip, his eyes warm and happy. "Good-bye, son, take it easy. If you want something different to eat, look in the canned goods. There might be something there to tempt you."

Clarence nodded shyly toward a paper box he had laid on the table when he entered. "There's the slab of pie Ma sent you."

Philip thanked him, remarking, as he did so, that he hadn't taken such an interest in food in years as he had since coming to the island.

4

HE WALKED down to the shore to help them push off and stood watching until the shimmering distance blurred the outline of their two bodies in the little white boat. Then he walked along the beach slowly until he came to the pine where he had seen his father seated. Here he sat down, leaning his back against the warm bole of the old tree.

He sat for a long time gazing into space, then found himself directing his eyes to objects near at hand. He studied with pleasure the exact but intricate shadow a green fern blade made on the surface of a gray rock; and, afterwards, the position of a single plume of weed at a distance, upthrust in an open spot as though determined to have all it needed of space and light.

It was going to be, he thought idly, one of those perfect summer days; a day not too warm, not too cool, enclosing all living things in a magic shell of golden light and movement. He saw a young maple near him with its powder-white underleaves lightly dipping into the waves of air like a lazy swimmer going under, coming up; and green porpoises of shrub and bracken in the distance rising and falling. Every green thing in sight seemed to him to be climbing, stretching, pulling itself on tiptoe to come nearer the arching sky. He could feel them straining at their roots, reaching out with long green arms, with trembling filaments of frond and leaf, to capture space, claim it, fill it full of their tossing and trembling grace.

Everywhere there was movement; but without disturbance, easy and true as breathing. The flecked water stretched and floated like a great bird between the near white shore and the dark band at the end of the inlet. Over everything lay the glowing light. Each blade of grass tossed its glitter back into the air, each crystal of salt, each turn of leaf—a vast dance, of unending, gay and stately measures.

He lost all track of time, all sense of himself. It was far past noon when, at last, he noticed he was hungry and rose from the ground to walk back to the house.

He began his meal with tomatoes plucked sun-warmed and blood-red from the vines in the garden, and finished off with part of Mrs. Bye's generous slice of pie. He looked again, as he ate, at the pictures in his father's books of the Zen fools and the seated quiet sages. When it was time for his nap he walked out through the orchard with a blanket and lay down at the edge of the woods in a spot from which the sun had just departed, leaving behind a warm scent of pine needles, huckleberries ripening, and last year's leaves slowly becoming the earth.

When he awoke he was immediately aware of a change in the atmosphere. The sky had darkened; everything had grown expectant. The air trembled and was still, whispered, listened, sounded a low murmur of warning. There was rain in the distance. He got up and withdrew a little into the woods, putting his blanket over his head and shoulders. The distant, murmured warning grew and grew. Little ripples of tension ran along the ground, and suddenly with a swish of green skirts the storm came rushing through the woods like a madwoman on some frenzied and fruitless search, looking under trees, under leaves, under fern and boughs, under shrubs and bracken, tossing, whirling, turning and swaying, departing as swiftly, as desperately, as she had come, leaving the forest drenched and exhausted.

Philip, watching the response—abject or resistant—of every living thing in sight, had discarded his blanket and let the downpour drench him too; fall into his face, soak his hair, beat lightly on the skin of his outstretched bare arms. It was the cleansing and restorative experience he had been waiting for for a long time. He remembered the moment in childhood when he had become aware of the cornstalks in his father's Milltown garden; how they seemed to stretch, whisper, plead for the moisture they must have to grow. "We'll need to have a rain dance pretty soon," his father had said, turning the hose toward them, and he saw the contorted Goya waifs of the New York sidewalks leaping in brief frenzy around the spouting hydrant.

He ran home like a boy through the wet orchard; stamped into the house whistling, shaking himself. But as he stood drying his wet body his mood altered. Suddenly the small house seemed cold, empty, isolated. He felt in it a lack, a want, as great as his own. For the first time he wondered what his father did (had done all these years) about loneliness. And he thought of Ellen, wished actively for her presence. Looking out at the gray water and the gray light—already brightening slowly where the sun was coming through again—he was glad he had an invitation for the evening.

CHAPTER **20**

*

* *

*

AS PHILIP made no noise coming along the pine-needled path in his rubber-soled sneakers, he reached the window of Lawrence Warren's house without being heard. He looked in and saw a young woman he took to be Clare Powers standing alone before an easel staring at a painting. Completely absorbed, she did not see him, and he had a moment to study her unobserved.

He tried to think of what her firmly defined yet delicate profile reminded him. Was it one of the Toltec heads reproduced widely in magazines during the past year?—a resemblance emphasized by the way she wore her hair, pulled up and back uncompromisingly from her face, resting in a flat pancake on top, a coiffure he normally disliked. Around the pancake she had tied a cerise cord.

Her appearance surprised him, for in her dark turtle-neck sweater and aquamarine shorts she looked much more like a painter's model than a learned anthropologist. He found this an immediate relief, realizing that he had unconsciously linked her in his mind with the stern-heeled guardian of the glass cases in the Indian museum. But this young woman stood bare-legged and casual, her feet—in ballet slippers the color of the cord around her head—crossed in almost a dancer's pose as, with her hands rammed in her pockets, she studied the canvas.

With no warning, but with undeniable directness, a stab of physical desire shot through Philip. He was amazed at its force; amazed to find himself so aware of a strange woman's body. At that instant she turned and saw him.

She spoke at once. "You're Philip Stewart."

He had for a moment the absurd feeling that he had been caught spying, that she knew of the sensation that had just surged through him. He managed to say, "I am."

She came lightly across the room and put her hand out through the window. "I'm Clare Powers. It's nice to see you. Come around to the door." Her face when she smiled surprised him by its warmth. There was in it a peculiar blending of elements; at once humorous and sensual, old and very young.

He walked around the end of the house and entered the one big room Lawrence had made—his father told him—by knocking out all the ground floor partitions. Three sides of the room were painted a crude white; one was left charred and gray-black, plainly showing where the house had been burned. Immediately Philip was aware of warring impressions—a sense of space giving way to a sense of clutter. There were several large tables covered with objects that he did not at once identify, except for some crude wood and wire experiments called "mobiles," presumed to be, he knew, the sole invention of a man named Calder. The canvases leaped out at him—dark colors, intricate unrecognizable forms. These would take some explaining, he told himself.

While the room registered its complexity he held himself firmly to amenities with the young woman. "My father couldn't come tonight. He sends his regrets and apologies."

"I'm sorry—but I was sure he wouldn't." She did not explain. "Lawrence isn't back yet from the store. He's gone for our week's supplies. I expect him any minute. Your father isn't ill, is he? I haven't seen him for days."

"No, tired perhaps. I think it must be something of a strain, having a city visitor—and a long-lost son."

"I don't think anything is a strain for your father. He is a very remarkable person." She said this with a special warmth and emphasis that pleased him.

"I think so too. It's quite an experience coming to know your own father after twenty-six years."

She gave him a slow look. "It must be. Still I suppose most people never know their fathers, so perhaps you will be one of the lucky ones." Without waiting for any reply, "I brought along some Bourbon for us," she said, lifting the bottle from the table. "Lawrence doesn't drink—or rarely."

She extended the bottle. "Will you pour your own?"

After he had poured for them both she lifted her glass solemnly. "Welcome to the island."

"Thank you." Philip smiled. "I appreciate that. My father has told me how you feel about strangers."

"Oh, has he?" She laughed. "We do try to guard our privacy. I'm quarreling right now with my conscience about using a publisher's advance to buy a few more feet of waterfront on either side."

"Extra protection?"

She nodded.

"Have you written a book?"

"Yes." Anticipating his next question she added, "It's a book on Indian ghost dancing."

Ghost dancing! What the hell! He decided not to go into it. He took a good stiff pull of the Bourbon and felt it hitting him instantly.

Clare Powers sat down quietly with her glass. The old high-backed wicker chair was fancifully woven in scrolls, circles and uprights, like penmanship exercises wrought in raffia. She folded one of her feet under her and at once the mottled yellow cat that had just minced in through the open door, jumped up and lay down on the aquamarine shorts. I wonder how often Lawrence paints her, Philip caught himself wondering, and, without meaning to, heard himself asking:

"Has Lawrence done your portrait with his cat?"

"Lawrence doesn't do portraits," she said. "He's strictly symbolic and subjective." She seemed to imply Philip should have known better than to suggest Lawrence would do a realistic portrait.

"Quite a description." His voice sounded acid even to his own ears. Was it the liquor filling him with these sudden feelings Ermenthal had labeled "hostile and aggressive?"

"Are these typical paintings of Lawrence's?" he inquired keeping his tone coolly detached so that she would not think he considered them of any undue importance.

"Typical?" She seemed to question the word a moment before accepting it. "Yes, I'd say so."

Philip rose and walked over to the nearest one. *"Disordered Universe,"* he read aloud. The name had been painted on the plain wooden frame. "What is it?" he inquired, looking at the canvas, "a brain or a mushroom?"

"Both," she said. She laughed. "That came out of the day your father talked to the local school kids on mushrooms—pointing out the difference between the edible Morel and the Brain mushroom—similar in looks, but poisonous. Lawrence rushed out of the schoolhouse as though he'd seen a vision and came home and painted that. Your father says he caught all the hidden meaning of evil in the brain-like lobes of a poisonous fungus." She laughed again, but not derisively.

"Quite a statement." He was again sounding hostile. He realized that he had deliberately avoided questioning his father about a small painting on his kitchen wall, *King and Early Star,* showing a diademed toad under a trillium.

Apparently Clare Powers did not notice the hostility for she went on, pleasantly conversational, "You've not met Lawrence yet, have you?"

"No. But I'm looking forward to it. My father's very fond of him."

"He's irresistible." She turned. "Are you not?"

Through the open door a tall, bearded man had noiselessly entered. Stooping a little as he cleared the frame, he dropped a burlap sack on the already overburdened table and extended his hand to Philip. "Glad to see you. We all love your father very much."

They make a point of appreciating the old man, Philip thought.

He looked closely at Lawrence. Why that beard? Did it conceal a wen, or some psychological trouble?

"Am I not what?" Lawrence was asking, looking at Clare.

"I said irresistible."

Lawrence's teeth flashed white through the smooth silky growth around his mouth and chin. The beard was at least two shades lighter than his hair. This man would be stared at anywhere, Philip said to himself, and he must know it. Why should a recluse . . . ?

"It's the beard," Lawrence was saying in answer to Clare. He spoke in a voice peculiarly low and soft, though not weak, not feminine. "Ladies of a certain age love it. Hard to explain, isn't it?" He looked directly at Philip. It was almost as though he had read his thoughts. "I know wearing one is supposed to indicate something amiss in the psyche. I never heard it properly explained. I suppose men were manly enough in the 1860's when they all wore them. The truth is I grow it every summer because I can't stand shaving every day. It's such a bloody nuisance. Drives me crazy. I don't see any sense in it. So—if I have to look like a tintype of a Civil War colonel or a cheap postcard of Jesus, then I have to, that's all. What do *you* do about it?"

"Shaving? Well, so far I shave," Philip said. "My father sets me a splendid example. He does it every morning with an old-fashioned long-bladed razor, the kind I thought were only used for murders."

"Your father's a highly disciplined character. How's his writing coming?"

"His what?" Did he imagine it or did he see Clare trying to flash a look of warning at Lawrence? If she did, Lawrence appeared oblivious.

"That story of his life he said he was going to embark on. Said he intended to take a sharp look at Thomas Cameron Stewart—on paper."

"First I've heard of it," Philip said. His voice sounded stiff and he saw that Lawrence, too late, had caught Clare's warning expression.

Lawrence mumbled something inarticulate about "probably hasn't got around to telling you," and immediately changed the subject, turning toward Clare. "I bought pork chops. Minnie Bye recommended them. I thought it was cool enough." Again he turned to Philip. "I hope you can eat pork. Clare does a dish with pork chops and sour cherries. It's very good. We thought we'd probably eat indoors tonight. It looks so much like rain again."

His way of speaking with simple declarative sentences gave Philip the impression that, in spite of his odd appearance and his weird paintings, Lawrence was essentially a very direct and simple human being. "But you'll probably be proved entirely wrong," he warned himself, staring around the room again.

"If it's to be the casserole," Clare was saying, "we'll go over to my place. I've got the kind of pot I need, and my stove's faster."

Philip felt relieved. He had wondered where in the confusion that he was now able to catalogue as paints, brushes, birds' nests, odd-shaped stones, driftwood, the bleached cranium of a mountain goat, the skulls of birds, they were going to find any place to sit down and eat. Yet, he had to admit, the room, though cluttered, was not without a certain style. Nothing was here, he felt, just to fill space. All the objects were placed for observation, apparently out of pure joy in the form. On a shelf there was a casual arrangement of barn owl skeletons; and the grass seeds and pine in the narrow-necked Oriental vase had obviously been created with a careless but artful eye.

"You go along," Lawrence said. "I'll feed Philomena and Simp first."

At the word Philomena, the cat jumped from Clare's lap and went to rub her body along Lawrence's blue denim leg.

"I didn't see Simp," Clare said.

"He came back with me. Outside now with the squirrels, I guess." Lawrence reached down and picked up the cat. He thrust his blond beard into the back of its neck, tickled its ears, turned it over to cradle it in his arms, scratching its stomach, smelling its fur, murmuring so amorously and displaying such an excess of affection that Philip turned away in embarrassment. This was very different from his own toleration of Edgarbergen. "Salmon for you tonight, sweetheart," Lawrence was promising.

Clare caught Philip's averted eye. "We're cat people," she said in an off-hand voice. "I hope it won't offend you. It does some people."

From the way she said "we," Philip felt sure they were lovers. He made no reply and she did not seem to expect any.

Just outside the door a mongrel dog, with a pronounced strain of Irish terrier, sat under a tree looking fixedly up the trunk. "There's Simpson," Clare said, "waiting for the squirrels. He never wins and he never learns."

"That's why I found dogs depressing to have around, once I grew to man's estate," Philip said.

"Too much like their masters?"

"Maybe that's it."

It was surprisingly pleasant to laugh with her, even at his own expense.

2

THE long main room of Clare's house had an air both of luxury and austerity, entirely unlike Lawrence's. Here there was no casual litter. All the objects were displayed with precision, a studied isolation. They reflected, he could see, the life she had lived among primitive peoples. There was a glass case on one wall filled with small crude stone figures that he learned later were fetishes. The rugs, gray and white, looked Navajo; the curtains and chair coverings, Mexican. There were two small Peruvian embroideries framed under glass. Behind an over-size couch hung a row of blown-up photographs of ancient ruins. Among them Philip recognized the familiar pyramid forms and serpent-guarded flights of steps of Old Mexico. In its entirety the room was cool, dignified, curiously abstract; an effect he decided that must come from the disciplined aesthetic components of the objects themselves.

"What are you thinking?" Clare Powers asked, as Philip stood by the fireplace deliberately looking about.

He tried to tell her.

She seemed pleased with his observation. "Yes, you're right. The work of primitive peoples does have restraint. Exuberance,

flamboyance—they come later. They belong to the Baroque—
the blending of unlikely elements . . ."

She was talking back at him over her shoulder as she walked
into her kitchen. Philip followed. With an efficient air she
began to pull salt, pepper, sugar, cinnamon, canned sour cherries, rice and a French casserole from the shelves and range
them alongside the pork chops. She put on the kind of white
smock that laboratory technicians wear and this added to her
look of efficiency, then turned on the oven of the kerosene
stove, addressing it as she did so, "Please behave yourself, baby."
At once she began to whistle something Philip did not recognize, music with a very involved rhythm, as she took a lemon
from the icebox and grated the peel into a bowl. She put the
thick pork chops into a pan to brown them, and a cup of rice
into a pressure cooker. "Short cuts," she said, as though in explanation. Philip became aware that he was staring at her rather
hard, smiling.

"Can I help?"

"Thanks, there's really nothing to do."

At this moment Lawrence entered softly and without a word
got silver, napkins, mats from a drawer and walked into the
living room where he proceeded to set three places at the end
of a long wooden table. Yes, Philip thought, he belongs here,
he is master. He was astounded to find the thought piqued him.
He began to feel ill-at-ease, subtly excluded, and immediately
the information they had inadvertently dropped about his
father's writing returned to his mind. Why had they acted so
disconcerted by his ignorance? And why was he ignorant anyway? Why should his father reveal something to his neighbors
that he did not tell his own son? Man of mystery, old Jim
Everett had said with his elfin cackle. The "story of his life".
What was there to tell?

He returned to the main room. Just inside the door there
was a full-length mirror and stepping back out of sight of the
two in the kitchen he took a deliberate look at himself. He was
astonished at the change tanned skin and the loss of a few
pounds around his waist had already made in him. In his gray
flannels and yellow linen shirt he looked younger and—he had

to admit it with satisfaction—physically strong; was "virile" the word? Actually, he thought, he appeared in better physical shape than Lawrence, who lived this kind of life the year round. Lawrence definitely looked undernourished. Maybe she didn't always cook for him, and he just opened cans the way men alone are apt to do.

Something about the sight of himself in the mirror restored his self-confidence. With an easy air, having nothing else to do, he began to examine the old woven Indian baskets in which Clare kept cigarettes, matches, pencils, fir cones for her fireplace.

"I wonder what became of my grandmother's Indian baskets," he said aloud. "And grandfather had a totem pole once—out back of the orchard on a hummock of ground. I wonder where it went."

"Chopped up for firewood by the Methodists maybe," Lawrence suggested. Philip, glancing at him, saw that he was speaking figuratively. "As for the baskets," he continued, laying the silver neatly beside each plate, "they probably went in a rummage sale for fifteen cents each. That one you're looking at now is a particularly fine one. I bought it for Clare at a sale and I paid just two dollars for it. It's worth ten times that much at least—or certainly will be before long."

Clare came in through the open door with a light green water pitcher of Mexican glass. It was almost the color of her shorts, Philip noted.

"My favorite Indian basket." She put down the pitcher and added, as though reciting from something. " 'The weaver of Klickitat looked into the water and found her pattern.' "

"Precisely," Lawrence said.

If in this moment the two of them had spoken some unknown foreign tongue Philip could not have felt more excluded. He caught the subtle communication between them; that communication of word, glance, murmur which only people of the closest intimacy and harmony can exchange together, and a feeling curiously like what he remembered jealousy to be, flashed through him.

"It will take about forty minutes for the casserole," Clare was saying. "If you're hungry we can open some sardines, and I've got cheese."

"I'm starved," Lawrence stated.

The three of them sat down around a small table before the fire where Clare placed beer for Lawrence, Bourbon, and a small dish of improvised hors d'oeuvre.

At first they groped a little for conversation. Then to Philip's surprise they began to ask him direct questions about things in New York, chiefly about art shows and concerts—questions to which, for the most part, he could not reply.

Clare sighed. "How rich New York is in things, things, things!" Her voice held a trace of envy, Philip thought. "Yet I cannot live there," she added positively.

Philip found himself absurdly wishing to defend the city; annoyed at the implication that anyone who wanted could avoid it. He experienced the same sensations that sprang up in him when magazines devoted pages to descriptions of happy young ex-Marine officers—stock-brokers—city-planners, who had "escaped" with their families to the country . . . "Borrowing $20,000 from relatives, the young Kerbys courageously staked their all in an Arizona cattle ranch!"

"Why can't you live in New York?" he demanded.

Clare shrugged. "It's no place for a creative worker."

"Lots of successful ones seem to manage to live there," Philip said.

She took care of this thrust with utmost coolness. "Maybe I'm not successful enough."

He felt, then, the need to defend himself further in the matter of his ignorance of New York art galleries.

"You know," he began lightly, "I think I should admit right now that I'm a typical New Yorker. I go nowhere, see nothing. I've always heard that it's the residents of Duluth or Sacramento who know which show's a top hit and what Bergdorf Goodman has in the windows . . ."

"Yes, I've noticed that about New Yorkers," Clare said. "There are no people more provincial. I suppose if you live at the hub of the universe you feel that's all you need to prove you're in the 'know.' "

She began then to speak with Lawrence about someone whose name was not familiar to Philip. Philip was excluded again—not rudely or deliberately, but quite definitely. He went back over the conversation, as he had learned to do with Ermenthal, admitting to himself that it was true he found some intangible but real pride in the fact that he was a New Yorker; a condition, a way of life that indicated sophistication, the assumption that you must know—by some unconscious process of osmosis—all the finer gradations of "what was what." He supposed that this, in its way, was what, years ago, old Jemma Bates had meant by provincialism. He tried to put his finger on the difference he felt between himself and these two people, and he saw one difference lay in the fact that he associated almost entirely with people who did things with other people's ideas—editors, publishers, producers—whereas Clare Powers and Lawrence Warren probably knew mainly originators, whether obscure or famous was beside the point. This distinction increased in him a subtle and uncomfortable feeling of having lived the life of a parasite.

As soon as he could he interrupted them with the manner of one earnestly seeking information. "Tell me just what it is you do among the Indians, Miss Powers. I know you said you were doing a book on ghost dancing. Just what is ghost dancing?"

Before answering him she said, "Why don't you call me Clare? I'm sure we're all bound to be friends." Then she looked at him with amusement. "To describe ghost dancing is a large order. You can't imagine how large! Better wait and read my book in a year or two."

He saw she was really trying to be pleasant and he told himself for God's sake, to get off his high horse, "I can't wait," he said. "Couldn't you give me just a hint?"

She hesitated. "Well, I'll try." She lit a cigarette and let it burn out between her fingers as she attempted, in a few careful, hesitant phrases, to say something about ghost dancing. What she said had for Philip the effect of some of Ermenthal's remarks in the hospital. Her words seemed to open up a wholly new aspect of life—one that he might have taken casually—or even indifferently—if read on a printed page, but coming from this young woman, swinging the cerise toe of her ballet slipper lightly up and down as she talked, they gave him a sensation of having entered an utterly unfamiliar world.

She spoke of how the Indians had resisted the whites, and how they had finally raised up a series of Messiahs, one in particular, who had visions and claimed guidance from Heaven for all the Indians of America. One prophet's worship had spread throughout all the West, uniting even warring tribes who danced in ecstasy together for days and nights on end. As she spoke of the natural gifts of prophecy and poetry among certain Indians, Lawrence cut in quietly to suggest, "Tell him what that one old chief said about the earth."

"Oh, yes," She looked straight at Philip. "He just remarked to the governor who was making the treaty to take over their lands, 'I wonder if the ground has anything to say. I wonder if the ground is listening.' Your father likes that speech." She smiled as though remembering something pleasant. "He likes even better a remark the Indian Messiah made to a white man: 'My young men shall not work, for men who only work cannot dream, and wisdom comes to us in dreams.' " She looked across at Philip in the firelight and smiled again.

"Yes," he said, "I can imagine my father liking that." He hastened to continue his show of interest. "And ghost dancing, is it still going on?"

"Oh, yes, though somewhat degenerated, of course—mixed up with Shakers and Holy Rollers . . ." She was plainly not anxious to discuss it.

"Holy Rollers." At last there was some point on which he could make at least a small conversational contribution. "I saw them once when I was a boy out here. I can still remember it. They scared the living hell out of me. The other kids used to sneak back to watch them in an old warehouse down on the waterfront. But once was enough for me. I had nightmares for a week. There was a gray-haired man foaming and jerking about, and a young girl with braids down her back, leaping like snakes. My God—those braids! I can still get the shakes just remembering them. Don't tell me that's what ghost dancing is like."

She hesitated. "Not always," she said quietly.

"Stay until the New Year," Lawrence suggested, "and we'll take you to a ceremony, not far from here, where the Indians dance with magnetized poles. Tell him about it, Clare."

When Lawrence spoke this time a slight frown crossed her face. Philip did not know whether she resented Lawrence's commanding voice or whether she was increasingly unwilling to talk about the subject. But after a moment she said to Lawrence, almost grudgingly, "I'll show him those drawings you made for the book."

She went to a desk at the end of the room and brought back a folder. In it were half a dozen crayon sketches. The style in which they had been executed was very free, but Philip could make out, with Lawrence's help, what the scenes were depicting.

There was first the interior of a long room with three fires of criss-crossed logs burning on a dirt floor. Around the fire, Indians were dancing, holding upright cedar poles, about twelve feet high, thin and round and hung with plumes of shredded bark. Drummers with faces as rigid as masks; singers with tortured and constricted expressions; the "shaman" with heavy black grease make-up on the lower half of his face, a red scarf knotted around his forehead; one dancer with his face almost entirely concealed by a bark head-dress, his mouth open, all the teeth exposed in a fixed grimace; the same man leaping high in the air over a fire; a woman being held by a band around her waist, apparently to prevent her from falling into the blazing logs.

Clare described how the poles the Indians were carrying during the dance became charged with some nameless force and, assuming a will of their own, pulled and led the dancers powerfully around the hall and, sometimes, out of the door and down to the very edge of the river flowing past, a few hundred feet away. "There are cases on record," he said, "of Indians going to their deaths in this fashion."

The whole story would have been completely unreal to Philip without Lawrence's sketches. These lent an air of authority that made dismissal hard, in spite of his scepticism.

"What was it in the poles?" he asked Clare. He tried to make the question sound casual and commonplace.

She had been sitting with her eyelids half-closed while she talked, as though this helped her create a clearer picture. Now she opened her eyes wide and looked at him with perfect candor.

"Who can say?" She shrugged, lowered her lids again, turned her face in profile as she lit a cigarette.

Her manner annoyed him. "You must have a theory?"

She made no reply. Her behavior now seemed genuinely puzzling, even irritating.

Lawrence spoke up with an air of pride. "Clare has danced with the poles herself." Philip looked from one to the other quickly. Clare's expression had not changed. When she said nothing, Lawrence continued, "The head of the tribe adopted her after she had persuaded one of his daughters—a born singer—not to resist her gift, but to go with it."

There was a short silence. "Of course," Philip said dryly, "I don't understand a word either of you is saying."

This made Clare laugh aloud. Her manner abruptly changed. She looked at Philip again and her face once more became friendly and natural. "I don't wonder. I'll try to make sense. But this, you see, is just why I don't like *ever* to talk about these things—but never mind!" She dismissed the half-finished sentence as though determined now to make the best of a difficult situation.

"You see," she said earnestly—and for the first time it was plausible to Philip that she could teach a class of graduate students—"being what is called an Indian 'singer' is a little like being 'possessed,' in our sense of the word. Singers get their songs from some ancestor, who visits them in a dream usually, or from some animal. It's a special gift, a power, and when it insists on using you, you can't very well get away with denying it. Not if you're an Indian, anyway."

She paused to give him a glance that was amused and a little mocking before she went on:

"This girl Lawrence just spoke about tried not to accept her —well, *fate*, is perhaps a good enough word. She resisted the power that tried to use her. Resistance made her sick."

She paused. Her manner said again: How did I let myself in for this?

Philip tried now to help her. "Why did she resist? Is it dangerous—this power?"

"Aren't all gifts dangerous?" Lawrence murmured. He did not look at either of them. Philip did not know what to answer and Clare acted as though she had not heard him.

"She resisted because she was going to marry an Indian who thought the whole business of being a singer was old-fashioned, something to be genuinely ashamed of. I finally persuaded her to go with the powers anyway. All her dreams showed that she really wanted to. And certainly her sickness was conclusive proof of the harm she was doing herself."

This woman is mad, Philip said to himself. He glanced at Lawrence. They were both mad.

"Clare's monograph on that girl might interest you," Lawrence commented. "It will soon be published."

"I'm sure it would interest me," Philip murmured. Then he could not resist asking, "And what became of her boy-friend? I suppose he got another girl."

That his dry emphasis was not lost on either of them he was certain, but Clare gave no indication she had noticed. "I don't know." She appeared wholly indifferent to this part of the story.

Yes, she's crazy, Philip told himself. Everybody around here is crazy. He thought of his father, of Clarence Bye, of the old man, Jim Everett, the first night he arrived. Imagine trying to tell anyone—Dick Fordyce, Lily Slade, Goldstone, even Ellen —about the talk he had already heard on this island: of murderous, jealous sea gulls, talking ravens, sensitive bears, "possessed" Indians, tobogganing humanity, Zen "idiots," egg teeth . . . And then he thought, What if I tried to reproduce one of my own typical office or lunch-hour conversations for my father, for Clarence and Minnie Bye, or even for these two worldly contemporaries with whom I'm about to eat dinner? How would it sound to them—that vocabulary of properties, personalities, deals, sales, prices, angles, pitches, slants and Anglo-Saxon monosyllables that make up my daily exchanges? Nevertheless, he persisted in arguing.

"Wasn't it hard to give the Indian girl advice like that?"

"Like what?" Her eyes were guarded.

"To give up normal life and go that—that other way?"

"Oh, she's quite normal," Clare said. "She goes to the movies and has a radio." She laughed maliciously. "In fact when she was telling me about the tutelary power that kept visiting her and trying to sing through her, she said to me, 'I watched it like in the movies.'"

Her voice had become mocking. Philip caught this and forced his tone to sound superior and critical in reply. "Well, I must admit I can't imagine being sure enough of myself to take such a responsibility."

He knew he had succeeded at last in annoying her, for her voice came back stern, flat. "That girl was a very gifted singer. There aren't many of them left nowadays. Indians are degenerating creatively, like everybody else. There was no one in the tribe like her. I'm sure the fact that she had been sickly as a child and kept from school made it possible for her to be *used*, if I can put it that way; or to be creative, if that sounds better to your ears. She wasn't swamped with alien stereotypes when too young and defenseless to protect herself."

She must have some doubts of the part she played in this girl's destiny, Philip said to himself, or she wouldn't be so defensive and expansive. She was sweeping on fiercely.

"I certainly thought—and still do—that a chance to develop as a real singer—the kind the tribe used to have—was much more important to this girl, and to the tribe, and to anthropology, than for her to marry some stupid beer-swilling Indian who would take her to live in La Conner where she'd develop a taste for needled beer herself probably, and probably have a full-fledged white-style neurosis in six months. Am I to infer that you think *that* would have been the civilized thing to promote?"

There was real tension now between them; the room was electric. Philip was pleased, enjoying himself for the first time. The tension he had created kept him from being ignored.

"I'm not sure," he said. "I'm just interested in your feeling that you had the right to influence so profoundly another human being."

As he spoke he glanced at Lawrence and found him sitting in

complete relaxed composure, wearing the air of a spectator at a mildly engrossing play.

Clare restrained her annoyance with difficulty. She replied calmly, though one fist drummed on the arm of her chair, "It is, I suppose, altogether a matter of one's viewpoint. In my opinion, you see, these forms of art, of religion, whatever you wish to call such cultural vestiges among the Indians, are important to preserve. Certainly they seem of more value than an imitation of the lowest level of white life: reading *True Confessions* and the comics, going to the cheapest films, listening to *Gang Busters* . . ."

She rose with dignity. "I think that casserole must be done by now."

As she walked toward the kitchen Philip had a sudden picture of her whirling around and around a firelit room with a troop of Indians, her long brown hair hanging below the shoulders, her feet in the cerise ballet slippers, in her hand an upright pole shaking wildly like a branch in the wind. The image produced in him an immediate, and powerful, emotional response. He jumped up from his chair.

"Don't give me up as hopeless!" He threw into his voice all the charm he could muster. He wanted to be near her now, to go on talking. She looked back at him from the kitchen door, amazed.

"Actually," he said, walking swiftly toward her, "all this interests me more than I want to admit." He saw her face soften. How seriously she takes it, he said to himself, surprised again. He hurried on, apologetically, "I suppose I've fallen into bad habits of arguing with people—as though that was ever any way to learn anything. But just let me ask you—and I put it very humbly, and forgive me if I sound like an unregenerate Babbitt: What is the real value in this kind of research?"

She leaned back against the lintel of the kitchen door for a moment, thoughtful now and very earnest. "The answer is a simple one. And I have it on my tongue's end because I'm asked it so often."

She walked then to the oven, took out the casserole, removed the lid, poked the chops, smelled them, returned the pot to the oven. "Ten minutes," she said.

Ramming her hands into the pockets of the laboratory smock, she spoke soberly and carefully, not looking at Philip but at Lawrence who was still sitting on the end of his spine, his legs thrust out, his head resting on the chair-back.

"I think it's revealing, more than a little revealing, to compare the myths that psychoanalysis has shown us modern civilized white people are still creating in their dreams—even living out in their daily lives—to the myths and dreams and mysteries of primitive people like the Indians."

Yes, Philip thought, she is a pedagogue, underneath all her charm and physical grace and animal vitality. And she is ruthless, too. Ruthless? Why did he think this so suddenly? Was it something about her cold intellectuality, her impersonal way of speaking?

She had broken off in impatience. "It's too big a subject! Some day, if you like and we have the time, we can talk about it at length."

"I'd like to very much." Philip smiled directly into her eyes. "I mean it," he added.

She returned the smile but said nothing as she went back toward the kitchen. This time Lawrence followed her, and Philip, watching through the door, saw him come up to her and without self-consciousness—almost as though in this moment he was unaware of Philip's presence—tip up her face and kiss her full on the lips.

Philip looked away, again uncomfortably resentful, resentful of their embrace, of Clare's sudden gentleness, of all that these two people so obviously had in common. *One and one and all alone.* The song of the girl in the night club that had so affected him just before his accident came back to him. He felt cut off once more, isolated and again inadequate, unequal to the demands of a whole set of circumstances he could not define, could not now even name.

CHAPTER *21*

* * *

THE moment Philip appeared the next morning his father asked, "What kind of a time did you have?" He quite obviously inquired out of genuine interest.

"Oh, we had a big argument," Philip answered half-irritably. "Or at least I think it was an argument."

"Oh, certainly," his father said easily. "Everybody always argues with Clare."

"Not with Lawrence?"

"Lawrence is not the arguing kind. Actually I think he dislikes all discussion. Not ideas, but discussion of ideas."

It piqued Philip to hear the note of affection in his father's voice.

"Well, I didn't know what the hell they were talking about half the time, and they probably think I'm a city boob." He pulled out his chair and sat down, frowning. There was white cornmeal for porridge.

"Use the brown sugar," his father suggested. "That white on white looks so sickly!"

"You too are an artist," Philip said. "Sensitivity even at breakfast."

His father only laughed.

"This Indian stuff," Philip said after a moment. "I never heard such hocus-pocus nonsense told with a straight face. Do you believe all that?"

"All that what?" asked the old man. "There are a lot of different kinds of Indian stories."

"Magnetic poles dragging Indians around and around a big room."

"Seeing is believing," said the old man, "and I've seen."

"You, too. I give up." He began to concentrate on the porridge.

"There are more things in heaven and earth than are dreamed of, Horatio," his father said, not using his quoting voice, just remarking it. But the cliché quotation made Philip wince, and he let annoyance seep down through his mind. He sat in silence.

His father went outside to the pump; stopped to address a few remarks in his Irish voice to a jay before re-entering. "And what may ye be doin' now, stealin' the very food from under me nose!" Philip felt ashamed of his irritation when he heard his father's good-natured address to the bird, and he looked up at a small ceramic figure in a monk's robe that stood on the kitchen shelf holding a nesting bird in the palm of his outstretched right hand. "St. Kevin, the only Irish Saint—except Patrick—I ever much cared for," his father had remarked, identifying it one day. He told the story: how St. Kevin, in prayer with outstretched arms, had stood so immobile that a blackbird came and nested in his palm. When the eggs were laid, the Saint first took notice, but since he did not wish to disturb the mother bird, he kept his hand outstretched until the fledgelings were hatched. . . . Remembering the story restored Philip's good humor. He reached for the salt and, as he did so, noticed that the card from yesterday, with the similar words from Buddha and Christ about the remarkable location of the Kingdom of Heaven, was still leaning against the saltcellar. He picked up the card and found a second one behind it.

He was reading aloud from it when his father came back through the door:

"There is no proof, there is only experience. There is no teaching, there is only learning. Do you believe that?"

His father put some wood into the stove, replaced the lid carefully and exactly. "I'm thinking about it."

"You mean the cards are here for you?"

"For whom, if not for me?"

Philip was disconcerted. "I thought maybe for me."

His father threw back his head and laughed. "I gave up preaching long ago." At once he denied this, sitting down, tilting back in his chair. "That's not true, quite. I've always been a preacher and a teacher of sorts and it's likely I always will be, since it seems to be my nature. What I mean to say is, I've given up preaching to convert, or—well, you might say—I don't try to prove anything to anybody who resists. Why should I?"

"You mean let the poor bastard stew in his own juice?" Philip spoke almost bitterly again.

His father did not appear to notice the tone. All he said was, "I think I ought to tell you before you hear it somewhere else, and maybe get a shock—for six weeks, beginning today, I go every Sunday, to a place near here called Venus, to give what I suppose might be called a sermon, since it's delivered at eleven o'clock in the morning on the seventh day of the week."

"You do?" Philip looked up, genuinely surprised. He noticed now that his father was wearing his best blue-serge trousers and a white shirt. "What do you preach on?"

"Practically anything." His father grinned. "The sixteen hundred varieties of moss, or what did Buddha and Christ really have to say about the spiritual life—as opposed to what it's *believed* they said. They're not real sermons, of course."

"Do many people come?"

"You'd be surprised."

Philip thought he detected a faint note of pride in his father's voice. He got up to fill the coffee cups and, as he did so, his father added, "There was a story about me in the newspaper a few years ago. Maybe it would amuse you to read it."

He brought from the sitting room a yellowed newspaper clipping. It showed a little ugly, cardboard-box church and his father on the steps, his binoculars over his shoulder. "*The most un-orthodox preacher in America*," the caption read.

The format was very much the same as the one Philip had seen in Seattle describing Lawrence. It was from a Sunday paper and had a woman's byline. Philip supposed someone had dreamed up a series of stories about "local characters." Yet the tone of the piece was not patronizing; it was, in fact, friendly, and surprisingly without mockery.

> "*Who are his audience? Summer visitors from Cali-fornia, people waiting for a ferry, Indians recovering from a Saturday-night drunk, farmers from down the road. Mr. Stewart says he doesn't worry about the num-ber of people because he's just thinking out loud any-way.*"

"Do you keep any record of what you say?" Philip asked, putting the clipping on the table and mooring it with the sugar dish, for a wind was coming in now off the water.

"After a fashion."

"I'd like to see it."

His father shook his head. "It's in no shape for reading." He took up his pipe. The thought crossed Philip's mind: "But does he let Lawrence and Clare read what he's put down?"

"So you're really a preacher." His voice was faintly accusing.

His father waved the burnt end of the match at him in depre-cation. "Not a bit of it. I don't do any talking about dogma. I don't believe in it. And it isn't possible to talk in so many words about a true religious experience. So I don't try."

" 'There is no teaching, there is only learning?' " Philip said, again glancing at the card. " 'There is no proof, there is only experience?' " He made it a question.

"Right," said his father. He attended to his pipe. Puffing, he went on with an amused eye, "You can get into a lot of trouble preaching from the Bible. A man with my kind of mind can, anyway. Not with the teachings of Jesus, they're pretty clear; but with the Old Testament. Full of a lot of stories might as well be forgotten. Clare Powers brought me Thomas Mann's story of the Jacob-Joseph legend. I thought he did a lot better job with his material than the book of Genesis. But even he couldn't make Jacob seem a very plausible character. Not a very bright one, anyway. It would take a pretty dull-witted fellow not to have known the difference between Rachel and Leah, even in a dark tent at midnight."

He pushed back his chair. "Better get at these dishes. Scotty McPhail's coming to pick me up with his outboard. He'll be here any minute."

Philip said he could easily do the dishes himself, but his father went right ahead stacking them in the ironware pan. Philip got the dish towels. "How far is it to Venus?"

"About three miles by water," his father said. "That's why Scotty picks me up."

"Where does Scotty live?"

"At the nearest point on the mainland by water. Sad case, Scotty . . ." and as he began the ritual with the dishcloth he told how Scotty, whose name was Jamie, had come fresh from a little town in the Highlands to a village in the Pacific Northwest. He had invested his money in a general store, but somehow people didn't take to him. No one could quite say why, but they found him uppity. It was, they decided, the way he had of walking, "grand-like," always looking superior. Finally Scotty's wife discovered what the trouble was: it turned out he'd worn kilts as a boy and so been taught how to swing them properly, grandly, as he walked carrying his bagpipes. "It was all very well to find out where the difficulty lay, but there was nothing to do about it. Scotty couldn't change. He went on swinging it. So the McPhails sold out and went away to a cranberry farm."

"That's quite a story," Philip said. The impulse to write it down stirred briefly in him.

"Aye, and a sad one in one way," said his father. His voice had become quite different as he told it, the accent deepening, a Scotch burr creeping in. He's a showman, Philip thought. He could imagine him now reciting in that San Francisco bar.

"Do you ever play your fiddle any more?" he asked abruptly.

"So you remember the fiddle?" His father appeared pleased. "No, not often. Sometimes for Clare's friends. Sometimes when I'm alone in the winters, just for company."

Philip could almost hear it; the little kitchen full of kettle bubble and fire breathing, outside the wind, the creaming water, the driving rain; *Garry Owen, The Arkansas Traveler* contending with the brush of boughs on roof and wall.

"Here's Scotty now."

His father got his coat, put on a dark tie. They went down together to where a tall man with a sandy face and iron-gray hair was beaching a boat. He had on rubber boots over his blue trousers, and on the seat of the boat Philip could see his polished black Sunday shoes.

"Scotty, this is my son, Philip."

McPhail extended a long hard brown hand. Philip felt briefly the softness of his own within its tough clasp. McPhail murmured; his gray eyes probed Philip. His father got into the boat. As they prepared to push off, McPhail spoke.

"Not coming?" He addressed Philip.

His father replied for him. "Philip's not a pagan like us, Scotty," he said. "He stays away from church like all the rest of the conventional Christians."

McPhail laughed, then pushed off the boat. Philip stood looking after them a long time. Once he raised his hand and waved to them.

2

TOWARD noon, as he lay sunning himself behind a big rock, Philip saw Clare Powers emerge from the trees on the opposite shore and sit down with a canvas beach pad and a book, her back against a madrona tree. She did not look across, and he watched her for a while remembering all the varied sensations of the evening before, feeling all over again the astonishment and strange unease her stories and manner had created in him. Once more he imagined her dancing with the magnetic poles and, as this thought lingered in his mind, again an excitement stirred in him. He told himself that he really owed her an apology and, easily persuaded, he put on his shorts, got up from the sand and walked down to where the boat was tied.

He rowed across in a few minutes. She waved when she saw him nearing the shore. The wave seemed perfectly friendly.

"I hope you didn't have bad dreams?" she cried, when he got within speaking distance.

"Why should I?"

"All the ghost dancing and the magnetic poles."

"I came over to say I think I must have acted rather like a bore," he said humbly.

"Not at all." She closed the book over a twig, put it to one side. "Lawrence and I agreed later we'd both acted rather silly. We're so used to talking to one another, or to people who have the same general interests, that we aren't very good any more with . . ." She looked up at him, hesitating.

"With outsiders?" he finished for her.

She laughed, neither accepting nor rejecting the term.

"I only want to say again that I'm really interested." He looked into her eyes and she met the glance, her expression open and sincere.

"I'm sure you are—or would be anyway. True Indian material is hard to get now—buried and corrupted—but there's still some to be found. People usually find it fascinating, once they get interested. I'm sure you would too."

He felt an exaggerated gratitude for this implication that the barriers were down; that he, too, could come inside the charmed circle where his father, the Byes, Lawrence and Clare lived and communicated with one another.

"Perhaps you will want to take some trips while you're out here when you feel stronger," she suggested. It was her first hint that she knew anything of the accident.

"I'm perfectly well now," he hastened to say. "I even think the sleeping jag I've been on since I arrived has come to an end."

She made no comment.

"What were you reading?" He stretched out at her feet and began to look at the earth, to explore and finger the infinite variety of minute nameless plants growing among the dried leaves and pine needles. He suddenly wished he had brought his father's magnifying lens.

She laughed. "The Indian explanation of why winters in the Pacific Northwest are mild." Her voice was teasing.

"I'd like to hear it."

"Very well, you shall."

She lifted the book, removed the twig and began to read. As she read, her mocking voice became quiet and sweet. She uttered the archaic and formal phrases of the translated myth with dignity.

The word sounds were pleasant Philip thought, lying on his back looking into the high blue sky—lyrical and onomatopoetic, like the flow of water, like wind in leaves; Umatilla, Walla Walla. He drifted back to his childhood, to the memory of his mother reading aloud in the winter evenings, reading legends of animals and men in a distant time when they spoke a common tongue, when trees had spirits and plants could talk, when mountains were White Maidens or Silent Watchers, and when these inland waters that he now lay beside were a living and breathing Presence.

He remembered waking in the night in his white-iron bed under the tacked-up muskrat skin, sensing a mysterious shift and stir in the atmosphere, a hush, a drip, the sound of the bell from Indian Henry's reef. The wind had changed to the south, promising rain; the Chinook . . . For the Chinook Brothers had won over the Walla Walla Brothers in the contest as to who should be most powerful, and so the winters in the Pacific Northwest were always mild.

When Clare stopped, he lay a moment silent, then rolled over on his elbow, one arm crooked under his head to look at her. She appeared relaxed and young in the soft light under the tree. He felt suddenly close to her. "Think how many American kids have the Indians in their souls. Even if it's only Hiawatha, or the name of some familiar lake or stream."

"Yes," she said quietly. "And I think it's probably more significant than we care to admit."

Another brick in the structure of a possible friendship seemed to be sliding into place. Philip was pleased because it had happened without his devising it, by a simple utterance on his part.

At this moment Lawrence appeared on the beach just below

them, emerging from the woods that hid his house. At sight of the blond beard, the bare sunburned torso, the frayed khaki shorts, Philip was faintly annoyed. Why must he come along now? But when Lawrence saw Philip, he immediately altered his course, though he waved in a friendly way before turning along the beach in the opposite direction. Clare and Philip stared after him.

"I hope I didn't disturb him being here," Philip said, trusting he sounded sincere.

Clare only murmured; neither denying nor affirming.

"I imagine he's moody, like all artists?"

"So only artists are moody?" She was again mocking.

"I didn't say only."

She did not pursue it. Instead, she looked down the beach after the retreating figure with what Philip thought was a worried glance. She seemed so abstracted that Philip quickly got the feeling that she wanted to follow Lawrence. He got up, made an excuse about having to return to Peachpit. Clare did not protest. When he got to the boat he looked around. She had disappeared.

3

BACK on his father's island a mood of restlessness seized Philip. He felt out of sorts now, somehow unable to put himself in tune with the day. He walked along the beach slowly toward the point, hoping the scene of sea and mountains would have its usual soothing effect, but it left him unmoved. He saw himself now as an outsider, even an intruder upon the two gulls who watched him with what he felt to be a cold and critical eye.

As he strolled along he observed Lawrence seated in the shadow of the opposite bank on one of the bleached logs that so obligingly skirted these island shores. He was staring off across the open channel. At sight of him Philip turned back to the cabin. And then, as he turned, he saw Clare again. She was walking slowly down her beach toward the quiet figure on the log. So he had been right, after all, to leave her alone.

He came back to the cabin, idly opened a can of fruit juice, drank some, then wandered into the little room they so rarely used, where his father kept his books. The moment his eye once more fell upon the faded photographs he thought of the remark Lawrence had made about his father's writing the story of his life. When did he do it? At nights? Early in the morning? Where did he keep it?

He opened the door of the old man's bedroom and looked in. On the rough pine table beside the bed, on the lower shelf, were two notebooks. They both had an old-fashioned look. Philip walked over and picked up the top one. On the outside, stamped on the worn leather, he read the word *Recipes*. Inside there was an illegible faded name; certainly not his father's. The book's pages seemed to be given over to quotations from a variety of sources.

He put this notebook down on the bed and lifted the one under it, a ledger several times larger, marked on the cover, *Accounts*. Although at the front the date read 190-, the writing was fresh, the ink new. His eye ran swiftly down the opening page and he saw that this was, indeed, the story of his father's life.

He closed the book and stood holding it, gazing out into the limbs of the madrona. The tree was rustling as it always did with a dry and stealthy sound like a creeping animal.

He had never been more tempted in his life. All his buried curiosity came up, pressed upon him. Why would it be wrong? After all, it was his father's life—as his son he had a right to know it, didn't he? What could his father possibly put down on paper that he would rather no one knew? Hadn't he told Lawrence and Clare he was doing it? Didn't this indicate that he meant eventually to show it to them?

This last thought was the one that determined him. He replaced the small book labeled *Recipes*, and, taking *Accounts* under his arm, went into his own room. Here he could not hear the stealthy creeping madrona. Here it was a cedar that floated softly, silently, in the breeze from the inlet.

He lay down on the top blanket, propped his head up on a pillow, opened the book and began, with mingled feelings of guilt and excitement, to read.

* *
*

Beginning in Ballymeaney

*
*   *
*

"IT WAS just after one of the periodic Irish famines, some years before the turn of the century that I, Thomas Cameron Stewart, ran away from County Antrim to America. My third year as a scholarship student at Queen's College·in Belfast lay just behind me, the summer holidays with my family just ahead. It was the thought of the holidays that had first stiffened my intention to run away six months before, and had set me to earning, in secret, the money to effect my escape.

"I could not endure another summer at home—to that my mind was made up: hot afternoons tutoring young Jock McDonnel, hot nights studying in my room where the neglected walls were green with mold and my eyes watered painfully with the poor light, mornings given over to all the many chores no one else could tend to.

"The worst of all the holiday tasks, the most shameful, the most unbearable, was the evening duty of going to the village pub to bring home my father.

" 'Your father's never yet spent a night from under his own

roof,' my mother would say when she timidly knocked on my door toward suppertime to remind me of my duty. It was the only point of pride the poor woman had left in the drunken eccentric that time—or nameless psychic misadventures—had made of her handsome husband.

"In spite of my love for her, at these moments I felt I almost hated my mother for her lack of spirit, her resigned and submissive acceptance of her fate. Yet I, myself, never stood up to my father, or spoke in disgust or anger to him. Gavin Stewart was not a man to cross. He had a quick fist and a quicker tongue. Somewhere I believed fearfully that if I challenged my father on the waste of his life and his strength, I might receive an answer—in words alone—too painful to endure.

"So I said nothing—even when I guided his crazy footsteps along the tattered hedgerows and heard the rooks commenting on the twilight spectacle. I held my head up, not down, with the bitter shame of it, my hand slack on his elbow, mechanically counting each mark my own shabby shoes made on the dusty path. I still remember there were three thousand footprints before we came to our stone wall.

"No mortification, at these times, touched my father. Gavin Stewart walked in triumph, a proud man and free, his mind on fire with ideas too big for coherent utterance, scraps and fragments from the inflamed brain of many a frustrated philosopher. His still beautiful voice rang out with startling resonance as he recited from the ancient classics. Greek, the big staggering man could speak—and often did to the fright of small birds—and Latin also for the benefit of the thorn trees—though he protested that he could not tolerate it spoken in a church where only a man's native tongue should ever be heard.

" 'Since 1611,' he would pause to shout, wagging a long soiled finger at folk along the road, 'The Stewarts have stood their ground and fought.' He seldom explained the nature of the battle. He assumed all proper Down and Antrim men would understand. The year 1611 was the year the first Stewarts came down out of Scotland in the great Ulster Plantation under James —and just where this descendant of theirs, a man of education and promise (one whose forebears had served the two Johns,

Calvin and Knox, as far back as the trials of the Scottish Reformation), had left the self-respecting path of a university graduate and a Presbyterian to start on the downhill grade, no one could rightly say. Certainly I could not.

"In moments of fierce resentment, I had tried asking my mother this question, but not once did she give me an answer I could use. She would only turn her head away and cry, and that was the end of it. When I thought of my mother and her hopeless tears it took all the strength I had—the desperate strength of youth—to make up my mind to run away to America.

"The night before sailing I walked as far as the slope of the hill overlooking the farm and waited there, hiding in the wild thorn until I saw my mother come out to feed the chickens. I watched her until she went back indoors with her empty dish, my heart near splitting in my chest at the thought that she could not, in her darkest dreams, imagine her eldest, the only one left of her five dead children, weeping above the ruined farm with a ticket to America in his upper breast pocket and no intention of saying any farewells. I can still feel how the rocks slid under me as I stumbled blindly down the rough slope and took the road to Belfast where the ship was waiting."

*

*

(Philip looked up, aware now that, uninvited, he was entering into the secrets of another man's life. He felt he should close the notebook, return it to the shelf, and hurry away. But even as he had this thought, the conviction returned that he had a right to know about his father's life, that, indeed, a more intimate acquaintance with the old man's history could only increase his understanding, his tolerance. He turned the page and glanced at the next few words: "In America I found" . . . He looked away from the page at the blank wall of his small bare room. In America he had found what? It was too tantalizing to resist, and assuring himself that his motives did not spring either from mere curiosity or from any childish or willful wish to intrude into forbidden places, he read on.)

*

*

"In America I found my formal classical education a most impractical equipment for a fast-growing and materialistic pioneer world. I came with no connections (at least none my pride would allow me to use), no friends, and no money—and I arrived in one of the new country's cycles of 'hard times.'

"Already exhausted from the labor of earning my fare, while keeping up my university classes, there were a few days following my landing in New York City when I thought I might collapse. The first week I only managed to feed myself by walking from the Bowery north all day long, cramming myself, for the price of a small beer, with the saloons' free lunches. When I felt my face was becoming all too familiar to saloon-keepers, I turned my back on the city and set out through the countryside of upstate New York.

"I walked, living on handouts and sleeping in hay fields and barns, until I came to the opulent farmlands of the Geneseo Valley. On a handsome barn I saw the name of Hector Dalrymple, and being sure thereby that one bearing the names of Cameron and Stewart would be welcome, I knocked at the kitchen door and begged a glass of buttermilk. It was the hour of the mid-day meal and the farmer was at table with his wife and daughter. Hector Dalrymple, after a quick appraisal, invited me to join them. And I—by way of singing for my sustenance— I devoted the meal to a vigorous and extensive discussion of the derivation of my host's name, making a shameful display of all those odds and ends of curious lore that filled my magpie mind. 'Dalrymple,' said I, 'No, sir, the name is not from the Gaelic *dail-a-chruimpuil* or valley of the crooked pool, the name of the Ayrshire hamlet lying in a bed of the Bonny Doon. No. Rather from the Saxon than the Gaelic, surely from *dahl* and *hrympel*, which is to say, sir, a rumpled landscape, as in the parish of Dalrymple itself; all little mounds and knolls, hollows and rises.'

"I stayed on with the Dalrymples.

"The farmer was an enterprising man, owner of the nearest

general store and possessor of an unmentioned number of stocks in the new railroads. He apparently thought he saw in me likely son-in-law material, perhaps even a possible surrogate for himself before the Throne of God, for at once he began to attempt to turn me back toward the ministry—a calling, I had admitted to him, that many of my ancestors had followed.

"In the first months, largely because of the Dalrymple daughter, Lucy, I didn't discourage her father's notions. I was perfectly willing to discuss the eventual possibility of my going to Union, or to Auburn, for theological training. But then some hidden perversity deep in my nature began to interfere. Lucy had a way of bringing up the subject of my future at very unlikely times; Saturday nights in the buckboard coming home from a dance, or when we were alone on the side porch in the twilight after supper. Then there would seem to me something so alien in this practical planned life (for so she and her father seemed to see the calling of the ministry) that I could not lend myself to Lucy's dreams and projects. I would surprise myself and, I'm afraid, shake and shock pretty Lucy by suddenly decrying all dogma, or quoting my own father, indulging as he had in wild outbursts as strange to her ears, no doubt, as Irish curses. I particularly favored the book of Revelations or Isaiah at these times. I'd fix poor Lucy with a distended eyeball and declaim aloud—silencing the peepers, setting a distant dog to barking: 'When flew one of the seraphims unto me, having a live coal in his hand which he had taken with his tongs off the altar: and He touched my mouth with it, and said, Lo, this hath touched thy lips: and thine iniquity is taken away and thy sin purged.'

"It was perhaps cruel of me to remind her—when, out of distaste of such mad imagery, she drew away her hand—that every word of it, and many more like it, could be found in the Bible. I'm ashamed to say that I enjoyed teasing Lucy Dalrymple.

"Still, for one year, I half-heartedly wooed her, listened to her father's mealtime prophecies of eventual American supremacy, strengthened my body, read borrowed books at night in the room over the kitchen, and rested content in the simple routine and the measured prosperity around me.

"In the second year a deeper stirring began in me. I was restless and dissatisfied. The ample white houses, the bulging red barns, the hum and bustle of reviving commerce at the cross-roads store began to affect my spirit as unhappily as the fallen chimneys, the untended yew hedges, the weed-grown gardens of my home place.

"Looking back on Ireland it seemed to me a perpetual twi-light hung over the land of my birth, where mists rose eternally from haunted bogs, where the caws crying from broken roofs announced only the fall of night. It seemed to me then that my tortured father had been right. He declared that, in Ireland, the old gods had long been forgotten, while the one True God had remained a biased bigot, or had become—depending on North or South geography—merely the ranking member of an elabo-rate man-devised hierarchy, a graded assortment of unlikely saints and deities.

"I used to dream a lot about my father. I'd be walking along the road with him in the white twilight and I'd see him take a shaky aim at a crow on a broken wall with a clod lifted waver-ingly from the road, and I'd hear him cry out, etching his Protestant scorn on the summer air, 'Saint Brighid is it then? A kitchen maid named Brighid, the foster mother of our Lord—if you can stomach *that*, lad! And Mary, the Virgin Mother, forever keening and weeping, for a' the world like any Connemara widow with her broken bleeding Son.' 'Shame on you, Gavin Stewart!' the twisted widow Murphy would cry, passing by to bring her own Patrick home from the same pub. 'Come along, Father, please come!' My hand would twitch in my sleep in the Geneseo Valley at the memory of my anxious fingers on the sleeve of Father's worn jacket. Yet, far away from the shameful reality of those evening scenes, I could at last begin to pity my father, could even account somewhat for his drunkenness. Where but in drink, in a decayed land, could a man find the gate to passion or poetry?

"Though I dreamed often about my home, I never wished to return to Antrim. I knew it lay behind me forever, yet I could not remain where I was. Wakeful in my bed above the Dalrymple kitchen, it seemed to me that the neglected property in Ireland, this over-tended farm in upstate New York, were but two faces of an identical coin; a coin for which, I said to myself, I did not yet have pocket space. As for entering the ministry, that too was out of the question. I had certainly made no peace with any dogma. Finally I knew I had had enough of the canny and cautious Dalrymples. I could well wait a bit for a roof, a hearth, a woman of my own."

*

*

"So I moved on from the Geneseo Valley, not much caring where I went or what I did to earn a living.

"At the Great Lakes I took a job on one of the boats carrying cargo between the States and Canada, and, for a time, this pleased me. In these first years of freedom, the American soil, the very earth and air of the new country, stirred my blood and imagination as they had countless thousands from lands of want and dead hope. Though I wrote my mother regularly, promising I was on the way to making my fortune, sending her money from time to time to prove it, and to ease the sorrow I had caused her, I found in myself no wish to lay my personal will upon this still expanding continent, to claim a piece of it, to search out its hidden treasures and store them up privately. I wanted only to fill myself with the great surge and pulse of the new continent's power, to move with it, unquestioning. In those first winey months I felt younger than ever in my life, even than when a boy dancing and fiddling jigs and reels the whole night through.

"But after many months of physical labor, labor that hardened my body but left me too exhausted for any reflection, I became dissatisfied again and determined to change my way of life. I took a train to Chicago. I had been in the city just two days when, standing reading a Latin copy of the *Iliad* in a bookstore on Michigan Boulevard, I fell into talk with a man associated with a New York publishing house. We went out, ate and drank together, and the next morning I had a job selling books for McMasters.

"To sell McMasters' books I had to travel, and in my travels I came to know the gentle valleys of the Ohio and the Mississippi. Although I liked this part of the States, I rapidly reached the conclusion that its people lacked some fire, some spirit I believed might be found on the hardier shores of the Western ocean. The more I thought about the Far West the more I longed to see for myself its golden landscapes. When word reached me of both my father's and mother's death from pneumonia—that curse of the damp Irish climate and the ill-trained, widely scattered Irish doctors—there was no reason to hang onto my savings. I set off across the country to San Francisco."

*

*

"In spite of the prosperous and festive air of this Western city, I, still an adventurer with more learning than muscle, found jobs in San Francisco hard to come by. At a time when my small savings had almost melted away, I chanced to drift into the famous saloon of the Widow Velvet Daly.

"On this night, Velvet, coming down the stairs from her apartment above the saloon, saw me—a young man in a theatrical waistcoat—leaning against her bar, gesturing like an actor and declaiming with passion. She came closer to listen. What she heard, I learned later, was 'The Charge of the Light Brigade,' as well as some of the argument I remember engaging upon with vigor the moment I finished. 'Theirs not to reason why, theirs but to do and die . . . Now there's a harmful and betraying philosophy for you! Down with it forever, say I!'

"I've always had the power to make my voice felt—something inherited, mayhap, from an exhorting Scotch dominie. I must have been reciting well that night, for I remember noticing how the liquor glasses were criss-crossing the bar as the group around me grew. On request I recited some of the things I'd been raised on: 'Ode to a Field Mouse,' 'The Cotter's Saturday Night,' 'out, out brief candle, life's but a walking shadow . . .'

"When I put down my glass for the last time, Velvet Daly summoned me. She gave me a good dinner in her little parlor, then put a question to me straight out. Would I come to help tend bar for her? She would pay me handsomely. The days of the 'girls' were over; respectability presumably in the saddle for good. Some places had singing waiters; she would have a reciting barman."

*

*

"I'm sure it had never been easy for any man to resist Velvet Daly with her melodious voice and frizzed bang, her necklace of assorted gold nuggets, her mounds of bosom and posterior, and her equally ample good humor. Although at her offer I laughed until the tears ran down my cheeks, I needed the money and something about putting my overstocked memory to this use appealed to the perverse in me. I looked with appreciation around Velvet's little snuggery with its smother of puce-velvet drapes, the open pink maws of her conch collection shining between the brass incense burners on the marble-topped table. Her belated respectability was as unyielding as the horsehair sofas on which she now entertained her gentlemen callers. I thanked her for her flattery and for her generous offer, and took the job.

"To my surprise the fame of Velvet Daly's reciting barman spread quickly. 'A young man with a voice like a bell, the runaway son of an Irish lord, no less,' was the way Velvet advertised me. So with every drink I poured I also poured out my stock of scripture and ballad, Shakespeare, Burns, Milton and the Romantic English poets. There was no show like it in town, 'twas said. 'Hail to thee, blithe spirit, Bird thou never wert,' I would whisper into a sodden ear amid shouts of wild mirth; or, darkly, turning the towel of Irish flax around and around inside a beer glass, 'For death is come up into our windows and is entered into our palaces to cut off the children from without, and the young men from the streets. Even the carcasses of men shall fall as dung upon the open field, and as the handful after the harvestmen, and none shall gather them.' After this sort of apocalyptic prophecy I soon found it was a strong man indeed who would not order another drink.

"Velvet Daly considered she had a prize in me. As long as she could, she tried to keep me, with raises and other bribes. But the day came when any pleasure I'd had in the rôle of entertainer grew dim. In the face of every derelict I began to see the features of my dead father. Too many of these men had come from the same race as my own. When they drank they drank as only men of warring conscience and a sense of sin can drink—darkly, fearsomely, steadily. Though their faces might light up with gratitude at hearing the lines of verse and prose out of their own youthful memories, this was no longer reward enough for me. I longed again for solitude, and, finally, I resolutely gathered up my savings and moved—north this time into the Pacific Northwest."

         *

         *

(Philip paused to find his cigarettes, lit one quickly and plunged on, knowing now that he would read to the end, must read to the end. The Pacific Northwest—that was where he came in; soon his own name must appear in these closely written pages. As his hands took up the notebook again he was startled to find them moist and clammy.)

         *

         *

"When I had my first look at the idyllic and heroic landscape called the Puget Sound Country, I knew I had found a resting place. Snow-capped peaks, giant trees, inland seas, wild rivers; the sudden tenderness of green meadows thickly embroidered with flowers, chains of ghost mountains floating on far skylines, the magic of live oaks on the slope of a gentle hill—this mixture of grandeur and intimacy captured my heart. Here were no extremes either of heat or cold to keep a man chained to weather. Here, as in my homeland, grass grew the year round. For the first time I wanted to possess something, a piece of this earth for my very own. Finally, after long searching, I became a homesteader in a green valley beside one of the many rushing streams that still carried an Indian name.

"Looking back now I can see that even my choice of a home-place was to affect the pattern of my fate. For had I chosen land with big trees I might have sold it at a profit—as many others did. But I chose prairie land—or what passes for prairie in this part of the world—a forest-bounded open stretch with a scattering of live oaks, a square of rich loam down by the river. And I chose it because of the river and the view of the mountains. For I could stand at my door on a clear day and see three giant snowcaps on three points of the sky—and the daily view of these majestic natural deities became almost a necessity with me.

"In this same valley, a mile away, I found a neighbor to my liking—Johnny Magee, a little gnarled bobbin of a man with legs as twisted as thorn-wood shilalaghs, with eyes as bright and darting as a wren's. I'd bought a violin in San Francisco with which, on my way north, I'd earned extra money fiddling and singing. Johnny Magee also had a fiddle, and the two of us would sit up half the night together playing the old airs of home; the sad sweet airs of the transplanted Scots: 'Bonnie Doon,' 'Loch Liel,' the 'Castle of Montgomery,' and 'My Highland Laddie.' Sometimes when there was liquor to pour we'd fall to talking of home and even crying together a little over our common memories, for Johnny, too, had run away—from County Down—without saying any good-byes.

"Other nights we'd sit till dawn arguing. Although agreeing on most matters of importance, frequently we would split apart just for the sheer pleasure of trying to prove points to one another.

"Johnny called himself a Philosophical Anarchist—a designation he'd picked up from a wandering knife-and-scissors-grinder, a dedicated but irreligious anchorite, who slept, if he had to, in barns, or hollow trees, in squatters' cabins or abandoned sawmills. I'd heard a man in Belfast speak on Tolstoi, so I called myself a Christian Socialist. Our joint ideas on the subject of both anarchy and socialism were, at this time, warm, vigorous, and spiritedly held, but nebulous too, very nebulous, and youthfully short of the facts."

*

*

"Then I met Johnny's friend, the anarchist scissors-grinder—a man who was to have more effect on me than any other man in all my life. As I write these words I stop to consider them and I realize that they are true, deeply true. He was a figure of destiny in my life. He was, in a sense, the father from whom I had run away—my father without the curse of a habit he could not control.

"From the scissors-grinder I began to acquire my first information about a many-fronted political battle being waged far away—or so at first it seemed—from our green valley by the Indian river. Through his talk there ran the red thread of violence. Around names like Homestead, the McNamara Brothers, Coxey's Army, he began to weave a new kind of American legend for us, the two young Scotch-Irish dreamers seated so cosily in our log cabins with our tobacco and whiskey, our fiddles and our books. He had pictures to paint of a very different way of life in distant cities, like Pittsburgh, where men and women worked in intense heat and coal smoke, in the unrelieved noise of steam and machinery, twelve hours a day for barely enough money to live.

" 'But they're free, man,' Johnny would protest with lively irritation. 'They're free. Let 'em get out, come away to the West. Tom and I, we landed without a penny in our pockets, too.'

" 'Aye, but we were speaking English,' I would have to remind him.

" 'Right!' cried the scissors-grinder, pointing his index finger with its broken dirty nail, wagging it solemnly up and down. 'Right you are, Tom, my boy. These people are Poles, Slavs, Italians. Sometimes they don't complain because they can't complain. No words to express it. Nobody will savvy. Sometimes they're just docile. Dumb, driven cattle—that's the phrase for 'em.'

"He would close his lips over his broken teeth, nod his head savagely up and down; a man of secret anger, dark information: a man with disturbing facts and figures at his tongue's end.

Traveling the countryside to sharpen knives and scissors, he had also sharpened the hidden blade of his fury.

"'. . . And at any time,' he would cry, 'at the drop of a pin, because of some scheme of the big operators, without any notice at all, their wages can be stopped. And there they are! Caught with their wives and children! Free men, you say?'

"There were many times when his violent tirades frightened both of us more than we would admit. Johnny would try to hold back the tide of our growing fear by simple counter-arguments.

"'Sure,' he would say, soothingly, 'I always said there was something sick at the core in the East. Couldn't wait to get away from there myself, man. Corruption—it set in early there, with the big machines and a'.'

"'The machine is it!' the scissors-grinder would explode. He would close a fist and split the air in front of him with it. 'Machines have nothing to do with it, man. I've nothing at all against machines. Machines have the power to free every mother's son of us from a lot of useless moil.'

"I'd find my pipe growing cold in my hands as I was carried away into an eddy of disturbing private thoughts. I'd miss whole torrents of rolling monologue, would float back into the main current again when I heard the old man crying out in mockery, 'Panics! Panics! Now what do you think of that for a name. *Acts of God*, they try to tell us.' This was a cue for him to roll his eyes to the rafters, constrict his mouth into a caricature of unctuous piety, fold his hands as though in prayer, and then suddenly, beating a fist on the table's edge hard enough to set the spoons rattling in our tin coffee cups, he would cry, 'Acts of Man and Mammon, call them rather!'

"Or again, in the voice of some tent-traveling evangelist—for it was indeed a regular show he put on—he would exhort us, 'Ah, friends, my friends with blinders, right here in the green West, in God's own country, in the land of Milk and Honey, the Land of Promise, in the very suburbs of Beulah itself you might say—and bless you, brethren and sisters, and a very hearty Amen —what do you find if you have the wit to look?'

"'What?' I would demand, dreading to hear, feeling nonetheless that I must learn the truth, the whole truth. 'What do you find if you have the wit to look?'

"The scissors-grinder knew how to play out any scene he started. He would lower his voice, as though someone were stooped outside with an ear glued to the keyhole, and launch into stories of people forced off their fertile farmland in neighboring valleys by railroad attorneys, sometimes even by armed agents of the government—and he gave the word 'government' a nasty twang of disrespect. He spread before us, his already glutted friends, a feast of dark facts about the Monopolies, Trusts, Railroads: how they had acquired the best land and what dodges they used for avoiding taxation. With the sure strokes of a born narrator, he would describe the foreigners he had seen, lured by stereopticon slides and smooth talkers, traveling west, ever west, on railroad promises; day after day, crowded on the hard wooden benches in the oven of full summer, or the ice of winter, without water or proper food, neglected, fearful, coming finally to their golden destination only to find more hardships and all the bright promises dissolving into empty air.

" 'There's an old Oriental law,' he said once, half-closing his burning eyes with their overhang of gray hairs, dry and twisted like grass in late November, 'an Oriental Law called the Law of Karma.' (And here he commanded my whole attention, for about the spiritual findings of the Orient, I had already acquired more than a Presbyterian's curiosity.) 'The Law of Karma says: "What you do you must pay for." Nations as well as men. So at least I take it, and so I say, America will pay for what she has done—misleading, misguiding, the poor and humble of the earth. The innocent son's sons of these villains will pay for this, mark you! Pay dearly! And in bloodshed! Just as they will pay for the sins of their grandfathers, for bringing slaves from Africa to cast a shadow on a free land!'

"I can see him now, leaning back to catch his breath, filling his mouth with the heel of the loaf that rested before him, as though by stuffing his oral cavity he would prevent himself from speaking for a while and so give his audience a chance to question further.

"While Johnny spoke, frowning, arguing that every man had

the right of choice and he, for one, could not abide blaming others for his own stupidity and ill-luck, I would fill my pipe again and stare into the dying fire. The scissors-grinder listened to my friend Johnny in a mournful silence, as though all his own oratorical effort had been wasted. But when I spoke, what I said made him light up like a brand renewed in a bonfire.

"For I demanded, 'But what's to be done?' As I asked it I was already hating and fearing the possible answer, remembering how short a time before this bright expanding land had been to me only a half-explored road to adventure, the promise to be fulfilled just over the next hill, in the next valley, around the bend of the New Year.

" 'That's the lad!' the scissors-grinder cried, gratified, extending his hand as though about to offer a reward to a prize speller. 'What's to be done, Tom wants to know! I'll tell you what's to be done—what's been done and being done—right now by good stout fellows not unlike yourselves . . .'

"And he began to list off on his cracked finger ends: Coxey's Army, Knights of Labor, the Grange . . .

"My imagination was most deeply caught by the stories he had to tell about the loggers; about the new social yeast that had begun to work in them. I had often seen the 'bindlestiffs' walking the rough frontier roads, carrying their own bedding since none was anywhere provided for them. They were all big men, with strong swinging bodies and a free way of walking and talking, careless, bold, like what they were, men without ties, wanderers, following the forests deeper into the West. Looking at my own wiry frame, I had envied them their easy strength, just as, when a boy, I had envied the shaggy and robust gypsies I had met on the Irish roads with their painted caravans.

"But my kind of romantic notion about loggers was not to be tolerated, even for a moment, by the scissors-grinder. 'So you think it's a good and enviable life—the logger's life! Then, I say, go and look at them in the waterfront dives in the slack seasons—in Seattle, Tacoma—flophouse and saloon, no place else to go—waiting for a job, their money running out, hopeless, helpless, rotting their very guts out with bad liquor while they hang around until some big lumber interest decides to ruin another forest!'

"His words filled me with a somber, almost painful premonition. Now when I thought of the loggers and the devastation they had wrought at the bidding of men who never saw their work but lived by its profits, I began to feel a sickness rising in me. The green beauty of the forests and the youth of good men, both soiled and broken by the new country's greed. I had never thought about commerce in this way. I often wished the scissors-grinder would go away, or else stop talking.

"But the unkempt man with eyes like embers would not stop. Like the showman he was, he would only change the subject when he perceived us lapsing into the paralyzed silence that comes from the possession of stirring information on which there seems little chance to act. So he would divert us, entertain us, with extravagant fables from a distant world.

"Addressing the bottle, holding it to the light to measure the remaining contents before he poured himself a fresh drink, he would cry, 'High life, my boys, high life! Let's take a look at this so-called high life—high, that is, as opposed to *low*.' After a long pull at the whiskey, 'Item Number One—I read it with me own eyes in the public press. It's reported an eminent Eastern citizen gave a birthday party for his pet dog. Engraved invitations he sent out, he did. And the present for the dog—what do you think? A diamond collar, my boys, a diamond collar!'

"Johnny and I sat staring, disbelieving.

" 'And it's sorry I am not to be able to tell you the animal's breed. But I do know this for a fact: it was fifteen thousand dollars' worth of blinkin' rocks went into that collar!'

" 'Go on with you!' Johnny cried. 'Into a dog's collar?'

" 'Sure, sure, so why don't you laugh, lads? It's laughable, ain't it—the way the rich ones carry on. It's Babylon! That's what it is! Maybe you'd prefer to hear about the Ball on Horseback! They're all very sporting, these rich fellows, live right with their animals; make a big fuss over them, treat them just like humans—better maybe . . . Well, at this Ball on Horseback all the millionaires and their ladies went riding around indoors on their favorite mounts, each with a little table attached to the front of his saddle

—very ingenious it was—to be able to ride around guzzling champagne and eating truffles and God knows what all else kind of dainties.'

" 'Ah, no, now! It's the circus you're describing,' Johnny accused him.

" 'That's right, lad, the Roman circus!' The scissors-grinder nodded in corroboration, winking his hot eye at me as one student of history to another. 'Another civilization—patterned on Rome —that's what looks to be built up in this country! Culture's for sale to Americans they say now—in Europe. I hear there's a fine business in castle panelings, staircases, even whole rooms. If you've the money—and the wish—you can even transplant a private chapel across the Atlantic, stone by stone and beam by beam for your estate on the Hudson.'

" 'For the worship of God?' I cried, and then I could really laugh, for indeed all these stories of America's new millionaires seemed too ridiculous, too fanciful, to rouse any anger in me. At that time I could even find a certain grim humor in grand-scale robberies enabling a man to import a private chapel for the worship of the Christian God.

" 'I can see, Johnny,' I said, 'that if we take to robbery it mustn't be Jean Valjean's loaf of bread. We'd better make it all the copper in Montana or all the coal in Pennsylvania.'

" 'You've got it!' cried the scissors-grinder. 'That way you'll be hailed as a public benefactor. And your descendants—they'll be able to create the illusion of a fine and beautiful world—all in the image of special privilege.'

" 'Ah, well,' I would say, ready to have the subject dropped, reaching for a handy tolerant generalization, quoting Bobby Burns, ' "The rank is but the guinea's stamp, A man's a man for a' that." '

"But the scissors-grinder was not so readily soothed. 'For my taste there are better lines than those in Robert Burns—lines about the man who must "beg his lordly fellow worm to give him leave to toil." '

"And having offered this with a flat finality calculated to leave me and Johnny speechless, like as not the scissors-grinder would burst out singing some bitter and violent verses, the music familiar, sacred or nostalgic, but the words far from the spirit of 'Auld Lang Syne,' 'Washed in the Blood of the Lamb,' 'Nellie Gray.' When his voice cracked, or he had exhausted himself, he would shoulder his pack and little grinding-wheel and set off down the footpath by the river that led to the town.

"We often walked with him to where the forest began. On the way back, and for days afterwards, Johnny and I would find ourselves singing these songs with their childishly simple rhymes about 'workers uniting,' 'the death of labor's heroes,' 'the villainy of bosses.' "

*

*

"I suppose it was, in part, my natural Scotch respect for learning that made it impossible for me to dismiss the dirty talkative wanderer as an eccentric vagrant. It was curious, I thought, that the scissors-grinder, so violently anti-church, so insistent on being called a Philosophical Anarchist, seemed at heart a most spiritual man. His pack bulged with books by Swedenborg, Ingersoll, translations from the Orient—China, India. Many of these books he lent me, and I read their unfamiliar pages eagerly, finding in them arguments to bolster my own secretly held conviction that all men in their searchings for truth must, inevitably, come upon the same basic answers, no matter what religion or race has formally claimed them.

"If this was true, if the same tenets of relationship—man to man, Man to God—lay beneath all religious faiths, what then did it mean to be a Christian? This question began to possess my whole mind and heart. To my astonishment I found that the scissors-grinder did not consider the Bible sacred. To him it was merely a compendium of folk literature, ranging from passionate and enduring prophecy and doctrine, to meaningless local and tribal incidents; a book of oracles, riddles, poetry, erotica, battle hymns, angry and tender monologues and dialogues dealing with murder, lust, love . . .

" 'The one great thing about the Bible—this translation,' he was fond of saying, 'is that there were fifty-four different men

to be found, alike enough in thought and speech to create the
beauties of the King James version. There's mystery for you.
There's brotherhood—of a real sort, man! And the language—
sure, the beauty of Biblical language is not to be excelled, man.
Not anywhere!'

"When he spoke directly of Christ, which was frequently, the
scissors-grinder made a point of stressing His plainer aspects.
He always referred to Him as "Jesus, the Galilean carpenter."
To be sure, he granted Him special gifts—gifts of spiritual understanding, of homely wisdom, even of supersensibility, but he
pointed out that these gifts were only comparable to special
musical or mathematical endowment in other men.

"It was precisely here that I fell into doubt, brooding, ponder-
ing. I was a good student of the Bible, like my father before me,
able to out-quote, if not out-think, the scissors-grinder on this
subject, yet his talk troubled me.

" 'I agree, yes,' I would begin, hesitantly. 'Between me and the
Source—whatever that Source may be—I, too, want no mediator,
no hierarchy, no priests, but . . .' Here I would founder.

" 'Man, it's a philosophical anarchist you are!' Johnny would
shout in triumph. 'Make no mistake about it!'

" 'Maybe it's a Buddhist he is,' the scissors-grinder would suggest, never revealing whether this comment was to confound me
further or point a new way.

"So I would sit, knuckles to chin, ignoring them both, searching. 'I'm a man,' I would bring out at last. 'That's it, and the
whole of it, and it's all to be found in the seventh chapter of the
Wisdom of Solomon—and a shame it is to have to look for it in
the Apocrypha and not in the Bible itself.'

"And dropping my eyelids, because the words moved me
enough to shamefully mist my eyes and send my voice down into
my chest, I would recite:

" 'I myself also am a mortal man, like to all . . . And when I
was born I drew in the common air, and fell upon the earth, which
is of like nature, and the first voice I uttered was crying, as all
others do . . . For all men have one entrance into life, and the
like going out. Wherefore I prayed, and understanding was given

me; I called upon God, and the spirit of wisdom came to me. I preferred her above sceptres and thrones, and esteemed riches nothing in comparison to her . . . I loved her above health, and beauty, and chose to have her instead of light; for the light that cometh from her never goeth out. All good things together came to me with her, and innumerable riches in her hands. For she is a treasure unto men that never faileth; which they that use become the friends of God.'

" 'Man, man, the beauty of it!' I would cry, springing up, filled with the power of the words. 'I'm telling you Shakespeare himself never equalled it—not even in Shylock's speech which says it too: "For hath not a Jew hands, organs, dimensions, senses, affections, passions . . ."' And I would continue my quoting, playing my themes back and forth between Shakespeare and Solomon, wedding them into a single symphony for my own, and, I hoped, for my friends', pleasure.

" 'You should have been a preacher, Thomas, that's a fact,' Johnny would say to me, almost in awe.

" 'Aye, I might have made a fair one,' I would admit, 'but my father wouldn't hear of it. A godless man—so they thought him. Too much John Knox in his youth, I suspect. Aye, I've come from a long line of preachers and rebels. Bad cess to them a'.' And I would laugh and pour myself a little more from the bottle."

*

*

"So the time in the green Western valley went by.

"With so many problems of a philosophical and spiritual nature to work on, neither Johnny nor I considered taking any routine job to waste our energies. Not but what we were willing to work hard at our own self-appointed tasks. I built my own cabin, set out fruit trees, put in a garden, got a horse and buckboard, chickens and a cow. Although the outlay took most of my San Francisco savings, I had, as yet, no real worries. The Far West was still a land of easy plenty: trout in every stream, salmon in every river at the seasons' turns, and plenty of deer, partridge, quail. Once a month I drove to town to get such staples as flour and sugar, coffee, whiskey and books. The rest of my needs I supplied myself.

"The nearest town had begun as a settlement around a tidewater sawmill. It was first called Crockett's Dream, after a wandering Maine sea captain by that name who had put in there from Hong Kong, found his wife waiting, and stayed on. It became the site of a tidewater sawmill and so changed its name to Crockett's Mill. Finally, when in the late Eighties, Cyrus Bachelder, a man of capital originally 'from the East,' selected it for the main office of his growing lumber operations it was called simply Milltown. Milltown it has been ever since.

"The social life of Milltown when I first encountered it was pleasant and democratic. The community possessed briefly an aura of what might, in time, have become a local culture—with the proper kind of interest and direction; which, to be sure, it never got. Milltown had its Reading Society, its Choral Society, its Debating Society. There were house raisings, harvesting 'bees,' weddings, picnics by steam launch on the adjoining bay, church socials. I began to find myself in demand on these occasions because of my fiddle, my singing voice, my memory for verse; even though my ways were believed by some—so I learned later—to be downright irregular; my ideas often verging dangerously near heresy. Also I was nearing thirty and not yet married.

"My cash supply, brought with me from San Francisco, was beginning to dwindle and I had need to supplement it in some way. So I decided to take a position teaching in the Milltown Seminary: Latin, Elocution and Mathematics. This seemed to me preferable to lending myself to any one of the various enterprises that local commerce offered. I had no talent for the prescribed ways of making money and I was perfectly willing to admit it—disgraceful as that kind of confession was in a growing American community.

"It was inevitable that I should come to know Flora Bachelder. I first met her old grandmother, who had traveled all the way from a fine house of strawberry-colored brick on a High Street in a Massachusetts town, to live out her days with her son Cyrus, who had electrified every branch of the family by going West to 'grow up with the country' and further surprised them all—

except his adoring mother—by making a fortune while at it. When Cyrus' wife—of Missouri ancestry on the wrong side of the Civil War—died suddenly, Hannah Bachelder, now a widow, packed up and left for the West to help her son rear his family —two grown boys and a near-grown daughter.

"Since Hannah Bachelder was a feminist, she naturally couldn't miss a debate in the town hall on the subject of the rights of women. I had the affirmative that night: 'Resolved: Women Must and Will Have the Vote.' I leaned rather heavily on Scripture, as I recall—knowing the kind of audience I was facing. I remember saying that even St. Paul, who had caused no small amount of trouble with his remarks on women, had gone so far as to state, 'Ye are all children of God. There is neither Jew nor Greek, neither slave nor free, neither male nor female, but all are one in Christ Jesus.'

"There was a round of applause at that, led by a stocky but imposing old lady in the front row. I looked right down at her and smiled, and I saw beside her the pretty girl I already knew was Flora Bachelder, Cyrus Bachelder's only daughter. I found their presence inspiring and I spoke with particular zest. I argued that the emergence of all creatures from slavery into light and equality was undoubtedly a Christian precept. Such Christian law had already freed the Negroes—and must certainly in time free women. This made a strong appeal to Hannah Bachelder— coming as she did from a line of New England Abolitionists.

"When I finished by saying: 'Your children and grandchildren will live to see women voting everywhere; *everywhere*: China, Italy, France—certainly throughout all of America and Great Britain,' Hannah could hardly contain herself. She rushed forward to be the first to grasp my hand when the debate was over. She presented me to her shy granddaughter and invited me to Sunday dinner. I had a feeling the young girl was a little nervous about the invitation. Later Flora told me what subsequently went on at home. She had said to her grandmother, 'I don't believe Papa knows Mr. Stewart.' 'What of that?' said the old lady. 'None of us does. That's why I invited him.' 'But you know how Papa feels about Irishmen, Grandma.' 'Of course I do. Just like his father before him.' For Hannah's dead husband, Cyrus

Bachelder's father, a New England gentleman, had been one
who worried excessively about the inrush of 'Shanty Irish,' the
Papists. He was afraid of the hold they were getting on Boston—
that stronghold of the one true Americanism. He had even been
haunted, according to Hannah, by images of the Swiss Guard, in
all their outlandish finery, posted, in time, outside Faneuil Hall.
Yes, Hannah Bachelder knew plenty about the prejudice against
the Irish. 'But Mr. Stewart's *Ulster* Irish, Flora dear. He said he
came from the North, from Antrim. He's Presbyterian Irish, Flora
dear, Scotch-Irish,' and to Flora's astonishment she laughed out
loud and quoted some remark she'd heard I'd made to the effect
that 'the wheelbarrow was one of the greatest inventions since
it taught the native Irish to walk on their hind legs.' Flora told
me later she thought the remark very coarse and was amazed at
her grandmother's pleasure in it.

" 'What does the fellow do?' Cyrus Bachelder wanted to know
of Flora, less interested in my racial background than in specific
and more tangible facts.

" 'He lives outside town somewhere,' Flora told me she had
put in, timidly.

" 'Homesteader?' her father had growled. This, I was to learn,
was with Cyrus Bachelder a term of final social opprobrium, de-
scriptive of those unambitious fellows who chose an irregular
independent way of life rather than making themselves a part of
some established business enterprise.

"The discovery that this was true—that I had indeed lived for
some years on a homestead and continued to do so, even while
I taught at the seminary—did not dampen Hannah's ardor over
my political and social sentiments."

*

*

"I began to go regularly to the big house across the bay. I, the
young upstart from Ballymeaney, struck it off at once with the
fiery old woman from Massachusetts. Hannah was dying for talk;
talk of something other than buying and selling, prices and
costs. Even the Unitarianism of one branch of her mother's

family had prepared her for my religious doubts and deviations. I was perfectly honest with her from the start. 'I was brought up a Presbyterian,' I said, 'but now I can't be one—not any denomination. It goes against my grain. Let men worship God any way they choose. The important thing is to let them choose.'

"These were happy days for me—so long used to 'batching,' taking care of myself. The Bachelder home had a special atmosphere. It smelled of dried rose leaves, of Japanned boxes, of imported tea, of starched white curtains and—faintly—of the very best tobacco. There was nothing pleasanter than sitting with the old woman in that transplanted New England parlor of a Sunday, talking on any subject that came into our minds, while Flora sat by, saying nothing, listening quietly, making French knots in embroidery.

"Toward evening Cyrus Bachelder, who spent his Sunday afternoons in his den with a newspaper over his face and his dog under his chair, snoring off his big midday meal, would often come into the parlor and ask for music. I would get my violin from the case, Flora would sit down at the piano and we would all sing—'Old Black Joe,' 'Swanee River,' 'Nelly Gray.' Even Flora's brothers, lofty young men who had been 'East to school' to satisfy their grandmother's ideas of polish, would frequently join in.

"Between the keen old woman with her eager mind and quick tongue, and the pretty young Flora with her soft glance and yielding ways, I began to think I had found what I was long looking for. I could sense that her grandmother's admiration for me and enjoyment of my company had begun to have their effect on Flora.

"And surely there would have been no one in the countryside to deny that aiming as high as Flora Bachelder was a bold stroke for a young man with no 'prospects' and nothing to recommend him but his charm. Yet Johnny Magee doubted my judgment. Johnny began with gloom and ended with insults on the one occasion of my speaking about it.

" 'Remember, it's not the old woman you're marrying. And the young one—she's not the lass for you, man.'

" 'And why not?' I demanded to know.

" 'She won't like your life, the way you want to live. She's spoiled. You're spoiled, too. You've been your own master too many years. But she—she's her father's darlin'. I've never seen it work, nor am I ever likely to. She won't want to live out here, so far from town, such a delicate young lass.'

" 'Plenty of others have.'

" 'Not that one.'

" 'She says she will.'

" 'Oh, aye, for a year.'

" 'Then what?'

" 'Then she'll heckle you, man. She's bound to. You'll end in the pay of Cyrus Bachelder and tight in his fist, too, I doubt not.'

" 'It's a taste of fist you're wanting right now, I'm thinking,' I cried. I struck my best friend with my closed hand and walked off, not looking back.

"Next morning, on my way to church (I had taken to going to Presbyterian services again since knowing Flora as it gave me an excuse to speak to her outside the Episcopalian church after services—and maybe get a dinner invitation) I came upon Johnny sleeping off his Saturday night on the edge of the woods. The church bells were rolling the warm air in curved cadences; it was spring and I was in love, yet my heart sank at sight of my friend. I remembered with burning shame the blow I had struck. That I should have struck a friend for offering an honest word! What kind of violence was this! (These are the things in a long lifetime of mistakes that burn the deepest and sear the memory.)

"That Sunday morning I stood gazing down at Johnny whose whiskey snoring—a thin whine—threaded almost pitifully in and out of the lilt of bird songs in the morning woods. I loved and pitied him then—knowing he was doomed to loneliness all his life. I looked about for some token to lay near him to let him know when he woke that I had been past. I found a four-leaf clover and thrust it into the half-clenched hand.

"Our friendship did not suffer, though our intimacy did. Somehow the shadow Johnny had cast on my mind with his suspicions I could not entirely shake off."

*

*

"But there was no turning back now. Before the summer was out I had begun, on the darkened terrace, behind the Bachelders' cedar hedge cut in the shape of a nesting bird, to kiss the frightened but responsive lips of Flora. And at last the day came when I faced Cyrus Bachelder in his downtown office and asked for his daughter's hand.

"Cyrus, leaning back heavily in his swivel chair, under brown-tinted photographs—the biggest tree his men had ever cut; Indians riding ponies into the sunset; his great-grandfather's house in faraway Massachusetts—was obviously prepared for the visit. His mother, I suspected, had been talking to him. She, I knew, approved the marriage. I did not believe that Cyrus would understand it at all. As a practical man he would surely recognize that I was a bad risk as a son-in-law—knowing more about Latin and poetry than about making money, or even saving it; having indeed, so I had told them all myself, nothing but a small amount of it hidden behind a brick in my fireplace, and this in spite of my nearing the end of my twenties.

"But evidently Hannah had worked hard on him, for Cyrus said to me that day, like a man bowing wearily to a willful child's fate, Yes, he was prepared to give his consent. But there were considerations. He wanted his daughter in town; his son-in-law employed in some regular business.

" 'You mean I'm to stop teaching in the winters?' I asked.

"Cyrus Bachelder made a brief gesture of corroboration, then quickly qualified the gesture. Let no one, he said, speak in his presence of the unimportance of education. Like all New Englanders he was proud to say he saw in it the backbone of a free and democratic country. Without education how could the foreign-born be trained in the American point of view, the historic traditions? Yes, indeed, he favored education—but it was for other men to give their lives to. He could see at a glance that his future son-in-law, Thomas Cameron Stewart, was not wholly the teaching type.

"Could he? The observation made me laugh inside. Instructing at the Seminary was hardly what I had thought of as 'teaching': Latin—poked arbitrarily down the throats of young men and women who had no use for it or pleasure in it; Elocution—'The Prisoner of Chillon,' 'Curfew Shall Not Ring Tonight'; Mathematics—well, there I had found myself less gifted than a number of my pupils.

"When I made no protest to Cyrus' statement he assumed we were agreed. Teaching was out! But he had a fine alternative to offer, a job in the mill office. When I asked him, 'What kind of job?' he was reassuring, but vague. He said he hadn't got it quite worked out—but I needn't worry about it; just trust him; he could use another man close in the business with him and his two sons. I could go up as fast as I chose.

"When I said I was sorry but I couldn't bring myself to work in the mill office, Cyrus Bachelder was both amazed and affronted. The more I tried to explain how I felt about it the more baffled and angry he became. For one thing, I was made to understand, no one ever turned aside lightly an offer of any kind from C. D. Bachelder. Finally I had to say that I had talked it over with Flora; that I had explained to her that I wanted to be 'free'; be my own master. He had a good snort at that word 'free,' but I stood up to him as best I could, telling him I didn't want my life cut up at some other man's will into little chunks and fragments of time. I wanted to stay on my own homestead which offered, I thought, a fair living, if well handled, and surely one of the best possible ways of life. Flora, I told him, had agreed to give it at least two years.

"It did Cyrus Bachelder no good to argue. Even Hannah's private misgivings, her argument to me that homesteading already belonged to the past—could not sway me. I was determined to stay where I was, and show Flora life through my eyes. And at that time Flora had the quiet courage born of first love. She said she wanted to do what I wanted, and that was the end of it."

*

*

(Philip looked up again. He had come to a break in the narrative. It was as though his father had marked a pause in his thoughts, arbitrarily, by leaving blank pages, though the writing continued further on. Philip was aware now that he was trembling slightly. There was still a faint fluttering sensation in his stomach, half-anticipation, half-unease, at having so far invaded without permission, his father's privacy.

How was it, he asked himself, that he could have had so little curiosity until now about the life of the man who was his father? Was it because of the neglected kinship between them, the unadmitted mystery of the bond of their common blood that he found himself so moved by this chronicle of chance, ill-luck, opportunity, love, sorrow—all the trials and experiences of living that, in some degree, were parts of every man's journey?

He heard a noise outside and started guiltily. Hastily he put the book under his pillow, rose and tiptoed to the window. It couldn't be his father back yet—then who? He stood looking a long time, immobile beside the window, but saw only the two gulls on the pilings and, nearer, a busy brown bird making a commotion in the salal beside the cabin.

When he had decided that it was probably the bird that was responsible for the noise he returned once more to his reading.)

*

*

"Since I first began to observe myself with the kind of eye I might bend on a stranger, I have been aware of a certain inner struggle, an eternal imbalance in my soul, a contention between the idle dreamer and the man who wants an answer. This inner struggle I have, upon occasion, attributed to my mixed environment, tangled in my youth in all that shimmer of Druid and faery, priest and lover, of ancient Eire, drowned in all the soughing poesy of her many legendary sorrows, solved in dream and violence; Scotch by blood and so chilled with the unyielding granite of those people from the high glens and fog-wrapped hills, those men who, like my father and his father before him, looked not for signs like faery rings on the lea or little men under a waterfall, or a saint who could give a wink or turn a miracle, but who had to have it worked out in man's own unbalanced ledger, his overdue account with God, an account to be reckoned only with his own conscience beside his own hearth and there dealt with personally without intercessor of any kind . . . Aye, war, war forever—so it sometimes seemed to me in my youth, and sometimes still does.

"Now that I was married, however, no doubt of it, I was, at first, all Irish: poet, singer and lover. I taught Flora to sing the wailing tender songs of the Old Country. I taught her the Irish Reel and the Highland Fling and—daringly—the taste of whiskey —a wee sippit in a medicine glass. I taught her to lie in the grass, to give herself to green slopes and the smell of clover, to forget ants and bees and all invisible things that creep secretly through the weeds, and to yield herself entirely to the lonely sundrenched landscape where we made love.

"Had there been longer before the first child, I believe Flora might never have slipped back into her staid New England ways. But with the second year there was a baby on its way and I had used up most of my money: used it for a new carpet and a brooch for my wife, a set of Carlyle and sundry other matters not easy to explain to my father-in-law, tapping the desk edge with blunt impatient fingers.

"Flora must come to town to have the baby, Cyrus insisted. Hannah backed him up. I was perfectly willing, wanting it even, having begun to feel afraid of the ordeal through which I knew I must soon pass. But Flora, as though with some intimation of what lay ahead on the hidden path of our life, could not bear to leave this spot in which she had known her first freedom and passion. She waited too long, and the wild ride we made in the buckboard through the dark night on the miry roads, with Flora moaning and, in the end, screaming . . .

*

*

"The baby was born dead. A boy, 'So like his grandfather,' everyone said.

"Flora recovered slowly. It was spring and I put in a late garden, coming into Milltown as often as I could to sit in Flora's room at her father's house and try to interest her again in living. Spring deepened into summer and I tried to insist that Flora return to the homestead. I believed the sight of the familiar places—the trees we had planted the month we were married, the big rock and the sunning hideaways, the banks on which we had lain in the clover-scented late afternoons—would restore her spirit. Flora listened to my pleadings without response. Finally she said, sobbing, that she did not want to leave her father's house again. And now no one supported me, not even Hannah.

"And this was a mystery—the change in the old woman's attitude. In her presence I found myself now inarticulate and ill-at-ease. It was—I felt—as though she blamed me for the whole tragedy of our baby's birth and death; not openly, a tacit criticism. I felt the two women arrayed against me; locked together in some speechless protest. Were they linked by the ageless anger, heavy and secret, of the passive female for the aggressor male? The thought occurred to me, but I was unwilling to accept such a generalization.

"I desired, above all things, to break down this mysteriously erected barrier. I would go out in the twilight and walk on the grassy terrace of Cyrus Bachelder's garden, hoping Hannah would come out and join me, as she often had in the past. Then I could link my arm through hers and say, 'Old woman, don't harbor dark secrets. Don't shut me out. If I've done wrong, help me to understand how.'

"But only the starched lace curtains trembled with her watching presence; the front door did not once open and close on her stocky body. I walked alone, bitter now in my loneliness. Could this be the same woman who had professed to me her belief in the equality of the sexes? Where was the equality, if women could still retreat together into some impenetrable fastness of blood, birth, tears, and moon rhythms to which no man might ever find access? Where had she disappeared, the keen old woman who so admired Margaret Fuller, who had dared to entertain Frances Wright, that bold advocate of birth control and the rights of women?

"Though, finally, I had to relinquish hope of support from the grandmother, I continued to try to persuade Flora to return to the homestead. When, at last, she consented, there was no joy in her return, for I found her trying to avoid the familiar places, as if the very memories were unbearable since the fruit of those hours of love had come to her only to die. She still found it impossible to accept the hard, the apparently meaningless, reality of the experience of bearing a dead child.

" 'But there will be others,' I would assure her. 'We are young, Flora. All of our life lies ahead of us.'

"She was not comforted. She seemed almost to resent the possibility of other children who might live, since the first one had not.

"Then I would lie alone by the dark river in the night-time seeking an answer, wanting, demanding something that went deeper and fed the heart more profoundly than the cold comfort of funeral scripture, 'The Lord giveth and the Lord taketh away.' Listening to the flow of the water over the rocks I would argue with myself. 'But passion must always bear death, for life itself bears it; it is the other face of life.' And I would ponder the mystery of the Word made flesh. 'Whoso eateth not my flesh and drinketh not my blood hath not eternal life.' Was this, then, to say that through flesh only might one come to that beyond flesh? Yes, surely this must be it—and for a moment the joy of a new understanding would flash through me. But there was no one with whom I could share this revelation.

"There was Johnny down the road—but we had quarreled over Flora, and anyway Johnny had never known what I had known with my wife. How could he—a wandering man never having a woman for more than a night? I often thought of the scissors-grinder whom I had not seen in a long time. Would he understand? It was not likely. The scissors-grinder was more concerned with the injustice of man to man than with the poetic torment of bloom and death, the mysterious source of the maiming will-to-destroy that lies hidden like a two-edged sword between men and women.

"My loneliness in those months seemed almost beyond bearing. I was never to be so lonely again—even living as a solitary on a remote sea-ringed island. Night after night I dreamt of my birthplace. I would see myself driving up to the door to present my first-born child to my mother. I would uncover its face and expose a skull; waken sickened, full of a guilt I could neither shake off nor understand. (Now to be sure, looking back I can say: How could you understand—you who were seeing for the first time at close hand—and all unprepared as we always are—those dark paradoxical affinities: Love-Anger, Birth-Death?)"

*

*

"Because Flora was still underweight, melancholy and quick to tears, the doctor had said there should be no more children for some time. He was not definite about it. He refused, indeed, to be specific; he merely gave forth his dictum, and I can see him now, closing with a cool indifferent click the lock of his sausage-shaped bag.

"Since no alternative was offered I practiced continence. Months passed. I determined at last that I would go to Hannah and insist she speak openly with me about the problem—since I could get nowhere with Flora. The very day I decided, Hannah had her first 'stroke.' She never spoke again.

"As a consequence of her grandmother's illness, Flora went once more to her father's house. In desperation, I called alone on the family doctor. What solution Doctor Tillney offered a desperate husband does not matter now, but I slammed out of his office, closing the door hard behind me. Walking away I said to myself I had been a lover once and I would be a lover again.

"I drove my wife home from her father's house on a night heavy with the aphrodisiac of blooming trees. Fortifying myself with Irish whiskey I took her against her will—to my eternal and undying shame—and out of this night of anguish and misunderstanding our daughter was conceived. Jane was born at her grandfather's in the upstairs east bedroom that had been her mother's in girlhood. She entered the world just at the moment her great-grandmother—blind now, and speechless—left it."

*

*

"After Jane was born, I yielded without further struggle to Flora's insistence that I sell the homestead. She had a right now to ask a sacrifice of me—and she did. We went to live in a little house near town, on land which Cyrus had offered us when we were first married. It was land from which, long ago, he had cut all the big trees. I accepted a job in the mill office, and determined to do my best to act as though I considered figures pertaining to lumber footage of eternal and lasting importance.

"Though I did not know as much then as I now know about the methods of the big timber interests and how they misused their power to ruin the land for generations to come—if not for-ever—I knew enough to realize that I had to put on blinders—and so for a time I did.

"Not that I didn't argue with Cyrus. Ah, no! We spent many a Sunday evening battling rather than singing. Much as Flora hated these arguments, she came in time to wish that her father's resounding bellows and my table-thumpings had continued. At least then he had considered me worthy of his best argumentative skills; had not dismissed me with silent contempt as merely one of a growing body of gadfly 'cranks' setting ourselves up as critics of the current social and economic order.

"Cyrus sincerely believed in his way of life. When I described monopolistic abuses and misuses—from my viewpoint—he would counter, 'What's wrong with any of that? It helped populate the land out here, didn't it? How else would you get six thousand people at a clip to cross the Rockies into unknown country?' I would say: 'Once you get them out here on false pretenses and promises, don't you owe them anything?' 'What?' he would de-mand in sincere exasperation. 'Tell me what! In God's name what? You've given them a chance—as good a chance as the next man—by making jobs for them. They're better off by far than if they'd stayed behind in the old countries.'

"While talking, Cyrus had an irritating way of fingering, one by one, the heavy links of the chain that festooned his sagging abdomen. Sometimes it seemed to me like a fourteen-karat rosary of Yankee aphorisms, particularly when he was chanting his copybook litany: 'You can't keep a good man down.' 'Always room at the top.' 'Time is money.' 'Competition is the life-blood of industry.' These were his stock answers to any criticism of the hurly-burly looting of the new country.

"For Flora's sake, I closed my mind and my mouth as best I could. I did my office stint doggedly, longing for five o'clock when I could ride my bicycle swiftly home to tend my bees and my garden. Only there did I feel at all alive. I grafted fruit trees, gathered eggs, picked berries, talked to my wife at suppertime about the mysteries of the queen bee and the drone ant, the polite manners of the cedar waxwing, the courtship habits of the mallard duck—all the many things I'd begun to learn in the days and nights on the homestead beside the river.

"At these times Flora was proud of me. 'Oh, Tom, how much you know!' 'I know nothing,' I would tell her. 'How can you say such a thing?' she would cry. 'There's not a person in Milltown, maybe in the whole state, that knows what you know.' And then I would see in her eyes the troubled question, why her husband could not put to better profit all his special gifts of memory and mimicry, the accumulation of curious information. Why was it that these particular traits seemed so useless in a booming pioneer society? What was my lack, my fatal weakness? Alas, I could not tell her, for I did not know myself. I knew only that I felt myself standing still; that nothing within me seemed really alive or used; that my life seemed to me to be flowing by like the river beside the homestead, leaving no mark as it passed.

"Yet I could not give myself to the quick greedy grab, or to the tight, well-laid plans, the careful schemes and enterprises of the prosperous world forming around us. This attitude toward life sickened and repelled me, and since I had no aptitude, or stomach for it, I finally withdrew and resigned myself to the role of observer, a move that, in time, earned me the doubtful designation of 'local eccentric.'

*

*

"On the day our daughter Jane was three, Flora gave her her first birthday party. It was at her grandfather's house. After it was over I went up with Flora to help put the little girl to bed. I remember now standing gazing down at the dark, warm, stubborn little face, thinking about the Spanish-Irish and wondering how else to account for her look. I caught the smile of love for her child on Flora's face and for the first time I dared to ask, 'Are you glad you had her?' Flora flushed and turned away, but she nodded—and I caught her to me and whispered into her hair, 'Oh, Flora, Flora, love me, forgive me!'

"And so that very night our son Philip was conceived out of a renewal of tenderness and trust. For this child Flora planned with joy. I know now that the babe in her womb seemed to her the fruit of our reconciliation, a promise for our future. That the child had been conceived in her father's house seemed to her, perhaps, an added blessing."

*

*

(Philip had to stop; had to get up, move his body. He took a nervous turn to the window and back, trying to avert the in-rush of some emotion he could not analyze; a mixture of awe and apprehension rising from the thought: "Now I am born. My parents have conceived me. My mother has borne me." "The babe in her womb—our son, Philip"; mysteriously compounded of Bachelder and Stewart and all the rest of those nameless ancestral "personalities," fading with the fixed spacing of generations, back into the oblivion of farthest time. In this instant Philip experienced a compelling sense of himself, of that living biological and psychical entity, inheritor of countless syntheses and affinities, emerging at last into this unique mystery, his own being. "A promise for our future." The words—reread—frightened him. He was glad to turn the page.)

*

*

"It was later that our real quarrels began.

"Their most apparent source lay in our difference of opinion about the scissors-grinder, a controversy which reflected, over a period of time, deeper, more fundamental differences between us; differences which, once a source of attraction, became, instead, a source of friction.

"My wandering friend had returned to the West and I insisted on inviting him for a meal to welcome him back. After that first time Flora always fought having him. She said he was a hobo. She hinted darkly that he was probably even a 'Wobbly'—the most dreaded name in her, or her father's vocabulary—a word beginning before the First World War to carry sinister weight in the Pacific Northwest.

"But if Flora opposed the presence of the scissors-grinder at our table she could not prevent my seeing him elsewhere. He would come and sit sometimes in my own orchard, or I'd meet him at a loggers' hall, or in the hobo jungle outside town. The old man was as fierce and fiery as ever. Now the flow of his anecdotes seemed to me—viewed from my new position as married man and responsible citizen with growing children and thus with a real stake in my country's future—more fearful, more challenging than ever before.

"The scissors-grinder had just returned from a long trek, as far as the Atlantic seaboard and back again, picking up tales as he went, in hobo jungles, at backdoors from Massachusetts to Montana, in the saloons and cheap flophouses of industrial centers. He had witnessed free-speech fights in Pennsylvania, New Jersey, California, Washington, and to supplement his observations, he carried with him a battered manila envelope full of newspaper accounts, clipped in each case, to what he called the 'true facts.'

"Yes, the facts! Everyone had the 'facts'—the only trouble was that one set of facts had nothing to do, as far as I could see, with another set of facts.

"There was my father-in-law, doubling up his right hand into a soft white fist, crying, 'Don't you try to whitewash those damned radicals to me!' There was the old scissors-grinder splitting the empty air with his fist and demanding, 'Stop them be-

fore it is too late, the greedy monsters, the heartless, evil de-
stroyers of the land that has been Europe's dream.'

"And then the image of my own father, sitting in his dusty
stale room in Ballymeaney, with its eternal look of disorder and
decay, smelling of the spirits with which he had tried to ease
his troubled mind, would rise before me.

" 'Sit down, lad,' I would hear him saying, pointing to the
shabby leather chair, 'sit down and listen while I read you a
pope's encyclical—a pope's encyclical against democracy.'

"I've never forgotten that papal phrasing—those astoundingly
bigoted and fearful words uttered by the head of Catholic Chris-
tendom—in which Democracy was described as 'that unbridled
liberty out of harmony, not only with the Christian law, but with
natural law also.'

" '*Christian* law!' my father had roared, striking the table until
his pipe-rack clattered to the floor. '*Natural* law! Now what the
bugger might that be, lad—*natural* law?' Tears ran from his eyes
into the stubble of graying hairs on his unshaved chin. 'Fight it,
lad, fight it for all you're worth! It's the oldest fight there is,
the right to think your own thoughts, speak your own words.
Do you hear me, lad?'

" 'Yes, Father,' I said, but I glanced quickly away from the
constricted face, longing only for escape from the stale room. I
saw the spider's lair under my father's table, the mummy flies
wrapped in the enemy-woven shrouds, waiting to be devoured.
How often this image, stamped upon my youthful consciousness,
has returned to my mind in later years: my father engaged in
fierce solitary encounter with the Church of Rome, the flies, the
spider, under the table—a tenuous symbolism here expressed;
one that I could not now, in Milltown, consider valid. For was
it not true that the Protestants who had supported democracy
when the Church of Rome had denied it, had nonetheless, become in time, History's fool, accepting the role of unquestioning
espousal of a society founded on freebootery, a social order where
to be able to amass money, to 'get ahead' was taken as a direct
sign of God's personal favor? Where, in such a scheme, could be
fitted those sayings about non-possession and poverty of the
original Christian—Jesus Christ himself? Oh, aye, these were

questions big enough to split open a man's heart. Aye, and his head, too, for that matter.

"Every Sunday before we went in to dinner with Cyrus Bachelder, Flora would pluck at my sleeve and beg with her dark eyes, 'Please, please, don't upset Papa today.' And I, remembering my own pleading hand on my own father's sleeve in the dusty twilight of my boyhood, would promise and try to keep the promise.

"But when I saw my father-in-law at table, reaching out for two more bloody slices of beef and a scrap or two of the forbidden crackling, his heavy jowl hanging down to his stiff collar like a separate face, like Face Number Two—it seemed to me—so much blind pendulous flesh, without eyes or mouth, but alive, and the embodiment of the greed, the slackened discipline he brought to his ample table three times a day (where he practiced the candid gluttony of one who has no other vices), then I would turn away trembling with an almost irresistible wish to plant doubt, like a worm, in this swollen fruit."

*

*

"Nothing in her lifetime, not even my faltering attempts to tell her about conditions around her, could ever possibly have prepared Flora for what finally happened. She knew, of course, that tension between owners and workers was rising. She knew her father had been given permission to arm himself when he went to his lumber camps. She knew that in nearby towns there had been violence—even, after the war, one shameful fracas in which men were killed, mutilated in ways only to be whispered. But somehow, in spite of my stated viewpoint and the dangerous friends I'd made, it was all remote from the little white cottage where she minded our two children, scolded, wept, sang, snatched moments of joy from nature: the first snowdrops (her favorite flower) pushing through the cold earth, the stars of Bethlehem hiding in the tangled grass, the flushed pink swell of peaches ripening in the orchard. Perhaps even under the chilly front she now invariably showed me, there was a woman who sighed at memory of the days when I had been content to lie by the hour in a field of clover, reciting verse while she plaited a wreath from the pink and white blossoms.

"The truth was, that though I had kept it from her, I was playing an ever more lively part in the organization of citizens' protest meetings. And on the one night that forever altered our lives I had gone to one of these meetings in a ramshackle hall down on the waterfront.

"I was on my feet speaking when the police and their 'special deputies' broke in.

"I remember well what I was saying, for I saw them enter, and their presence gave me added fire. 'I'll get in a lick or two before they break us up,' I said to myself, and I shouted aloud: 'There was plenty of talk to striking men about patriotism and un-Americanism during the war. Who talked about the *patriotism* of the lumber profits that were made then by a few timber barons? Is there patriotism in wartime profiteering? How do they explain the fact that, during the war, spruce shot up from sixteen dollars a thousand to sixteen hundred dollars a thousand? Who profited by that plunder? Not you, certainly—not even indirectly—though that's what the newspapers will try to tell you. Not you, and certainly not our country. No, this country and all its citizens— except for a handful of the rich—are the poorer for that plunder.'

"A cheer went up. Everyone present knew, some had even personally witnessed, the shameful waste and denuding of the last great spruce forests of the Pacific Northwest during World War One. There was stamping, howling, pounding of chair legs. The special deputies—ordinary citizens of the town, armed for the 'emergency'—moved forward with their guns and clubs, Flora's brothers among them.

" 'Break it up, boys! The meeting's over. Break it up! Clear the hall! Get out now. Go on home.'

" 'Home!' somebody yelled. 'You mean that stinking lousy bed at Bay Street Fanny's?'

"I cried for order. There was one last moment of quiet. I used that moment to say—to the amateur deputies as well as to the men seated in the hall—that 'All Americans were guaranteed the right of assembly and of free speech by the American Bill of Rights.'

"(Oh, how many times has this been said before and since!) I did not speak long. It was said I resisted arrest. When they shoved me through the door of the jail I had a black eye, a mashed face, an aching groin, and a broken hand.

*

*

"That first night in jail passed quickly, for it passed in a blaze of emotion: anger, amazement, resentment, the sense of my own innocence and the injustice I had received set my whole being throbbing. When, however, I thought of other men who had gone through this same experience, I was lifted to a plane of such exaltation that I hardly felt the ache of the bruises, the pricking of the scratches and cuts on my face and body. I did not feel alone that night—though I was alone; no one else had been arrested at the meeting. I thought a great deal about other men in solitary vigils, including even the passionate vigil of Our Lord at Gethsemane.

"That night I felt that I was one of many, an army, a mighty and invincible band of men, not great in numbers, but great in the sublime power that comes from suffering in a just cause to the very point of imprisonment and death. I felt, in the darkness, the sustaining presences of all those other men whose names and faces I did not even know, lying on prison floors in other Western towns, waiting sentence, sometimes for as much as twenty to forty years, for crimes they had never committed, for crimes that were not—in my opinion—crimes at all. I was one, inseparably, with these men, now and forever! In that dank prison cell smelling of faulty drains and dead air, with an invisible rat gnawing secretly, persistently, at some nameless object just out of my reach, I dedicated myself to what I believed was the common cause of justice.

"But when the first gray light came, followed by the bowl of gray gruel from the restaurant next to the jail, I began to think with worry and pity of Flora and my children. I asked for paper and was writing a note to send home when Cyrus Bachelder's lawyer, a deacon in the First Presbyterian Church, came with the money for my bail. I refused it, making no explanations, saying simply that I did not want it, that I chose to remain in jail.

"An hour or two later Flora came. She walked straight up to the bars of the cell and looked in at me. I shall never forget her face. Her eyes were sunk deep in her head. She had no color, and her mouth hung in a slack arc—not angry, just shocked, ashamed and sick. She gave a little gasping cry when she saw the dried blood on me, but her voice when it came was without feeling.

" 'Tom, come home with me.'

"I shook my head.

" 'You must.'

" 'I can't.'

" 'Father has paid your bail.'

" 'I cannot accept that.'

"She set her lips in a thin anguished line. 'I beg you.'

"I shook my head again.

" 'I shall stay until you do.'

" 'It will be a long wait.'

" 'I am going to kneel right here and wait.'

"I saw she meant it. She was beyond all possible embarrassment or shame. She was determined on only one thing: to get me out of that cell. I groaned, hiding my face from her. I prayed. 'Oh, God, help me.' I cried out. 'Flora, please, I beg you, I ask you.' But she had knelt down outside the cell on the stone-cold, filthy floor. I saw the old jail guard, worthless, drunken Peter Cary, turn his head away and shuffle off, after one long incredulous stare at the kneeling daughter of Cyrus Bachelder.

"Flora remained kneeling. I held my head in my broken fingers and waited. The minutes dragged past; became hours. Flora remained where she was. I had already begun to feel the penetration of the damp cold through the walls of the ramshackle jail, and I knew she must feel it even more than I. But she made no complaint. Neither of us spoke. When I looked through my fingers at her white face and closed eyes on the other side of the iron bars I saw her lips were moving. She was praying. I had been praying, too. Were we addressing the same Power?

"When Flora spoke at last it was to say, sobbing as she fell back to rest her knees, rubbing them pitifully in pain and despair, 'I know now you wish to punish me. You hate me, and you hate my father, and this is how you show it.'

" 'Flora, I beg you, don't, for God's sake,' I cried. 'It isn't that at all. I've tried to explain to you. There's a principle here.'

" 'Principle,' she cried, she choked on her sobs. 'There isn't any principle except something sick in your own mind.'

" 'Go home,' I begged, 'please go. It's hard enough. Don't make it harder.'

"Finally she went away. She said she had to go home to the children, but she would be back. And she was. She came every day for six days, pleading, begging, weeping. On the seventh day she lay down flat on the cold dirty floor. She did not kneel—she lay prostrate.

" 'I said I would stay until you remember your children and come home to them, and I shall. I don't care for myself. Nothing matters to me now, or ever will again. It is the children. Only the children.'

*

*

"What could I do? I gave in. I accepted bail and walked out a free man, knowing I would never come to trial because Cyrus Bachelder had the power to prevent this final family disgrace. This seemed to me the greatest shame I had to bear—this unwanted protection for the sake of my wife and children.

"I went to bed in my room and stayed there for a night and a day, sick with the knowledge of my weakness and failure. I told myself that other men had obviously resisted the entreaties of their wives. Pleas about their children had counted for less than their own sense of the meaning and dignity of suffering endured in a just cause. Had not Christ himself said: 'He that loveth father or mother more than me is not worthy of me; and he that loveth son or daughter more than me is not worthy of me'? Had he not said that a man's foes shall be they of his own household; and that he came bringing not peace but a sword?"

*

*

"By the second morning I had made up my mind what I must do. I waited until the children had gone to school and then I came out, lit a fire in the fireplace I had built with my own hands, and asked my wife to sit down with me and let me talk to her.

"She came, a frozen mask, and for the last time I tried to make her understand the erratic character she had married—married, in part, because of her grandmother's admiration for the very quality of mind that led me to the conduct she could not now forgive. Once more, for the last time, I tried to make her understand what it meant to be driven by the belief that you could not remain a non-participant in a just fight and come out with your eternal soul still alive.

"All she could see from my talk was that her greatest fear had come to pass; her husband had become that most dreaded of all living creatures, a 'radical.'

"I tried once more to reach through her terror. 'Flora, help me,' I begged her. 'It's a big fight, a long one, I think a noble one. I don't know how I'll manage—or what I'll finally do. All I know right now is, I must go this way. And you can help me.'

" 'But what way is it?' She twisted her hands in her anguish. 'I don't understand you.' She was crying again. 'Why is this fight your fight? You're not a laborer or a logger. You're a man of education. No one here has had the schooling you've had.' She stopped, then added, accusingly, 'Though you've never done anything with it.'

"I admitted it. 'No, I haven't. But maybe now—maybe at least I can use it to help others wake up.'

"I leaned forward then, trying to take her hands, but she pulled away quickly to cover her face. When I saw the helpless tears dropping through her fingers into the lap of her blue-cotton dress, I felt weak and miserable, wholly unable to comfort her.

" 'Papa's right. I think you're really lazy,' she said finally.

" 'Maybe,' I agreed. 'Though I think it's just that I haven't known how to use what I have; to be what I am. Now I think I do know a little. One thing at least I know, I don't want our children growing up with the idea that making money is all that counts. It's a low instinct. Men who have it seldom have anything else.'

"She turned her head away. 'I suppose now you're criticizing my father again. He doesn't deserve it. He works hard. I admire him. So does everyone else.'

" 'For his powers of concentration, for his ability to work around the clock—yes, I admire him for that too. I only think what he's working for doesn't mean much.'

"She whirled on me then as though this was what she'd been waiting for. 'It doesn't mean much to give your wife and children every comfort? To make their lives pleasant and happy— free of worries?'

" 'Don't you think a life can be happy without a growing bank account as its chief goal?' I asked her. I went on groping for a way to reach her. It wasn't easy to talk against her set face and lowered lids. What I said faded into abstractions; descriptions of a man's search for—for what? His self; his meaning?

"I tried to take the subject off myself, hoping to make her see her husband wasn't alone in his idiosyncrasy. 'All men must feel this way at times, Flora, must ask themselves the question that plunges down below all the quick and ready answers; the question: Who am I? Where am I going?' I hoped she would say something then, but she didn't, and so I went on as best I could: 'Lately, for some time now, the question has come to me with more force than you can ever imagine. Right in the office sometimes. Right at my desk, I find myself suddenly faced with it, suddenly asking myself, "Man, what are you doing here?" and I don't have any answer.'

" 'You're working for your living.'

" 'For my pay check! Is that all it is? Am I alive just for that? For a pay check. No, I can't accept that answer, Flora. There must be something more. I'm sure there is . . . I have to find what that something more is. Maybe it won't look like an answer to anyone but me—maybe, in time, not even to me. But I know I have to start looking. Yes, I've come to the place where I must take the first step.'

"I could see how much this last had frightened her.

" 'And what is that first step?' She looked up, her eyes without pupils—distended with fear.

" 'To quit. To quit everything I'm doing.'

" 'Why?'

" 'Because then maybe I can see better what it's all about; where I'm going, and what I want to do.'

"Her bewilderment was pitiful. 'You mean you aren't going to work any more at all?'

" 'Oh, yes, I've had a job offered to me.'

" 'What?' Her voice—usually so soft—was drawn fine and thin now. But I had to say it.

" 'To cook for the boys at Thompson's Lumber Camp—and fiddle for them maybe on Saturday nights.'

" 'You wouldn't do that!'

" 'Why not?'

"The look she gave me was so full of incredulity, of anger, contempt, despair, that I could not meet it. Without a word she got up and walked into the bedroom, closing the door behind her. I saw my mother with the pan for feeding chickens walk into the house in Ballymeaney, not seeing her only boy hidden in the thorn on the hillside ready to go to the New World and leave her forever.

"And yet I could not turn back now, any more than I could have, years before, run down the thorny slope, among the scuttling pebbles, to take the feeding pan from my mother's hand and sell the boat ticket for America."

*

*

"When Cyrus Bachelder died of his second stroke he left his daughter Flora only the silver and china that had been her mother's, and a small annuity to expire at her death. For this act of exclusion he made no explanation, but to the rest of the family no explanation was necessary. *I* was the explanation.

"I think this cold and unjust deed of her father's toward her children killed her. She had no place to turn. How often I have felt my heart twist thinking how it must have been with Flora in those years. She had been ailing since the time of the prison incident. The disgrace of my taking a job as a cook at a lumber camp was followed by a deeper disgrace. I had begun to travel for 'the Cause.' Sometimes I went as far as Chicago or New York. The little money I sent home came from men she considered her own, and society's, enemies.

"When at last she took to her bed she faded rapidly. As she faced death she turned in desperation outside herself for help. She appealed to her father's oldest sister in faraway Massachusetts—an aunt she had never seen—to take the children and bring them up."

*

*

"I was at home for her last illness. Certain violences I had witnessed, certain attitudes among co-workers on my own side of the fence, had set me to tilting again with those by now familiar—even banal—adversaries, ends and means. Once again I, Thomas Cameron Stewart, had to face the truth that for me the use of destructive and violent means toward an end called good, was an insupportable paradox; for by such means the end was transformed, ceased, indeed, to be the aim the ideology appeared to endorse. This sent me back to solitude again—the solitude of a night-watchman's job in a brewery.

"And in this recurrent eddy of question and counter-question my wife died, my son went away forever, my daughter chose to stay with me for reasons that might have been quite as wrong as right, but which lay, I felt at that moment, beyond my final understanding or power to change." . . .

*

*

(Philip had come to the end of his father's writing. He closed the ledger and put it down on the bed, lay back on the pillow, one arm across his eyes. He wanted to weep but he could not, though he sensed the moisture under his tight lids and the sting in his throat. "Oh, Dad," he said aloud, "Dad, Dad!" He felt the tears come from his eyes then and roll very gently down his cheeks onto the pillow. He did not wipe them away and they did not last long. He felt them drying slowly in the wind that now lifted the green trailing sleeves of the cedar outside the open window.

"And Mother! Poor Mother!" he said aloud and for a moment identified himself again with her confusion, with what must have been her despair and shame at his father's conduct. He thought of Jane and her stubborn blind unyielding loyalty to her father, the pain she too must have suffered. "It's too much to bear! Too much—because it's all too late!"

He lay on his back looking up at the water-stained ceiling for a long time, feeling the ache of bewildered regret through all his being. A slow anger at the waste, the blind cross-purposes, the seemingly useless misery of the characters revealed in his father's narrative, began to rise in him, but he could find no object on which to vent the anger. For whom could he truly, justly blame? The skeins of the chronicle were too interwoven, the balance of any possible guilt too shifting. Was, then, one of the painful truths of any life the truth that everyone came to understand his own family too late—if at all? Too late? The familiar phrase now caught his attention. What did it mean—too late? Was any understanding ever *too late*? This was the kind of question Ermenthal might well have put to him—and when he thought of the little man who had passed so swiftly, so fatefully through his life, he too seemed to belong among his immediate intimate circle, with those few in his life who would matter forever to him on some ultimate level of significance.

The banked tears were suddenly released. He turned on his pillow and cried as he might have cried in the days when his mother rocked him in the old Windsor rocker, while the unbearable blind grief of childhood possessed his whole body. When, much later, he rose and went out onto the beach in the fading afternoon, he felt purified, curiously lighter, as he remembered he had felt once or twice after sessions with Ermenthal in the hospital.)

*
*   *
*

PART SIX

The Lost Island

*
* *
*

WHEN his father came in early that evening Philip had supper almost ready, and his father's, "Ah, mighty good!" when he entered and appreciatively sniffed the air seemed to him a real reward.

"My turn tonight, Dad." The instant he said "Dad" he was aware it was the first time since boyhood that he had called his father by this simple homely term.

He wondered if his father had noticed, but all the old man said was, "I think I should leave home oftener," and sat down rather heavily in the rocking-chair. Philip saw he looked tired.

"One swallow of Bourbon to begin with—even if it is Sunday?" Philip held up the bottle.

"Don't mind if I do," the old man replied, "though Jehovah, they say, observes every swallow. Or is it sparrow?"

Philip grinned and poured the whiskey neat, flanking each double jigger with a glass of water, then sat down. He now felt completely relaxed in his father's presence.

"How'd the sermon go today?"

"Not a sermon, son. I told you I don't dignify it by such a name. It went well enough."

"What was it about?"

Tom turned the Bourbon once in his hand, holding it firmly, lightly, with an air of mastery before he lifted the glass and tossed the liquor down his throat. Philip thought this must be old San Francisco theatrical expertness. "Ah," his father said. He let the kindly bite warm his tongue before replying.

"I talked about Henry George, son. Nobody reads him any more. But—well, I think his basic ideas can stand reviewing from time to time. I suppose you must have heard about him."

"Only a name to me," Philip admitted. "I'm not an educated man, Dad. I just went to college."

"I know," his father said, grinning. "It can be quite a handicap. Makes a man think he's had it—when he isn't even on the fringes." He paused and ran his tongue around the rim of the jigger glass, settled back a little in his chair. "Take George— he didn't get any formal education. Lived in poverty all his life. But that didn't keep him from becoming a thinker." He held out his glass again. Surprised and pleased Philip filled it, and then his own.

"What were George's thoughts?" he inquired, setting the bottle back on the table. "What did he believe?"

"He believed two things that we haven't come much beyond in our thinking—and nowhere near in our actions. He believed the ends toward which men and society are moving have been established by religion. The means of getting to those goals lie in the province of economics and politics."

Philip considered the statement. "Seems to pretty well cover it."

His father nodded, suddenly abstracted, looking down into the liquor which he did not drink this time in a single swallow, but sipped very slowly. He appeared to have finished with the subject of Henry George. Philip cleared his throat rather self-consciously and said in a rush of words, "Dad, tell me simply and briefly, if you can, what you've come finally to believe—here alone on this island."

His father glanced up at once, amused, quizzical, his blue eyes brightening.

"Briefly, eh?" he said. "Maybe it's not a brief subject." Having made this point he did not press it. They were both silent. The old man appeared to be sorting his thoughts.

"In the first place," he said at last, looking up and giving that fiery level glance Philip found so difficult to meet, "what I have learned, or come to believe, didn't just grow out of my life here on this island. I *earned* this island." He spoke almost fiercely, with an edge a little like anger. "I paid for this peace, this beauty. I think the price was high enough. Maybe I'm wrong. Maybe I've still got some further price to pay."

Philip thought, "This is the moment to tell him I've read his journal," but he lacked the courage to say so.

His father crossed one knee over the other, fixed his eyes on a point on the floorboards. "I paid for it with a week in prison. That's a terrible experience for a free man in a free country." The fiber of his voice was suddenly tremulous. "But," he hesitated, then his face stiffened, "but I went down quoting the Bill of Rights."

As he spoke Philip saw again the comment in the ledger; he had a deepening apprehension of what it must have cost his father to write those close-packed pages.

"Yes, in my day I was a fighter." The old man raised his eyes and looked full into Philip's face. "While I was fighting this battle I lost many things I held dear; my wife among them, and my only son." He paused, shifted his glance again—out the window this time where the dusk was flowing now under the trees like a slow green liquid.

The silence lengthened awkwardly. Philip wanted another drink but he could not bring himself even to reach for the bottle.

"Ah, I suffered," the old man said at last. "You may be sure I suffered." His voice quivered, and, as if to steady himself, he took off his glasses and wiped them with slow care before continuing. "But I learned something, I guess. Through this suffering I was forced to see things that are hard to see—hard to see and harder to endure. Yes, I had periods of sureness, and periods of doubt. In one of the blackest hours of doubt this island came

to me—as I told you—came to me like a miracle, which perhaps
it was."

He had seated himself in the rocker when he had entered
the kitchen and now he began to move it back and forth deliberately until its homely soothing creak rose above the purring of
the water in the double-boiler where the rice for their supper
was staying hot. Back and forth, back and forth, a long time he
moved in the old chair and when he again spoke his voice was
natural, without strain or bitterness, or even regret.

"When I first came away here—and many times later—people
called me selfish. Maybe you'll agree. And maybe you're right.
But I've lived my life—and is it any more selfish than the life
of the man who does nothing all day long but think how he's
going to make money?" He paused, rocking his chair once more.
"Still, selfish or not, it was the life I had to live; something as
unavoidable—or so it seemed and still seems to me—as the meeting and marrying of your mother."

He was again silent. The fire in the stove crackled violently, a
small explosion of gases in an alder log. Philip started nervously.
His father took no notice.

"I have grown humbler with the years. Here I sit. Into my life,
in the summer months, come people from the outside. Sometimes we speak together. I say what I think, what I feel. Perhaps
I plant a seed. Perhaps not."

"But they plant no seeds in you?" Philip could not help asking. "For you—you've found the answer?" He realized that his
voice had taken on a faintly derisive note.

His father did not miss the tone. He looked up and smiled
and Philip saw there was nothing humble in that smile. "Maybe
not *the* answer, son, but an answer, or *my* answer. . . . Can I
say that?"

Philip half-shrugged, not knowing what to say, yet feeling
something was expected of him.

"Arrogant, isn't it?" the old man said with maddening serenity. "As arrogant as the Chinese sage on the mountain top, or
as the statue of the meditative Buddha, or—and this is the crux—
as arrogant as the man who painted the sage and carved the
Buddha. For, to express this condition, wasn't it necessary for the

artist to see the same truth his subject saw?" He addressed
the question to Philip, but promptly answered it himself. "That
much we surely know."

"I don't," Philip said dourly. "I know nothing."

His father made no denial; but he paused, giving his son a
chance to continue. After a moment Philip said, "You didn't
answer my question, you know."

"That's right. What was it again?"

"I asked you what you'd come to believe living on this island."

"Ah, yes," said the old man. "I'm not as sharp at dialectic as
I used to be. Give me a moment."

He took several. Through the open window Philip heard the
hermit thrush uttering its cool evening notes far off in the dim
woods, and as the sound, sad and tender, melted into the air
Philip longed to leave the kitchen, to go into the woods, walk
quietly among the trees and listen to the birds preparing for
sleep; to have done with perplexing memories, with all discussion, with all effort to crack the hard kernels of meaning. The
thought of his father's "*Accounts*" swept back over him and for
an instant he was again on the verge of blurting out that he had
read them. It was his father's voice that saved him.

"I'll tell you what I said today in church," the old man began
again briskly. "I can just about give it to you in two sentences."
He paused a moment and suddenly his index finger shot away
from his folded hand in the way Ermenthal's had, only with
more expressive vigor, and Philip said to himself, "Are people
going to be finger-wagging at me from now on in?"

"Two sentences," his father repeated. "We must somehow
find a way for all men to share the goods of the earth, and we
must find a universal religion." He struck the table a light blow
so that one of the forks rang sharply for a moment against the
edge of a plate.

"Away," he cried with growing passion, "away with all these
warring creeds and dogmas, these inflexible notions of the One
Final Religious Truth! That's what I said this morning in
church." His voice became calm again. "You know, son, with
all our talk, we're little better today than they were in the Old
Country in the seventeenth century when the Presbyterians

hanged Aikenhead, the Catholics burned George Wishart, and the Episcopalians drowned Margaret Wilson."

(The martyrdom of Margaret Wilson—another of the stories Philip's mother had not wished him or Jane to hear, disliking their morbid gloating over the details of poor Margaret strapped to a stake on the shore in the incoming tide for her refusal to give up Presbyterianism, though her father saved her younger sister Agnes by paying one hundred pounds. And how did the father ever choose between them? A Greek story, Philip thought, recalling it now, a tragic drama, infinitely removed from the First Presbyterian Church on the corner of Main and Maple, with the eight-sided dome and the stained-glass window showing Christ in a belted negligee carrying a lost sheep.)

"This One and Only Prescribed Way to Salvation!" his father was crying scornfully. "Have we not yet passed beyond such nonsense? There's no such thing—and never has been. Any commonsense reading of religious history will show you that. Trouble is people don't know anything about religions except their own brand. No, no! There are only certain great common truths—and they are obtainable by any man who sets out to find them for himself. For *himself*—that's the main point!"

How fiery he was, Philip thought. He could imagine him lashing forth from the shabby pulpit in the Venus church. "But how are all these changes to be brought about?" His voice suggested that he had no expectation of receiving a usable answer.

His father waited to hear again the cool lilt of the thrush. When it had come and gone he produced his reply with the air of a man who has thought it through long ago and often spoken his conclusions aloud.

"We'll have to have some kind of world organization, I'm afraid."

Philip groaned.

His father looked at him sympathetically and a little whimsically.

"Never has worked yet," Philip said gloomily.

The old man leaned forward and tapped him on the knee. He lowered his voice as though about to reveal a secret. "Listen," he said, "there isn't any other way!"

Philip sat rigid as his father leaned back, removed his glasses, tapped the frames on the arm of the rocker and stared ahead. "Yes, lad, we've got to have at least an outer symbol of unity."

Philip still found nothing to say. He was struggling with the scepticism current in his world where such simple basic convictions as his father's had become debased by glib repetition. Easy phrasing had robbed such ideas of any possible vitality or force. From Philip's point of view it was no longer possible to believe that a single word could be uttered on the subject of world organization in any form that could wholly command the heart and mind of the fact-glutted and disillusioned modern man.

"You see," his father was saying softly, and his voice was as dreamy as though he had contacted a distant oracle and was merely repeating what it said to him, "there's danger here. Man's time, clock time, is running out."

Philip was tempted to ask how this statement squared with a favorite one to the effect that there was plenty of Time; in a way, "nothing but Time," but instead he said, allowing a note of truculence to creep into his voice, "If you believe all this so urgently what are you doing hidden away on a remote island?"

The moment he had spoken he was sure his father had had this question put to him frequently, for without a breath of hesitation the old man answered, "Working. In my own way." He looked directly at Philip again and, although his voice remained serious, Philip could see the familiar flicker of humor in his eyes. "Who'd have thought," he said, "that I'd have a chance to influence a man connected with one of the very biggest mediums of modern education? That he'd sit right here in my kitchen and ask me what I thought could be done, should be done? Yet that's just what happened to me. And it came about miraculously, you might say."

Philip was interested. "Who was that? And what medium of education?"

"You!" said his father. "You and the movies."

"Me!" Philip cried. Then he got it. He looked at his father and saw, with astonishment, that the old man was not joking. He began to laugh as harshly and angrily as he had laughed at Ellen in the hospital.

"Oh, God, Dad!" He jumped up, awkwardly knocking over his chair, walked to the window, then turned back. "You just can't imagine how naive you are to believe I could do anything about ideas like yours in the movies. Particularly in the seat *I* occupy in that complex hierarchy."

"I'm not convinced," said the old man, looking straight at his son again. Philip felt the piercing blue glance like a hook caught in his flesh. He turned his face away, absurdly agitated, feeling his heart begin to beat now as though at some physical challenge he could not possibly meet.

"I'm not convinced," his father repeated. "I've given it some thought, and what I say is, doesn't one small piece of yeast make a whole batch of dough rise and work?"

"Now, Dad," Philip began. He tried to laugh again, more gently this time, looking toward his father with a mocking and affectionate glance which he hoped would mask his sudden feeling of worldliness and superiority. "It may all appear very easy to you—sitting here on this remote island."

"Oh, no, not easy," the old man interrupted. "I never said that. Hard—harder than anything."

Philip stood up. "Let's eat, shall we? It's all ready." But as he began to dish up the rice and stewed chicken he was ashamed of his abruptness. "I just don't want to talk about it," he said lamely, "because there's no use in it."

"You began it," the old man reminded him affably. "We were getting along nice and peaceful until you asked me what I'd learned on this island, and one thing I learned was that every man is a responsible human creature, responsible to himself and to all his fellows, and he can't get off that hook once he's caught on it!"

Hook? The conviction that his father had read his mind stirred uncomfortably in Philip. "I'll take the blame then for introducing the subject," he said in a tone of dismissal, "but let's drop it for now, shall we? Maybe later sometime—when I'm in better shape."

He felt ashamed of himself for offering his physical disability as an excuse for stopping a simple discussion. It was absurd. He hadn't felt or looked so well in years.

The old man made no response as Philip began to serve him, putting the chicken wings and backs—Tom's favorite pieces—into one of the old bright Cantonese plates they used for stews, measuring out the rice by mounding it in an inverted cup.

His son was serving, Tom noticed, as he himself invariably did, in a style almost Chinese in its precision, a style that had taken Philip back, the first time he saw it, to old Sam shuffling about his grandfather's kitchen, slicing thin hairs of ginger from dun-colored lumps, dropping the eggs so deftly into the clear soup to make the curdled patterns for which he was famous. Philip remembered now suddenly, as he lifted his own still empty green-and-pomegranate plate, the time he had taken Goldstone to Chinatown in New York to order a real Chinese meal, and how the appearance of an unfamiliar oversize fish with its head still on—the main *plat*—had mysteriously upset Goldstone so that he hadn't been able to eat. At the memory Philip laughed aloud, but sourly, without any real mirth.

"I'd like to hear you pass on your ideas to my boss, Dad," he said. "One hour with him and you'd know just how crazy you really are."

"If he's your boss," said the old man calmly, "he must be a bright fellow, and I'm never afraid of the bright ones. It's the stupid ones we all have to fear."

"Well, Ellen would be on your side. She thinks it's as simple as a-b-c to do what you want and still earn a living."

The old man spoke placatingly. "Perhaps it's because she never had to earn a living herself."

"Perhaps." Philip hoped the moment would pass with no further reference to Ellen. But after a pause in which he detached some of the chicken from a wing with unnecessary concentration, the old man asked bluntly, "Son, are you still in love with your wife?" It was his father's first direct personal inquiry and it startled Philip. He found it hard to answer; not so much from embarrassment but from the difficulty of speaking the truth out of his own mixed feelings. "Yes," he said, and then, "I don't know." He hesitated. "We've had our difficulties." He wanted to suggest that perhaps Ellen was not wholly unlike his own mother in certain basic attitudes, but he could not say this because it seemed to suggest an indirect comparison of himself with his father, and this he felt was in no way valid.

"What kind of a girl is Ellen?" his father pursued. "You haven't told me much. I don't seem to have a very clear notion."

"She's—well, I guess she's typical," Philip said. He tried to speak of her as impersonally as though she were not an intimate appendage of his life. "As typical as I am," he added ironically. "She's a product of a certain kind of upbringing. Sheltered, well taken care of, protected. Some education, intelligent, charming, quiet, patient. She's put up with quite a lot from me."

"What, for instance?"

This sudden unexpected probing Philip found both puzzling and a little disconcerting. "Oh, irritability, boredom, beefing about my job . . ." He shrugged, got up to pour coffee and get his cigarettes. "City life is quite a strain, Dad," he said. "A kind of dissociation sets in in the family—you all live together but somehow you aren't a unit. Perhaps it's the pace. I don't know—it's hard to explain. Maybe it isn't just the city. Maybe it's the twentieth century."

His father seemed to show no inclination to comment and after a silence Philip said, as though reassuring himself, "Yes, I still love my wife."

Then the old man said with a gentle dignity, "I hope the next time you'll bring them both—Ellen and the little girl." He did not say "my grandchild." He had apparently returned to his usual impersonality.

In spite of himself some still unreleased, some unformulated, bitterness lay behind Philip's reply, "There probably won't be another time, Dad. I'll be paying for this holiday for years to come."

They finished the meal in silence. His father applied himself to his rice and chicken with seemingly wholehearted interest. "I was downright hungry," he said when he had finished. He did not appear to be brooding on any of the conversation of the last half hour. He was quite calm and cheerful, and this too was characteristic, Philip thought—that the old man never seemed to harbor any vague ill-will if he failed to make a point, never seemed to need to have the "last word."

THE next day at lunchtime Clare Powers beached her canoe
and came across the sunny gravel to their cabin. She was wearing
a black maillot and a sombrero so enormous that it gave her a
ridiculous top-heavy look. Philip, going out to greet her, thought
her face under the huge brim of woven straw looked tired and
drawn. Even before she spoke he was sure she had come on a
sudden impulse.

"Is your father here?"

"Yes," he said. "Is something wrong?"

"No, not really." But her tone was not convincing. Philip
followed her into the kitchen where Tom was just washing up.
Clare took the cup of coffee he offered her, dropped down on
the bench beside the wall, pushed back her absurd hat and said
without preamble, "Tom, Lawrence is in a terrible mood. Could
you come over?"

"The usual thing, I suppose," Tom said calmly, hanging up
the dishpan.

Clare nodded. "He can't paint. He has to get away. He's

311

empty—used up—no new ideas . . . I'll take you over if you can go now."

"Give me five minutes." His father left the room, went into his bedroom, closed the door.

Something in Philip felt pleased by the news of Lawrence in the dumps. It was heartening to learn that, even on these islands, he was not the only victim of recurrent depressions. Yet he found something puzzling in the whole scene; in Tom's immediate familiarity with the problem and in the hint it offered of their three-way intimacy, closer than he had yet suspected. Clare made no attempt to explain. She remained on the bench against the kitchen wall, looking forlorn and solitary, like someone being punished for a minor misdeed.

"What can my father do for Lawrence? What *does* he do?" Philip asked finally.

"He talks to him," she said.

Though she answered in a voice so dull and remote it invited no further questioning, Philip persisted, "About what?"

"Oh, different things."

He tried again. "You mean like, Buck up! Be a man!"

"Oh, God, no!" When she looked at him and saw he was joking, she made an effort to relax. "I mean just things to stir his imagination—things you can't explain about Nature. . . . You know your father's a mine of strange lore, don't you?"

"I'm beginning to gather that." He was tempted to add, "You know you all puzzle the hell out of me," but he restrained himself.

With a perfectly straight face she said, "Once when your father told him about the compulsive tumbling of tumbling birds, Lawrence got a canvas out of it. He called it 'Acrobatics.'" She took off her sombrero and dropped it beside her on the floor, ran her fingers through her hair. It was tied behind like a schoolgirl's with a piece of purple twine. "It's strange how your father's stories always seem to have the power to drive Lawrence back to work," she added.

Philip sat staring as she lit a cigarette, wondering if she had any idea at all of how her—their—casual talk frequently affected him. Suddenly the tumbling bird, of which he had never heard, linked

up in his mind with an ornithological wonder of his boyhood—
the moa bird of the primordial New Zealand forest.

"Did the old man ever tell you about the moa bird?" he
asked Clare.

"I don't remember that he did."

"Quite a character." Philip began to describe the gigantic
feathered but wingless creature, fourteen feet tall, with the leg-
bones of a dray horse, silently stalking those ancient woodlands.
. . . "He used to stalk my dreams too when I was about ten
years old."

His father reappeared just then carrying in his hand his
frayed straw hat—his binoculars, as usual, hanging around his
neck.

"I was telling Clare about the moa bird. Remember that old
book of natural curiosities Jane and I used to pore over?"

"Of course I do," said his father. He looked delighted. "Must
tell Lawrence about the moa bird some day," he said.

Clare, who had risen to go, looked at Philip and said suddenly, "Why don't you come along too? I'm not working today."

"Yes, why not?" said his father. "You can row me back and
save Clare another trip."

He followed them out of the house saying to himself, amused,
"Guess it was the moa bird that got me the invitation."

2

As HE rowed behind them across the inlet toward Madrona,
Clare's last remark returned to Philip and he wondered if
Lawrence's mood had prevented her from working. He felt a
prick of jealousy that Lawrence should be able to command the
full attention of both these people and he wondered if his moods
were serious, perhaps manic or suicidal.

When they had crossed the inlet Philip was startled to see
Lawrence seated on a log at the shore calmly waiting for them.
If his father and Clare were surprised, they gave no sign.

As they approached, Lawrence, without rising, pointed down
the beach toward the old fir that hung above the water and said,
"I've been watching those birds. Can't recognize them from this

distance. What are they doing anyway—holding a conference?" His voice and manner seemed to Philip perfectly natural, but he was quite prepared to see moa birds when he followed the pointing finger.

Tom lifted his glasses and stared down the beach. "Evening grosbeaks," he said promptly, handing the glasses to Philip for a look. "Don't often see them hereabouts. Mountain birds." He joined Lawrence on the log. "Strange time for them to be traveling. But Clarence assures me all the signs are failing this year. Too bad he isn't here. He'd have some fine story to tell about what they're up to."

He had settled down beside Lawrence as though there was nothing on his mind and all the time in the world. "I never did care much for grosbeaks—in spite of the way they sing," he was saying. "Anyway, not for the female. She always acts so darned no-account and careless. Making her nest she just throws a few sticks together and drops her eggs in among them."

Clare, who had accepted the binoculars from Philip and was also looking at the grosbeaks, put in, "But I thought you liked the goldfinches just for that reason—because they're so casual."

"Yes," Tom admitted, "but that's because goldfinches are always having too much fun to settle down early in the season when the other birds do. It's different with the grosbeaks. They do their duty, but in a sort of unfeeling way."

Clare laughed. She offered the glasses to Lawrence and he got up from the ground in one lanky easy motion and took them from her. At that moment the grosbeaks gave a loud scream and deserted the fir, sailing off down the inlet, riding in formation.

"Well," Lawrence said, "I guess I wasn't supposed to see them." He dropped back on the grass and seemed to want to stay where he was.

Tom was going on about the grosbeaks. "Maybe their bad manners have something to do with their natural strength. They've got the strongest beaks of any bird I know. Can even break dogwood seeds—just about the hardest seeds in Nature."

As he talked he was hanging the binoculars again around his neck. He's rather like a priest, Philip thought; never at ease without his rosary dangling; or was it the cross that dangled? Philip walked to the shore line and began to skim stones over the water. He felt restless, unable to understand either Clare's or his father's apparent anxiety over a problem that now appeared no problem at all.

"Just like J. P. Morgan or F. D. Roosevelt," he heard his father saying as he came slowly back.

"Who?" Philip demanded, dropping down on the log again.

"I was just telling Clare and Lawrence how the bower birds of the South Pacific Islands resemble some of our leading citizens," Tom explained. "They're collectors. Collect berries, animal bones, parrots' feathers—probably stamps and coins too, if they find any lying about. What's more, they build a kind of Gothic pavilion of twigs to display their collections." His voice took on a note of genuine longing. "I've often wished to see them, and the gardener bird too. He's a sort of cousin. He even builds a turf lawn in front of his private entrance and brings his offerings there—flowers, fruit, fungus, berries—for his female's pleasure. Not for her palate, mind you, but for her eye."

"Is that really true?" Lawrence asked. He was listening with obvious pleasure, very relaxed and interested.

"I do love you, Tom," Clare cried. She leaned forward impulsively and kissed the top of his hat. "You should write down what you know."

Philip listened to his father's even voice, hardly hearing the words as he looked out from the cool shadow of the wood-edge to the bright glitter of the sun on the water. He thought how like the soothing of a child this whole scene was, like telling fairy stories to someone who is running a slight temperature, or has had a disappointment, or broken a pet toy. Although he wished to resent Lawrence, wanted to feel superior again, to be above this sort of "spoiled-child handling" as he now phrased it, he knew in his own heart he longed, had often longed in moments of depression, for just such attention himself. When he looked at Lawrence in the shadow under the tree he suddenly saw the suffering in the man's face, the war between elements he could not easily identify; fear, perhaps, buried fear; and anger, cloudy and sullen, beneath an almost childlike innocence. It was easy now to understand Lawrence's devotion to his father. Who else, with such complete impersonality and lack of self-consciousness, would have taken the trouble to come over, as now, and sit on a bleached log in the sun yarning gently about eccentric birds until such time as his presence was no longer needed?

Yet the unreality of the situation grew on Philip moment by moment. It was a relief to have his father's voice stop at last, to hear Lawrence say quietly, "Want to come up to the house, Tom?" and to hear—for he did not turn around—the two of them moving off through the salal and huckleberry.

When Philip shifted his position and glanced toward Clare, he found her face hidden in the sombrero. She was staring fixedly at the water. But she must have sensed he was looking at her for at once she turned and said, "Shall we walk down to the point? You've not seen the view yet from our shore, have you?"

They walked to the point, looked out toward the pale silhouette of the mountains. From this level it was hard to imagine the sea of peaks that lay behind that silhouette: a land of sharp verticals, clefts of deep canyons, the silence of ancient, still-untouched forests, the roar of glacier-fed rivers—so his father had described it. Philip said something of this to Clare.

"That's why the region went unexplored so long," she said. "You may be sure the Indians wouldn't risk the anger of the Thunderbird who lived on the peaks above them. They stuck to the shore line, wherever it was flat enough." Philip was recalling the baleful black eye on the blanket in the Indian museum when Clare broke across his recollection with the abrupt question, "Are you going to make the trip over there with us?"

He stared at her. "What trip?"

She looked surprised. "I thought your father had spoken to you. We've been planning one all summer."

She turned and started back along the shore. Philip was about to ask for more information on the projected trip when she said, frowning, "I'm to blame for Lawrence's mood." She spoke in the manner of one who feels it necessary to confess a mistake. "I invited some people here for the week-end without asking him first. It was wrong."

"For God's sake, why?" Philip demanded shortly. He had heard just about enough on the subject of Lawrence's sensitivity.

What was so special about Lawrence? What about his own sensitivity? What about the plans Ellen and Bob Scott and Goldstone —even Ermenthal—had made behind *his* back?

Clare answered his sharp question without glancing at him. "Because he was working well. And people can throw you off frightfully when you're deep in your work, don't you think so?"

"I don't work," he said sullenly. "I just earn a living at a job I hate."

"Well, that's work," she said quietly.

He was ashamed of himself.

"Why do you hate artists so much?" she asked, after a silence broken only by the sound of their feet moving on the loose stones of the beach.

He was surprised. "I don't know that I do."

"You seem to. At least I thought I noticed it the other night."

Philip picked up another handful of stones and skipped them across the water before he replied, "My psychologist would say it was jealousy. He told me I'd repressed my creative side. The truth is I haven't any creative side." He knew, when he said this last, that his voice had become flat and resentful.

Clare took off her sombrero as though to get a good look at him. "As a Philistine," she said, after her scrutiny, "you are a terrible flop. I suggest you try another disguise." And then, without waiting for a reply, in a tone warmer than she had yet used to him, "Will you come over Saturday for dinner? I've asked your father, and he said he would."

"More artists?"

She laughed with genuine amusement. "No—professors."

"Of course," he said. "I'd like to."

CHAPTER 24

*
*   *
*

THERE were three people at Clare's Saturday night: a tall, stooped, prematurely gray man with enormous shell-rimmed spectacles that he kept pocketing and putting on all evening with compulsive repetition, his wife, a handsome, aggressive young woman with a crisp bob and a husky voice (the man taught something in the Social Sciences—Philip couldn't make out what), and a professor of English literature with a mop of blond baby hair and a petulant asperity edging the easy phrases that rippled from his pursed pink mouth.

The English professor was talking when Philip and his father arrived, and, after the interruption of greetings—Tom knew all the guests—the professor went right on, flinging himself back from time to time in his chair in an attitude of semi-crucifixion which apparently marked his chief points of emphasis. He was delivering a monologue on Kafka, and although Philip knew little about Kafka beyond his name and a play he had once read for *Suprema*, since it was said to have been a great success in Europe, he listened with interest. The man appeared amusing, even, he supposed, brilliant, had he known enough of the subject to judge. When at last the final gesture had been made, the last embroidered phrase uttered, the professor lounged back in exaggerated ease like an erudite and decadent cherub and proceeded to devote himself to a private bottle of old port, rather conspicuously undusted, that he had carried all the way from Seattle in a wicker wine basket. Altogether, Philip said to himself, an incongruously Proustian character for the Last Frontier. He must remember to describe him when next he wrote to Ellen. Philip was amused to find that the English professor made no further contribution to the evening's conversation. It was as though having performed his act early, he was relieved of any further effort. Indeed, within an hour the professor retired to a corner with a book looking as though a book—any book—would always possess for him far more reality than any conversation.

Philip had decided to be very careful about what he said this evening, to reveal as little as possible of himself, for he fancied the visitors all eyed him with not-very-well-concealed curiosity, hoping perhaps, he would in some manner commit himself, make it possible for them to pass judgment. He had again—though not so disturbingly as on his first visit to Clare's (for now he was more willing to be merely the observer and listener)—the feeling of living a life alien in all respects to these particular people. Was his own life better, worse, or merely different? It was another self-posed question he could not answer.

The conversation that got under way, after the Kafka monologue, between his father and the professor of Social Sciences and his wife—with bits from time to time contributed by Clare —was by no means as fantastic or unfamiliar to Philip as that first evening's account of Indian ghost-dancing. In fact, if it had not been for what the talk further revealed of his father's life and philosophy, the general conversation would have had, for Philip, a familiarity bordering on that same inescapable banality he was forever noting. The rights or wrongs of dedication to a given political point of view (which seemed to be in general what they were hammering at) had been the subject of many a book and manuscript he had been forced to read in his fifteen-year search for material for magazines and films.

Now only the new setting and the personalities involved lent any added drama to the familiar subject matter. It was plain that the professor and his wife found it difficult not to make an outright personal attack on Tom. The professor admitted he was doing a series of articles on the early history of labor in the Pacific Northwest, a series which, upon publication—he said with bitterness—might well cost him his job. It was quite apparent that he had made up his mind about the authenticity of his historical facts and, when the old man's views didn't tally, he was disinclined to accept them, even though Tom had lived through the events about which the professor had only read or heard. When Tom quietly contradicted him and his wife a few times they settled down to baiting him on what they considered his "desertion," his "escapism."

Philip watched with interest how his father handled the situation. He answered their charges in a very special way, a way Philip felt had been carefully devised to quiet critics without open argument. By freely confessing to certain old-fashioned qualities and attitudes, he made it easy for them, if they wished, to dismiss him as merely an aging crank.

"I was an evangelist of the labor movement," he said half-humorously, half-apologetically. "Not unlike Debs—though nowhere near as important. And maybe the truth is, the time for evangelists has passed. At least that's what I came to think some years ago. Everyone's tougher now—less sentimental. America's changed. It wouldn't be possible for any labor group in this country to raise up today a man who'd be the subject of the kind of poem James Whitcomb Riley once wrote about Debs." He looked around, smiling almost apologetically, certainly with compassion, at this angry earnest young couple.

A feeling of love for the old man rose in Philip and caught like a wad in his throat. He had to look quickly away.

"Just about the worst poetry you ever read," Tom went on in a rueful, half-laughing voice, "but full of feeling, capable of tapping something in that big juicy pie-heart of the Middle West."

"The big juicy pie-heart of the Middle West! That's quite a phrase," the professor said with a trace of admiration.

"Riley on Debs I'd certainly like to hear," his wife remarked grittily. (Why did she seem so permanently embattled? In a whisper from Clare, as they were in the kitchen getting ice, Philip learned that the woman had been teaching in her husband's department when they got married, and the university, because of some rule about husbands and wives on the same pay roll, had dropped her.) "Of course that's not all of it," Clare added. "She's a perfectly sincere . . ." She broke off to listen. In the room behind them the professor's wife was just posing another question to Tom.

"Can you remember what Riley wrote?" Her voice indicated faint doubt.

Clare called out. "Of course Tom can remember." She sounded almost truculent. "He has the memory of an educated elephant." Philip followed her back into the living room. She assumed, he noticed, a rather proprietary air toward his father in this company—alternately protective and proud.

"I think I can give you one stanza anyway," Tom said, willingly enough. "It should illustrate my point, I hope." And, although his eyes glinted in amusement, there was no mockery in his voice when he began the recitation.

> "Go search the earth from end to end,
> And where's a better all-round friend
> Than Eugene Debs?—a man that stands
> And jest holds out in his two hands
> As warm a heart as ever beat
> Betwixt here and the Mercy seat."

They all laughed. The aging cherub, coming out of his book as soon as the recitation started, cried aloud, "Marvelous! Supreme!" The professor's wife said, "The purest, the *very* purest corn."

"What did you expect?" her husband asked. "True to type— 'The Ole Swimmin' Hole,' 'Little Orphan Annie' . . . Still, I don't know, maybe that's what makes it surprising. You know it is amazing, when you come to think about it, the effect Debs had, still has, on the American imagination. It makes his failure all the more remarkable. How do you account for it?"

He turned again to Tom, somehow softened, as though the old man's willingness to recite such a monstrous verse about a friend had taken the edge off his wish to attack.

"Debs' failure?" Tom repeated. Philip got the notion that his father was suddenly very tired of the whole discussion. Without any great air of conviction or interest he remarked with an air of conclusion, "I think Debs wasn't finally doctrinaire enough. He was a passing American type, soon to be extinct, the essentially rural philosophical mind."

"Yes," the professor's wife said. There was something almost complacent about the way she spoke. "Times are too grim now for men like Debs."

Instantly Philip saw his father take fire. "I'm not so sure about that. I think Debs expressed it all pretty finally when he said that, 'As long as there remained a man in prison, he was not free, as long as one man was hungry, he was not fed.' "

"An abstraction," murmured the professor, but his voice had lost its flat authority.

"Yes," Tom said, "maybe." He looked around, as though measuring in advance the possible effect of his next remark, "An abstraction like most of the pithy remarks of Jesus the Galilean carpenter."

Philip couldn't help being amused at the sudden change in the room. Some embarrassment, some hesitancy and uncertainty, had fallen over the professor and his wife at this religious reference. Had his father, quite deliberately, made the remark in order to abandon once and for all the socio-political vocabulary, with its fixed and prescribed terms, that had been imposed on the evening's talk?

Suddenly, out of the silence, Lawrence spoke. He, like Philip, had contributed nothing so far to the conversation. Indeed from the moment he had entered—a little after Philip and his father—it had been apparent he was a man who had brought only his body to the gathering, that his mind and spirit were far away. Now, with a wild springing movement—making Philip think of the sketches of the "possessed" Indians—he jumped from his chair. In his face Philip thought he saw the same fear he had imagined that afternoon on the beach a few days before when his father had tried to soothe him with talk of grosbeaks and bower birds.

"Maybe all this," he began wildly, his voice intense, his eyes clouded—"maybe it's an eternal fight! Maybe it can *never* be won!"

Tom spoke up quickly, his voice quiet, reassuring. "Oh, I doubt that, lad, I think it can be won. It will be won."

But the professor's wife, much less interested in Lawrence than in Tom, saw her perfect opening. "It won't be won if all men as informed as you take to the woods, or find their private islands and retreat," she said pointedly.

Before Tom could reply, if, indeed, he intended to, Lawrence burst out again in the same tone of worried violence, "It's war in Heaven! We're the victims of war in Heaven!"

Philip stared in amazement. How had Lawrence's imagination carried him so far afield? As the painter stood like a bearded prophet hurling some visionary utterance, a shiver ran down Philip's spine. He saw the old Doré engravings in Milton's *Paradise Lost*—the winged men falling with contorted faces, the scales of writhing creatures, bright-winged angels with swords, with wide halos of streaming light, contending for some mysterious power; he heard again his father's voice reading aloud the long flowing passages of Milton's mighty theme. He thought also fleetingly of Clare's description of the poisonous "brain mushroom" Lawrence had painted, and he asked himself, is Lawrence mad? Or is his madness—all madness—a kind of higher sanity, a further vision?

Lawrence's outburst had produced a peculiar effect in the room. The atmosphere grew tense, rigid, ready to splinter into a thousand fragments. Even the learned cherub held his book suspended, frozen in his plump little hand. Had Lawrence's cry, his inflamed appearance, suddenly presented to everyone the image of a long-denied, outmoded Heaven and Hell?

It was Clare who saved them. She rose swiftly, and in a voice both strong and anxiously gay, said, "Tom, you promised to play for us. If it is 'war in Heaven' give us your number about

Casey Jones at the Pearly Gate." They all turned toward her with gratitude, acknowledging that by her words she had jerked them back from the very brink of some momentarily frightful and apocalyptic vision.

Clare darted across the room, snatched up the fiddle, thrust it into Tom's hands. Tom smiled up at her in open admiration, took the fiddle from the case, tuned it, lifted it to his chin and in the silent room began to saw out the old childish folk-song with its blasphemous verses.

"When Casey Jones got up to Heaven to the Pearly Gate
He said I'm Casey Jones the guy who pulled the S.P. freight,
You're just the man, said Peter, our musicians went on strike,
You can get a job a-scabbin' any time you like."

Tom finally got them all to singing with him—even Lawrence, who could not resist when the end of the old man's bow waved commandingly in his direction. The tapping foot in the rough shoe, the faded shirt, the clean corduroys—why should this aging fiddler, his father, seem to Philip now a figure of power? Again he felt a surge of pride toward the old man, seeing how he bent, turned to his mood like a kindly wind moving through a grove of trees, these other humans. He began to feel sad, to be filled with pity and regret, that such a personality should have chosen to live out his life in an orbit so limited, so confined and unrewarding. Unrewarding? Philip could almost hear his father's ironic answer.

2

ON THE way home, rowing in the dark across the inlet where the retreating tide tugged at Philip's oars, his father said, "Sorry about the evening, son. Total waste of time."

"I'm used to wasting time," Philip said. "Anyway, I don't think it was." He wanted to say something then about his feeling of pride but all he managed was, "I thought you handled it very well."

"Thanks," his father said. "I've had a good bit of practice."

"I—there's something I have to tell you," Philip began hesitantly. He was glad he could not see his father's face in the darkness. "While you were gone Sunday I read what you'd—you'd written in that book called—*Accounts*."

There was a silence. If his father was shocked he did not reveal it. At last he spoke in a voice calmly matter-of-fact. "That's all right, son. Nothing to hide—though plenty of mistakes. Just part of the story of a man's life—a life that happened to be mine." He paused, then added more lightly, "Only scratched the surface, of course, didn't know how to get down under. That's where writing technique comes in, I suppose."

Philip rowed on in silence, hardly able to believe that his guilty revelation had been so lightly accepted.

As they beached the boat they still did not speak. When they came into the kitchen and were drinking a glass of water and having some cheese and crackers before retiring, the old man said, "Don't worry about having read that writing of mine, son. I would have given it to you, if you'd asked me." And then without waiting for any reply he added, "I want to take you on a little trip, if you feel up to it. Want you to meet an old friend of mine. An Indian. He's got a story I think you might like to hear."

Philip was touched. "Don't tell me I've got you gathering material for me now, Dad."

The old man looked at him amused but did not answer.

"What kind of story?" Philip asked.

"Story about fate," said the old man, "blind fate. Something to stretch your mind on. A clock-time jolter."

What did he mean? At these moments it was seemingly impossible to comprehend his father. It was necessary merely to accept what he said as though it made reasonable everyday sense. Philip recalled again Jim Everett's words, "Man of mystery."

"Of course, Dad. I'd like to go." Then he added, "But we'll have to make it soon. I'll not be able to stay much longer."

His father regarded him with an appraising air.

"Don't rush it, son," he remarked quietly. "Remember what I told you—every man is entitled to his forty days in the wilderness."

"That's easy to say," Philip began, but since his father did not seem inclined to discuss it he let it drop.

"We'll take Clare," the old man added, his mind still obviously on the trip. "She's been wanting to go all summer to collect an old carving this Indian promised her. And she wants to hear the story, too."

"And Lawrence?" Philip asked. He spoke casually, but he could sense how his whole body alerted itself for his father's reply.

"He'll be leaving any day now."

"He will?" Philip was surprised. "Where to? Will he be gone long?"

He spoke eagerly, realizing he wanted the answer to the last question to be "yes," for only in Lawrence's extended absence, he felt, could he ever possibly come to know Clare as now he admitted he wanted to know her. The painter, it was all too plain, commanded her full attention. Lawrence—Lawrence and her work: this was her life.

"It depends," the old man was replying evenly. "Once he went off for six months—but it's not usually so long in the summer. Fact is, I've never seen him this restless in the summer. It's winter when he usually gets these spells."

Philip was tempted to refer to Lawrence's outburst about "war in Heaven," to ask his father if he considered Lawrence unbalanced, but remembering his defense of Clarence's eccentricities, he was sure he would only be told that Lawrence was specially gifted and so, of course, not required at all times to act like ordinary folk.

"The truth is," the old man said, again creating in Philip the uncanny notion that his thoughts had been read, "Lawrence is two people; he's a saint and a satyr—and that's a mythical conjunction of qualities not often found on this particular slope of time."

Well, at least here was a line about Lawrence that he could quote to Ellen, Philip thought to himself, as they left the kitchen. She had written in some excitement asking what the painter was "really like," had said that Betsy James was "terribly thrilled" by Philip's proximity to Lawrence, and by his father's long friend-ship. "I told Mother your father had been a great influence in Lawrence's life and even she was quite impressed. He's *really* famous, you know," Ellen had ended, as though she thought it might be necessary to warn Philip not to dismiss Lawrence too casually.

CHAPTER 25

*
*   *
*

ON THURSDAY Clare, Philip, and his father set out for the
trip to the old Indian.

Lawrence had left on Monday. He had come across to say
good-bye, but Philip was away from the cabin and did not see
him. His father said he had no idea where Lawrence was going
and had not asked. Apparently he accepted Lawrence's abrupt
departure with total unconcern as he did all aberrations of human
conduct.

It was early in the morning when the three of them left Clare's
house and started off through the woods toward the Byes' ferry.
Clare and Tom walked ahead with an even steady pace, pausing
only occasionally to point—the ghostly bloom of Indian pipes,
the yellow warbler who floated before them doling out its motley
scraps of song. The sunless air along the wooded path carried a
sweet coolness, a blend of secret scents from earth, sea and air.
Philip heard himself humming under his breath.

They passed the stone called The Squat, with only a side
glance at the intricate lichen landscape, and went on down the

328

sloping springy path into the hollow just beyond. Suddenly Tom, the lead, stopped. When Clare and Philip came up, he was kneeling beside the path. He broke off a fir bough and laid it on top of a mound of leaves, then stood up and walked on.

"Dead chipmunk," Clare explained softly over her shoulder.

Philip, frequently made aware of likenesses between his father and Lawrence in their intense concern with Nature, saw here, in this simple act, an obvious difference. Lawrence would never have stopped to bury a dead chipmunk, though he might have stopped to study it. Philip recalled the scene he had witnessed between the painter and his cat the evening before the last party at Clare's. He had been on his way back from the post office when Lawrence, meeting him on the path near his house, had invited him to share a beer. They had been sitting on the ground under the cedar by the half-burned back porch when Philomena, the cat, appeared suddenly from the brush carrying a dead bird. She had laid the bird at Lawrence's feet and he had thanked her gravely, as though she had rendered him a service. Then he had taken up the dead bird and examined it with detached clinical care. "I'd like to sketch this," he had said.

Just this morning, while waiting for Clare to close her pack, Philip had seen in her living room the completed canvas of the dead bird. "Lawrence worked fast on that one," he had remarked. "Without stopping for hours," Clare answered.

Philip had studied the picture with particular care, amazed at the suggestive power in the dead bird lying at the center of a green and black vortex—amazed, for he was unused to deriving illumination or even pleasure from modern paintings. It seemed to him that some part of the fathomless riddle of the universe had been caught by the painter in the open beak, the tiny stiffened claw, the silent feathered box from which the incredible morning song had so recently issued. To Lawrence, then, the dead bird had been merely a subject, a study of the phenomenon of death? He had felt interest first, before pity? Was this, then, the way artists invariably were—objective, impersonal, recording life as if it were only a relentlessly fascinating abstraction?

Now, looking back at the mound above the dead chipmunk,

Philip knew that his father was incapable of looking at any dead animal with the cool eyes of a clinician. How then could he maintain toward humans and their struggles his almost unbroken detachment?

This thought disturbed Philip in a way he could not analyze. For one thing he was annoyed with his new habit of turning over and over in his mind such detailed and self-conscious speculations about people and life. How could this idle examining be of any importance or use to himself or anyone! In the world outside these islands there was certainly no time for introspection of this order, and a man did well to avoid the habit. It led inevitably to sleepless nights peopled with a hundred half-forgotten incidents, names, faces . . .

Through the shaded arch of the trees he caught now the first distant gleam of the flat sunlight on the Byes' meadow. Immediately some unpleasant recollection stirred in him, a vague wish to flee, to retreat from the sun-filled open place ahead. Not until they were halfway through the meadow, past the black-eyed susans and low-growing wild-rose bushes, did the explanation for his apprehension come to him. The arch of trees: it was the Tunnel, the Tunnel in which he had lain in the hospital fearing the light ahead, resisting any movement toward it; forced to, only at last, by the threatening Thing behind him.

As soon as he knew what the memory was, he felt relieved. His fear dropped from him as quickly and easily as the pack he put down on the weathered porch in front of the two beaming Byes who now stood welcoming them from their kitchen doorway.

Minnie Bye insisted on their having coffee and blueberry muffins before Clarence started the boat. His father had a glass of fresh buttermilk with oatmeal mixed through it. "Old Country treat," he said, raising his glass.

2

THERE was no one else crossing on the early morning ferry. They picked up Clare's car beside the ferry landing and were off at last down the highway. The sense of imminent adventure that had risen in Philip on the night of his arrival, when he and Clarence had rattled down a stretch of this same road, returned, setting his pulses up.

His father too seemed to be in a particularly expansive frame of mind. After he had entertained them with impromptu verses, using the larruping Indian names of the rivers that rushed through the wild countryside: Lilliwaup, Hamma Hamma, Duckabush, Dosewallips—Philip thought again of Goldstone sitting in his country tweeds on the six-by-four terrace that looked out on the trees and benches and strollers of Central Park West. "Must drop my boss another card," he said. " 'Miss you on the old Dose-wallips.' " This seemed very funny as he said it, yet almost at once his amusement vanished. A warning voice in his interior reminded him, "Your time here is coming to an end. You can't possibly stay on much longer."

He saw that it was going to be hard to leave this country. Every time they stopped the car to get out and stretch and look, the drowsy landscape seemed more appealing. There was something haunting here, something untouched, enduringly nostalgic like the ghost of the silence the first settlers had found. Delicately melancholy the silence lay like a visible shimmering skein—half-memory, half-promise—over the little farms tucked away in the sunny rifts of high green valleys, over the gas pump at the lonely crossroads store where white dust rose unexpectedly to film the huckleberries the tow-headed children along the way were now dropping into tin buckets.

3

IT WAS mid-afternoon when they came to their destination. They caught their first glimpse of Spaniard's Bay from the slope above. Philip, who was driving, stopped the car and they sat looking down at the half-moon of white beach, the small fishing boats of the Indians riding at anchor—and, beyond them, past the guardian headlands of rock and wind-torn trees, the blue straits that led to the open Pacific.

From the hilltop the Indian village had appeared to possess a picturesque charm, but on closer view it resolved into a huddle of ramshackle dwellings. Not even the line of carved wooden totem poles fringing the beach—impressive relics of a less degenerate day—improved the drab and dispiriting effect.

They stopped in front of a small shabby bungalow that served as a general store and dwelling house, a typical Indian store, so Clare said as they got out to go in. When they opened the door a tall dignified Indian came forward at once to greet them. He was introduced to Philip as "the grandson of Old Doctor"—the Indian they had come to see.

The grandson, in a voice surprisingly clear and cultivated, said, "My grandfather is expecting you. He had a dream and was expecting you, but not until tomorrow. Tomorrow in the late afternoon."

Philip glanced over at Clare, amused. It was all just as she had prophesied: the old Indian would not appear the first day, they would have to make an appointment to see him. "They can be very formal when they wish," Clare had said. "This is an important occasion to Old Doctor and he's going to give it full ceremony." Philip was not prepared, however, for the statement about their arrival having been foretold in a dream, though Clare and his father accepted the news as something entirely commonplace.

"Please ask your grandfather to plan to have supper with us tomorrow," Tom was saying. "Tell him I've brought my son to hear the story of the island. Miss Powers wants to hear it too."

"And I've come for the carved figure, you know," Clare put in. She spoke a little uneasily, as though not certain how much she should say of this to the grandson.

The Indian did not appear surprised. He walked to the rear of the room and lifted a dirty flowered curtain that admitted to an alcove. "It is here," he said. As he lifted the curtain the sun, slanting toward evening, struck full through the dusty side window of the little shack.

Philip started in surprise and Clare cried out in instantaneous pleasure at what the shaft of sunlight revealed: a wooden statue of a man about four feet high, with a tall hat and a great nose. Though crudely carved, and painted like a clown with large coin dots in faded green and red, the statue possessed, Philip felt at once, a strength that sprang like a living force from the close-set bright black eyes. These eyes—whether of glass or obsidian he could not make out in the first quick glance—stared out fixedly from the primitive figure, projecting an uncanny, almost mesmeric power.

Philip saw by his father's and Clare's expressions that they were similarly affected. He thought it took real courage for Clare to advance, as she now did, and lay her hand with dignity on the wooden figure. She stepped forward with the formal air of an appointed emissary claiming a gift for some distant potentate. No longer the pedagogue, or the professional anthropologist, she was a great lady, representing her whole race at an important ceremonial moment.

"It is finer than I imagined it could be." She looked directly at the Indian. "Please tell your grandfather how pleased and proud I am; how much I appreciate his trust and his generosity. Tell him we will be here tomorrow afternoon."

She then turned her back on the figure, and the Indian dropped the dirty curtain.

At once the atmosphere became less formal. They all went into the front room where, among the nondescript miscellany of small objects for sale, Clare purchased some dusty chewing-gum packs, six boxes of toothpicks, and three bottles of warm soda pop. She caught Philip eyeing her in astonishment.

Outside the store she gave the soda pop and the gum to some dirty-faced Indian children sitting among broken beer bottles and burdock near the sidewalk. They accepted the gifts silently without any change of expression. The toothpicks she put in her pocket.

"They'll be useful for canapes. Poor Joe! He can't say No. Some salesman sold him five hundred boxes of toothpicks once. Every time I come here I try to deplete his supply."

Tom was walking along not listening. "So that's the carving," he said. "What a beauty!"

Clare's face lit up again. "Imagine Old Doctor giving it to me at last."

"Why did he?" Philip demanded.

"A dream told him to."

"He seems to have particularly compelling dreams."

She laughed. "Yes. Thank goodness for his dreams."

Tom turned off the broken sidewalk and led the way down through the tangle of weeds and tin cans to the clean shore.

"What was the carving, anyway?" Philip asked. "And why the stovepipe hat?"

"I wondered about that hat, too," Clare said. "Sign of dignity maybe. Important whites wore them in the old days. The carving was made years ago. I've heard the story. Old Doctor met the little man—he was a god, of course—in the deep woods when he was only a boy. It was after a ritual fast. Old Doctor had been fasting to get the vision in which he would acquire his adult name. He expected an animal, but instead it was this little man. He—the god—gave him the name of Old Doctor and revealed to him the arts of healing. Then Old Doctor didn't see him for over eighty years." She turned to Tom. "Old Doctor must be at least a hundred, himself—wouldn't you say?"

"Easily," Tom said.

As they walked along the shore looking out across the water, riffled now by a mild wind sketching bands of white scallops as far as they could see, Philip wondered again about his father's motive in arranging this trip, this whole experience. What did he have hidden in his mind? Was it going to prove to be some embarrassingly solemn hocus-pocus—a long session spent listening to a yarn about supernatural powers? Most Indian legends bored the hell out of him—and had for years. He felt his irritation rising, tried to check it when he recognized it sprang from the same subtle unease he always experienced when faced by a situation in which he might prove inadequate. He tried to let go of these cloudy feelings, to listen without annoyance to Clare who was continuing with her story about the carving.

"Then the god reappeared in a dream last spring, and it was at that time he said I was to have the statue of him that Old Doctor had made years ago in his boyhood. The grandson sent word by a young Indian who came all the way to Seattle to deliver the message to me. I was told to come for it at the end of the summer. Well, I simply couldn't believe it—can't believe it yet."

His father, still walking along as calmly as though listening to some prosaic report from a news magazine, said to Clare, "Well, you worked for it. Every bit of it. You earned it." He raised his eyes and regarded her with affection and pride.

She shrugged, obviously pleased to be praised, but making light of it. "Well, if we are rewarded for endurance I guess I earned it." She addressed Philip. "I spent part of three summers in this place."

He was shocked. "Where?"

"In a room above the general store. Not the one we were in, but the white man's general store. It's even dirtier. I'll never forget the bed bugs. Nor the smell of stale beer."

"How did you know you'd find material here? It looks the most unlikely place to me."

"Ah," she said mocking, "but I have my guardian angels too."

At Clare's words the feeling of unease rose again in Philip. A curious newspaper heading on which his eye had once fallen flashed into his mind: *Annual Shower of the Perseids to Begin After Moonset Tonight*, and there was surely no line any stranger in his father's moldy book on transcendental magic. A glaze of unreality fell on the beach, the sea, the figures of his father and Clare. For a moment he had a passionate desire to close his eyes, open them and find himself settling down by the radio in the corner of the familiar room on East Seventy-second Street, an ice-cold Tom Collins in his right hand, the noise of the city below him.

4

THEY planned to spend the night away from the Indian village, off the reservation at a place called Bright Pebble Beach where on a wild rocky shore an old woman had rustic cabins for rent.

Facing the beach beside each little house were rustic tables and benches, but there was only one other party making supper —a father, a mother and two young boys. They came and went— the four of them, absorbed, busy, happy—threading from fireglow to watery green twilight, carrying frankfurters, roasting ears, coffee. The smell of singeing corn husks, boiling coffee, lay cradled in the sharp briny smell of the sea and in the scent of the pine needles relinquishing the day's warmth slowly into the cooling air. There was something about the scene, its homeliness and simplicity, the curving gentle strands of relationship expressing— in voice, gesture, attitude—the one word "family" that suddenly affected Philip. He longed for Pammy—to put his arms around her bony shoulders, tweak her pale braids, look into her anxious and adoring eyes: "I think you're beautiful, Daddy." "I wish Pam were here," he said aloud.

"Next time perhaps you could bring her," Clare said.

Next time! Philip saw himself again walking on the black-and-white tiles of the Seventy-second Street foyer, past the carved Italian furniture, into the green box that would receive him and indifferently lift him for deposit in the second green box (an unavoidable progression) where the three black buttons beside the three black doors . . .

He heard Clare saying, "We'll find some agates to send to-morrow. We'll look in the morning. And probably she's just the age to adore one of those dreadful pine-cone and twig storks?"

"Who?" he asked absently.

She looked amazed. "Your child."

He felt that he had been gone an immeasurable time from this campfire into which his father—who had carefully built it—was now casting a sea-wracked box on which could still be read the fading words, NATURE'S WONDER.

"Yes," Philip said quickly, "she'd love it—this kind of thing." And from loyalty he added hastily, "Ellen would too. She even enjoys picking pine needles out of the sugar."

5

AFTER supper his father disappeared, walking slowly away from them along the beach toward the rocks of the far headland where the sunset tides were flinging spray high onto the banks. He had departed with the air of a man who does not desire company. Philip suggested to Clare that they too take a walk—for the pale green twilight of this northern country seemed magical now, a twilight lit from within as though a radiance rose out of the very ground itself to suffuse the atmosphere and the sky.

Behind their beach lay another protected shore line, a sandy half-moon where whips of kelp with blunted onion ends floated hypnotically in the tide. The place was deserted except for the sea birds, still coasting and gliding with idle pleasure in the translucent air. They strolled back toward a farm they had passed in the afternoon and came, to their surprise, on an old weed-grown cemetery whose crude wooden tombstones slanted rakishly on the earth. Unlike the substantial enduring graveyards of New England, this one was plainly destined, in a short time, to disappear altogether. When Philip remarked something about the easy loss of family records in a new country, Clare explained that this was the graveyard of an abandoned and forgotten Utopian colony of the Eighties.

They pushed their way through the stubborn and resistant grass to try to read the words carved on the weathered headstones. Clare stooped, scraping away gray lichen with a bright nail. " *'Archie, infant son of Mary and'*—the rest of it is gone." Philip found himself saddened in the way a certain kind of romantic verse from the nineteenth century had once affected him: ruined abbeys revisited; Lucy Gray, the solitary child; elegies in country churchyards. When they moved on, the long tough grass pulled at their ankles as though to detain them. "I never find the infants as sad as the adults," Clare said. "It's those women of thirty lying buried in the middle of a dark forest . . ."

Philip took her arm and firmly turned her away from the tombstones. He was glad to escape the clutch of the graveyard grass, to feel his feet again on the hard-packed path the farmer's cows had made around the crumbling fence up the hill from the lonely bay. He began to recite half-mockingly, half-seriously, " *'The curfew tolls the knell of parting day, the lowing herd winds slowly o'er the lea.'* " He was surprised to find that it all came back to him, and as they leaned, with the last lines, over the farmer's moss-grown stile, Clare looked at him—almost tenderly, he thought—as she said, "Sometimes you're very like your father."

CHAPTER 26

*
* *
*

THE next afternoon Old Doctor was waiting for them at the store. He was sitting in the back room on a packing case near the carved figure. The dirty flowered curtain had been drawn back, and the dusty room, with late light slanting through the window, had an eerie quality. The heavy upright figure of the old Indian seated alongside the carved image of the god he had met so long ago in the forest, gave Philip—in spite of his resistant scepticism—a sense that they were interrupting a vigil; that some symbolic act was about to be performed, far deeper and more impressive than the mere transfer of the crude wooden figure to the luggage compartment of Clare's car.

The old Indian greeted them without any visible signs of pleasure or displeasure. He looked unlike any Indian Philip had ever seen: his skin the color of pale tobacco, his hair hanging to his shoulders; and the whole cast of his face decidedly Oriental; not the delicate, birdlike, small-featured Oriental, but rather the bland, full, rounded style of certain Bodhisattvas of Hindu influence that Philip had observed in his father's Eastern books.

338

The similarity was heightened by the Indian's remarkable ear-lobes, long, thick and full, almost as exaggerated as in figures of Buddha. Looking at him Philip uncovered some vague memory about the "Oriental origins of Northwest Indians."

Old Doctor rose slowly from the packing case and haltingly offered to each one in turn his horny crusty old man's hand. His face remained impassive as a schoolbook's traditional description; his dark glance appeared to have no center: it was, Philip thought, like a blind man's.

"Your son?" he said to Tom, accepting Philip's hand, but barely clasping it. It was as though a handclasp was a rite he had learned late in life and could neither take lightly, nor place much faith in.

Clare was more formal with the old Indian than Philip had ever seen her. "I can never thank you enough. You know what it means to have this figure, and how grateful all my colleagues will always be. For years to come students will be looking at it in the museum, and reading the story of your night in the forest."

A picture of the neglected Indian museum in Seattle rose in Philip's mind.

Old Doctor nodded. "I was told to give it." His tone—though not grudging—seemed to imply that without this instruction he would never for a moment have considered doing so.

"You'll have supper with us," Tom said. His father's manner was easy—the manner of one old man to another.

Old Doctor inclined his head, indicating acceptance.

There was an awkward silence. Clare now seemed faintly ill-at-ease, affected by the Indian's unyielding gravity.

"When shall we move the figure?" she asked finally. Philip thought he detected a tremor of uncertainty in the question.

"Best time now," said the old Indian. "But we must cover it."

He moved over behind the wooden statue and lifted from the floor some lengths of soiled sailcloth. He began very deftly, though slowly, to wrap the body in it—only shaking his head at Tom's offer to help. The grandson stood by passively. He seemed to know that this work was the old man's private concern. Old Doctor proceeded with care and exactness to bind the wooden figure like a mummy. It occurred to Philip suddenly that he might not want any of the other Indians at the Bay to see what was being carried out of the musty back room and into the waiting car.

When he had finished with the wrapping, he silently indicated the figure could now be removed. Philip took one end and the grandson the other. They stepped outside the door into a flood of yellow light—a garish and sulphurous glow where the setting sun struck the water along the shore. They walked around to the open luggage compartment almost furtively. Philip began to feel that he had robbed a tomb by stealth, and he glanced quickly up and down the dusty road to see if they were being observed. But the street was deserted. Perhaps all the Indians were at their evening meal, or perhaps—and his thought showed him how he had changed in the last weeks—perhaps they had caught some underground tremor about the transfer of a god and were hiding indoors from any possible fateful retaliation.

The wooden figure proved too long for the luggage compartment. In the end it had to sit upright, like another passenger in the rear of the car, like a dead man in one of the early gangster movies—whisked away, propped between living men. This macabre image flickered in Philip's mind while he propped the stiff carved figure against the back seat and held the door so that Old Doctor, at Clare's suggestion, could climb in beside it.

They drove through the village, past the unpainted ugly wooden houses, and turned off down a road that led into the forest. They saw no one; not along the streets, in the windows, nor on the graveled road that wound into the dark woods. When they had gone about a mile, they came to where a grove of tall alders opened toward the sea.

"Here we are!" Clare cried.

Philip saw some crude tables and benches and several outdoor stone fireplaces.

"What is it?" he asked, getting out of the car, "a public park?"

"Indian park," said Old Doctor, descending with dignity from the rear seat. "Gift of Old Man Sam." He gave this remark no special emphasis, but Philip, looking into the somber face, caught a glimmer of something he thought might pass for humor.

Clare burst out laughing. "*Uncle* Sam," she said. "Not Old Man Sam."

She was still laughing when she went off with Philip to gather driftwood from the beach. "The old fox," she said. "Didn't you love that barb? The Indians had it all once—now Uncle Sam—Old Man Sam—grants them a picnic ground."

"With fancy stone fireplaces I suppose they never use."

"Maybe the young ones do."

Philip glanced about at the wild shore. "Well, Old Man Sam gave them a beautiful spot at least," he remarked. The pale sand was smooth and hard as enamel; the rocks, standing in the slow wash of the tide, shone in the spray like huge lumps of jet. One immense tree root—alone, without the trunk it had once served—hung suspended against a bleached chalky bank; an intricate cabalistic *mandala* speaking of a vanished age, of great forgotten cataclysms of Nature that had uprooted giant trees, shelved the high banks and thrown the rocks up out of the ocean's depths.

At first glance he had called the scene beautiful, but now he found it terrifying too, as though some unexorcised primordial spirit dwelt here, fiercely resenting intruders. He could imagine Spaniards landing, hopeful, lustful, homesick and quarrelsome; Indians ambushing their enemies, leaving their bodies on the sand to wash out to sea, putting their heads on high poles for the birds to plunder, warning all other marauders in their great sea-going canoes to be wary of this angry tribe. Philip looked into the sky and was relieved to find it serene and blue, with a few cloud puffs and the first star of evening.

"You should see it here in winter," Clare was saying. "Fog you couldn't cut with a knife. But it *is* wonderful at this time of year—haunting and sinister too . . ." She stood for a moment, driftwood in her arms, looking about her as though she, too, was aware of the secret life of the place. Then she said briskly, "We've got to get the fire going. Old Doctor won't stay late; he won't talk until he's eaten, and I must get that story out of him tonight."

At times like this she wore her determination, her inflexible will, as visibly as a garment. A thought he had had before returned to Philip: She is a ruthless woman. But she looked so young and eager in the dying light with her load of driftwood, hurrying across the damp sand leaving the marks of her small bare feet, that he could not wholly believe it.

2

CLARE had warned him that he must not offer liquor to the old Indian. She had said it was a government rule and one she took good care never to break. "But why?" he had protested. "It's a silly rule, isn't it?"

"Maybe," she said, "but I don't intend to give any of my enemies a chance to make trouble."

"Have you enemies?"

"Of course." She was quite bland about it.

"Professional or personal?"

"Both, I suppose. But I was speaking of professional ones!"

"Well, if you don't mind," he said, "I shall retire and take a solitary slug. I have a feeling that the evening's rites may be a little hard for a city paleface."

"What are you afraid of?" she taunted him.

"You," he told her.

She turned away and went back to unpacking the picnic kit. Philip sensed that his one word had set up some new silence between them.

Tom prepared the supper, a steak with which he fried slices of a giant puffball he had found in the woods. They had bread, tomatoes, cheese, and an elaborate breakfast pastry dotted with pecans and crystallized sugar of which Old Doctor ate at least half. It was obviously the high point of the feast for him. Clare wrapped the remains in a paper napkin and insisted that he take it home, that it had been purchased for him. While they were drinking their coffee Tom brought out a cigar and offered it to Old Doctor whose gratification was now unmistakable.

They were silent for a time after they had eaten. A screech owl came to a tree near them and rippled and murmured plaintively. Old Doctor cocked his head, listening. When the owl moved off, Clare spoke.

"Now, Old Doctor, you told me last year that the next time

While Philip was studying the Indian's face—over which there had fallen a veil of even more marked detachment, separating him from his audience—he did not catch the first sentences, the very identifying sentences that would—he thought afterwards—mean the most to Clare, helping her to place the legend properly in relation to a specific tribal culture. Philip only began to move with the story when, in the old man's slow sing-song, he heard the solemn words: "He could not shake the dream from him."

It was a commanding sentence. Half-shaped memories of his hospital nightmares formed at the back of Philip's mind.

. . . "Powerful as he was," the old man was saying, "the greatest of the medicine men, he could not forget his dream. When he was feasting, laughing among his people, when he was alone in the dark forest shaking his wooden rattle, beating his drum, chanting his chant—he would remember. Though he was the strongest man on all the North Pacific slope, though he was mighty and very tall with muscles like those of the timber wolf, he could not rid himself of his dream."

Again the old man paused. When he spoke next he broke up each sentence into a separate statement:

"He could go for many days without eating.

"He could meet his enemies without fear.

"He had killed a tribe single-handed.

"He had the strength of a giant.

"He did not know fear.

"He could drive away and kill enemies and wild animals.

"Only the dream of the white man's camp he could not drive away. It was an enemy he could not destroy. It was only a dream but its power was more than the power of anything he had ever known on earth."

Again the pause. A little wind had come up off the water. Overhead the boughs weaved gently in the light from the rising moon. At a distance Philip heard the sea striking the rocky point past which the Spaniards had once sailed, searching gold and hidden ways to the Orient. The fire moved on the logs with little puffs of velvet sound. He glanced at Clare. Her face was as impassive now as Old Doctor's. She was concentrating all her forces to give an exact accounting of the legend. His father's face was now in shadow, the eyes closed. He, too, seemed completely under the spell of the old Indian's voice.

"At last the great chief went away from his people. He walked many days through a pathless forest. He climbed to the top of the highest mountain in the land. There he camped. Many days he went without food or water. Then, once more, the vision of the white man's world rose before him. He saw it stretching farther than any human eye could reach. He knew there was no weapon by which it could be destroyed."

In this fresh pause Philip shivered. It was a moment of nameless, rootless fear, fleeting but very real. He tried to account for the feeling. Was it the sense of fate, of the implacable and inescapable forces that in retrospect are called historic—whole peoples ploughed under, no more chance than the land to be spared its destiny? . . . Ermenthal. He, too! Gone without a message of hope or confidence; gone without promise or answer . . .

Why, he asked himself, should his father have wanted him to hear this legend? Was it his father's hope that it would help him acquire some special "perspective" on his own troubles; help him see himself small against history? If so, he had to admit that he found no personal sustainment in any such obvious revelation.

The old Indian was continuing, "Then he knew. Then he accepted his dream. He looked into the sky and spoke: 'I am old, O Sagalie Tyee. Soon I shall die. Do not let my strength die with me. Keep it for my people so that they may endure the rule of the paleface. Keep my wisdom for them. Show me where I may hide it where the white men may not destroy it.'"

Again the pause. Again the sea striking the rocks, the fire whispering, the boughs swinging. Far away a noisier bird than the owl screeched and was silent. Once more a shiver passed through Philip. He leaned toward the fire. No one else moved. The old Indian had scarcely stirred since the story began.

"Then the chief left the mountain. He came down to the water. Chanting a medicine song he entered his canoe and began to paddle. It was sunset. He paddled toward the dying light. Just as night fell he came to an island in the sea. It had gray rocks. On the top he saw great pines and firs. As he came nearer the island he felt his strength leaving him. He felt his power and wisdom leaving him. He felt them drifting from him. They were like a cloud and they drifted from him. They drifted to the island and rested there. He saw them resting on the island like low clouds. When he knew they had left him forever he turned his canoe and came back through the dark night.

"He came back to his village. He was weak now as a woman. When he came to his lodge he called his people. He told them what he had done. He told them they must go and search for the island. When they found it they would find his wisdom and his strength. His wisdom and strength would remain there forever to be found, to be used.

"In the morning he did not wake. He was dead."

And now at last the old Indian stirred a little. The set and masklike face relaxed. He seemed to return from the world to which he had departed with the first lines of the legend, to draw near again in space to his audience.

But he had not quite finished.

"For many years young men and old looked for this island," he said, using again the voice with which he had first spoken. "They knew it was there, somewhere up some lost channel of seawater. But they could not find it."

The pause that followed was longer than any so far, lending the next words even darker weight.

"They have never found it. Maybe now it is too late. For they do not look any more. Yet the old chief told them that his strength and wisdom would remain there. For they can never die. They live forever. They are what is passed on to children and grandchildren."

And now Old Doctor had concluded, but still he did not move. His impassivity held them fixed. It was like a ritual in which they were all participating. Until the old man moved they were forbidden to so much as shift their positions. Philip began to feel cramped. He glanced at his father. Had he fallen asleep? Clare was still looking into the fire on which the old Indian had now also bent his gaze. Just as Philip felt he could not endure the rigidity of the scene one moment more, the old man rose with dignity. At once, but slowly, Clare and his father rose, too. Philip found his left foot was asleep. Leaning against a tree he shook it vigorously.

"I want to thank you very much, Old Doctor," Clare was saying solemnly. She held out her hand to the Indian; her face soft and gentle in the firelight. "It is a very beautiful story. I shall never forget this night."

The old Indian inclined his head. He touched Clare's hand, next Tom's, then Philip's. "Good-bye," he said. As he touched Philip's fingers he looked with a brief questioning glance into his face. It was a look Philip could not read, but it made him feel again a stranger, an alien.

"I will go now."

"Let us take you," Clare said.

"No." His headshake was firm.

"At least take a flashlight," she begged. "It's dark in the woods."

"I'll go with you as far as the road," Tom said firmly. Old Doctor neither assented nor protested. The two old men moved out of the circle of light made by the fire and disappeared into the darkness of the trees.

4

As THOUGH by spoken agreement, Clare and Philip turned together toward the shore. The moon was well up now, heightening the drama of the wild beach, silvering the bleached tree root they had seen in the afternoon, turning the bland rocks to figures of menace. Philip looked into the sky to search again for the Dipper and the Bear of childhood evenings. The long shining blades of two white clouds, with the fins and heads of sharks, approached the moon on either side. They seemed to bring with them a wind, for at once the air stirred, the water curled nearer.

"Ah," Clare said.

Philip saw her shiver. She reached out and took his arm, linking hers tightly through it. He pressed it against his side, holding her hand, grateful for the spontaneous contact.

"Did the story frighten you?" he asked.

"Of course."

They began to walk slowly along the sand. When they were out of sight of their fire glowing behind them like an ember in the dark cave of the trees, they sat down on a log some ancient storm had cast up out of the water.

"We've all seen a terrifying vision, too," she said softly, almost whispering the words, "and we can't avert the doom and we can't find the island. Perhaps for us there isn't any island?"

"You've found an island, haven't you?"

"I?" She laughed almost harshly; the bitter sound, the single word, denied his suggestion.

But Philip went on. "You, Lawrence, my father—each of you has an island. So it seems to me."

"Your father—yes, I'll grant that."

"Not Lawrence?"

"Only sometimes. When he paints." She was again silent.

"Anyway, I envy all three of you," Philip said.

She made no direct reply. After a moment, out of her own thoughts, "Yes," she said to herself, "I will put down the legend to gather dust on a few shelves. Lawrence—had he heard it— would have been moved to paint some strange canvas whose source only he would have ever been able to trace. And you— what will you do with the legend?" There was no thrust in her question, but he did not like it.

"I? Nothing. Not a thing."

She began quietly to sift the white sand through her fingers. In the moonlight her face was gentler than he had ever seen it. As he looked at her, his longing to take her in his arms grew so strong he could hardly restrain it. Then he asked himself why there was any question of restraint. Certainly it was not because of Ellen. It had been a long time since the thought of Ellen had held him back at such a moment. Yet if in this same moonlight, shining just as compellingly three thousand miles away, Ellen

. . .

He tacked away quickly from the painful image that rose before him of his wife in an embrace not his own. And she might well be, he thought. After all, their relationship had been pretty thoroughly on the rocks weeks before the accident. And even afterwards they had not been able to find one another again. She had persisted, he remembered, right up to his departure, in treating him like a patient, and her letters to the island had been, though frequent, very general in tone, full of small news, certainly without passion or even any very extensive affection! What was there left between them? Habit? A friendly intimacy based on years of sharing a life together? One child? If this was all, why then did the thought of her possible unfaithfulness arouse in him such sharp protest and distaste. He could not answer.

Without knowing he was going to, he cried out, "Help me, Clare!"

He seized her hand and laid his face on it, hiding from her amazement. She put her free hand instantly on the top of his bowed head. After a moment she began gently to stroke it.

"What are you afraid of?"

"Of everything! I feel so alone!"

After a moment she said, "Everyone is alone—finally."

"But you have Lawrence!" The words burst from him.

She was silent. "No one has Lawrence," she said. "No one will ever have him."

The pain in her voice reached Philip even through his own misery. He knew in that moment what she meant. He saw Lawrence going away—right in the same room going away, closing a door, departing as palpably as though he moved his body from view. Whatever most completely stirred and interested him, this led him away; away from everyone, even the woman he loved, into the solitary cavern where he painted his bloodless fancies.

Philip took Clare in his arms. When she rested against him, without protest or question, his blood began to pound. He lifted her face in the moonlight and looked into it. He felt he had never before looked into the eyes of a woman. The wonder and beauty of the human eye swept over him; the deep dark pool of the pupil, the petaled corolla. Where did it come from— from what source—the look of tenderness and sadness that he now read there? He kissed her. She did not reject him, but he was conscious that she did not wholly respond either—not as he had quickly imagined, hoped. There was something tentative—even elusive and questioning—in her face, seen in the flooding moon-light.

After a moment she turned her head away. Philip dropped his arms. They rose and walked in silence back to the camp.

Long after Clare and his father were both asleep by the dying fire Philip lay wide awake, hearing the little owls far off in the woods, the trees at their green weaving overhead, and the unrest-ing tide beyond the clearing. He had never been lonelier, never more confused and bewildered, more removed from what he had once thought was the unquestionable reality of his life.

CHAPTER 27

＊
＊　　＊
＊

THEY had been home a day when Philip told his father he was going to row across the inlet for supper with Clare. The old man only nodded. Something in his silence, in the nod, indicated he knew his son's visit was more than casual but that he would neither interfere nor pass judgment on it.

2

PHILIP pulled hard at the oars, aware of how much he wanted to see her, of how alive he felt. He beached the boat quickly and ran up the path to her house.

There was a smell of baking in the kitchen. He knocked at the door, then called Clare's name. Surprised to get no response he entered. The house was empty. Had he misunderstood her invitation on the ferry coming home? Had he not been definite enough in his last glance, or in the pressure he had laid on her arm when they parted? The weight of his disappointment, immediate and intense as a child's, shocked him.

352

He was about to go outside again when he looked out the back window and to his relief saw her coming from the direction of Lawrence's house carrying the cat. She was wearing a black dirndl with bold magenta embroidery and a black halter. Her throat rose smooth, sun-burned from the folds of dark cloth. He could feel himself begin to tremble.

Clare came up to him calmly. "Hello. I thought I heard you beaching the boat. I brought Philomena over for her supper."

He wanted to reach out and take her in his arms at once but he felt awkward and unsure. "What can I do to help?" he asked, as she went over and looked in the oven.

"Get out the ice, if you will. I'm making *pizzas*. Anchovy ones. I think you said you liked them."

"*Pizzas!* I'm terribly impressed."

"Really very easy."

As he took the ice cubes from the tray and filled the pitcher, Philip had a sudden comprehension of the quality in his father's movements when preparing a meal, or washing up, that had so arrested him, this performance of simple physical actions with a kind of completeness and joy. He held the ice tray immobile, groping for the lines he had read only that morning in one of his father's books on Chinese philosophy. "What is the Tao?" And the answer, "Usual life is the very Tao." (Tao, the final Meaning, the Way, the Path, Enlightenment . . . Then it was everyday life that held both the mystery and the meaning, was both question and answer?)

Clare was lifting down a bottle from the shelf. "Chianti. One bottle. Small but adequate, I hope." She looked at him and smiled. He forgot the problem of the Tao.

Through supper they were both constrained, making polite conversation. It was a direct question from Philip which drew her first personal remarks:

"I spent many years explaining myself to people—or trying to." (He looked at her mouth: sensual, proud, angry.) "First my father—the president of a bank; then my mother—the president of womens' clubs; then my husband—an archaeologist without imagination. I even had my turn with a psychoanalyst. He took me apart but he didn't quite put me together again."

Who did that for you? he wanted to ask. Who put you together again? Something told him that he knew the answer—and did not want to hear it.

"What came next?"

"That's a long and boring story," she said lightly. She had obviously decided to drop this talk about herself.

While they were having their coffee a sudden thunderstorm blew up. Philip ran out to turn over the rowboat. A fierce wind whipped at the beach and the rain began to fall with a staccato beat on the stones. He looked over where the lightning flashed, scrawling its cryptic signs on the black sky above his father's house. As he stood with the rain striking his face he was aware of a kind of physical exultation and strength, some harmony between himself and the elements as on that other day in the woods when he had allowed the storm to drench him.

When he came back into the house, shaking the rain off his head, Clare was standing by her case of stone animal fetishes. She held one up to view. "Beautiful?"

He went up close to her, looking not at the stone animal but at her face. He reached out and closed his right hand firmly on her wrist. "Yes, beautiful." He pulled her against his body with all his force, pressing his mouth hard on hers, forcing her lips open with his tongue. This time she did not turn away.

3

IN THE dark and the silence, he lay hearing the sea. The wind was high—and the tide. The waves beat forward toward the house, retreated, sucked back down the gravelly beach, rolled forward again, cracking on the shore like a giant whip. The glassy sea of his childhood memory, that Sunday morning with the fixed eternal dip of the oars and the eternal fixed motion of the tide, had gone. The waves pounced, snarled, gnawed with a physical rush and ferocity that slashed and tore at the green banks.

He turned over and lay with the tears hot on his face while Clare's hand stroked the back of his head, moved along the nerve ends over his shoulder blades, down the arms to the fingertips.

Suddenly her gestures were hateful to him. From what intimate source had she learned these quieting and accomplished subtleties? He sat up suddenly, rose, walked to the window and looked out. Across the inlet through the streaming rain he could see the faint gleam from his father's kitchen window.

"I must go back," he said.

"Go back now?"

He nodded.

"Why?"

He did not answer.

"No, Philip, the tide's running terribly strong and—no, don't try to. Your father won't worry."

"How do you know?"

Her voice was quiet. "He just doesn't worry, that's all."

After a long silence, while he stood with his face close to the splattered pane staring at that unwinking light through the stormy darkness, he turned back into the room. "I suppose this had to happen to me." The words seemed to burst from him without his will.

He heard her strike a match, saw the end of her cigarette dot the darkness. "Why?"

"Punishment." The word sounded excessive, embarrassingly extreme, the moment he had said it—like a bad Russian novel, his mind quickly told him.

"Punishment for what?"

"For general stupidity." He deliberately chose the banal unrevealing words. In her quiet question he had felt the same directed pressure-from-underneath he had detected at times in Ermenthal's voice, the pressure which, in the first days of analysis, he had so irrationally resisted.

"Oh, God damn it!" He returned to the couch, thrust his face into his hands and groaned again. "I have to face it. I'm in love with you, Clare."

She said nothing. He had expected her to deny it, to argue, to question, but she did not. He wanted then to be angry; to tell himself that this was arrogance, this calm assumption of love as a thing due her, a gift readily extended by many men.

After a few moments she came back across the room and

stood pressing his head against her. And this time he felt her sympathy extended to him and he thought: she can feel my suffering because Lawrence has made her suffer. But what he said aloud, when finally he spoke, was, "I don't understand."

After a moment, "Don't understand what?" she asked.

"You—this—tonight."

Finally she asked, "Does that really puzzle you?"

He thought he caught a faint mockery in her voice. "Yes," he said stubbornly, "it does."

She withdrew from him and sat in the chair near the couch. "What really puzzles you about it?"

He dropped back on the pillows. Instantly he saw himself flat on his back in the hospital bed, with Ermenthal across from him. He tried to struggle up, but could only sink back farther, feeling the need of support under his head and shoulders.

"Can you tell me?" she asked.

"I'll try." His voice was dry and muffled, again the resistant voice of his hospital sessions. He felt two warring impulses: to run out of the house into the dark night, take the rowboat, start rowing wildly against the wind and the tide, finally letting go, to drift, to be carried by the dark elements of wind and water far away from this woman stirring beside him in the shadowy room, far away also from the light in his father's window: or else—the second impulse held him to the couch, to the wish to understand something difficult and evasive he now must solve.

He wanted to question Clare but he was afraid to, afraid of her answers; afraid she would make explanations he could not bear. He wanted to say to her: If you love Lawrence so much, why did you need and want this with me tonight—for I know you did; in these things it is impossible to be fooled. Yet he would not ask it because he could remember once, more than once, a voice saying, "But your wife . . ." and tapering off, never finishing. That way, yes, that way lay awkwardness, sadness, a hundred questions he could not answer. Maybe there were no answers.

And now, by Clare's calm silence, by her obvious conviction that there was nothing she need explain, he was forced to experience an emotion he was sure he had often roused in others: the feeling that to question was to be blind and stupid; that about some things you did not speak—things too puzzling, too painful, in a given situation for the human heart and mind to consider.

Yet he could not keep from asking, "What are we to do?"

"To do?"

"I mean—I won't be able to stand it when Lawrence comes back."

"But you will be gone soon." There was astonishment in her voice.

"No, I'm not going! I'm staying right here!" He knew he sounded like an angry schoolboy and hated himself for it. He was equally angry and astounded by this confession of an intention that had not occurred to him before this moment.

"Your wife?" she asked simply.

There it was, the old question. "My wife and I are complete strangers," he said.

"Have you always been strangers?"

He thought a long moment. "I don't know. I don't know because I never knew anything about myself until—until a short time ago. So how can I know anything about my wife?"

"Quite true," she said.

"Oh, Christ!" he exclaimed. "Must you always be such a sibyl? Don't you ever feel anything?"

She laughed. This time her mockery was open. "No," she said. "I am quite cold and dead. Couldn't you tell that?"

He wanted to strike her for the pain her words gave him. "What are you then? Just an intellectual whore?"

He knew this had shaken her. In the darkness, the width of the room, he could feel her stiffen. She made no reply.

"Forgive me," he said, after a moment. "Forgive me, Clare. I—I feel beside myself tonight. I . . ." ("Beside myself," his mind repeated—two selves then—split. How apposite the tired phrase was when you examined it!)

He groaned again. "I'm really so god-damned bewildered and tangled up!"

"Do you know why—what it is you want—or need?"

"I need love," he said. "Love!" His voice was desperate now in its sincerity. "Or maybe I want to give it. Maybe that's it—

and I want to know something—really *know*—just one single final truth about myself, or my wife, or you, or Lawrence . . ."

After a silence, "You love him, don't you?" he added, as though he had just seen the truth and was accusing her. "And you always will."

"Yes," she admitted. "In a strange way, that's the truth. And it's baffling. At least sometimes—to me. For he's difficult, God knows, and we're very unlike and—and he can hurt me more than anyone . . . He's not always even a satisfactory—partner."

(Did she mean lover? Had she spared him that word not wanting him to think she had given herself so freely tonight because of some failure on Lawrence's part?)

She was going on quietly. "As I told you once, I spent years of my life trying to explain myself. Lawrence helped me to drop all that. When I got to know him, saw how he just quietly lived in the main stream of his own life, did what he wanted, let other people do what they wanted—well, a great load rolled off me." She looked at him almost with defiance as though reliving some remembered scene. "That's what I need! I said to myself. To do what I want to do! What are the things I want to do? Live alone and work; study Indian mysteries; be near Lawrence . . . So, in time, it has all come about."

"Just what you wanted?"

"Yes." She was still defiant.

"Isn't that pretty completely selfish?"

"Is it? Who am I harming?"

Philip shrugged. "Well, I don't know. But, in the past—what about your husband?"

"Much more happily married to a girl who worships him."

Philip was silent. "No wonder you and my father get along so well," he said at last, hearing the resentment in his voice. "He took the selfish way too."

"Selfish?" Clare raised her brows. "And you find him a less mature personality for that?"

Philip could not answer immediately, yet he knew he was going to say to this woman things that he had not been able to force from his lips even in his hospital sessions. "My father killed my mother," he said. "That's the truth."

"Perhaps she killed herself?"

"Well, anyway, he warped and twisted me."

"More than your mother did?"

"Well, let's say he warped and twisted her, and she, in turn, did the same to me." (But who was it really on whom the blame could lie: his mother, his father, Jane, Aunt Hetebel, Uncle Logan, his grandfather, his great-grandmother? . . .)

Clare jumped up impatiently. She crossed the room and threw some pine cones into the fire. "And who warped and twisted your father?—his parents, I suppose. And who warped and twisted your mother?—her parents, no doubt. Oh, there's no end to it *that* way!" She flung more cones into the fire. "We have to cut through all that," she cried. "We have finally to stop dead still and take stock and say, I go on from here alone! Here I toss off the Old Man of the Sea—whoever and whatever that particular burden may be—for we've all had him, at one time or another, strapped to our backs . . ."

As she spoke, Philip, watching the pine cones glowing in their perfect fiery silhouettes, heard Ermenthal's voice that last day: "No guide can go all the way with you. Somewhere you have to go on alone."

He said hollowly, "It sounds fine. But not everyone can do it —toss off the Old Man of the Sea."

Her voice was suddenly very quiet, undefensive. "Anyone can who wants to pay the price." There was nothing glib in the way she spoke the over-familiar words.

"So what do you recommend for me?" He was surprised that he dared put this question.

She was silent. Finally, with hesitation, "I can't recommend for you," she said. "Who can tell you what to do with your life except yourself?"

"Are you completely happy?" He had to ask it, though he knew how it sounded.

She replied quickly, "No, of course not."

"Then *what* are you?"

"I've told you." She was becoming impatient again. "I'm living my life. Nobody else's! Mine! That's all I can say—and that's all I ask."

"Or will ever ask?"

"How can I tell? How do I know what lies around the corner tomorrow? I may *have* to change. My notions of what I want may change—but the river of my life won't change—it will just run along a different bank—maybe."

"You make it all seem so easy." He spoke half-angrily. "There are people who have responsibilities, you know—responsibilities they don't feel they can just toss overboard—children, families, wives, husbands . . ."

"I know." She turned her face in profile and looked at the framed photographs of ancient Mexican ruins as though studying them for the first time. "It's this kind of argument that proves to me one should never discuss any of it." She turned back toward him abruptly. "I didn't say it was easy," she said, her voice rising again. "I certainly don't recommend *my* life for general practice."

She got up then and stood by the fire, her hands stretched out behind her toward the flame. Her pose reminded Philip of the first night he had entered this room, when she had talked about Indians dancing with magnetic poles, when he had first considered her a pedagogue. He could imagine now how she must have been as a willful girl; headstrong, stubborn, concealing her uncertainty and even—it was possible—her pain under this brittle exterior.

In a moment she said, as though she really wanted an answer, "Don't you think choosing *anything* comes at a price? The very word choice—doesn't that suggest the difficulty?" Her voice was suddenly gentler. "And your own father—he paid a price, didn't he? He didn't see his own son for over twenty years."

A month ago, Philip said to himself, he would have flinched from such a personal comment, have replied lightly, or hastily changed the subject. Now he said, after a moment, "I wish I could hate my father. It would make it easier. I used to. Now, since seeing him, I can't feel any hate at all. Maybe it's still there—just temporarily buried—for I *should* resent him. I still think he let me down. Yet I find myself respecting him—loving him, even . . . It's a mystery."

"Maybe it won't always be a mystery?"

"You mean I may find myself acting like him—and so come to an understanding of him?"

"I didn't say that—but who can tell?"

He shook his head vehemently. "Oh, no, not that! I've got a lot of the Bachelders and the Jessups and the Davises in me—and they upheld the church, and the state, and the banks, and the status quo through hell and high water!"

He recognized that his voice had somehow lost its strain. She must have noticed it also for she said, rising, going to the fireplace and poking up the dead logs, "Let's have something to eat, shall we?"

He looked at her across the room in the light of the reviving fire and smiled. "Sometimes you're very male," he said. "It's very male to be hungry at times like this."

"Is it?" She too seemed amused.

He got up from the couch and came across to her. He put his arms around her and without tension or self-consciousness she freely returned his embrace in the firelight. It was now as if they had known each other a long time.

"I love you," he said solemnly. "I don't understand it, but don't forget it—and we won't question it."

"I'll not question it," she said. "It's you who will. You'll want it all cut and dried—like that New England grandfather with the ledger and entries that had to balance. But in life"—she hesitated—"do they ever balance? They didn't—they don't. Not for me anyway." Her rueful expression made her again look young and bewildered. He stretched out his hand to her and together they went toward the kitchen.

CHAPTER 28

....

*
*   *
*

PHILIP spent the following morning writing letters. He wrote
first to Goldstone and said he needed a few extra weeks, and to
take him off salary for this additional time if he wished. Then
he wrote Ellen, enclosing a duplicate of his letter to Goldstone.

He waited for the familiar prick of irritation that invariably
came when he thought of Ellen's calm acceptance of his "duty"
as job-holder and provider; that fixed responsibility of the male
that she had never questioned—he told himself—until his collapse. But, for some reason, today his usual irritation did not
appear. Perhaps, he thought, it was absent because for the first
time in his life he had dared to act independently about his
return from a holiday.

In a mood of relief he wrote Ellen more expansively than he
yet had. Not only did he tell her in detail about the trip to the
old Indian, but he made an attempt to correlate some of the
intangible, yet increasingly "real," experiences that had come
to him from living so close to nature and to his father. "I haven't
felt this alive mentally since college," he wrote. "Spider geometry

and mountain peaks, Zen riddles and Indian myths, Christ and Freud . . ." When he reread the letter he found it garbled, but he sent it anyway.

He did not mention Clare in this letter as he had in all earlier communications. When he observed this unconscious omission he searched himself for feelings of guilt. There were none. "Maybe this is what Ellen needs," he thought, "a new experience; something to shake off the numbness of her years with me." For a moment he expanded the idea that every human being had a right to these experiences; the right to participate in what the world considered unconventional behavior, if from it there could spring such impulses of generosity as he now felt. But almost immediately he asked himself again how tolerant of Ellen, in any similar situation, he would be. He wasn't sure.

He decided that some part of his reason for his own guiltless feeling came from his father's dignified reticence about his daily trips to Madrona. And because of the old man's silent understanding, his complete detachment, Philip found himself wanting to confide in him. Once he even spoke at length about Ermenthal. Haltingly he mentioned the conviction of special meaning, sacrificial meaning, which the death of Ermenthal had seemed at the time to imply. This feeling he was amazed to discover, had begun to intensify. It was as though it had gone underground to become a part of some deep inner conviction. Yet he had in fairness to ask himself what action he had taken to justify this arrogant and mystic interpretation of Ermenthal's death.

2

BEYOND the private place where his father so often sat looking at the mountains, Philip had found his own spot, a retreat with a similar pine back-rest. Here he would lie for hours in the sunlight, the gentle air brushing his exposed body. The swing of the tidewater no longer soothed him to sleep; now it continuously created in him a state of heightened perception where things that had long troubled him seemed about to disappear forever, like the fading shapes of dreams in morning light. He understood now what his father had meant once when he said that he wished his daily life to be "like the bird in the sky which moves freely, but leaves no track."

On one of the afternoons under the tree Philip began to sense, with special awareness, his own body: his spine against the tree trunk, the stretch of his legs on the pine needles, the way his head fitted his shoulders, how the breath moved his blood. He became aware of a humming, a singing, around him, everywhere, nowhere: insects and heat, sand and water, wind in the branches, the air itself, a rhythmic breathing of which his own breath was counterpart. He felt himself flowing away, melting into the air, the sky, the mountains, the hour of the day.

Yet at the same time, with equal awareness, he felt these elements melting back, returning into him. In this rhythmic suspension, he rested—a leaf in a still pool, a toad blinking in the sun, a human body leaning against a pine tree. It was late afternoon and through the atmosphere there came, like the turn of great silent wings, a magic shift in sky and earth, the signal of approaching evening. The mountains toward which he had been gazing steadily still lay ghostlike, floating milkily on the horizon; but this stir in the air was bringing them, he knew, slowly nearer, nearer, through the deepening sky, until soon they would stand waiting for him at the very foot of the inlet, as on the night he arrived.

How long the spell held he could not have said. But when the union was dissolved, he knew he had experienced a moment of security in Time, an identity with, and simultaneously, an oblivion to, the universe moving around and through him.

He attempted later to tell Clare of the experience. She listened attentively, nodding. "The Southwest Indians have a word to describe that state, and I suppose your father has his terms too."

"Are the Indians always your frame of reference?"

She smiled, her face suddenly wistful. "Yes, I suppose they are. I guess it's because they—the Indians—restored me to something I'd lost, a kind of naivete and wisdom that children have and don't hold on to."

"But I thought it was Lawrence . . ." Philip began. He stopped short.

She finished for him, "Who put me together again?" He nodded. "Yes, he helped, too," she said.

Philip forced himself to refer to Lawrence from time to time, though mention of him, even thought of him, was always the signal for some inner distress which he could not entirely explain. He had said to Clare on their first night that he would not be able to bear it when Lawrence returned; and this he still felt. Complete as Clare's surrender to him had been, he was puzzled by her. Under her physical freedom, under a certain wild intensity that she alternately checked and released, he sensed an untouched, unyielding core in her nature which he knew he had not reached. Had anyone? Could an abstracted dreamer like Lawrence . . . ? He knew better than to question Clare. She had said, apparently, all she intended to about Lawrence's place in her life. She had admitted, he reminded himself, that Lawrence was not always a satisfactory "partner." This was the one comment that now conveyed to him any lasting solace.

3

ON AN afternoon in early September when the wind scudding down the inlet flicked the water into little caps of foam, Philip rowed as usual across to Madrona. It was mail day, and as he pulled across the channel he thought with apprehension of the possibility of a summoning note from Goldstone, or at least a strong hint that it might not be wise to postpone his return too long, a repetition of Goldstone's recent warning that things were "toughening up" in the film industry. Ellen's answering letter had already come. He had found it almost stiltedly perfunctory. She had said that it was his "decision"; she would write him more about it soon.

He stopped to look in Clare's window, hoping she would be free and want to walk with him to the Byes'. But she was not in the house and, with a faint—he told himself—a foolish deepening of his vague apprehensions, he set off through the woods. He walked rapidly over the path that had by now become so familiar to him.

There were only two letters: one from Jane to his father, one from Ellen to him. He did not open Ellen's in the store, but waited until he came to the wood's edge, where he dropped down in a sheltered place and tore open the envelope.

It seemed, as he remembered it later, that the entire contents of Ellen's brief note registered on him in one moment of shattering comprehension. He had no sensation of reading separate words and phrases; it was as though he saw it all in one single illumination as one sees a landscape revealed by lightning: *I think I should tell you, Philip, that I have gone to a lawyer about a separation. I was afraid you might hear it from someone else— since your new delay in coming back—and I'd rather be the first to tell you. It isn't anything special—or anyone in particular— though I have been seeing quite a lot of Bob Scott. This isn't necessarily final, but just that I think it's the next step. Maybe this will do for me what your trip away has apparently done for you—give me some perspective and clarity. God knows I need it!* . . .

His first clear thought was, "But she can't! It's monstrously unjust! She wanted me to come here herself—she urged it!" He cried aloud, his voice echoing, coming back through the trees, "No! No! She can't!" And he got up from the ground and started to hurry through the woods toward Clare's, feeling a consuming need to find her at once, pour out his story, call upon her sympathy, demand from her the kind of unstinted loving attention he had seen her give Lawrence in moments of crisis.

When he came to Clare's windows and looked in she was not at her desk. For a moment he thought the room was still empty —and then he saw her. She was lying face down on the couch. At first he decided she was sleeping; then, as he put his head against the window, he was shocked to hear the strangled ugly sound of heavy sobbing. He stared, unbelieving, and in that same moment he became aware of another presence. In the corner watching her, with his wooden imperturbability, with the terrible dead fixity of his obsidian eyes, stood Old Doctor's god of healing. At sight of him Philip felt a sensation of primitive terror.

Suddenly—as though sensing Philip's presence—Clare sat up on the couch. She turned toward him a face swollen and blurred. Her hair fell in strands across her eyes, and her expression, wild

and distorted, terrified him even more than the wooden image.
"Go away!" she cried. "Go away!"

He was too stupefied to move. But when she cried out again,
"Please, please, go away!" he turned and came quickly through
the door into the living room.

As he entered she jumped up like a humiliated and angry child,
jerked one edge of her scarf over her face and attempted to run
past him into the kitchen. He caught her and spun her around,
trying to hold her in his arms. She beat at his hands. "Let go!"
she cried. "Let go!" When he held on, trying to soothe her, her
voice became angry, out of control, spiteful. "What were you
doing anyway—spying through my window?"

He dropped her arms. "Oh, for God's sake!" he said in disgust.

She ran from the room and he heard the kitchen door slam.
When he looked out the windows opening on to the woods behind the house, he saw her disappearing down the thin path that
led toward The Squat.

For a moment he stood debating whether or not to follow her.
He took a cigarette, lit it, decided that whatever the source of
her uncontrolled weeping, she would probably rather be alone
until the storm subsided. Certainly, he thought, Ellen was like
that.

Ellen! Abruptly he heard his wife sobbing in the locked guest
room that night four months before. He attempted to shut out
this memory by staring intently at the tree outside the window.
The boughs were hanging heavily, lifting and falling slowly in the
wind like seaweed in a tide of dark air. "She will have to come
back soon," he thought. "It's going to rain. She didn't take a
coat." He sat down to wait.

The room was cold. Judging from the look of the hearth, there
had been no fire all day. He could smell the acrid ashes of the
night before, the aromatic scent of cedar boughs on the table,
and faintly, from the pillows of the couch, the perfume Clare
used on her hair. He studied the imprint her body had left on the
cover, looking at it a long time as though it might now contain
a clue to the mystery of her identity; like a fingerprint, a track in
the sand. "You, too!" he said aloud. He realized that he had
often—though until now he had never admitted it—wished that

he might see her like this: broken, unsure, her discipline shattered, the pedagogue in her become only a puzzled sufferer. Now that it had happened he wondered why he felt no triumph, no exultation, nothing but a heavy despondency. It was as though, slowly and finally, another invisible prop was slipping away from him.

He sat pressing his hands hard to his skull. Again he thought he heard the sound of sobbing and looked up, half-expecting Clare. It was no one.

He walked over to the cupboard, found the Bourbon, poured himself a drink.

As he stood with the glass in his hand there was a step in the kitchen. The door between the rooms opened and Lawrence appeared on the sill. In his surprise Philip could not speak. Lawrence greeted him warmly, naturally, "Phil, how are you?" Philip moved toward him and they shook hands. He managed to ask, "When did you get back?"

"This morning."

"Good trip?"

"Fair. I went to Death Valley."

Philip stared. "Death Valley," he repeated. The name seemed to him, in this confused moment, to have a symbolic, rather than a geographic, reality.

"The desert," Lawrence explained. He looked at Philip intently for a second before he added, "It's good for the painter's eye—that emptiness—restores the vision. I'm looking for Clare. I thought she came over here."

"She . . ." Philip began thickly. He cleared his throat. "She —was here when I came but—she just went into the woods." He forced himself to add, "Seemed very upset when she left."

Lawrence showed no reaction of any kind. He looked out into the fir boughs. "It's going to rain," he said. "I suppose she went without a coat. I'd better take her one." He walked to the closet, removed Clare's hooded mackintosh. "See you later." Philip watched him take the thread of path that led into the woods.

After Lawrence had disappeared he stood quietly looking again into the green wall of trees. He felt stunned now, mercifully encased in an armor of non-feeling. This, he told himself, was the mood he must by all means sustain. He walked to the cupboard and poured himself a second drink. As it burned its way into his stomach he felt his control, his encasing armor, melting away. In its place came all his unadmitted jealousy of Lawrence. He stood looking into the woods with the glass in his hand and he felt a wave of hatred toward Clare, Ellen, Lawrence and—finally toward his father—the old, long-buried inexplicable hatred and anger twisting and winding its way through him. He was completely alone now, completely stripped, deserted and abandoned in a cold and unfamiliar room, with night descending, a storm rising. Ellen—even Ellen! He had no place to go—no home. "I have no home." All at once his sense of isolation, of pain and loneliness became so intense, so acutely physical, that he could no longer remain still. He rushed from the room to his boat, got in, pushed off and began to row toward Peachpit. But as he rowed he knew he did not want, could not bear, to face his father now. He prayed the old man had not yet returned from his fishing trip with Clarence.

He found the house empty. He scribbled a note and laid it on the kitchen table. *Feeling punk. Am napping. Don't worry. Just let me sleep.* He went into his room, turned the bolt that, for the first time, he noticed on the door, opened his valise and got out a bottle, a raw brand bought in Venus, he had told himself, "against emergencies."

He took a long pull, shuddered, then found himself staring fixedly at the bottle's distinguished label—a kindly Southern gentleman in a wide-brimmed straw hat snipping a rare rose for his buttonhole. *Smooth as rose petals*, the label read. The words filled him with unreasonable fury. One more lie! One more elaborate deceit in a world full of illusions and pitfalls. He took a knife and began to scrape the label from the bottle. He poured another long drink. His head was pounding now, his heart racing the way it had in London during the bombings. "What is it? What is it?" he demanded. "Why am I so afraid? Why am I so upset? My life—this situation in which I find myself—it can't be this bad. Nothing, *nothing*, is this bad. What does one call it? It must have a name." Rejection? Was that it? "Fear of rejection because of the guilt of rejection": Ermenthal. But Ermenthal too had rejected, had abandoned, disappeared, left him to struggle on alone. It was unfair, a horrible injustice—his father, Lawrence, Clare, they were all so smug and contained in their strangeness and self-centeredness. They had never really accepted him, he knew it now. They rejected him and his feelings, abandoned him, just as his mother had years ago when she took to her bed and died, making her escape in a coffin as he had tried, in those first days of pain and confusion in the hospital, to make his escape by going underground. And then his father after the funeral, looking on coolly at his son's struggle, at his childrens' decision to stay or go; never gesturing, never beckoning or nodding, never once pleading, or even suggesting, saying merely, "Make up your own minds, children!" What was this but consummate unflinching cruelty! "Make up your own minds"—with Aunt Hetebel's purse and the train ticket East lying on the table between them . . . And now this further cruelty—Ellen, Ellen signing a cold piece of paper testifying that the separation, so long apparent between them, was now neatly and legally bona fide.

He raised the bottle again; began to drink slowly, steadily, methodically, aiming at total oblivion.

4

FROM a half sleep he heard his father return with Clarence, and then there was silence and he slept again. When he awoke the second time it was to a question that seemed to have asked itself aloud in the room, "Why was she crying?" He sat up. "Who crying?" he demanded. His confused and tormented mind swung back to the thought of Clare, her body outstretched on the couch not in an abandonment of grief but of passion. And then it was Ellen in the same attitude and with someone else . . . Bob Scott? He jumped up from the bed. He could not bear to lie there a moment longer; inaction, reflection—they were now beyond his endurance.

He looked at his watch. It was two o'clock and suddenly he knew that he had to go back across the inlet and find them. He must bring this situation out in the open, hurt them as they had hurt him. Ellen was out of his reach—but these people—they would have to answer him. Who was Lawrence that he should be protected by everyone? Clare, he was certain now, had not been crying over him, Philip. Oh, no, his pain was of no consequence to her. It was Lawrence of whom she was thinking. Or was it of herself?

Anyway, he would find out. Action! That was what he wanted, that was what was called for now. He took another drink and left the house, got the rowboat and returned to Madrona. It was a hard pull, the wind from the north came in gusts that tossed waves over the sides of the frail dinghy, but he rowed on.

He stole up the familiar path to Clare's door, opened it and said softly, "Clare." There was no answer. He had a flashlight with him and in a shaking hand he aimed its hooded beam around the room, picking up the obsidian eyes of the Indian god. He went into the kitchen. There was no sign of cooking, or of anyone having eaten in the past hours. With a cleverness that in his drunken state he admired, he opened the closet door and looked carefully for the mackintosh Lawrence had carried with him into the woods. It was not there.

Abruptly he left the house by the back door and crossed the pine-needle path toward Lawrence's. He tried the side door, the one by which he had entered the night he had first seen Clare through the window standing before Lawrence's easel. The side door was locked. He tried it again several times, and, when he was sure it had been bolted from the inside, he stumbled around the house through the low-growing bushes to the door opposite. Locked, too! He stood then, short of breath, leaning against the house wall, listening to the crazy thumping of his heart.

Suddenly he lifted his fist and struck at the house wall. "Clare!" he shouted. "Clare!" That would bring her. He was certain now that his voice sounded imperious and commanding. He pounded with his fist again, raised his voice even louder. "Clare!" He heard the trees screeching behind him, locking and unlocking their boughs.

When there was still only silence from within the house, he began to imagine Clare and Lawrence behind the door, consulting, whispering what to do. "Be quiet! He'll go away."

The third time he shouted "Clare" and pounded, the door opened suddenly. "What do you want?" She did not seem angry. She simply stood, wrapped in her coat, waiting.

"You!" he answered. He seized her by the shoulders and shook her back and forth. "It's you I want! You know damned well! You, Clare, you, you, you!"

She detached his hands from her shoulders. He lunged awkwardly toward her again, but she stepped back out of reach. Then, as though she did not want to offend or wound him with her withdrawal, she put out her hand and touched his arm.

"Don't, Philip! Don't stand here torturing yourself. You can't talk now. You're in no shape. I'll see you tomorrow. We can talk then."

"To hell with tomorrow!"

"Philip, please! Tomorrow—I promise. I want to talk to you—but not now. Go home now!"

"Home!" he hooted. He gave the word his full drunken scorn. "Home! Where's that? I've got no home!" He could hear his voice bellowing, echoing through the night.

"Don't shout," she said. "Your father'll hear you. You don't want to upset him, do you?"

"Oh, no!" He became exaggeratedly quiet, he put a finger to his lips. "Shhh! Let's protect my kind old saintly father as long as we can. You bet!"

He belched. It was not intentional but it seemed to him, at this moment, singularly appropriate. "My father," he said, "now I'm glad you mentioned him. He's an interesting subject to me and, I'm sure, to you." He leaned nearer, lowered his voice confidentially. "He's really the Devil, you know. Or did you?" He raised his voice a little and spoke with conviction. "He's the Devil disguised as an old man—a sage." He half-fancied the poplar trees applauded this statement with a thousand soft green palms. When Clare made no comment, he said abruptly, stiffly, "I'd like to speak to Lawrence."

The door opened on his words. Lawrence had obviously been waiting behind it, listening. "Well, Philip, what is it?" Was he as composed as his manner indicated? Philip thought not, though the voice held no trace of strain.

"You know god-damned well!" Philip was near enough to see the steady dark eyes swimming up out of the pallid oval of the face.

Lawrence shook his head. "No, I have no idea."

Somehow, even through the liquor, Philip realized that this was the truth, but he could not restrain himself. "You're a liar!"

Lawrence stepped back then, inside the door. There was a short silence. "Look, Phil, can't we talk about it tomorrow—whatever it is. You're in no shape now . . ."

"I'm in as good shape now as I'll ever be!" He tried, with self-conscious defiance, to straighten himself, but the effect was carried through by his shoulderblades alone. He could feel his knees sagging.

"All right," Lawrence said agreeably. "Let's walk down to the shore. What do you say?" When he made a movement to take Philip's arm, Philip jerked back, almost rocking off balance. "I don't care where the hell we go!" he said and started running toward the beach.

He rounded the house uncertainly. When the force of the wind struck him, he kneeled like a broken ship in a gale but plunged on. Once he heard himself, as though at a distance, crashing down on a log near the bank and, after he was down, he sat there trying to control the spasm of nausea that struck his stomach. He began to shake, unable to quiet his quivering muscles. A confused succession of blurred images and ideas—accusations, pleas for help, murderous threats—rocked through his brain. Their clamor was too much for him. He clapped his hands over his ears.

Lawrence came up to him, stood waiting in silence as Philip remained on the log with his hands still clutched to his ears. Everything around him was in movement now: advancing, retreating, pulling, pushing. He could dimly feel Lawrence helping him to his feet; was aware that he was walking again. Yes, here was the shore, and here the boat, the good old scrubby tub of a boat. He heard Lawrence say, "I'm going to row you home, Phil."

"Not going home." He jerked his arm away again. The abrupt movement seemed to clear his head briefly. He stared hard at

Lawrence trying to still his wavering image. "I can't go home because I have no home." There! What could be more plausible? Now Lawrence would certainly go away and leave him. When he did not move, except to continue weaving back and forth as though blowing in the wind, Philip added thickly, "*You've* got a home. Go on back to it. I'll be all right."

"Come on back with me then and I'll make you some coffee," Lawrence offered.

Philip shook his head elaborately, decisively.

"Then come over to Clare's and lie down. You can't cross over tonight. Not feeling like this. Come on, will you?"

Even through his sick and drunken despair Philip felt the hard impact of Lawrence's suggestion. Clare's house! What a monstrous joke! What a stupid monstrous affront! What kind of character was this painter anyway? Did he really think . . . ? Lawrence was trying to look into his eyes. Philip could feel his gaze on him, calm and quiet.

"I'm all right," Philip muttered again. "Just leave me alone." He started walking off unsteadily down the beach. He heard Lawrence coming after him again. He walked faster; he felt Lawrence's hand on his shoulder.

"Look, Philip," Lawrence said. "I'll leave you. But promise me—don't cross over tonight. Will you promise that? Will you?"

"Promise," Philip finally said thickly. He was suddenly exhausted from the walking; he felt any time now he might drop on the sand and be unable to get up.

"Good," Lawrence said. He turned away.

Philip heard him go. Lawrence's shoes on the loose shale— gigantic teeth crunching melba toast. Then the sound stopped abruptly, too abruptly. Ah, so Lawrence was watching him, was he? Waiting to see what he did. Well, it would be simple— childishly simple—to fool him. Philip turned and, with an ease that amazed him, crossed the small stretch of beach toward Clare's. He opened the kitchen door and closed it behind him with a loud noise. Then he stood leaning against it, perspiring, laughing, the silly cracked noise of his voice coming back to him like a demonic echo.

He slid down slowly to the floor and rested there, leaning

against the door, catching his breath. It was very silent now. There was no one here. No one but Philip Bachelder Stewart, Philip Bachelder Stewart, Philip Bachelder Stewart . . .

The sick misery of the afternoon began to stir in him. It was like—like the slow erupting of a hundred minute volcanos in a dish of cooking porridge. "Mush," he said aloud. His father's morning mush. Only this was black. From the throat down, black mush—a bubbling tumult of a hundred open mouths of misery; a hundred mute moving portals of black wretchedness. He struggled to his feet, opened the door wide, caught a draught of the wind again, full in the face. It steadied him; recalled caution. He must creep stealthily from the house; enter the woods at the place just beyond the spring where he would not be visible to Lawrence.

5

THE path through the woods had always seemed easy by day. By night it lay waiting with a battery of concealed traps, foot mines, tricks of shadow and motion to signal the eye, clutch at the chest, deal the breath a sudden hard fist of terror. Twice he came up against a tree that had moved, wraith-like, menacing, directly into his path. Three times he stumbled headlong, catching his toe in one of the half-exposed roots of Oregon grape. Or was it cedar? Must be accurate at all costs; botanic accuracy, like his father's. He got down, felt along the path with his hands —tactile revelations: scrape, prick, cut, scratch—until he found the cedar roots, tough, strong as steel wire. With a desperate necessity, digging his heels into the ground, cutting his palms, summoning all his strength he pulled at the loosened thong until it came free at one end, then he felt it far away, strike him, strike his eye. He lay down moaning, his hand over his stinging flesh. "Blinded," he moaned aloud in agony. "Blinded." The tossing trees—the Greek chorus of the tossing trees—what were they saying? Blinded? He listened. "Mush," they chorused. "Mush." Or was it, "Hush"? "Mush-Hush, Mush-Hush!" It was only the wind.

At last, covering his right eye, he dared to force the lid of his left up over the hot flood that still poured from it. Dimly he could make out shapes of dark and light—yes, they were there, they registered, even through the watery wall. Perhaps, then, the injury was not fatal. But oh, it might have been, oh, yes, it might. It was a close call. "Close call?" Where had he heard that before?

When—he could not have said how much later—the pain and the uncontrolled weeping had lessened, he got to his feet again. Something told him it was very late and he must make the Byes' meadow in time to see the sun come up. The thought of that meadow, the sprawl of the old house, the Bye kitchen, made him feel better. He began to recite aloud, his voice thick, mawkish. " 'The foxes of the earth have holes, the birds their nests, but the Son of Man hath not where to lay his head.' " Only fox holes, love nests . . . He quickened his stumbling steps to hurry away from his spurious self-pity. He tried to laugh. He wanted to laugh as he had that first night of his arrival on the island when listening to Clarence Bye's tall Nature stories. To laugh? Why did he want to laugh? About what? What was funny? What was funny about Nature? Didn't spiders embrace and devour? Didn't the wild male turkey gobbler destroy its mate's eggs? Didn't tom-cats eat their offspring? And didn't people lie in bed together, locked in the dark intimacy of physical union, only to rise from it and speak like strangers, like enemies? No, there was no balm in "Nature." Nature—it was terrifying, cannibalistic, cabalistic, unbearably impersonal.

He stopped suddenly, frozen. Ahead, on the path, was a great lumpish form—an animal waiting. A bear? Yes, a bear surely, because it was nearing apple time and Clarence had said— and the fruit in the Bye meadow was almost ripe. His heart began to beat like a wild drum, louder, louder, a steadily deepening clamor that gradually filled the whole woods. Overhead a dark shape detached itself from a tree and moved off silently, floating, a phantom in a slow-motion nightmare. "Owl." And in that moment he knew it was not a bear ahead of him. It was only a clump of huckleberry. Yet when he passed it, he began to run.

Just before he saw the glimmer of pale light that announced

the meadow, he stumbled for the last time and fell, badly wrench-
ing his knee. He crawled out into the open and lay in the dew-
soaked salal, smelling the sickish breath of the waxy fruit crushed
under his body. He felt the damp and the chill penetrate through
his thin shirt, his torn trousers, but he could not move. He tried
to remember where the hammock hung in which he had napped
the day of his arrival, the fine comforting hammock between the
madrona trees, swinging, swinging . . .

6

HE awoke stiff and cold in the dawn. His head was still throbbing, an engine laboring up a hill, but he forced himself to
think. Yes, he had to think. He had to think and plan—plan his
escape, for now he thought only of how he could get off the
island; how he could get away from his shame and rage and disappointment. Clarence? No, Clarence would never take him in
his present condition; not with a black eye, a wrenched knee,
torn clothes, bloody palms. Not without an explanation.

While he stood trembling, reviewing the night's damage to
himself, trying to formulate some plan, the light grew steadily.
Behind him, in the woods through which he had just made his
frantic stumbling progress, the birds were already running scales,
clearing their throats, exchanging morning greetings. Their bright
chatter seemed stupid, meaningless, without pity.

He looked down the path. He knew he would have to go back
the way he had come; pack, clean up, change his clothes, bandage his knee—and surely his eye. Then he would borrow his
father's boat and row around the point to the Madrona landing
in time for the afternoon ferry. One thing was certain, no
matter what the difficulties, he would not stay on Peachpit
another day.

He turned and started back through the woods.

When he emerged once more on the shore opposite his father's
island he was trembling with exhaustion and the pain in his leg.
But he did not stop. He had left the woods cautiously just where
he entered them—behind Clare's spring—out of sight of Lawrence's windows. He hoped one thing with all his heart; that

neither of them would see him in his present condition, try to stop him, even speak to him.

He was shaking with cold when he got the boat into the chan·nel and began, in spite of his torn palms, to row quickly across the inlet—smooth now and gentle as though the wild wind of the night had stroked away its fury. He looked back once from mid-channel and was sure he saw a human figure pressed against Clare's house. He felt a return of his formless rage against them all: "They know you don't belong here! They've just been tolerating you. They'll be glad you're getting out. Glad to be rid of you—just as Ellen is!"

When he grounded the boat he pulled it well up on the sand, farther than usual, as though proving thereby some point about himself to an invisible audience. Winded, he sat down for a moment. He heard the birds again in the woods behind him and, from habit, looked toward the end of the inlet where the mountains stood. In the growing light they appeared to belong to a world of cool purity, of repose and wisdom that he now felt was forever closed to him, and in a panic he tried to recall the moment he had had under the pine. It seemed if he could even as much as touch the fringes of this experience the mountains would not be lost to him. But the memory would not come back—the sensation of belonging, of being a part—and suddenly the snowcaps across the blue water were enemies. He got up and started for the house.

It was then he saw his father. The old man rose from the pine down the beach and walked slowly toward him. Though he was still at a distance, Philip felt sure his father must have seen him. But the old man did not hurry, did not even wave or call out. Nothing in his appearance or his movements gave an impression of agitation. Hadn't his father worried about his absence? Could nothing shake him from his established routines, his cheerful impersonalness? "God damn him!" Philip cried to himself. "He doesn't give a damn! Never has, never will."

He slammed into the kitchen and tramped, limping, through the house to his room where he cast himself face down on the bed. The moment his head touched the pillow he realized how sick and weak he felt, and he longed, like a child, to have his father come to the door and rap and ask him if he was all right. But he did not come, and when after some minutes Philip was convinced that he did not intend to, he forced himself off the bed and began his packing.

In the mirror of his shaving kit he examined his eye. It was not badly discolored. His knee and palms looked worse; they were bloody, black, with dirt ground into them. He cleaned the flesh as best he could with shaving lotion and pasted a few band-aids across the torn surface. When he had managed with his shaking hands to get his bags packed, he decided on another swallow of whiskey to stop his body's trembling.

He took a long gasping draw on the crude liquor. As soon as he put the bottle down he knew he could not face his father in this condition; did not want to answer any questions, make any explanations, endure that steady gaze. Well, he didn't have to face him. He could just sneak off quietly, take the boat, send Clarence back with it later on with a note of some kind. If he was careful, if he left by the window instead of the kitchen door, his father would not see him. He pushed the window to its limit, dropped the bag outside, waited a moment, listening. There was a blurred whirring in his ears but no sound in the house. With infinite caution and some pain in his bandaged knee, he lowered himself to the ground. Then crouching, so that his head might not be seen from the kitchen windows, he crept out through the madronas toward the beach.

His father was sitting on the shore. He had pulled the boat up higher and tied it firmly to a log.

Philip limped over to the boat, and, without speaking, threw in his bag, walked to the rope and began to untie it. His father got to his feet then, put his hand on the rope and held it.

"What are you doing, son?"

"You can see what I'm doing! I'm getting the hell out of here!"

"Not with this boat," the old man said quietly.

"Who's going to stop me?"

"I am."

"You!" Anger as bitter as vomit rose in him. "Nobody's going to stop me this time! It's my life and I can do with it what I god-damn well please!"

"That's true," said the old man with maddening calm. "It's your life but it's my boat."

"I warn you," Philip said wildly. Even his voice was trembling now, shaking like his body. He could feel the liquor taking hold again and he knew he could not control himself. "Don't try to interfere with me. You're too late." He looked straight at his father, hardly able to see him. What he saw more clearly was an image of himself in the Seattle boat with Aunt Hetebel, his father on the dock—casual, contained, seemingly indifferent. "The time to have interfered with me was twenty-six years ago. But then—then you didn't raise your hand. Now you're too late. If you're so god-damned wise and knowing, why haven't you been trying to reach me all these years? But no! No, you didn't want to. You didn't even want me to come this time. You just took me in because you were forced to, because you thought it was your Christian duty! Well, now you're really rid of me. This time it's final."

The old man came near enough to lay his hand on Philip's arm. "Stop it, son! Stop it now. You're not yourself. Let's sit down and talk about it a little."

"Don't call me son! You've never been my father!" Philip cried. He gave a yank at the rope with his full strength. It was as though the pain inside him moved into his hands with fiery force. He felt the rope cut through the band-aids and into his torn palms. The old man—still holding the rope—was unprepared for this sudden movement. As Philip yanked the cord, his father lurched forward, wavered, slipped on the wet stones and —with an unexpected clownlike reversal of movement—fell backwards, striking his head and spine. He made a sound between a grunt and a groan, and then lay motionless.

The wildness went out of Philip so suddenly he felt sick. After one stunned second he was kneeling beside his father. "Dad! You're hurt!"

The old man's lids flickered. With difficulty he opened them. "No, I don't think so." He made an attempt to rise—pain in his face, his eyes cloudy. "Struck my back pretty hard. Took my breath . . . ." After another moment, "Give me a hand. Let me sit up."

Philip raised him, keeping his arm around him. "You're hurt," he repeated like a child in fear.

"No, don't think so," said the old man. "Just my breath. Maybe a bruise. Let's get back to the house."

Philip helped him to his feet and, supporting him as he walked leaning over—for the old man now admitted one spot felt rather queer—they made the kitchen. Philip got him out of his shirt. Low on the right side there was already a discolored place. It looked ugly and was swelling rapidly. There were several smaller cuts where the barnacles and stones had scraped through.

"How does it look?"

Philip described it.

"Arnica for the bruise," said the old man, still speaking with some thickness. "Iodine for the cuts. I'll be all right in a jiffy. . . . Maybe a cold compress first on that spot over the kidneys." His voice was light, cheerful, but Philip saw he spoke with effort and realized his father had never expected such violence from him—that this, as much as the fall itself, had shocked him.

They sat together in silence then, Philip holding the compress to his father's back, watching without shame his own tears making dark stains on the knees of his gray city flannels.

When he had the old man rubbed and bandaged and in his bed, he brought him a swallow of liquor. "I'll get us some breakfast now."

"You go ahead for yourself, son. I'd better just lie here alone and quiet for a little while. Pull myself together."

Philip hesitated; he did not want to leave the room until he had made an attempt to explain his conduct. But his head was still churning with liquor and his confused emotions of shame and despair. After a moment he turned and walked back to the kitchen and stood for a long time in the middle of the floor like a man unable to make the next movement, even the next step. Finally he became aware that he was shivering. He went over to the woodbox, got the wood and paper and lit the fire. When he poured on the kerosene—as he had so often watched his father do—and the flame roared up, he was so strongly tempted to throw on the whole explosive contents that he frightened himself. He hastily put the lid on the stove and sank down weakly in his father's chair.

"Breakfast." He spoke the word aloud. The thought of food was nauseating, yet he knew he needed something immediately sustaining or his shaking body would fall apart. His dead eye, roving slowly, came upon the liquor still standing on the table where he had poured the drink for his father. He reached out and grabbed the bottle by the neck, clenching his eyes shut as he forced a raw swallow down his throat.

For a moment the warmth revived him. Then he was sick. He ran to the kitchen door, barely got outside. When the nausea had passed, he lay a long time with his head among the maidenhair ferns his father had planted at the corner of the house, his mind blurred, no longer able to tell him whether he was in the Bye meadow or back on Peachpit. He saw the ferns, recognized them, felt momentarily reassured. Ferns. It had been salal in the meadow. As the memory came to him it brought the sickish smell of the crushed berries again and he retched once more and lay where he was. He longed now for unconsciousness, longed to lie here alone and unnoticed, like a man freezing in the snow, or a sick animal creeping deeper into the forest to find death.

After a while he thought of his father and pulled himself up and went back into the house where he stood listening outside the door. When he heard no sound of any kind he grew apprehensive. He did not want to waken the old man in case he had fallen asleep. Clumsily he got down and looked through the wide keyhole.

The bed was empty. His heart jumped—and then he saw his father's head and hands. The old man was kneeling; kneeling on the far side of the bed, and, although his face was hidden, Philip realized that he was praying. It was the first time he had ever seen his father praying alone. The privacy of this moment seemed far more intense, more immediate and real than any prayer he had ever witnessed. It seemed far away from his father's meditations under the pine. Philip rose and crept quietly back into the kitchen.

He sat down by the stove, his hands clasped hard between his knees. He wished he too could pray but he had no idea how to begin. He was oppressed now with the thought of his own unworthiness and was sure he was the object of some petition on his father's part, some placing of his son's troubled spirit before a source of judgment even more impersonal than his own. Or was the old man asking help—general, non-specific help? "In praying set no limits." His father had said that in his "sermon" the day they had come back from the trip to Old Doctor—the one occasion that Philip had entered the shabby little box in Venus where he spoke. "If you turn to the Will of God, then leave it to the Will of God." He had been speaking on prayer—its abuse, its meaning. Little of what he had said then had touched Philip; the subject seemed too remote, belonging to another era, other ways of life.

As he sat huddled near the stove he heard a noise on the beach outside. It was again the giant's teeth scrunching—the monstrous shoes approaching over the shale. At the sound all the horror of the night returned. He looked out and saw Lawrence coming toward the house. He was moving with a certain hesitation, almost timidly, Philip thought, and this wariness made him ashamed. He longed to jump up and hide, but instead he forced his body to the door and opened it to the visitor.

"Come in."

"I just came over to . . ." Lawrence began hesitantly.

"Come in, will you?" It was as though by the repetition of this formal phrase Philip believed he could spare them both embarrassment. When Lawrence stood inside the kitchen door, Philip said, "My father has had an accident. He slipped and hurt his back."

A tide of brown color flooded Lawrence's eyes, darkening, dilating them. "Badly?"

"No, I don't think so. He says not."

"You're sure?" Lawrence's concern—so genuine, so instantaneous and warm—sent a wave of affection, and after it a fresh wave of shame, through Philip.

"Yes, it's only a bruise. If it isn't absolutely all right by tomorrow, though, I'll let you know."

"I'll gladly go for a doctor—or any medicine."

"Thanks. I know."

"I can't bear to think of your father in pain."

Philip said nothing. A cloud passed over the sun and the room was in shadow. As it brightened again Lawrence said, "Clare was worried. She sent you a note."

He extended a small white envelope. For a moment Philip could not even put out his hand to accept it. The nerve, he thought, the bravado, to act like this, without feeling—or was it without feeling?—anyway, calmly taking up the threads again, acting as though this was the way it was—life—and one needn't expect it to conform to the obvious or the anticipated any more than one need expect him, Lawrence, to paint a naturalistic toad under a naturalistic trillium flower—and he looked at the kitchen wall where the warted monarch sat under his trifoliate star. Lawrence was still standing by the door holding out the envelope, waiting. "The note," he repeated.

Philip took the piece of paper from him. He felt compelled to open it, read it in Lawrence's presence. *Would you like me to come over? Or will you come here? Or shall I write? Clare.*

Lawrence's unshaken calm, his poise, his matter-of-factness, made Philip angry again. "They've asked for it," he said to himself. He did not feel revengeful now but he was going to get matters settled between them once and for all. He looked straight at Lawrence.

"Tell her I want to ask her just one question. Why was she crying?"

Lawrence's expression did not alter. "Is it so unusual for a woman to cry?"

"Clare—yes."

"Oh, no," Lawrence said. "I haven't often seen her cry—but I have often heard her."

"And you don't know why?"

Lawrence seemed faintly surprised at this question. "Yes," he said, "I think I know why. Things get too much for her. She works too hard—lives too hard. She never runs away, like I do. So when it all piles up she has a crying spell."

He waited, like a messenger, Philip thought, who expects further questions and is prepared to answer them.

Philip checked an impulse of impatient dismissal. He stood

immobile by the kitchen stove, Clare's brief note in his hand, trying to capture the elusive shades of meaning that now seemed present in Lawrence's last words, in this whole episode. Parts of that intimate personal acrostic on which he had been at work since his hospital days began to fit with sudden deceptive ease into their appointed spaces. Lawrence's steady calm highlighted his own tension; revealed the exaggeration of his own response to Clare's scene of tears. "Lack of proportion," he accused himself. Underestimating Ellen's tears, overestimating Clare's—both responses springing from that "maladjustment in values" (Ermenthal), from that amateur status in the realm of "feeling" which created, which had always created, his distortions, his false evaluations? Not then: *Why* was she crying?—Ellen, Clare, even his mother—but rather, Why *shouldn't* she cry?

He had no idea how many minutes passed as he carried on this inner dialogue. When he again saw Lawrence (though he had been looking straight at him) he could tell himself, "Yes, they belong together." He was able then to fold Clare's note calmly and put it in his pocket.

"Thank her for writing," he said, and added, "tell her to send me that book on ghost-dancing." Lawrence's steady, faintly troubled gaze did not leave Philip's face. After a moment Philip said, "I'll be leaving the island as soon as the old man feels fit again—in a day or two, at most. I'm long overdue."

"We'll miss you." Lawrence's tone was unmistakably regretful. His brown eyes, with their glinting mica centers, were clear, grave.

"Thanks," Philip said, wanting to say something more. They clasped hands silently; Lawrence turned and walked away.

He watched Lawrence cross the beach, step into the boat, start the short pull to Madrona. Suddenly he seemed to Philip like a figure in a legend. The departure by boat, the shifting play of light on the water where the wind had now returned, the sudden skimming dip and volplane of Tatoosh the Gull above the ruined piles of the old dock, gave the scene the merciful air of a myth. This was not a rival, this strange emissary recrossing the inlet toward the far shore. Was it not rather what Ermenthal might have called his alter ego, or the child he had once been—the young boy who could lie all day on his stomach on the floor, drawing hawks, moths, Indians—or dreaming beside the stream where the dragonflies and the darning needles unraveled time in the long afternoons of summer?

When Lawrence beached the boat on the far shore, he turned back once toward Peachpit, peering from under the palm of his right hand. Although he could not possibly have seen Philip looking from the kitchen window, Lawrence waved, or rather, he lifted his hand—the hand with which he had screened his eyes—lifted it and moved it back in space slowly, then ahead, as though giving a signal to invisible powers. Then stooping—a characteristic gesture—(Philip had seen it many times) he gathered a handful of gravel from the beach and walked away shaking the bits of stone lightly in his closed hand, dropping them one by one like markers in some game of chance. Yes, that was it; he was a magician; reading from stones, studying the skulls of dead birds and the entrails of sea animals for prophecy of coming events; finding, at last, nothing more to express than that slow gesture of his right hand—an inescapable, inevitable, "Hail and Farewell."

CHAPTER 29

AND now finally Philip knew it was over; his time on the island. He knew it calmly now, not in anger. He must go to his father, fall on his knees, ask to be forgiven. He saw his father urging him to his feet, urging him forth, not like that Kipling figure of his youthful reading, not that romantic *Vortraeger* in riding boots and sun helmet, but more like a plodding Diogenes casting his lantern's beam now here, now there, searching, searching even in the mottled heirloom mirror on Seventy-second Street, for his own face floating like something long undersea, rising at last whitely to the surface.

2

HE OPENED the bedroom door and looked in. The old man was pushed up on his pillows, his face serene again, his eyes clear.

"Fit as a fiddle," he said. "No pain at all."

"Let me take a look at your back."

Philip removed the bandage and gazed at the injury. It was still raw and ugly.

"I tell you I'm all right," said the old man. "I know."

"Will you have something to eat? I'll bring it here."

"I can get up perfectly well."

"No," Philip said firmly. "You stay right here today. You've had a shock—and I know it. Dad—I . . ."

The old man held up his hand, palm out, in a quick gesture. "Forget it, son," he said. "Let's forget it. I'd rather have coffee than talk at this point, anyway."

Philip walked back to the kitchen and prepared a tray. As he turned the bacon, scrambled the eggs, he continued to feel such acute shame and need to speak that when he again appeared in the bedroom he said, as soon as his father had had a swallow of coffee, "Dad, I—I wish there was some way to abase myself—really abase myself, for what I did this morning—last night."

"I know," the old man said, nodding cheerfully. He acted as though Philip's confession was of small moment. "But just leave it be, lad."

Philip groaned. "No, don't try to make it easy for me."

"Maybe I'm just trying to make it easy for us both," the old man said simply. He picked up a slice of toast. "You know there's a theory been advanced that people enjoy confessing because it gives them a chance to relive the crime, or the sin." He paused to spread some blackberry jam on the bread with evident relish. "That way you get not just one experience but two. Kind of an extra dividend, so to speak." His eyes flickered with amusement. "Something in it, maybe."

"Maybe," Philip said dully. He was grateful to his father for trying to spare him, but he could not keep from saying, "I thought I'd learned something here—grown calmer . . . Now this lack of self-control . . ." He stopped speaking. After a moment he said, "I can't believe other men go to pieces as badly as I have in the last months."

His father held the slice of toast suspended again for a moment as he looked gently at his son. "I've a notion a good many men are being knocked out of their cocoons these days. The war alone . . ."

"Oh, I can't blame it on the war," Philip said tensely. "I had a very good war, taken all in all."

"I doubt anyone having 'a good war.' " The quiet way his father spoke made Philip realize the cheapness of the current phrase.

"Well, all I know is," Philip said, "I was getting along all right—at least I was going along in an easy rut—and all of a sudden . . ." He stopped, uncertain whether to speak now about Ellen.

"You were tossed out of the rut," his father said. "You can't ever go back—you know that. It isn't there to go back to. Even *looking* back is foolish—that's just spilt milk. You've got just two possibilities: stop dead in your tracks, or go on."

He paused a moment. "All of which doesn't mean that you may not go right back to what appears, on the outside, to be the same situation," he concluded.

"Oh, paradox, paradox!" Philip muttered, and at once was sorry about the impatience in his voice.

His father turned his head away. Philip had to strain to hear him. "Maybe you'd better decide to come to terms with paradox, son. Maybe where we are now as human creatures, paradox is what it all has to be."

"But that's no help, damn it!" Philip cried.

His father said nothing. After a moment Philip spoke again in a voice that he deliberately held level, as if only by this discipline could he say what he had to. "Dad, I've got to talk with you whether you want me to or not. I'm cut adrift. I can't find my bearings—you don't understand, Dad. Before I came out here, not long before the accident, I quarreled with my wife about a basic thing. I may even find when I get back that she doesn't want to go on living with me. I quarreled with her because she wanted another child and I couldn't face having it."

"Why?" asked his father. The word was absolutely without overtone of any kind—no astonishment, criticism, curiosity.

Philip jumped up, "Why?" he cried, "Why? Why? Because I've no belief in anything—that's why. No faith in life. That's the whole thing. I've had it for a few moments here on this island under ideal conditions, but even here I can't hold it—didn't hold it. Even here, with all the help, I've had—failure! I've failed . . . Why did I fail? Because I haven't had—still haven't got—any final direction, final answer. Nothing—no one—has told me convincingly that my life—*my* life—has meaning."

He was afraid to look at his father. He stared down at the floor.

After a moment the old man said softly, "But that's terrible, lad." There was no censure in the voice. "Maybe that's because of the way you were educated—expecting the answers in the back of the book, or to get it from some teacher who'd be able to *tell* you the answer. The truth is we don't know enough yet—about anything. And we have to admit that to ourselves. Maybe life itself is just the search in one way or another, by one kind of man or another . . ."

Except for the difference in accent it could have been Ermenthal: "life itself is finally your only guide." Once more the vision of some mysterious winding gyre of time and experience rose at the back of Philip's mind—a moving track on which he passed and repassed the destined figures of his individual fate, seeing them, in the shifting light and at different points of the spiral, now this way, now that, now enemy, now teacher, now alien, now brother.

And now the old man's voice changed, grew speculative, even faintly melancholy. "Aye," he said in the voice of the Old Country. "The search! That's where you need, laddie, the 'stiff heart for the steek brae.' "

Now for Philip everything seemed to stop. He could imagine nothing existing beyond the confines of this bare room, or at most, the house and the little island on which it stood. It seemed now beyond the bounds of possibility that within a few days he would be in the stratosphere thundering back toward New York and whatever remained of his other life. There was a long heavy silence.

When his father spoke again Philip knew at once to what the old man referred. "You know the truth is, son, people aren't fit to be parents. It's without doubt the most trying and exacting and important of the professions—yet any man or woman whose ovum and sperm are fertile can achieve it—play the role without a single thought of what they're undertaking, and without any specific training . . . On the other hand, of course, people can begin to think so much about the hazards and the responsibilities of parenthood that they decide just to avoid the trouble at all costs."

After a moment in quite a different voice, one that was full of pain and regret, he added, "I probably shouldn't have been a father myself."

"Don't say that!" Philip blurted out. "It's not true. I honor you—you've taught me—I was learning from you even when I didn't know I was—and Jane—she certainly wouldn't agree either." He blundered to a pause. Then he said, "Do you know the last word Jane ever spoke to me was the word 'coward'? It's never stopped ringing in my ears. No, actually it wasn't the last word—three from the last. The last words were, 'I hate you.'" Tears rushed into his eyes. He was silent, fighting for control. "I shall have to write her and tell her she was wrong. I chose the hard way. I didn't know it then—but I know it now."

He looked at his father then and saw that his face had suddenly grown slack and old. "I said the other day I might have to pay a little more for this island, son, and now I know it's true."

"Oh, Dad," Philip protested. "Don't! If I had half your wisdom . . ."

But the old man shook his head, turning his face away, "I'm no wiser than the next one. We're all in this together."

To Philip's amazement this remark, which should have depressed him, revealing as it did a weakness in his father's unfailing armor of calm detachment, gave him instead a feeling of strength. He had the sense of sharing something; he believed for the first time in his father's capacity to suffer—not in memories of the past, but in the living present. An enormous relief began to wash through his heart and mind.

"Look, Dad," he said, "that's the most helpful thing you've said yet."

At that the old man turned his face toward him. "Is it now? And how's that?" (Those Irish triads, Philip noted.)

"I don't know. It just is. Sense of inclusion maybe." They were both silent.

"But *can* I go back?" Philip cried aloud, fresh doubts suddenly assailing him. "Convince Ellen? Face that damned job I hate?"

"Yes, of course you can," the old man said.

What did he mean? The little spear of fear thrust into Philip's flesh; the expectation that too much was going to be asked of him; some unbearable demand laid on him.

"How?" His voice was tremulous.

"How can I say?" said his father. "I don't know enough about it. It's not my life, it's yours." He spoke without sharpness. Then he added, doubling back on his tracks, "You can go back, you will go back. Yet you're not going back to the same thing because something has fundamentally changed. Right in the midst of your life suddenly everything is different. It happened to me, too—though more slowly, gradually. It came again and again, like a whisper, the question: Is this all life is? And finally I had to go with the question all the way, to the very end. Your life will never again be matter-of-course because you have questioned it. Probably increasingly you will question it."

Philip was silent a long time. He had traveled a course he could not himself trace when he spoke again.

"And some day find my own island?"

"You've already got an island," his father said with peculiar emphasis. And then, as though his remark could also be taken literally, he added, "This is yours, whenever you really want it. When you can use it."

It was a long time before either of them spoke again. The windows were open and Philip, seated on the bare bench with his head in his hands, could hear the familiar sounds of the island world; the feathery tapping of the poplars, the faint rustle of the tide, the dry persistent dropping of madrona leaves.

He rose and walked over to the window. "Maybe I've learned something here. Something I'll know, in time, how to apply." He said it as if anxious to reassure his father, but the words were more for himself. He looked toward the end of the familiar mountain chain that his father's window framed.

"About fate." He groped for words. "About how to change it . . . . The inner attitude—is *that* what alters the outer form?"

Because he seemed to be speaking to himself his father made no answer. After a moment Philip went on.

"So you don't need to think so much about changing the situation, or the people? You try instead to change your own attitude toward it—and them?" He looked at his father then, hoping for correction or corroboration.

The old man nodded. "I believe that's how certain Hindus assert they can even alter what they call their Karma."

He reached out to the table beside the bed and took from the lower shelf the small leather notebook marked *Recipes*.

"I had a friend once who, when he died, left me a little book in which he'd written what he thought to be the great truths. Among them all—and they are from men in all times and lands— is something that was said by Meister Eckhardt, of whom you may have heard."

"Vaguely," Philip said.

"He was born in the thirteenth century," his father went on, leafing through the shabby notebook, "but you might well say he was timeless." He put on his glasses and read in his clear steady voice:

" 'That I am a man, this I share with other men. That I see and hear and that I eat and drink is what all animals do likewise. But that I am I is only mine and belongs to me and to no one else; to no other man, not to an angel, not to God— except inasmuch as I am one with Him.' "

His father closed the book with a slow dignified gesture. "That's a big responsibility—that kind of thought—but I don't know—somehow I find it comforting." He paused, added in a lighter tone, "Maybe you don't derive the solace from words that I do?"

"I've abused words," Philip said, "all my life."

They sat again without speaking. Outside, breaking the silence, they heard the sound of many birds keening shrilly in the still air.

"Listen," said the old man, holding up a finger, "the gulls are back. It's autumn—the season of the soul."